THE BEST OF
Archie®
COMICS BOOK TWO

TH BEST O

Archie®

COMICS BOOK TWO

Published by Archie Comic Publications, Inc.
325 Fayette Avenue, Mamaroneck, New York 10543-2318.

ArchieComics.com

ISBN: 978-1-936975-20-4

Publisher / Co-CEO: Jon Goldwater
Co-CEO: Nancy Silberkleit
President: Mike Pellerito
Co-President / Editor-In-Chief: Victor Gorelick
Senior Vice President – Sales and Business Development: Jim Sokolowski
Senior Vice President – Publishing and Operations: Harold Buchholz
Director of Publicity & Marketing: Adam Tracey
Executive Director of Editorial: Paul Kaminski
Project Coordinator & Book Design: Joe Morciglio
Production Manager: Stephen Oswald
Lead Production Artist: Carlos Antunes
Editorial Assistant / Proofreader: Jamie Lee Rotante
Production: Steven Golebiewski, Jon Gray, Suzannah Rowntree, Jonathan Betancourt, Shannon Goldwater, Emma Goldstein, Kari Silbergleit, Duncan McLachlan, Pat Woodruff

Stories written by:

Frank Doyle, George Gladir, Al Fagaly, Al Hartley, Bob Montana, Joe Edwards, Harry Lucey, Bob White, Bill Woggon, Bob Bolling, Dexter Taylor, Bill Golliher, Fernando Ruiz, Mike Pellowski, Tom Root, Andrew Pepoy, Michael Uslan, Ian Flynn, Mike Kunkel, Stephen Oswald, J. Torres, Alex Segura

Artwork by:

Bob Montana, Al Fagaly, Harry Lucey, Dan DeCarlo, Bob Bolling, Samm Schwartz, Fernando Ruiz, Holly G!, Stan Goldberg, Dexter Taylor, Jeff Shultz, Rudy Lapick, Rex Lindsey, Rick Burchett, Joe Edwards, Henry Scarpelli, Dan Parent, Marty Epp, Bill Woggon, Andrew Pepoy, Tania Del Rio, Chad Thomas, Art Mahwhinney, Joe Staton, Walt Lardner, Francesco Francavilla, Pat Kennedy, Tim Kennedy, Bill Vigoda, Jimmy DeCarlo, Sal Trapani, Jim Amash, Jon D'Agostino, Vince DeCarlo, Rich Koslowski, Dan DeCarlo Jr., Terry Austin, Bob Smith, John Workman, John Costanza, Bill Yoshida, Teresa Davidson, Jack Morelli, Barry Grossman, Matt Herms, Glenn Whitmore, Joe Morciglio, Rosario "Tito" Peña, Jason Jensen, Mark McNabb

Welcome to
The Best of Archie Comics Book Two

When readers made the first volume of ***The Best of Archie Comics*** our best-selling Archie book ever, we couldn't wait to take on the challenge of making a fresh and fun follow-up edition. In choosing from over 25,000 stories, in addition to a big helping of the classic Archie humor stories we all love, this time we added into the mix a large dollop of adventure, Archie style – from King Arthur's court to Robin Hood to pro wrestling, superheroes, the Loch Ness Monster, and visitors from outer space! Room has been made for slightly longer stories that wouldn't fit into the first volume, and there are dozens of brand-new story introductions by artists, writers, comics specialists, and Archie staffers who have shared some unique insights into the stories, the characters, and their creators. As we did the first time around, we've worked from the best available materials we have for each story. Most of the stories are scanned straight from the artist's original art or from vintage proofs (and combined with modern recoloring), but when they were unavailable, we worked from scans of the original printed comic books, some dating back over sixty years. Of course, with so much great material, there are plenty of our and your favorites that didn't make the cut, and we look forward to featuring them in future volumes. We hope you enjoy the journey as we travel together over seven decades of classic Archie comics.

Thanks for reading!

THE BEST OF Archie COMICS BOOK TWO

the 1940s

Archie
Pep #25, 1942
by Bob Montana

In this classic story, written and drawn by Bob Montana, Archie has just learned how to drive. He has a car that's in constant need of repair and asked his father for one too many advances on his allowance. Archie needs to come up with a plan to earn enough money to keep his car out of the junk yard. Now I'm sure many of our older readers can identify with this problem. I know I can. I spent more time in a repair shop with my first car than I spent in the car. But Archie does come up with a plan to keep his car on the road. A plan that will take you from one hilarious panel to the next. It's Montana at his best (and one of my favorite stories) with an ending that might surprise you. Just thought you might be interested to know, Bob owned a car just like the one he drew in this story.

--Victor Gorelick
Co-President/Editor-in-Chief, Archie Comics

Daily Newspaper Strips
1946
by Bob Montana

When Bob Montana began writing and drawing the newspaper strip in 1946, most of Bob's gags were based on his experiences during his high school days. If it happened to Bob, there's a good chance it would happen to Archie! However, when Archie caused trouble he usually got away with it, Montana did not. Bob also had a treasure trove of humor beyond high school... experiencing life as a parent. These newspaper strips are not just about Bob Montana's life, they're about your lives, too. While reading these strips, you might find old friends, teachers, parents and children that are part of your past, present and future. I handpicked these gags with the hope that they bring a smile to your face.

--Craig Yoe
Founder, YOE Studios

Archie
GEE, ARCHIE, YOU'RE GOING AWFULLY FAST!
YEAH! ISN'T IT GREAT? AND I JUST LEARNED TO DRIVE YESTERDAY!
KEEP 'EM FLYING
RHS
61W35
HANG ONTO YOUR HATS, RIVERDALE...HERE COMES ARCHIE WITH HIS FIRST JUMPIN', JIVIN', JALOPY! BETTY COOPER SAYS EVERYTHING MAKES A NOISE BUT THE HORN.... AND RIGHT NOW SHE'S FINDING OUT THAT THE ROUGHEST DISTANCE BETWEEN TWO POINTS IS A RIDE WITH....... ARCHIE!
Words and Music by Montana

HI, MA! WHEN DO WE EAT?
YOUR FATHER WANTS YOU IN THE LIVING ROOM!
TRIG
DID YOU WANT ME, POP?
OH, YES! IT'S ABOUT THAT-UH CAR. YOU'LL HAVE TO GET RID OF IT! IT'S COSTING TOO MUCH AND YOU'RE WAY OVERDRAWN ON YOUR ALLOWANCE
AW, GEE, POP, I JUST GOT IT RUNNING! DON'T MAKE ME GIVE IT UP. I'LL DO ANYTHING! I'LL MAKE IT SELF-SUSTAINING!
HMMM! SELF-SUSTAINING, HUH! AND HOW WILL YOU DO THAT?
I'LL- I'LL MAKE IT A TAXI!
EARLY SATURDAY MORNING---
YOU KNOW, JUGHEAD, I THINK I'LL MAKE IT AN EXPRESS, TOO- SO'S NOT TO PASS UP ANY BUSINESS!
DANGER HAIR BRAKES
HERE COMES THE 9.20 NOW-- I'LL GET A FARE FOR SURE!
RIVERD
SO THIS IS RIVERDALE! HUMPH!
TAXI! TAXI-CAB HERE! I'LL TAKE YOUR BAGS, MISTER!
IS-IS THAT THE ONLY TAXI?
YUP! IF YOU WANT TO TAKE THE LIBERTY OF CALLIN' IT THAT!
OOPS! THE DOOR CAME OFF!
OH, DON'T MIND THAT--IT'S A CONVERTIBLE! IN THE SUMMER, I TAKE THE DOORS OFF! SAY, DO YOU MIND GIVING IT A LITTLE SPARK?
TAXI

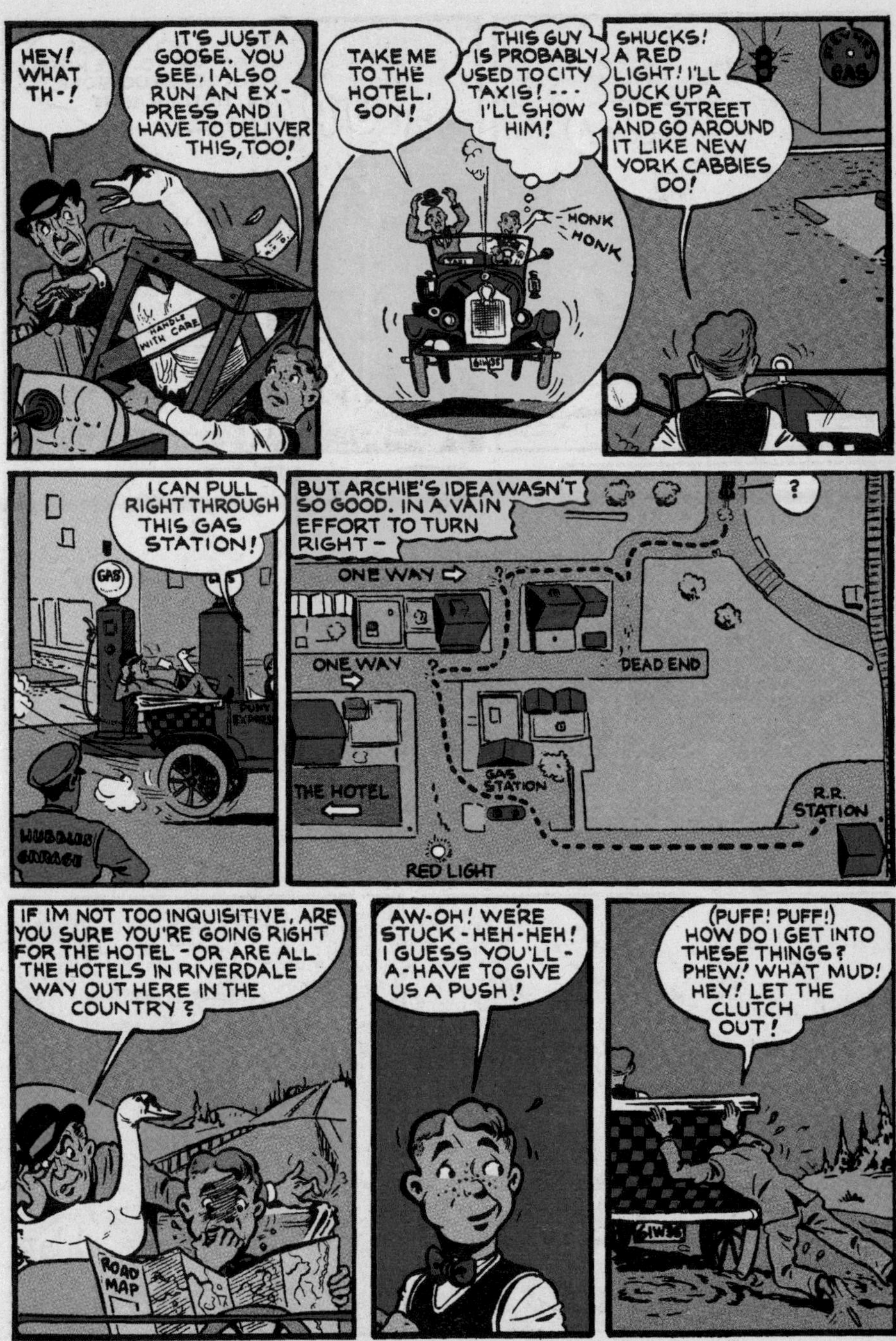
HEY! WHAT TH-!
IT'S JUST A GOOSE. YOU SEE, I ALSO RUN AN EX-PRESS AND I HAVE TO DELIVER THIS, TOO!
HANDLE WITH CARE
TAKE ME TO THE HOTEL, SON!
THIS GUY IS PROBABLY USED TO CITY TAXIS! --- I'LL SHOW HIM!
HONK
HONK
SHUCKS! A RED LIGHT! I'LL DUCK UP A SIDE STREET AND GO AROUND IT LIKE NEW YORK CABBIES DO!
GAS
I CAN PULL RIGHT THROUGH THIS GAS STATION!
GAS
BUT ARCHIE'S IDEA WASN'T SO GOOD. IN A VAIN EFFORT TO TURN RIGHT -
?
ONE WAY
ONE WAY
DEAD END
THE HOTEL
GAS STATION
R.R. STATION
RED LIGHT
IF I'M NOT TOO INQUISITIVE, ARE YOU SURE YOU'RE GOING RIGHT FOR THE HOTEL - OR ARE ALL THE HOTELS IN RIVERDALE WAY OUT HERE IN THE COUNTRY?
ROAD MAP
AW-OH! WE'RE STUCK - HEH-HEH! I GUESS YOU'LL - A- HAVE TO GIVE US A PUSH!
(PUFF! PUFF!) HOW DO I GET INTO THESE THINGS? PHEW! WHAT MUD! HEY! LET THE CLUTCH OUT!

YIPPY! SHE'S STARTED!
YEEOW!
SLUP!
WILL YOU PLEASE GET ME TO THE HOTEL BEFORE I DO SOME-THING RASH?
OKAY! OKAY! I'LL TEAR UP THE ROAD!
I THINK THEY ALREADY HAVE!
LOOKOUT FOR THOSE CHICKENS! PUT ON THE BRAKES!
WHAT BRAKES?
CLUCK
CLUK
CLUCK
WHACK!
BUCK! BUCK!
BA-GAWK!
HONK! HONK!
HOLY COW! THE FEATHERS STUCK TO THE MUD!
HURRAY! IT'S RAINING! NOW I CAN WASH THESE FEATHERS OFF!
THAT'S NOT RAIN - IT'S THE *RADIATOR*!
TAXI

HMMM! STOPPED DEAD! WE CAN'T BE OUT OF GAS. I PUT IN A QUART YESTERDAY!
AND HERE COMES THE LIMITED -
HEY! THE TRAIN - THE TRAIN IS COMING!
WHAT DID YOU SAY?
JUMP! JUMP!
CRASH!
OH, WELL - IT BURNED TOO MUCH GAS ANYWAY!
OOOOH! MY FEET! IF THEY WEREN'T SO SORE I'D KICK YOU ALL THE WAY BACK TO RIVER-DALE!
RIVERDALE
17
MILES
HOTEL
IF I NEVER SEE YOU AGAIN IT WILL BE TEN YEARS TOO SOON!

NEXT MORNING ARCHIE ENTERS HIS SCHOOL ROOM
HEY, ARCHIE! I HEAR YOU WRECKED THAT CEMENT MIXER OF YOURS! WHAT'S A MATTER-CAN'T YOU DRIVE?
OH YEAH!
WISE GUY!
OUCH!
I SAW THAT, ARCHIE ANDREWS, AND YOU CAN MARCH RIGHT DOWN TO THE OFFICE! TSK, TSK, AND ON THE FIRST MORNING OF OUR NEW PRINCIPAL, TOO! A FINE WAY TO MEET HIM!
PHOOEY! WHEN WILL I LEARN NOT TO DO THINGS LIKE THAT IN HASTE? I SHOULDA GOT HIM AFTER SCHOOL!
OFFICE
BASKE
BALL
FEB -
OH MIGOSH! IT'S THE GUY I PICKED UP AT THE STATION IN MY TAXI! HE'S THE NEW PRINCIPAL!
RIVERDALE HIGH SC
?
ZIP
SLOW
SCHOOL
ZOOM
THAT NIGHT
YOU KNOW, POP, I'VE BEEN THINKING! YOU'RE WORKING TOO HARD AND I THINK IT'S TIME I QUIT SCHOOL AND WENT TO WORK-- --STARTING TOMORROW!
NOW, WHAT GAVE YOU THAT IDEA ?
THE END
IF YOU LIKE FUN (AND WHO DOESN'T?) DON'T MISS THE NEXT ADVENTURE OF COMICS' GREATEST LAUGH NOVELTY---------
"ARCHIE"
in "PEP" and "JACKPOT" COMICS!

TO ATTRACT ARCHIE YOU MUST DO NOTHING!– IGNORE HIM! BIDE YOUR TIME!
MADAME SMOG KNOWS ALL
FORTUNE TELLER MIND READER
ASTROLOGER BABY SITTER
YES AND BIDE MY NAILS!
POOF! YOU ARE TOO GOOD TO HIM– TOO SWEET!
WELL DON'T FORGET– YOU CAN CATCH MORE FLIES WITH SUGAR THAN WITH VINEGAR!
MONTANA 3-11
YOU WANT FLIES– –OR ARCHIE?
SOME CHOICE!

ARCHIE! WILL YOU HOLD THAT CHALK SO IT WON'T SCREECH!
SORRY, MISS GRUNDY!
SCREECH SCREECH SCREECH
SCREECH!
ARCHIE!
MONTANA 9-13
ARCHIE! SIT DOWN! AND LET SOMEONE ELSE DO THE PROBLEM!
YES, MA'AM!
SQUEAK
SQEAK!
SEE? I TOLD YOU IT WOULD WORK WHEN YOU DON'T KNOW THE PROBLEM!
S
D
Copr., 1947, Archie Comic Publications, Inc. Dist. by McClure Newspaper Syndicate

OOMPH!
ARCHIE! DO YOU SEE THAT SIGN? IT DISTINCTLY SAYS DOWN! OR DON'T YOU BELIEVE IN SIGNS?
DOWN
STAIR
Y-YES, SIR!
NEXT TIME YOU SEE A SIGN-OBEY IT! UNDERSTAND? DO EXACTLY WHAT THE SIGN SAYS!
MONTANA 10-20
Copr., 1947, Archie Comic Publications, Inc. Dist. by McClure Newspaper Syndicate
?
KICK ME!

BROWN AND GOLD
RIVERDALE HIGH SCHOOL'S PAPER
STUDENT S' DAY
PUPILS TAKE OVER SCHOOL!
THE FACULTY IS BUSY PICKING STUDENTS TO ACT AS TEACHERS WHEN THE BOYS AND GIRLS OF OUR SCHOOL RUN THINGS ON 'STUDENT S' DAY! EVEN THE ROLE OF PRINC PAL WILL BE TAKEN BY SOME WORTHY PUPIL.
DILTON DOILY
WORTHY CANDIDATE
THE PRINCIPAL'S
SUPERINTEND
I HOPE MR. FLUNKEM, PICKS ME FOR HISTORY TEACHER!
HE SHOULD! YOU'RE TERRIFIC ON DATES!
Copr., 1948, Archie Comic Publications, Inc.
Dist. by McClure Newspaper Syndicate
ARCHIE! DO YOU THINK MISS GRUNDY WILL PICK ON YOU FOR A TEACHER?
WHY NOT?
ABEUNT STUDIA IN MORES
SHE PICKS ON ME FOR EVERY-THING ELSE!
MONTANA
2-16

OH, I'VE NEVER HAD SO MUCH FUN AT A DANCE!
WHY NOT! YOU'RE THE ONLY CHICK HERE AND UP TO YOUR EARS IN WOLVES!
WHERE **ARE** ALL THE GIRLS??
OH! THEY ALL HAD TO GO TO A *SPECIAL* MEETING THAT THE "SCREAMIN' MEAMIE CLUB" CALLED!
BUT YOU'RE **PRESIDENT** OF THAT CLUB... SHOULDN'T YOU BE THERE??
WITH ALL THE BOYS **HERE**?
WHY DO YOU THINK I CALLED THE SPECIAL MEETING?!
MONTANA 5-1
Copr. 1948, Archie Comic Publications, Inc. Dist. by McClure Newspaper Syndicate

Goat Radio
Super Duck #17, 1947
by Al Fagaly

The late 1940s offered few comics as crazy and popular as writer/artist Al Fagaly's rough, fast-paced Super Duck. Largely forgotten today, back in 1948, it was voted the 10th favorite comic book of over 120 titles among 18-20 year old males in a Gilbert Youth Research survey commissioned by Archie, just ahead of Superman (and with over three times the votes cast for Donald Duck).

For me, Fagaly's sometimes recklessly violent stories are at their best when tempered with a big dollop of good-natured silliness, and boy, does Al get silly here. By the time I reached the goofy floating head close-up of a cross-eyed, hiccuping goat named Uncle Sam captured between dance moves, I was laughing out loud.

--Harold Buchholz
Senior Vice President – Publishing and Operations, Archie Comics

No Body's Dummy
Pep #62, 1947
by Bill Vigoda

When Veronica laments to Archie, "You always say you'd die for my sake, but you never do," it is the perfect encapsulation of the entitlement she feels toward everything in her life, most especially Archie. And that's just the opening line in the most outrageous Archie story I've ever read!

--Paul Castiglia
Writer & Archivist, Archie Comics

SUPER DUCK
THE COCKEYED WONDER

FINISHED! SUPER DUCK'S MIDGET PUSH BUTTON PORTABLE RADIO! IT'LL REVOLUTIONIZE THE - - -
RING RING!
HELLO? OH, HIYA, HONEY! WHAT'S UP?
EVERYTHING! WOULD YOU PLEASE AMUSE UNCLE SAM FOR ME THIS AFTERNOON? I'M UP TO MY NECK!
I'D LOVE TO, HONEY! YOU KNOW ME!
YOU'RE A DARLING, SUPE! BYEEE!
CLICK!
!!! WHAT DOES SHE TAKE ME FOR? A DOPE?
THAT'S TELLING HER, KID!
SLAM!

HELP ME STRAIGHTEN THIS PLACE UP, FAUNT! QUICK!
WHO'S SHE BRINGING, ROYALTY?
HER UNCLE SAM, WHOEVER HE IS! I DON'T WANT THE DODDERING OLD GOAT TO··
LOOK OUT, SUPE!
S. DUCK
WHAMO
MEET UNCLE SAM, SUPE! SORRY HE GOT AWAY FROM ME LIKE THAT!
UNCLE SAM, EH?
VERY FUNNY!
WELL, ENJOY YOURSELVES, BOYS! I'LL PICK UNCLE UP LATER!
OH, SURE!
S DUCK
2.

WAIT A MINUTE! WHAT IF HE GETS HUNGRY?
ARE YOU KIDDING?
DUCK
GOATS WILL EAT ANYTHING!
CRUNCH!
YI! MY NEW RADIO!
GULP!
COUGH IT UP, YOU BEWHISKERED GARBAGE COLLECTOR, BEFORE I TURN YOU INTO A HATRACK!
CLANK
I'LL GET YA FER THIS, YA RAT!
FAUNT! IT'S A TALKING GOAT!
BANG!
MMF! HE GOT ME!
3

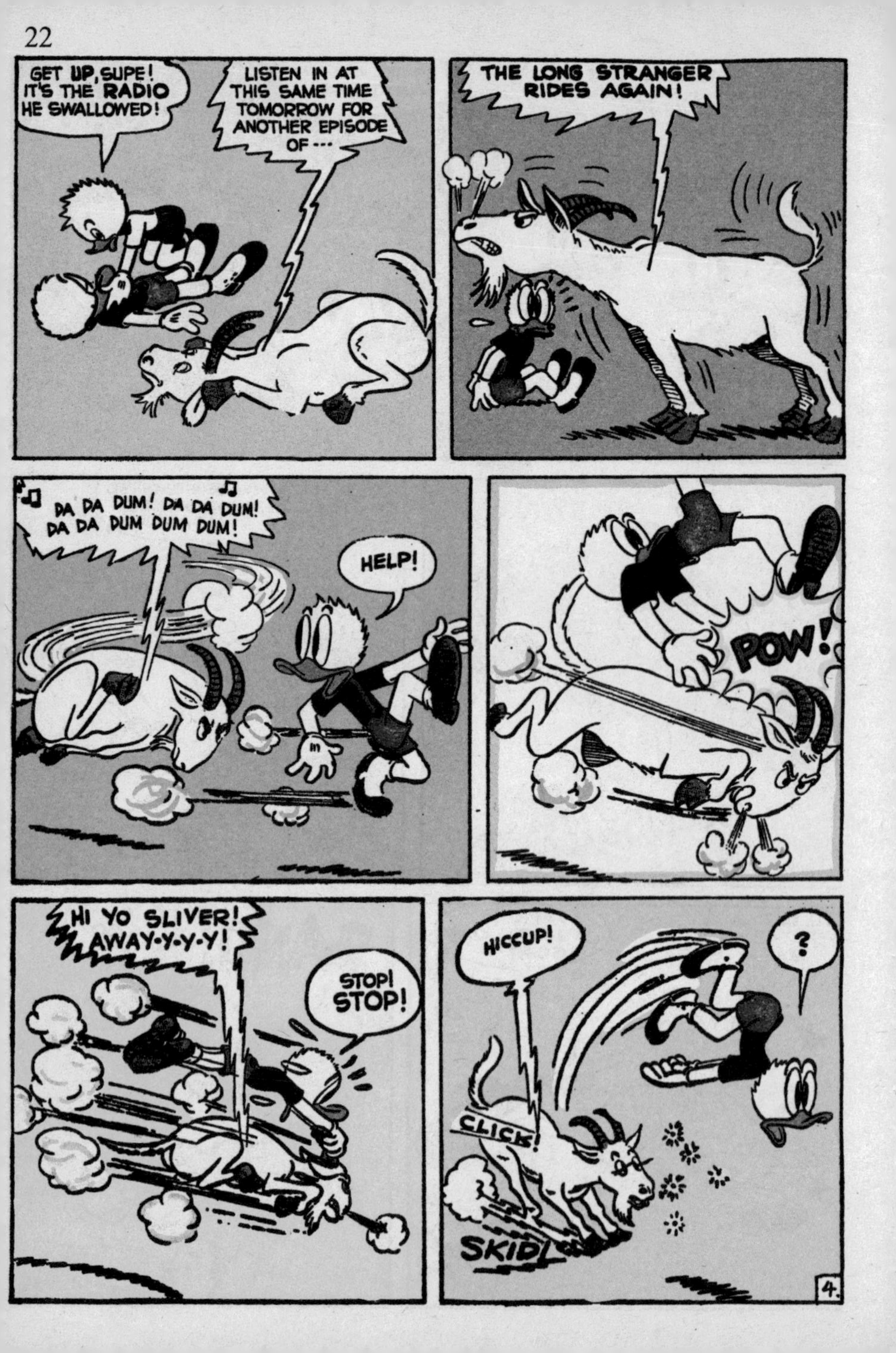
GET UP, SUPE! IT'S THE RADIO HE SWALLOWED!
LISTEN IN AT THIS SAME TIME TOMORROW FOR ANOTHER EPISODE OF ---
THE LONG STRANGER RIDES AGAIN!
DA DA DUM! DA DA DUM! DA DA DUM DUM DUM!
HELP!
POW!
HI YO SLIVER! AWAY-Y-Y-Y!
STOP! STOP!
HICCUP!
?
CLICK!
SKID!
4.

OH, HOW WE DANCED
HIC-UP!
CLICK!
HOLD THAT TIGER
I'LL BE DARNED!
HIC!
HE CHANGES STATIONS EVERY TIME HE HICCUPS! HA HA!
BONNG! THERE GOES THE BELL FOR THE TENTH ROUND! BATTLING BILLY COMES OUT OF HIS CORNER LIKE A WILD BULL!
WHAT THE--?
A LEFT TO THE JAW! A A RIGHT! A LEFT! ANOTHER LEFT! THIS IS BRUTAL!
A TERRIFIC RIGHT --- AND THE CHALLENGER IS DOWN!
SPLAT!
5.

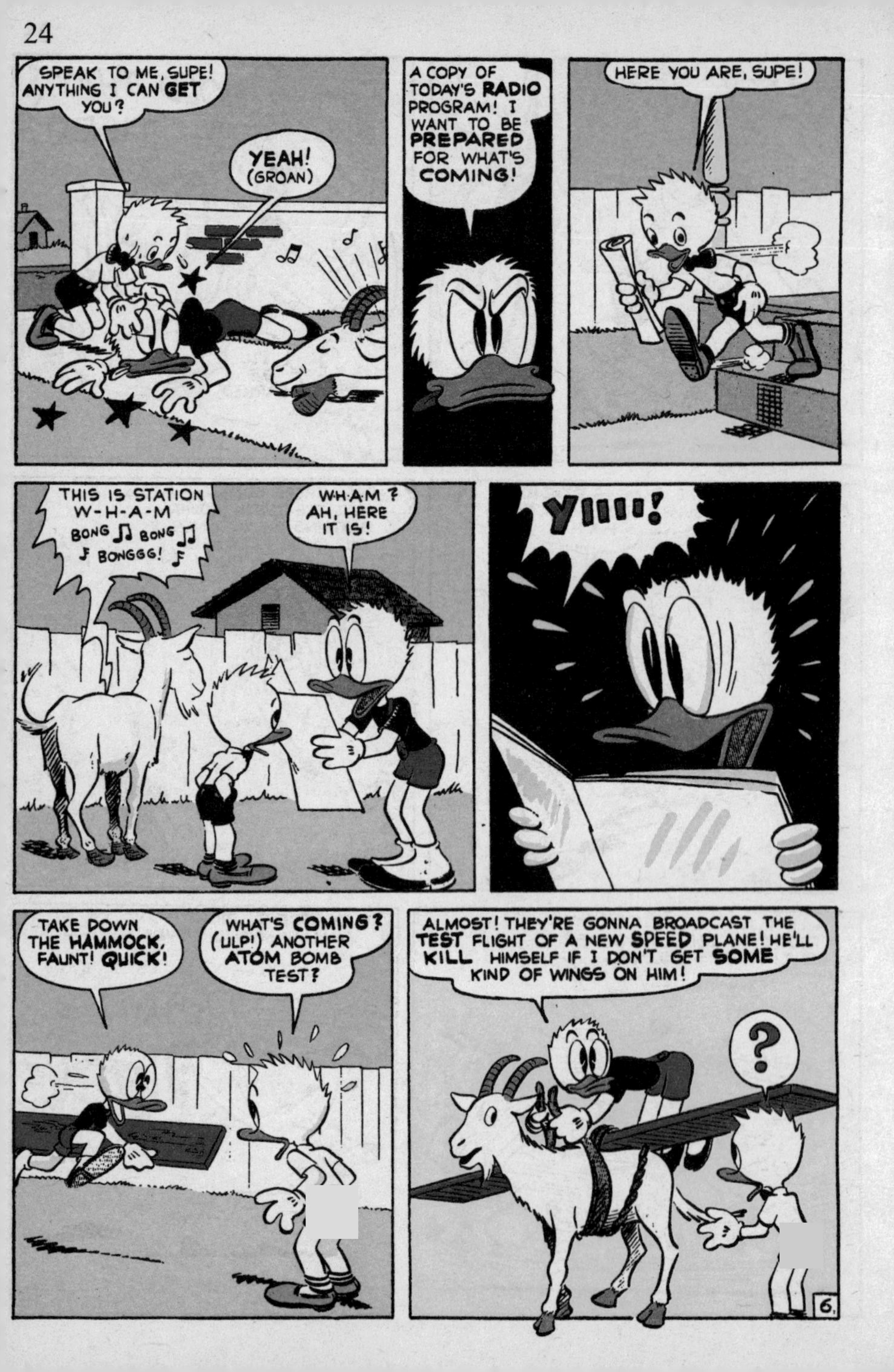
SPEAK TO ME, SUPE! ANYTHING I CAN GET YOU?
YEAH! (GROAN)
A COPY OF TODAY'S RADIO PROGRAM! I WANT TO BE PREPARED FOR WHAT'S COMING!
HERE YOU ARE, SUPE!
THIS IS STATION W-H-A-M BONG BONG BONGGG!
W-H-A-M? AH, HERE IT IS!
YIIIII!
TAKE DOWN THE HAMMOCK, FAUNT! QUICK!
WHAT'S COMING? (ULP!) ANOTHER ATOM BOMB TEST?
ALMOST! THEY'RE GONNA BROADCAST THE TEST FLIGHT OF A NEW SPEED PLANE! HE'LL KILL HIMSELF IF I DON'T GET SOME KIND OF WINGS ON HIM!
?
6.

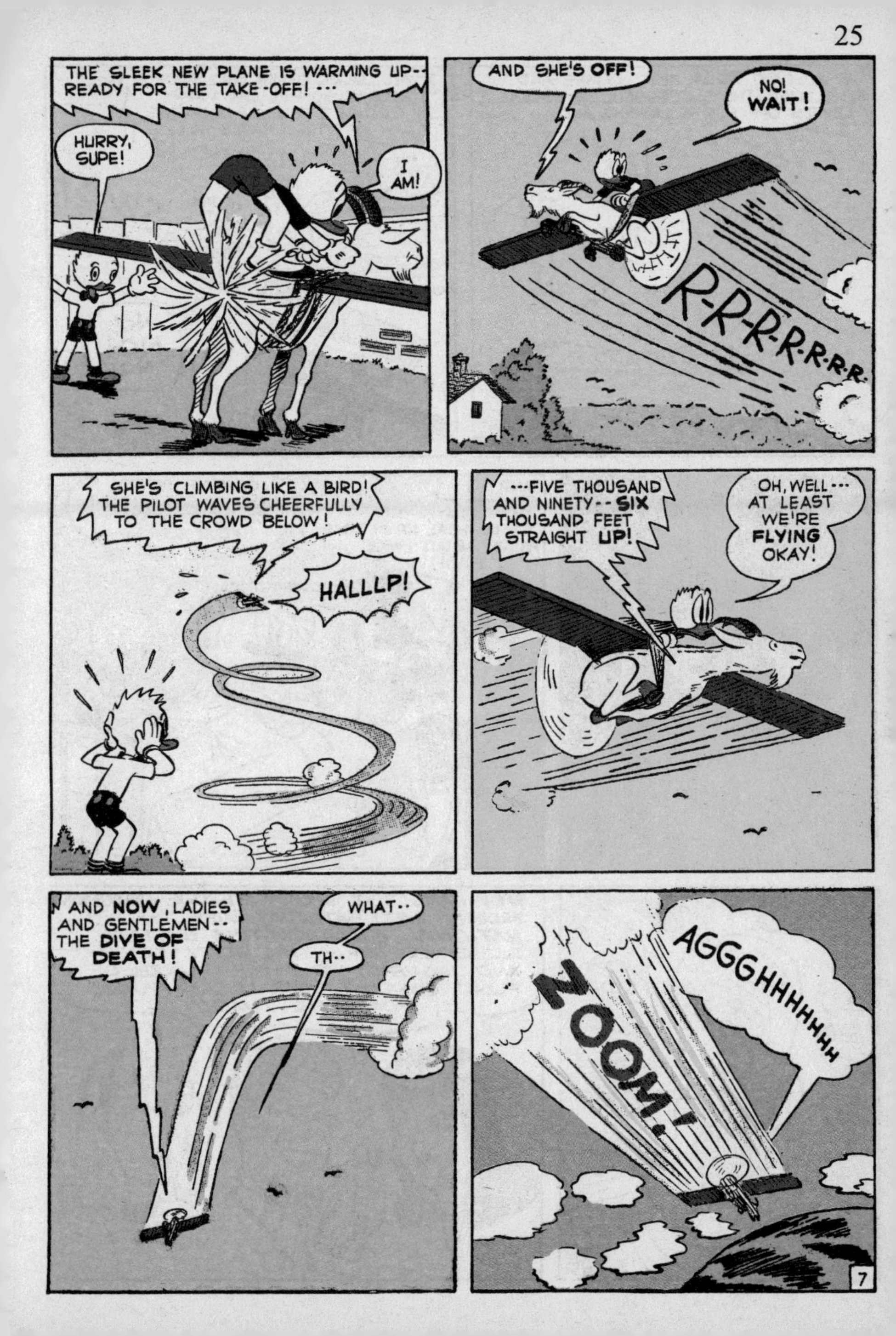
THE SLEEK NEW PLANE IS WARMING UP-- READY FOR THE TAKE-OFF! ---
HURRY, SUPE!
I AM!
AND SHE'S OFF!
NO! WAIT!
R-R-R-R-R-R-R-R-
SHE'S CLIMBING LIKE A BIRD! THE PILOT WAVES CHEERFULLY TO THE CROWD BELOW!
HALLLP!
---FIVE THOUSAND AND NINETY--SIX THOUSAND FEET STRAIGHT UP!
OH, WELL--- AT LEAST WE'RE FLYING OKAY!
AND NOW, LADIES AND GENTLEMEN-- THE DIVE OF DEATH!
WHAT--
TH--
ZOOM!
AGGGHHHHHHH
7

AT A SCANT FOUR FEET, LADIES AND GENTLEMEN, THE SUCCESSFUL NEW PLANE LEVELS OFF FOR A LANDING AND ...
RRRRRRRRRRRRRRRRRR
HIC!
WILL JACK'S OTHER WIFE DIVORCE GEORGE SO PHIL CAN MARRY CYNTHIA? WILL MR. ANDREWS GET THE CHAIR? WILL --
SWISH
NO! NO! NO!
CRASH!
AND SO--
OKAY! OKAY! YOU'LL HEAL UP IN TIME! WHAT ABOUT UNCLE SAM!
OH YEAH! THE DOC SAYS TO GIVE HIM ONE OF THESE EVERY FOUR HOURS ---
POWER TUBE
THE END
HEY GANG! TUNE IN ON THE ARCHIE ANDREWS PROGRAM EVERY SATURDAY OVER THE NATIONAL BROADCASTING SYSTEM. I'LL BE THERE WITH MY GANG, BETTY, VERONICA, AND JUGHEAD! WE'LL HAVE A BARREL OF FUN!! CONSULT YOUR LOCAL PAPER FOR THE TIME!!
NBC

Archie
IN
no Body's Dummy
YOU ALWAYS SAY YOU'D DIE FOR MY SAKE, BUT YOU NEVER DO!
BUT YOU WANT ME TO BE A.. PIN CUSHION IN SEWING CLASS.. WHAT DO YOU THINK I AM, A DUMMY? (DON'T ANSWER THAT!)
RIVERDALE H.S. A.D.XIIIV
SAY! I KNOW THE WINDOW TRIMMER AT THE FAIRTEEN SHOP! I'LL GET YOU A REAL DUMMY!
A MANIKIN?
MANIKIN, GIRLIKIN.. WHO CARES! I'LL SHOOT BACK AND GET IT!
DON'T BE LATE FOR SCHOOL!

TAILOR
THANKS, JOE! I'LL THROW THE DUMMY IN THE BACK SEAT!
THAT'S WHAT I DO WITH MY MOTHER-IN-LAW!
BUMP!
ZIP
HENRY! CALL THE POLICE! THE POOR GIRL'S BEEN RUN OVER!
YETH, DEAR! (LUCKY GIRL)
NUTS! AN ARM CAME OFF! MAYBE I CAN HAMMER IT ON WITH A WRENCH!
EEKK!
HURRY POLICE! HE'S BEATING HER OVER THE HEAD WITH A WRENCH!
I KNOW JUST HOW IT FEELS!

THERE HE GOES-- MUST BE A BODY SNATCHER!
I'LL TAKE A SHOT AT HIM!
KEEP 'EM FLYING
P.D.
AW CHIEF! JUST ONE LITTLE SHOT?
I SAID NO! NOW PUT THAT AWAY!
HE'S GOING INTO THE SCHOOL!
CAN I TAKE A SHOT FROM HERE CHIEF-- HUH-- CAN I?
CRASH!
ARCHIE! IS THIS ANOTHER OF YOUR CONFOUNDED PRANKS?
OF ALL THE IDIOTIC THINGS! BRINGING A DUMMY TO SCHOOL--AS IF WE DIDN'T HAVE ENOUGH HERE!

YIPE! NOW WHO PUT A BOTTLE OF RED INK UP THERE?
GET READY.. HE'S MAKING A GETAWAY!
CAN I SHOOT, CHIEF?
DAD RAT IT! I'LL HAVE TO WASH THIS RED INK OFF!
KONK!
AH, WEATHERBEE ISN'T HERE! I CAN GET MY DUMMY BACK!
DARN THESE SYNTHETIC RUBBER GARTERS.. BROKE AGAIN! UMMMM... NO ONE IN THE OFFICE!
I'LL DUCK BEHIND THIS CLOSET DOOR AND USE A PAPER CLIP!
4

I TELL YOU, I CAN SHOW YOU IT WAS A DUMMY!
OKAY, BUT DON'T TRY ANY FUNNY STUFF!
YEAH! OR I'LL PLUG YA!
THERE... SEE!!
HMM..
HOW DARE YOU-- YOU... OLD WOLF!
I QUIT!
HEY! MY GUN!
CLUNK
ISN'T THIS WHERE WE CAME IN?
EXIT
WHERE HAVE YOU BEEN?
I RAN INTO SOME TROUBLE--ABOUT 200 POUNDS OF IT!

WELL, PUT THE DUMMY BEHIND THAT SCREEN AND I'LL GET IT WHEN WE ARE READY!
I'LL STOP IN THIS EMPTY ROOM AND STRAIGHTEN MY WIG!
EEEK!
RIGHT IN SCHOOL-- KISSING AND HUGGING-- WELL! I NEVER!
SHE'S RIGHT--SHE NEVER!
HA! I KNEW IT! ARCHIE!--AND I'LL BET THE HUSSY IS VERONICA!
6

THE MATERIAL IS ALL CUT, RONNIE!
WILL YOU GET THE DUMMY--ARCHIE LEFT IT IN THE NEXT ROOM BEHIND THE SCREEN!
FRONT
BACK
I KNEW IT! HERE COMES BETTY! SHE IS SO JEALOUS OF VERONICA!
OH! THERE'S A SPIDER ON THE DUMMY!
I'LL KILL IT!... UGH!
EEEEEK! SHE STABBED HER!
PLOP!
OOOOOHHH
7

CHIEF—LEMME TAKE ONE SHOT?
SHUT UP! WE HAVE TO FIND THE BODY--OR WE DON'T HAVE A CASE!
WOW!
DID YOU FIND THE BODY?
I'LL SAY... WOW!
OBOY! NOW WE'RE GETTING SOMEWHERE! WHERE IS IT?
THERE IT IS! SOME BODY, HUH, CHIEF?
GET AWAY FROM THAT CALENDAR, YOU DOPE!
ENTER NOW!
SWIMMING OPEN TO ALL STUDENTS
WELL NOW, THOSE LEGS LOOK LIKE THEY BELONG TO A DUMMY!
EEEEEEEK!

THERE'S NO BODY HERE!
BUT I SAW BETTY STAB HER AFTER ARCHIE LEFT!
I THOUGHT SO! LET'S GO TO THE SOURCE OF ALL TROUBLE...
LATER...
HONEST! IT WAS A DUMMY! IT'S UP IN SEWING CLASS... COME ON, I'LL SHOW YOU!
SEE! WATCH, I'LL PROVE IT'S A DUMMY--WITH THIS PIN!
YEOWw!
JUGHEAD!
THERE'S THE DUMMY-- IT WAS TOO LARGE--SO WE USED JUGHEAD!
9

WELL, IT LOOKS LIKE WE WERE ALL DUMMIES!
JUST GET THAT THING OUT OF HERE! TAKE IT WITH YOU!
NOW, CHIEF, NOW CAN I TAKE A SHOT?
YES! GO AHEAD! YOU CAN SHOOT THE DUMMY!
O'BOYOBOY! I'VE WANTED TO SHOOT THIS GUN EVER SINCE I GOT IT!
CLICK!
HEY, CHIEF--WHEN CAN I START LOADING IT?
THE END

THE BEST OF
Archie
COMICS
BOOK TWO
the 50s
R

Sir Walter Wilkin
Wilbur #42, 1952
by Joe Edwards

People may say chivalry's dead now, but it looks like it wasn't that easy to come by back in the '50s, either! America's other typical teen, Wilbur Wilkins, shows everyone who's boss – or at least tries to – in this hilarious story. While the ending may have a funny twist, the '50s were actually marked by many milestones in women's boxing! Barbara Buttrick, known as the "Mother of modern women's boxing," won the first Women's World Boxing Championship in 1957. That same year, she suffered the only defeat in her career – against Joann Hagen, a woman whose femininity often contrasted with the tough boxing scene. In 1952, Hagen fought against a male boxer, Norm Jones, and defeated him in a four-round decision. It looks like Wilbur's "li'l bunny" Laurie was in good company! In addition to being great for laughs, Archie Comics always had its finger over the pulse of pop culture and current events!

--Jamie Lee Rotante
Editorial Assistant / Proofreader, Archie Comics

Horizontal Heroes
Ginger #5, 1952
by Harry Lucey

Harry Lucey was the man. The Archie that I grew up with was drawn in the house style established by Dan DeCarlo, so I didn't discover Lucey's work until I was a little bit older. I was old enough to know that I wanted to make art professionally, but not old enough to really understand what incredible quality I was looking at when I read his stories. Fortunately it didn't take long for me to learn to appreciate the true merits of his work. Funny? Yup. Dynamic? Yup. Pretty, descriptive, exciting? Yup, yup, yup. I'm glad we have collected books of Lucey's works available now – I would have lined my shelves with them when I was fourteen if they had existed then. No two panels of his stories ever look the same, and you always know what's going on in the stories, whether or not you stop to read the word balloons. Lucey drew the character of his subjects – this is one of the reasons why his work on Ginger is so much fun to read.

--Suzannah Rowntree
Features Editor, Life With Archie *magazine*

Wilbur in Sir Walter Wilkin
...AND I'M YOUR LI'L OLE BUNNY, LAURIE!
...AND I'M YOURS, WILBUR-KINS!!
JO EDWARDS
NOTHING WILL COME BETWEEN US...
WHEEEET

THE VERY IDEA WHISTLING AT ME!
?
WHY YOU LI'L PIPSQUEAK! WHISTLING AT MY GIRL! WHY I'M GOING TO SOCK YOU SO HARD YOU'LL HAVE TO OPEN YOUR SHOE LACES TO BLOW YOUR NOSE!
Y--YOU'VE GOT IT ALL WRONG! I WASN'T WHISTLING AT YOUR GIRL---
--- I WAS ONLY (GULP) WHISTLING FOR MY DOG!
?
?
WELL-L-L- IT WAS A LUCKY THING FOR YOU--- VERY LUCKY!
OOOH-- MY L'IL WILBURKINS IS SO STRONG--- AND MANLY---
AHEM!
2.

GRR-R.. RR NOT AGAIN!
EE EEEE WHEEE
EET
WHY
I'M
GOING
GULP
"MUSCLES" THE FOOTBALL CAPTAIN OF THE SCHOOL---
WOWIE! HI, GOOD-LOOKING!!
ARE YOU GOING TO LET HIM TALK LIKE THAT!
GULP IF HE WANTS TO CALL ME GOOD LOOKING-- LET HIM---
HEH! HEH!
...IF YOU'RE NOT GOING TO DO SOMETHING...
BUT LAURIE...
...WE'RE THROUGH!!

NOT ONE WORD!! NOTHING! HE DIDN'T EVEN BOTHER TO DEFEND LI'L OLE ME! I'LL TELL YOU I'M DISAPPOINTED IN WILBUR!
LOOK, CHIVALRY IS ONE THING, LAURIE, BUT SUICIDE IS ANOTHER!! ANYONE IN SCHOOL WHO HAS TANGLED WITH MUSCLES HAS BEEN PULVERIZED!
I KNOW ALL THAT!
HUH? THEN WHY THE BIG FREEZE ON WILBUR!
IT'S JUST THAT A GIRL LIKES TO BE SHOWN HOW MUCH A FELLOW LIKES HER! BUT WILBUR JUST STOOD THERE GULPING...
WILBUR WAS LUCKY! MOST BOYS DON'T EVEN GET AWAY WITH THAT MUCH BEFORE MUSCLES CHANGES THEIR ADDRESS TO THE GENERAL HOSPITAL!
YOU'VE GOT ME ALL WRONG! I WOULDN'T WANT WILBUR HURT FOR THE WORLD!
I DON'T GET IT! FIRST, YOU WANT A GUY TO GET HIS BRAINS KNOCKED OUT AND THEN YOU DON'T! I CAN'T FIGURE THIS ONE OUT, WOMAN AS I AM!
IF WILBUR DOESN'T WANT TO SPEAK TO YOU, I WOULDN'T BLAME HIM!
MAYBE, I HAVE BEEN TOO HARSH WITH THE POOR BOY!
4.

...AND THAT'S THE WHOLE STORY, RED! NOW LAURIE WON'T TALK TO ME BECAUSE I DIDN'T STAND UP TO MUSCLES!
STAND UP?? WHY YOU'D BE LYING DOWN! IT'S SUICIDE TO FIGHT THAT GORILLA!
MAYBE I NEED SOME BOXING LESSONS!
LOOK MY CHIVALOROUS PAL--- THE ONLY THING YOU NEED IS A SUITCASE AND A TIMETABLE!!-- THAT IS IF YOU'RE THINK-OF CHALLENGING MUSCLES!!
CHALLENGE?? HEY YOU'VE GIVEN ME AN IDEA!
I'LL CHALLENGE MUSCLES TO A DUEL! THAT SHOULD APPEAL TO LAURIE'S VANITY!
HEY! YOU'VE CRACKED YOUR CAP!
JUST GET ME A PEN AND PAPER! I'M GOING TO WRITE A LETTER!
HOW DOES THIS SOUND? "DEAR MUSCLE BRAINS, "FOR INSULTING MY GIRL, I'M GOING TO KNOCK YOUR BLOCK OFF THE NEXT TIME I SEE YOU!" SIGNED WILBUR." -- GIVE ME A STAMP!
WELL, HOW DOES IT SOUND!?
LIKE YOUR LAST WILL AND TESTAMENT!
5.

I'D LIKE LAURIE TO TAKE A LOOK AT THIS LETTER TO MUSCLES!
YOU WON'T HAVE TO WAIT LONG -- HERE SHE COMES!
RED, WOULD YOU SHOW THIS TO LAURIE BEFORE I MAIL IT! IT CONCERNS HER!
HUMPH!
WILBUR!! OH NO!!
WILBUR WILKIN!! IF YOU GO THROUGH WITH THIS NONSENSE, I'LL NEVER TALK TO YOU AGAIN!!
?
I'M GLAD I STOPPED YOU FROM DOING THIS FOOL-HARDY THING!
YOU MEAN YOU DON'T WANT ME TO FIGHT FOR YOU!
LET'S FORGET ALL ABOUT IT! COME, WE'LL GO TO MY HOUSE TO CELEBRATE OUR RE-UNION!
BOY, AREN'T WOMEN FUNNY?!
6.

I'D HATE TO THINK OF WHAT A MESS YOU'D HAVE BEEN, IF YOU MAILED THAT LETTER!
HEH! HEH!.. WHO WAS GOING TO MAIL IT!!
YOU CAN HAND OVER THE LETTER NOW! YOU WERE THE LAST ONE TO HAVE IT!
GOLLY, I DON'T HAVE IT!
YIKES!!
IT'S PROBABLY STILL AT THE SODA SHOP!!
?
DID YOU SEE A LETTER.. GASP! ?
YES! I FOUND ONE! I THOUGHT YOU FORGOT TO MAIL IT!
SO I MAILED IT FOR YOU!!
R.I.P. WILBUR WILKIN

GULP.-- I HOPE I'M NOT RECOGNIZED! I'M A DEAD DUCK, IF MUSCLES CATCHES ME!
HI, WILBUR!! WHERE HAVE YOU BEEN HIDING LATELY!
S-SH!! SSSH--!
WELL, I KNEW IF I FOLLOWED LAURIE, SHE'D LEAD ME TO YOU!--- MY LETTER WRITING FRIEND!!
SOCK!
BAM
SOCK!!
SO YOU WERE GOING TO KNOCK MY BLOCK OFF?..
YOU HIT HIM!!
YOU HIT MY WILBUR!! YOU BRUTE!
BOP!
BOY! I NEVER KNEW YOU HAD SUCH A LEFT HOOK!
I DIDN'T BECOME CAPTAIN OF THE BOXING TEAM FOR NOTHING! NOW I'LL TEACH YOU HOW TO JAB...
GIRLS BOXING TEAM
The End

Ginger
"HORIZONTAL HEROES"
FOOTBALL PRACTICE TODAY
ICKKY! MY HERO!
DON'T WORRY, GINGER!
HE'LL LIVE!
...BUT HE'LL NEVER PLAY FOOTBALL!
FIRST AID
HARRY LUCEY
C-COACH.... YOU MEAN HE'S THAT BADLY HURT?
WHO SAID HE'S BADLY HURT? I SAID HE'D NEVER PLAY FOOTBALL! TIDDLY WINKS MAYBE, BUT NOT FOOTBALL!
SO! JUST BECAUSE HE MADE ONE SMALL MISTAKE, YOU DON'T WANT HIM ON THE TEAM?!
WHO SAID LIVING IS SUCH A SMALL MISTAKE?!

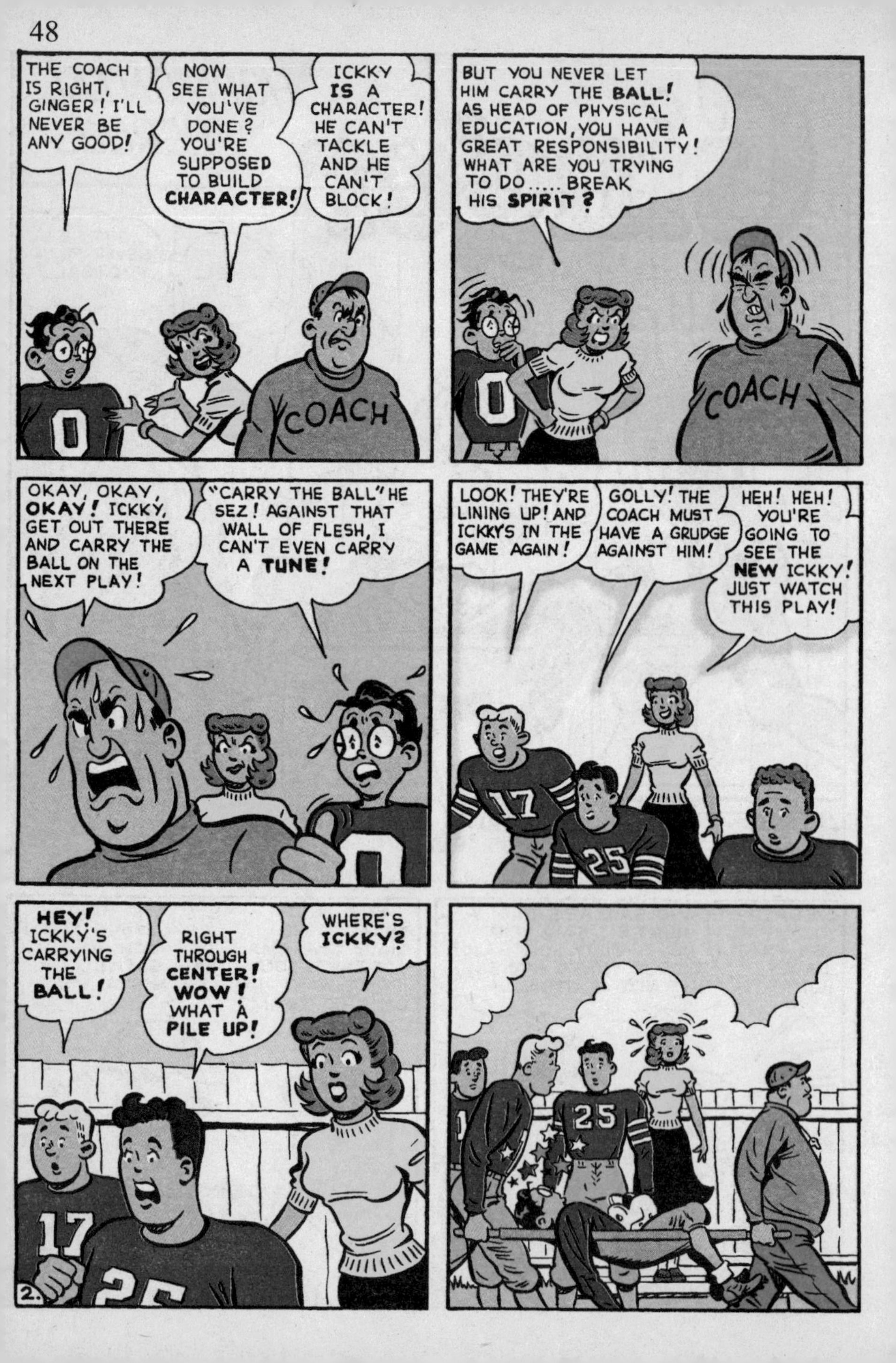
THE COACH IS RIGHT, GINGER! I'LL NEVER BE ANY GOOD!
NOW SEE WHAT YOU'VE DONE? YOU'RE SUPPOSED TO BUILD CHARACTER!
ICKKY IS A CHARACTER! HE CAN'T TACKLE AND HE CAN'T BLOCK!
COACH
BUT YOU NEVER LET HIM CARRY THE BALL! AS HEAD OF PHYSICAL EDUCATION, YOU HAVE A GREAT RESPONSIBILITY! WHAT ARE YOU TRYING TO DO..... BREAK HIS SPIRIT?
COACH
OKAY, OKAY, OKAY! ICKKY, GET OUT THERE AND CARRY THE BALL ON THE NEXT PLAY!
"CARRY THE BALL" HE SEZ! AGAINST THAT WALL OF FLESH, I CAN'T EVEN CARRY A TUNE!
LOOK! THEY'RE LINING UP! AND ICKKY'S IN THE GAME AGAIN!
GOLLY! THE COACH MUST HAVE A GRUDGE AGAINST HIM!
HEH! HEH! YOU'RE GOING TO SEE THE NEW ICKKY! JUST WATCH THIS PLAY!
HEY! ICKKY'S CARRYING THE BALL!
RIGHT THROUGH CENTER! WOW! WHAT A PILE UP!
WHERE'S ICKKY?
2.

BUT, COACH, IF I DON'T HELP BEAT YOGURT, GINGER WON'T GO TO THE VICTORY DANCE WITH ME!
I'M SORRY, JONES, BUT WITH THE TEAM WE HAVE IT LOOKS LIKE THE DANCE WILL TURN INTO A WAKE!
CO
IF I ONLY HAD A MAN TO SCOUT THE YOGURT TEAM AND FIND OUT WHAT PLAYS THEY'RE RUNNING WE'D HAVE A CHANCE!
WOULD THAT BE A DANGEROUS JOB?
DANGEROUS? WHATEVER GAVE YOU THAT IDEA? THEY'D PROBABLY ROLL OUT THE PLUSH CARPET AND PIN A MEDAL ON YOU!
YEAH?
OACH
HEY! MAYBE I COULD FIND OUT WHAT THE COACH WANTS TO KNOW AND HELP WIN THE GAME!
THEN GINGER WOULD STILL BE PROUD OF ME!
AND I WOULDN'T GET KILLED!
BUT, ICKKY, THEY MAY NOT LIKE ANYONE SNOOPING AROUND!
IT'S NOT SNOOPING! I'M GOING AS A REPRESENTATIVE OF THE SCHOOL PAPER, SPORTS WRITERS ARE ALWAYS WELCOME!
3.
IT'S LIKE BEING A VISITING DIGNITARY FROM ANOTHER COUNTRY! THEY SHOW YOU EVERY COURTESY! YOU HAVE DIPLOMATIC IMMUNITY!
OH! LIKE AN AMBASSADOR!

THEN YOU OUGHT TO LOOK THE PART! YOU KNOW....STRIPED TROUSERS....CUT-AWAY COAT!
I COULD WEAR MY PIN STRIPES AND MY TUX JACKET!
HOW DO I LOOK?
WONDERFUL! I BROUGHT DADDY'S BRIEFCASE! ALL AMBASSADORS CARRY PORTFOLIOS!
HERE WE ARE....BUT I DON'T SEE ANY PLUSH CARPET!
MAYBE THEY DON'T EXPECT YOU! YOU SHOULD HAVE PHONED YOU WERE COMING!
YOGURT H
THIS IS EXCITING! HE LOOKS JUST LIKE ADAMIN EDEN GOING INTO TEN BROWNING STREET!
I'M GLAD I THOUGHT OF THIS! ICKKY IS A BORN DIPLOMAT!
YOGURT H.S.
I WONDER WHAT SORT OF A MEDAL THEY GIVE VISITING DIGNITARIES!
4.
RT H.S

I GUESS THEY DON'T APPRECIATE DIPLOMACY! WE'LL SHOW 'EM! THIS WINDOW LEADS TO THE LOCKER ROOM!
IT MAY LEAD TO TROUBLE! SUPPOSE THEY SHOOT SPIES!
'REMEMBER NATHAN HALE' SHE SEZ!
THEY HUNG HIM!
HEY! A WINDOW ON THE OTHER SIDE!
MAYBE I COULD CLIMB UP AND SEE THE FIELD FROM HERE!
GEE, COACH, OUR BOYS ARE REALLY IN TOP FORM! THEY'RE MURDERING THE SCRUB TEAM!
YEAH, WE'RE RUNNING OUT OF SCRUBS! BETTER SEE IF YOU CAN ROUND UP SUBSTITUTES!
OW! I CAN SEE EVERYTHING FROM HERE AND EVERYTHING I SEE IS BAD! THEY'RE CARRYING OFF ANOTHER MAN FROM THE SCRUBS!
HEY, YOU!
C'MON! GET INTO THOSE PANTS AND PUT ON THIS WHITE SHIRT! WHERE'S YOUR SCHOOL SPIRIT? THEY NEED YOU ON THE FIELD!
BUT..... BUT.... BUT.... BUT.....
5.
STOP ARGUING! HERE'S YOUR HELMET!
GET OUT THERE AND FIGHT!
WUMP!
YOGURT

COACH, HERE'S ANOTHER VICTIM ....ER.... SUB FOR THE SCRUBS!
GET IN THERE! WE'RE WAITING TO RUN OFF THIS LAST PLAY!
HEY, WAIT!
17
OKAY, LET'S TRY THAT POWER PLAY AGAIN!
AND YOU SCRUBS TRY TO HOLD THAT LINE THIS TIME!
9
YEAH..... ....TRY!
SIGNALS..... 1-2-3-4-5 HUP!
ULP!
Wham!
COMES THE DAY OF THE BIG GAME!
OH, OH! MONK'S HURT! NOW I'LL GET INTO ACTION! I'M GOING TO BE THE STAR OF THE GAME!
ICKKY..... YOU? YOU MEAN YOU'RE STILL ON THE TEAM? WHAT POSITION DO YOU PLAY?
6.
THE END

All Keyed Up!
Pat the Brat #21, 1957
by Bob White

As much as I love Little Archie, I think I love Pat the Brat even more. Sure, he's Archie's answer (or should I say response) to Dennis the Menace, but as much as I love Hank Ketcham's art (especially early Ketcham), I think I love Bob White even more. The other thing is, I seem to relate to Pat more than Archie or Dennis. Maybe it's because I didn't have two girls fighting over me when I was a kid. Maybe it's because I didn't have a dog, or an elderly neighbor to annoy. Maybe it's something as simple as having black hair. Whatever the case, I don't have a lot of Pat the Brat comics (hint: I'D LOVE A COLLECTION) but the ones I do have include a lot of stories that I not only relate to – I lived them! Case in point, one of my favorites, "All Keyed Up" from Pat the Brat #21. I've had a misadventure or two with keys and locked doors to my parents' chagrin!

--J. Torres
Writer,
Archie Comics series Jinx

Venus Bound
Cosmo the Merry Martian #4, 1958
by Bob Montana

I loved *Laugh Digest*. This was the book that wasn't only filled with Archie stories, it also included stories from other characters like Sabrina The Teenage Witch, That Wilkin Boy and even really bizarre characters like Super Duck. *Laugh Comics Digest #7* introduced me to Cosmo the Merry Martian. Cosmo had his own series which ran for seven issues back in 1958. I'd never heard of him when I ran across "Venus Bound" in *Laugh*, but it was an adventure story and a sci-fi story so I was there! Sure, it wasn't Star Wars but it took place in outer space so that was good enough for me! Cosmo looked like a bowling pin with legs but he had a spaceship, a martian dog, and he encountered crazy aliens on really wild planets. I loved it! I dug Cosmo so much that to this day I'm always sneaking Cosmo into the backgrounds of the stories that I draw. Keep a sharp eye out!

--Fernando Ruiz
Writer / artist,
Archie Comics

PAT THE BRAT
IN
"ALL KEYED UP!"
OSWALD! WILL YOU GO SEE IF THERE'S ANY MAIL?
I WOULD IF I COULD FIND THE KEY TO THE MAILBOX! WHERE DID YOU HIDE IT THIS TIME?
I HID IT ON THE HALL TABLE WHERE I ALWAYS HIDE IT! ...ON THE RING WITH THE CAR KEYS! IF IT HAD TEETH IT WOULD BITE YOU!
LEMME GET THE MAIL, POP! HUH, POP? I CAN USE THE KEY! HUH?
ALL RIGHT, PAT!
IF IT BITES ME, I'LL BITE IT BACK!
SMITH
U.S. MAIL
HEH, HEH! THE LITTLE RASCAL! HE SURE CAN FIGURE THINGS OUT!
HERE YA ARE, POP! JUST A LOT OF BULLS!
BILLS, PAT! THAT'S ALL WE EVER GET!

DON'T FORGET TO PUT THE KEYS BACK WHERE YOU FOUND THEM!
I FOUND A SAFER PLACE FOR 'EM, MOM!
WHERE'S THAT, PAT?
I DROPPED 'EM IN THE SLOT IN THE MAIL BOX!
FIVE DOLLARS! A BRAND NEW BOX, TOO!
ZZZZZ
SMITH
U.S. MAIL
GOSH, POP! WHY ARE YOU CUTTING THAT BOX IN HALF?
CAN YOU THINK OF A BETTER WAY TO GET THE KEYS OUT?
SURE! OPEN THE DOOR AN' TAKE 'EM OUT!
OH, NO!
Y-YOU D-DIDN'T LOCK IT? W-WHY DIDN'T YOU SAY SO?
YA DIDN'T ASK ME!
SMI TH
(SIGH) OH WELL, LET'S GET INTO THE HOUSE! IT LOOKS LIKE RAIN!
YOU WANT I SHOULD LOCK THE GARAGE DOOR, POP? THE CAR MIGHT GET WET!

THAT HEAP'S COVERED BY SO MANY MORTGAGES THE RAIN WOULD NEVER GET TO IT!
WHAT MORTGAGES, POP?
NEVER MIND, PAT! LET'S GO CLOSE THOSE GARAGE DOORS!
HERE'S THE KEY, POP! CAN I LOCK IT? HUH? CAN I?
6430
WATCH OUT, PATTY! WE DON'T NEED THE KEY TO LOCK THE GARAGE DOOR! ONLY TO OPEN IT!
YOU SEE, SON! THIS KIND OF DOOR LOCKS BY ITSELF WHEN YOU CLOSE IT!
GEE!
6430
NOW STEP OUT OF THE WAY! I DON'T WANT YOU TO GET HIT BY THIS DOOR!
OKAY, POP!
6430
SLAM!

THERE! NOW LET'S... LET'S........ OOPS!!!
PAT! I MEANT YOU SHOULD STEP OUT OF THE GARAGE! I SUPPOSE YOU'VE GOT THE KEY?
SURE, POP! RIGHT HERE!
OH GREAT! AND THAT WINDOW HAS BEEN STUCK FOR YEARS! STEP BACK, SON!
CRASH!
GEE, POP, THAT WAS KEEN! WERE YOU EVER A FIREMAN?
NO! BUT I GET PRETTY HOT UNDER THE COLLAR AT TIMES!
MARY! WE'VE GOT TO DO SOMETHING ABOUT PAT! ALL HE WANTS TO PLAY WITH ARE KEYS AND LOCKS!

OH, THAT'S JUST A STAGE! ALL CHILDREN GO THROUGH IT!
BUT IT'S DANGEROUS! I READ JUST THE OTHER DAY THAT A BOY HAD LOCKED HIMSELF IN THE BATHROOM!
...AND HIS PARENTS FOUND HIM ALMOST DROWNED IN THE BATH TUB!
POP! MOM!
I LOCKED THE BATH-ROOM DOOR!
OMIGOSH! OUR PATTY DID IT!
OHH! M-MY POOR BABY!
ZOOM!
COME ON, SON! OPEN IT UP!
P-PUT THE K-KEY IN THE L-LOCK!
H-HE DOESN'T ANSWER!!!
D-DO SOMETHING MAYBE HE FELL IN THE TUB!

AN AXE! THERE'S NO TIME TO LOSE! I NEED AN AXE!
I HEARD YA YELLING, POP! HERE'S YOUR AXE!
(SOB) T-THANKS, PAT!
(SOB)(SOB) DADDY W-WILL BE RIGHT THERE, SON! I'LL........
CRASH!
.....THANKS, PAT ???
YOU'RE WELCOME, POP!
PATTY! M-MY BABY! YOU'RE SAFE! W-WE THOUGHT YOU WERE LOCKED IN THE BATHROOM!
SMACK!
GEE, NO, MOM! I LOCKED IT FROM THE OUTSIDE! ...BUT I COULDN'T GET IT OPEN AGAIN!
THE QUIET AFTER THE STORM!
WHO DID YA BULLY BEFORE THE STORK BROUGHT ME?
THE END.

CHAPTER ONE
VENUS BOUND!
DEEP INSIDE THE MOON CITY OBSERVATORY, A SOLAR SPOTTER SEES SOMETHING ON THE GIANT SKYSCOPE...
OMIGOSH! A FOREIGN ROCKET SHIP...! HEADED THIS WAY!
CALLING ALL MOONLINGS! FLASH RED! ROCKET SHIP APPROACHING
CONDITION HELP!
CALL OUT THE MARINES! CALL OUT THE MARINES!
WE CAN'T! WE DON'T HAVE ANY MARINES!
OH, NO!
WHAT'S ALL THE FUSS ABOUT? TRY TO KEEP CALM!
DON'T BE SILLY, COSMO! RULE NUMBER ONE ON THE MOON IS- "WHEN IN DOUBT... PANIC!"

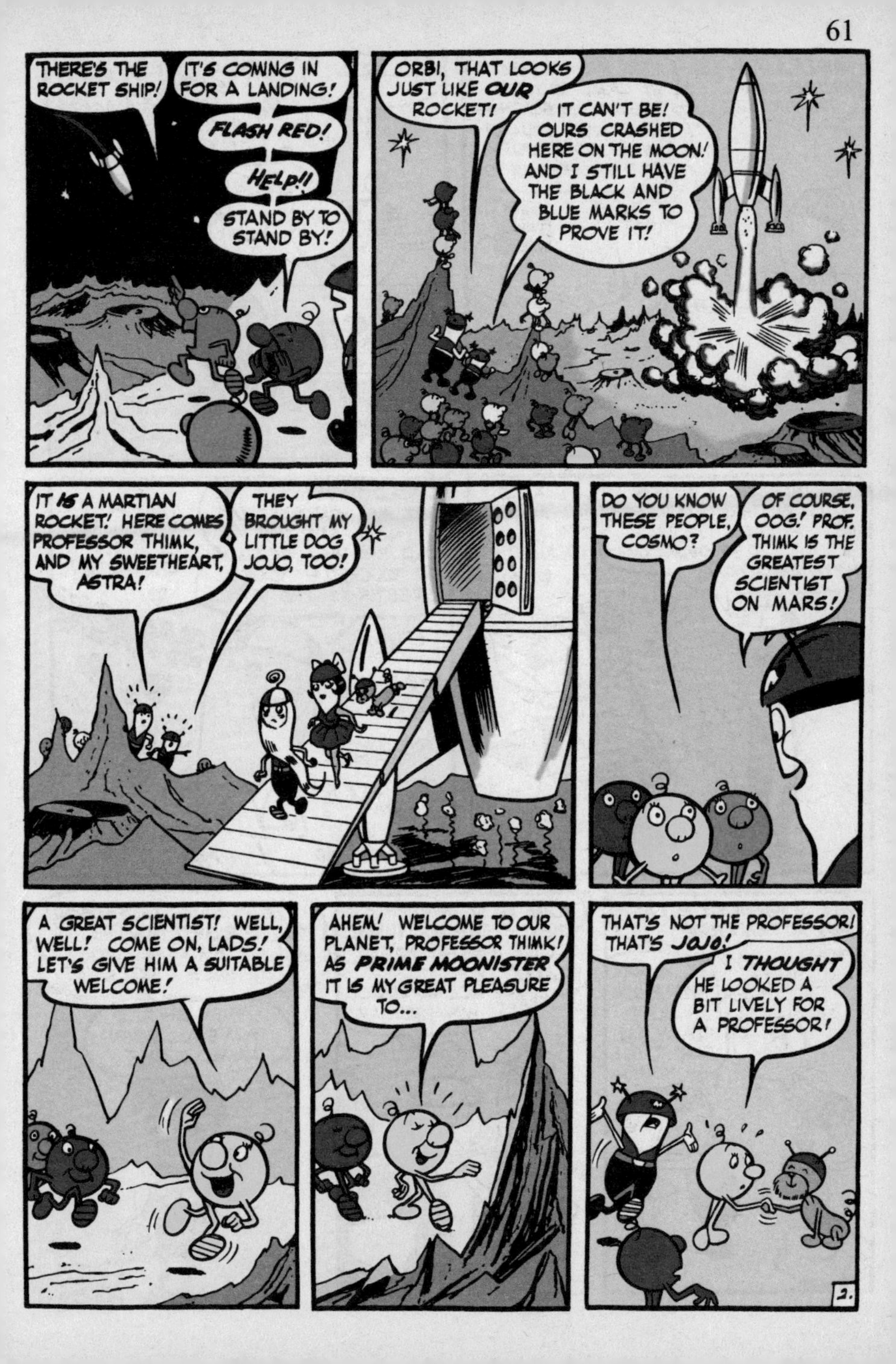
THERE'S THE ROCKET SHIP!
IT'S COMING IN FOR A LANDING!
FLASH RED!
HELP!!
STAND BY TO STAND BY!
ORBI, THAT LOOKS JUST LIKE OUR ROCKET!
IT CAN'T BE! OURS CRASHED HERE ON THE MOON! AND I STILL HAVE THE BLACK AND BLUE MARKS TO PROVE IT!
IT IS A MARTIAN ROCKET! HERE COMES PROFESSOR THIMK, AND MY SWEETHEART, ASTRA!
THEY BROUGHT MY LITTLE DOG JOJO, TOO!
DO YOU KNOW THESE PEOPLE, COSMO?
OF COURSE, OOG! PROF. THIMK IS THE GREATEST SCIENTIST ON MARS!
A GREAT SCIENTIST! WELL, WELL! COME ON, LADS! LET'S GIVE HIM A SUITABLE WELCOME!
AHEM! WELCOME TO OUR PLANET, PROFESSOR THIMK! AS PRIME MOONISTER IT IS MY GREAT PLEASURE TO...
THAT'S NOT THE PROFESSOR! THAT'S JOJO!
I THOUGHT HE LOOKED A BIT LIVELY FOR A PROFESSOR!
2.

ASTRA!! PROFESSOR THIMK!
HERE WE ARE M'BOY! WE CAME TO YOUR RESCUE AS SOON AS WE COULD! YOU CAN ALWAYS COUNT ON THE OLD PROFESSOR TO..
.....ER.....
SMACK! SMACK! SMACK! SMACK! SMACK! SMACK! SMACK! SMACK!
SWISH!
YES INDEED! I KNEW YOU'D BE THRILLED TO SEE ME! I TOLD THEM BACK HOME YOU'D BE OVERCOME WITH EMOTION!
SMACK! SMACK SMACK! SMACK! SMACK!
I TOLD THEM YOU'D GET ALL CHOKED UP WHEN YOU SAW THE OLD PROFESSOR! I'M SO TOUCHED BY YOUR GREETING! IT'S VERY...
SMACK! SMACK! SMACK! SMACK! SMACK! SMACK! SMACK! SMACK! SMACK!
WILL SOMEBODY PLEASE PAY ATTENTION!
ER... SORRY, PROFESSOR THIMK! I REALLY AM GLAD TO SEE YOU!
COME ALONG AND MEET OUR FRIENDS, THE MOONLINGS! ALL OF THEM ARE NAMED OOG!
ALL NAMED OOG? HOW PECULIAR!
IT IS PECULIAR, PROFESSOR! YOU'RE RIGHT! IMAGINE ALL OF 'EM NAMED OOG! BOY, THAT'S A HOT ONE!
THEY SHOULD HAVE ALL BEEN NAMED SAM!

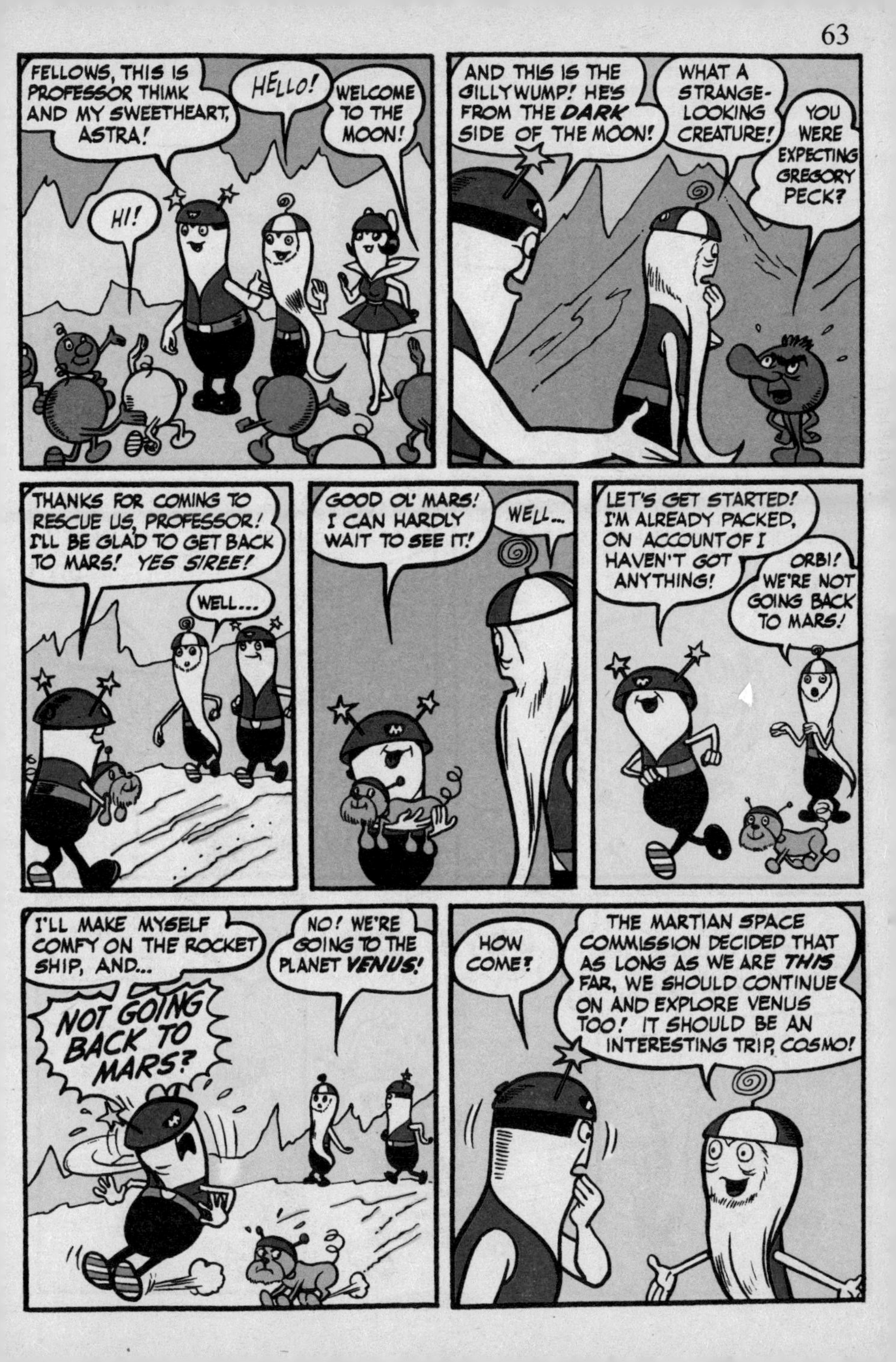

FELLOWS, THIS IS PROFESSOR THIMK AND MY SWEETHEART, ASTRA!
HELLO!
WELCOME TO THE MOON!
HI!
AND THIS IS THE GILLYWUMP! HE'S FROM THE DARK SIDE OF THE MOON!
WHAT A STRANGE-LOOKING CREATURE!
YOU WERE EXPECTING GREGORY PECK?
THANKS FOR COMING TO RESCUE US, PROFESSOR! I'LL BE GLAD TO GET BACK TO MARS! YES SIREE!
WELL...
GOOD OL' MARS! I CAN HARDLY WAIT TO SEE IT!
WELL...
LET'S GET STARTED! I'M ALREADY PACKED, ON ACCOUNT OF I HAVEN'T GOT ANYTHING!
ORBI! WE'RE NOT GOING BACK TO MARS!
I'LL MAKE MYSELF COMFY ON THE ROCKET SHIP, AND...
NO! WE'RE GOING TO THE PLANET VENUS!
NOT GOING BACK TO MARS?
HOW COME?
THE MARTIAN SPACE COMMISSION DECIDED THAT AS LONG AS WE ARE THIS FAR, WE SHOULD CONTINUE ON AND EXPLORE VENUS TOO! IT SHOULD BE AN INTERESTING TRIP, COSMO!

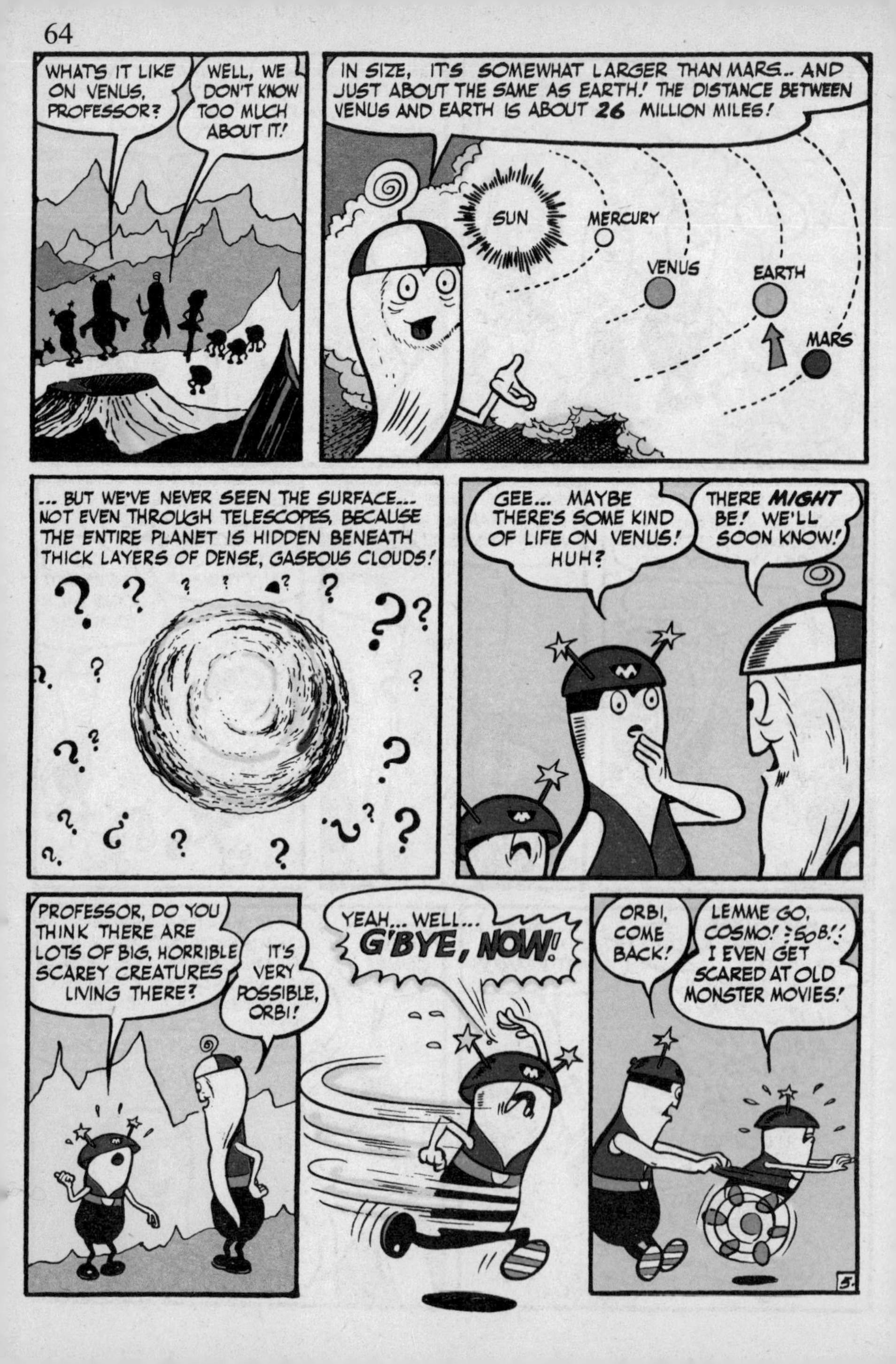
WHAT'S IT LIKE ON VENUS, PROFESSOR?
WELL, WE DON'T KNOW TOO MUCH ABOUT IT!
IN SIZE, IT'S SOMEWHAT LARGER THAN MARS.. AND JUST ABOUT THE SAME AS EARTH! THE DISTANCE BETWEEN VENUS AND EARTH IS ABOUT 26 MILLION MILES!
SUN
MERCURY
VENUS
EARTH
MARS
... BUT WE'VE NEVER SEEN THE SURFACE... NOT EVEN THROUGH TELESCOPES, BECAUSE THE ENTIRE PLANET IS HIDDEN BENEATH THICK LAYERS OF DENSE, GASEOUS CLOUDS!
GEE... MAYBE THERE'S SOME KIND OF LIFE ON VENUS! HUH?
THERE MIGHT BE! WE'LL SOON KNOW!
PROFESSOR, DO YOU THINK THERE ARE LOTS OF BIG, HORRIBLE SCAREY CREATURES LIVING THERE?
IT'S VERY POSSIBLE, ORBI!
YEAH... WELL... G'BYE, NOW!
ORBI, COME BACK!
LEMME GO, COSMO! SOB! I EVEN GET SCARED AT OLD MONSTER MOVIES!
5.

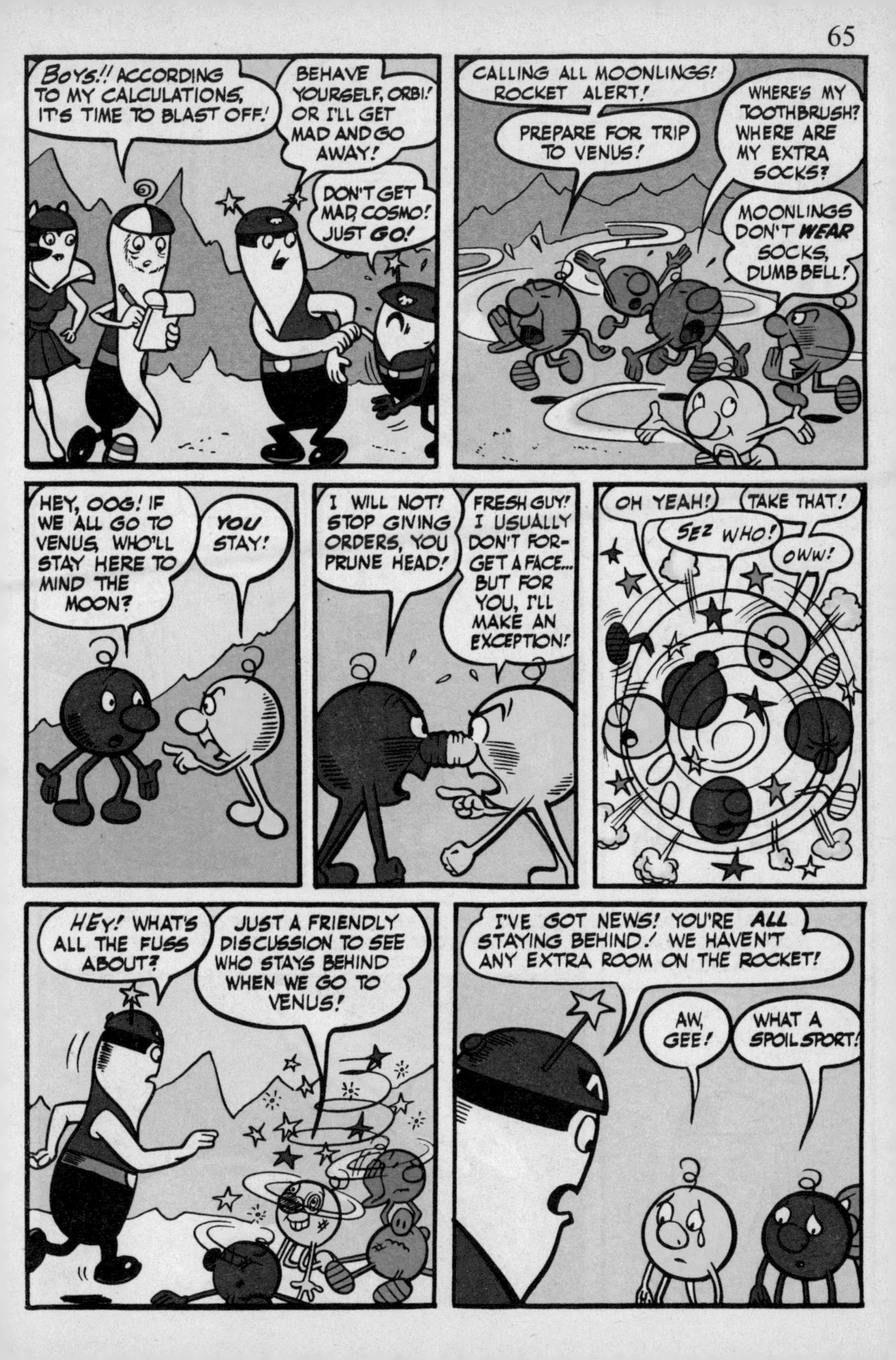
BOYS!! ACCORDING TO MY CALCULATIONS, IT'S TIME TO BLAST OFF!
BEHAVE YOURSELF, ORBI! OR I'LL GET MAD AND GO AWAY!
DON'T GET MAD, COSMO! JUST GO!
CALLING ALL MOONLINGS! ROCKET ALERT!
PREPARE FOR TRIP TO VENUS!
WHERE'S MY TOOTHBRUSH? WHERE ARE MY EXTRA SOCKS?
MOONLINGS DON'T WEAR SOCKS, DUMBBELL!
HEY, OOG! IF WE ALL GO TO VENUS, WHO'LL STAY HERE TO MIND THE MOON?
YOU STAY!
I WILL NOT! STOP GIVING ORDERS, YOU PRUNE HEAD!
FRESH GUY! I USUALLY DON'T FORGET A FACE... BUT FOR YOU, I'LL MAKE AN EXCEPTION!
OH YEAH!
TAKE THAT!
SEZ WHO!
OWW!
HEY! WHAT'S ALL THE FUSS ABOUT?
JUST A FRIENDLY DISCUSSION TO SEE WHO STAYS BEHIND WHEN WE GO TO VENUS!
I'VE GOT NEWS! YOU'RE ALL STAYING BEHIND! WE HAVEN'T ANY EXTRA ROOM ON THE ROCKET!
AW, GEE!
WHAT A SPOILSPORT!

COME ALONG FOLKS!
GOODBYE, OOGS!
HAVE A NICE TRIP!
SEND US A PICTURE POSTCARD FROM VENUS !!
... ZERO MINUS FOUR ... ZERO MINUS THREE... ZERO MINUS ONE ...
BLAST OFF!
THERE, THEY GO!
WE'RE ON OUR WAY, COSMO!
Y'KNOW... I'M REALLY GOING TO MISS THOSE CRAZY MOON-LINGS!
SURPRISE!
GALLOPIN' GALAXIES!
TWO OF US STOWED AWAY, COSMO!
ME TOO! A GILLYWUMP MAY COME IN HANDY IN OUTER SPACE!
OH, NO!
FOUR MARTIANS... A DOG... TWO MOONLINGS NAMED OOG... AND A GILLYWUMP!
THIS CERTAINLY IS AN UNUSUAL CREW!
BREAKING FREE OF THE MOON'S GRAVITATIONAL PULL, THE GREAT ROCKET TRAVELS IN "FREE FALL TOWARD VENUS...

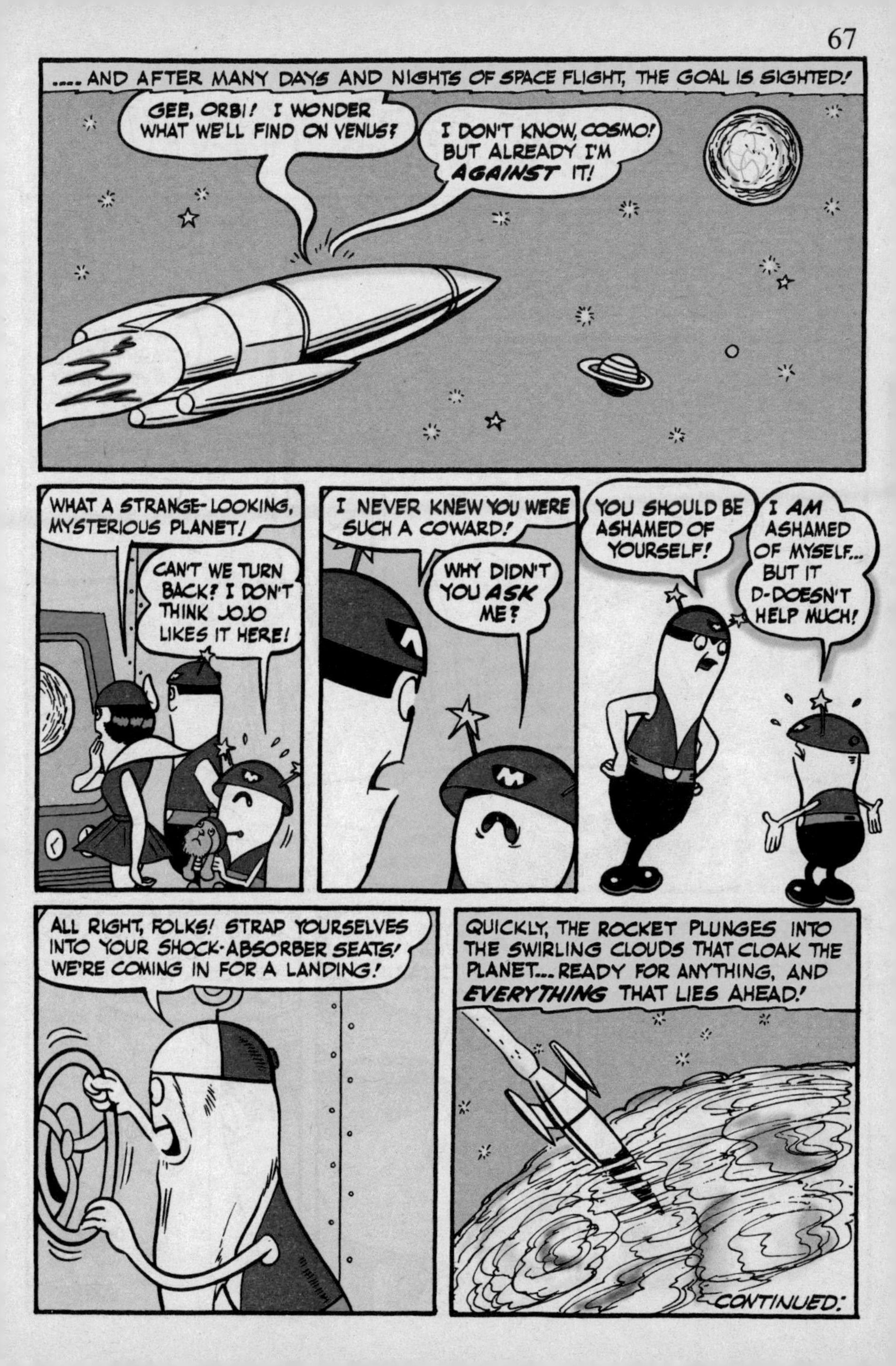

.... AND AFTER MANY DAYS AND NIGHTS OF SPACE FLIGHT, THE GOAL IS SIGHTED!
GEE, ORBI! I WONDER WHAT WE'LL FIND ON VENUS?
I DON'T KNOW, COSMO! BUT ALREADY I'M AGAINST IT!
WHAT A STRANGE-LOOKING, MYSTERIOUS PLANET!
CAN'T WE TURN BACK? I DON'T THINK JOJO LIKES IT HERE!
I NEVER KNEW YOU WERE SUCH A COWARD!
WHY DIDN'T YOU ASK ME?
YOU SHOULD BE ASHAMED OF YOURSELF!
I AM ASHAMED OF MYSELF... BUT IT D-DOESN'T HELP MUCH!
ALL RIGHT, FOLKS! STRAP YOURSELVES INTO YOUR SHOCK-ABSORBER SEATS! WE'RE COMING IN FOR A LANDING!
QUICKLY, THE ROCKET PLUNGES INTO THE SWIRLING CLOUDS THAT CLOAK THE PLANET... READY FOR ANYTHING, AND EVERYTHING THAT LIES AHEAD!
CONTINUED:

CHAPTER TWO

TROUBLE FOR ORBI!

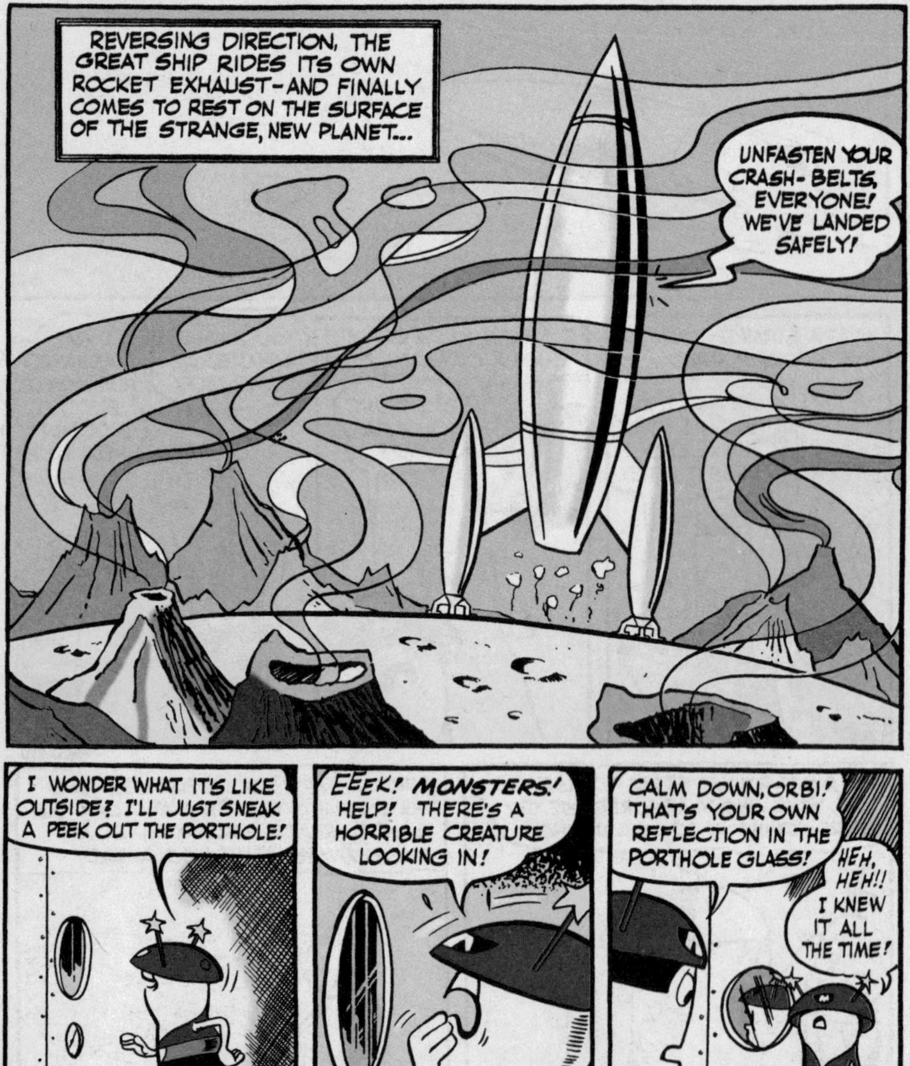

LET'S DO A LITTLE EXPLORING, FOLKS! IT'S PERFECTLY SAFE FOR US TO LEAVE THE SHIP!
HOW CAN YOU TELL, PROFESSOR?
BY CHECKING MY RADIATION METER, MY ATMOSPHERE METER, AND MY TEMPERATURE METER!
H-HOW ABOUT Y-Y-YOUR MONSTER METER?
ORBI, STOP ACTING SO SCARED!
WH-WHO'S ACTING?
WELL, WELL! LOOK AT THESE POCKET-SIZE VOLCANOES, ALL PUFFING SMOKE! THIS IS WHAT CAUSES THOSE DENSE CLOUDS AROUND VENUS!
THE WHOLE PLANET IS COVERED WITH THEM!
HERE'S ONE SHAPED LIKE AN INDIAN TEPEE!--IT'S MAKING SMOKE SIGNALS!
... AND HERE'S A CIGAR-SHAPED ONE... BLOWING SMOKE RINGS!
WHAT'S WRONG WITH THIS ONE? THERE'S NO SMOKE COMING OUT!
MAYBE IT'S INHALING!
2

LATER:
VENUS IS A FASCINATING PLANET! YOU KNOW, COSMO... IT WAS NAMED AFTER THE GREEK GODDESS OF LOVE!
I LIKE LOVE, ASTRA DEAR!
STOP THE MUSH! STOP THE MUSH!
WURF!
DON'T BE A GROUCH, ORBI!
I CAN'T HELP IT! MY FEET ARE TIRED! SO ARE JOJO'S..... AND HE'S GOT FOUR OF 'EM!
I'M A LITTLE TIRED TOO, COSMO!
OKAY, ASTRA! LET'S ALL CLIMB UP ON THIS HILL AND REST A WHILE!
WHOOPS!
UP YOU GO!
WELL, THERE'S ONE THING ABOUT THIS PLANET THAT REALLY DISAPPOINTS ME!
WHAT'S THAT, ORBI?
NO MONSTERS!
zzzzZZZzzzzz
3

zzzzZZZzzzzz
?
?
?
GEE! WHAT'S THAT FUNNY NOISE?
PROBABLY A BUZZ-SAW!
OF COURSE! THAT'S WHAT IT IS ALL RIGHT! I SHOULD HAVE.....
HEY! WAIT A MINUTE! WHAT'S A BUZZ-SAW DOING ON VENUS??
ZZNNNN
YOU'RE RIGHT! LET'S INVESTIGATE!
AFTER YOU, C-COSMO!
BE CAREFUL, BOYS!
YIP, YIP!
LOOK! THE FUNNY SOUND IS COMING OUT OF THAT CAVE!
ORBI, I'VE GOT NEWS FOR YOU! THAT ISN'T A CAVE...
ZZZZZZ
... IT'S A MOUTH!
4.

ΔϘΩ!!
HELP! HELP! MONSTERS! SPACE CREATURES!
RUN FOR YOUR LIVES!
HEAD FOR THE SHIP, ASTRA!
OH, DEAR! I'M FRIGHTENED!
WAIT FOR ORBI! WAIT FOR ORBI!
(PUFF! PUFF!) THAT'S FUNNY! I'M RUNNING AND RUNNING... BUT I'M NOT GETTING ANYWHERE! (PUFF! PUFF!)
NO WONDER! I'M OFF THE GROUND!
HELLLLP!
5.

I'M BEING CAPTURED BY A MENUSIAN VONSTER! I MEAN, A VENUSIAN MONSTER!
ΦΔΚΩ!!
LET'S RUN AND TELL THE PROFESSOR! QUICK!
WURF!
PROFESSOR THIMK! PROFESSOR THIMK!
POOR LITTLE ORBI!
AH, THERE, COSMO! I HAVE INTERESTING NEWS FOR YOU! ACCORDING TO MY INSTRUMENTS, THERE ARE NO LIVING CREATURES ON VENUS!
THAT'S WHAT YOU THINK!
WHAT DO YOU MEAN?
ORBI WAS JUST CAPTURED BY A VENUSIAN EIGHTY FEET HIGH!
IMPOSSIBLE! MY INSTRUMENTS ARE VERY ACCURATE!
BUT IT'S TRUE! WE SAW HIM!
WELL! I MUST SAY THIS IS MOST IRRITATING!
YOU'RE IRRITATED? THINK HOW ORBI FEELS!
CONTINUED!

CHAPTER THREE
TO THE RESCUE!
IN THE GRIPS OF A HUGE MENUSIAN VONSTER.... OOPS, SORRY.... WE MEANT VENUSIAN MONSTER... LITTLE ORBI IS CARRIED OFF TO AN UNKNOWN FATE!
HELP!! PUT ME DOWN! I DIDN'T EVEN WANT TO COME TO THIS CRAZY PLANET!
POOR ORBI!
FOLKS, WE'LL HAVE TO ORGANIZE A RESCUE PARTY!
RESCUE PARTY! RESCUE PARTY!
CALLING ALL VOLUNTEERS FOR THE RESCUE PARTY!
PIPE DOWN, OOG! I'M IN CHARGE OF PANIC AROUND HERE!
I'M IN CHARGE OF PANIC! YOU'RE IN CHARGE OF HYSTERIA!

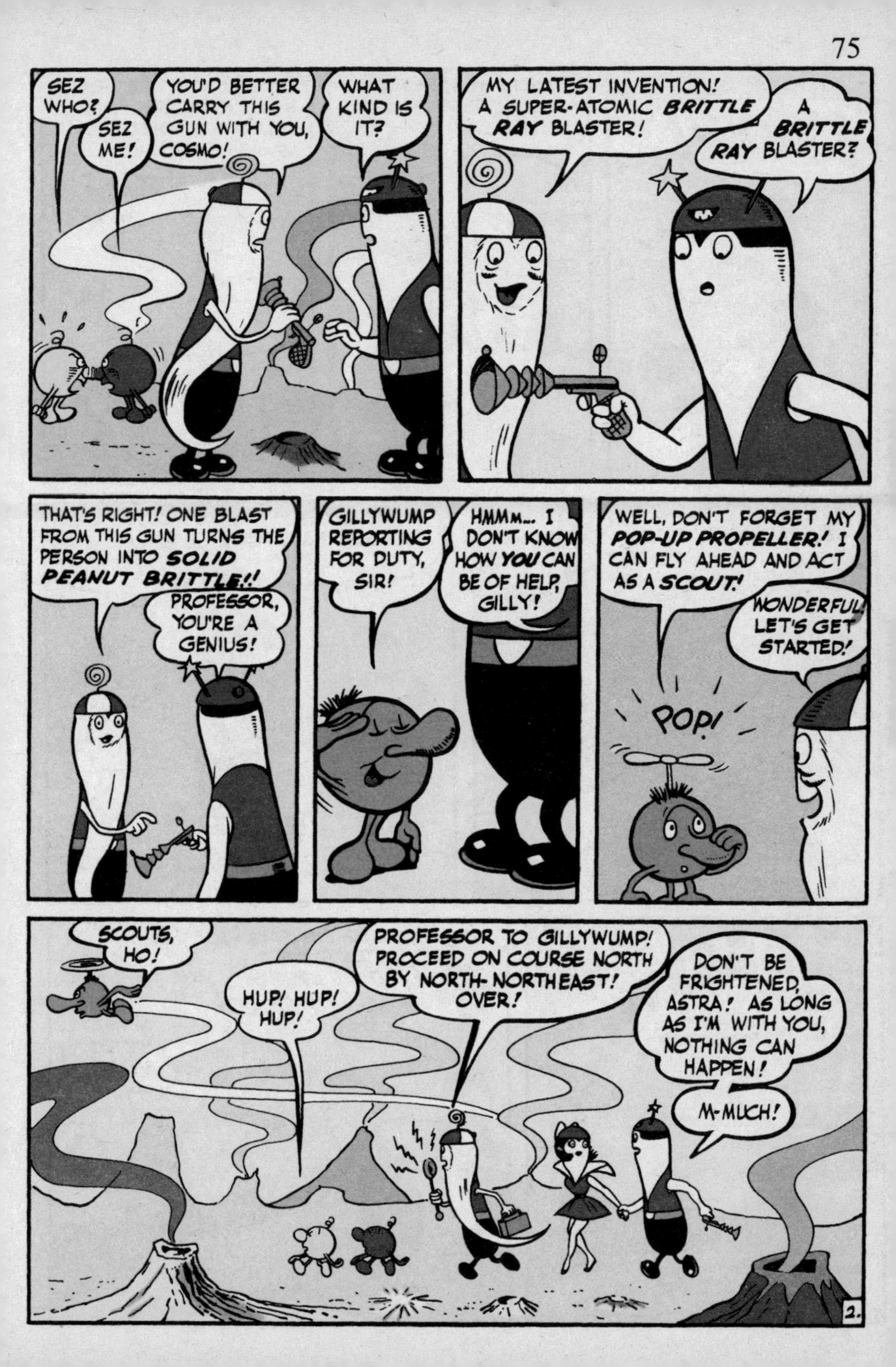
SEZ WHO?
SEZ ME!
YOU'D BETTER CARRY THIS GUN WITH YOU, COSMO!
WHAT KIND IS IT?
MY LATEST INVENTION! A SUPER-ATOMIC BRITTLE RAY BLASTER!
A BRITTLE RAY BLASTER?
THAT'S RIGHT! ONE BLAST FROM THIS GUN TURNS THE PERSON INTO SOLID PEANUT BRITTLE!!
PROFESSOR, YOU'RE A GENIUS!
GILLYWUMP REPORTING FOR DUTY, SIR!
HMMM... I DON'T KNOW HOW YOU CAN BE OF HELP, GILLY!
WELL, DON'T FORGET MY POP-UP PROPELLER! I CAN FLY AHEAD AND ACT AS A SCOUT!
WONDERFUL! LET'S GET STARTED!
POP!
SCOUTS, HO!
HUP! HUP! HUP!
PROFESSOR TO GILLYWUMP! PROCEED ON COURSE NORTH BY NORTH-NORTHEAST! OVER!
DON'T BE FRIGHTENED, ASTRA! AS LONG AS I'M WITH YOU, NOTHING CAN HAPPEN!
M-MUCH!
2.

ONE HOUR LATER...
WOW!
THREE M-MONSTERS!! THE BIGGEST THINGS I EVER SAW!
GILLYWUMP TO PROFESSOR! THREE MONSTERS ABOUT HALF A MILE AHEAD... EACH AS BIG AS A HOUSE!
MERCIFUL MARS!
D-DID YOU HEAR THAT, OOG?
THREE MONSTERS!
EACH AS BIG AS A HOUSE!
COME ALONG, EVERYONE! WE MUST SAVE POOR LITTLE ORBI!
COSMO, WAIT FOR ME! I'M AFRAID TO...
EEEEEEEEEEEEEEEE
GALLOPING GALAXIES! ASTRA SLIPPED INTO A CREVICE!
IT'S SO BLACK DOWN THERE! W-WHAT'LL WE DO NOW?
CONTINUED:

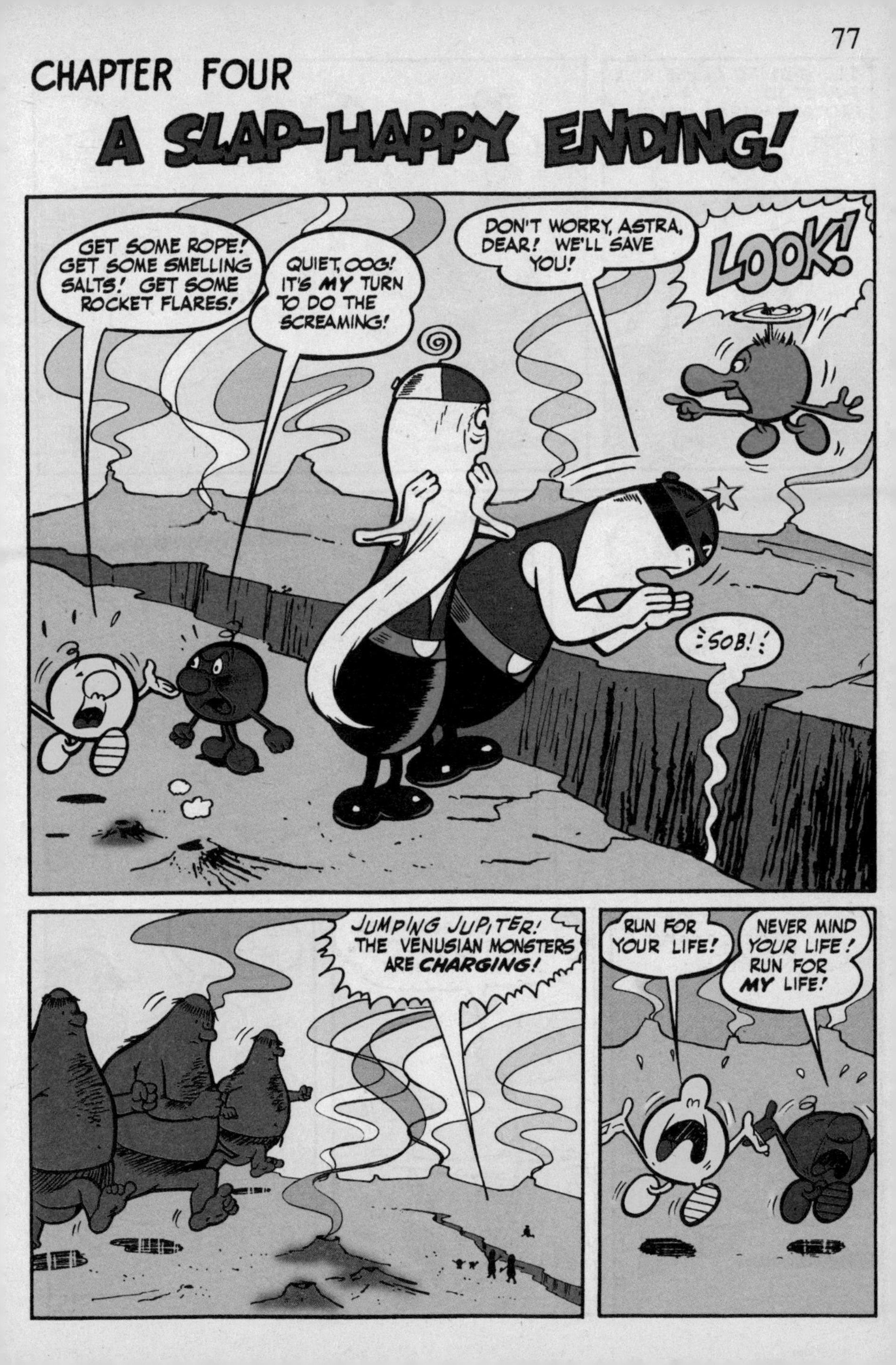
CHAPTER FOUR
A SLAP-HAPPY ENDING!
GET SOME ROPE! GET SOME SMELLING SALTS! GET SOME ROCKET FLARES!
QUIET, OOG! IT'S MY TURN TO DO THE SCREAMING!
DON'T WORRY, ASTRA, DEAR! WE'LL SAVE YOU!
LOOK!
SOB!
JUMPING JUPITER! THE VENUSIAN MONSTERS ARE CHARGING!
RUN FOR YOUR LIFE!
NEVER MIND YOUR LIFE! RUN FOR MY LIFE!

I'LL S-STAND F-FAST TO PROTECT ASTRA!
USE YOUR R-RAY GUN ON THEM!
BLIP!
OM!GOSH! THE RAY GUNS AREN'T STOPPING THEM!
YOW!
JUMP, COSMO!
EEEEEK!
LOOK! HE'S GOT ASTRA! HE'S PUTTING HER DOWN ON THE GROUND!
2.

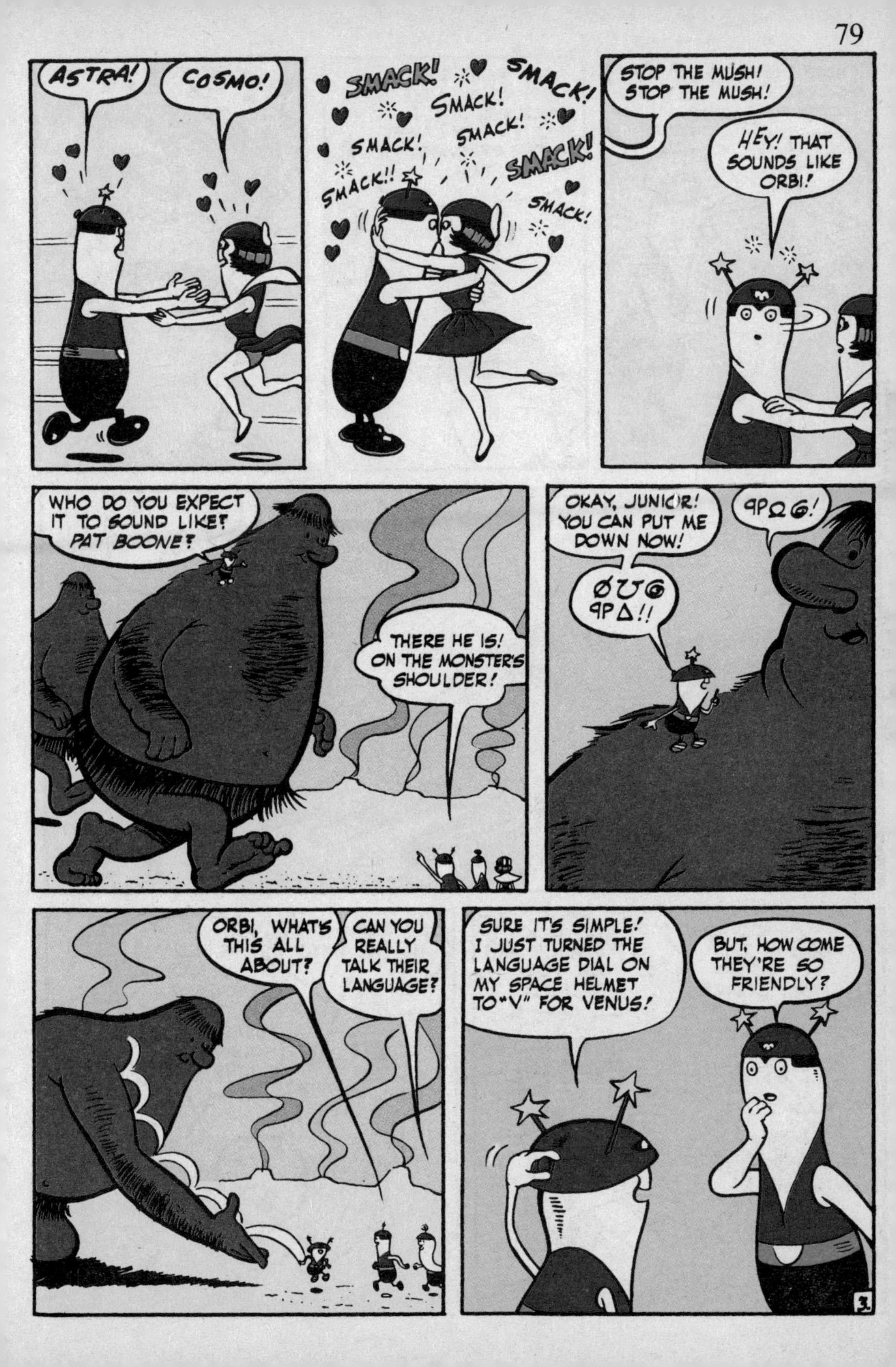
ASTRA!
COSMO!
SMACK!
SMACK!
SMACK!
SMACK!
SMACK!
SMACK!!
SMACK!
SMACK!
SMACK!
STOP THE MUSH! STOP THE MUSH!
HEY! THAT SOUNDS LIKE ORBI!
WHO DO YOU EXPECT IT TO SOUND LIKE? PAT BOONE?
THERE HE IS! ON THE MONSTER'S SHOULDER!
OKAY, JUNIOR! YOU CAN PUT ME DOWN NOW!
ORBI, WHAT'S THIS ALL ABOUT?
CAN YOU REALLY TALK THEIR LANGUAGE?
SURE IT'S SIMPLE! I JUST TURNED THE LANGUAGE DIAL ON MY SPACE HELMET TO "V" FOR VENUS!
BUT, HOW COME THEY'RE SO FRIENDLY?
3.

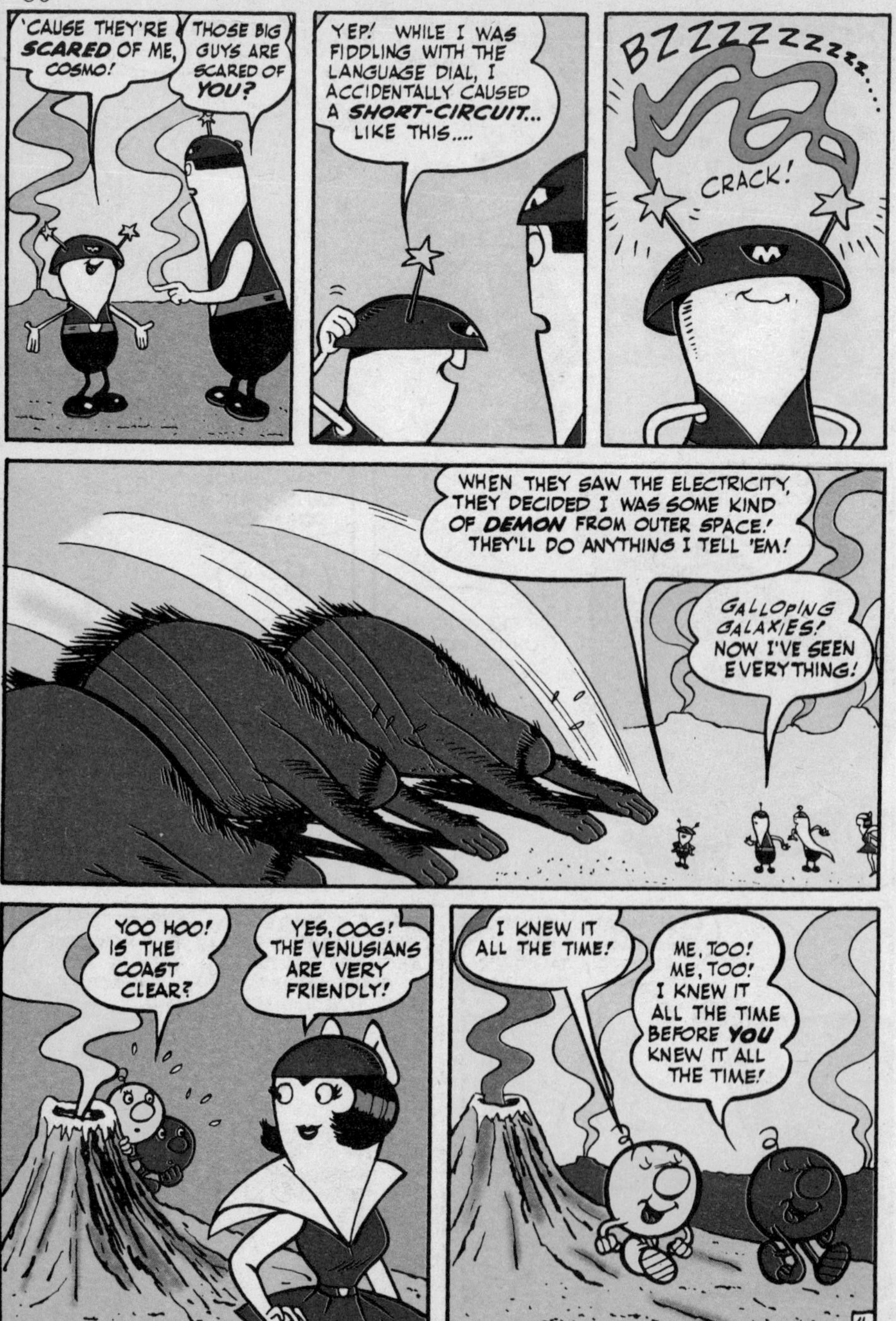

'CAUSE THEY'RE SCARED OF ME, COSMO!
THOSE BIG GUYS ARE SCARED OF YOU?
YEP! WHILE I WAS FIDDLING WITH THE LANGUAGE DIAL, I ACCIDENTALLY CAUSED A SHORT-CIRCUIT... LIKE THIS....
BZZZZZZZzzz....
CRACK!
WHEN THEY SAW THE ELECTRICITY, THEY DECIDED I WAS SOME KIND OF DEMON FROM OUTER SPACE! THEY'LL DO ANYTHING I TELL 'EM!
GALLOPING GALAXIES! NOW I'VE SEEN EVERYTHING!
YOO HOO! IS THE COAST CLEAR?
YES, OOG! THE VENUSIANS ARE VERY FRIENDLY!
I KNEW IT ALL THE TIME!
ME, TOO! ME, TOO! I KNEW IT ALL THE TIME BEFORE YOU KNEW IT ALL THE TIME!
4.

OH, YEAH! I KNEW IT ALL THE TIME AHEAD OF TIME!
YOU DID NOT! YOU DIDN'T HAVE TIME TO KNOW IT ALL THE TIME!
ØΔΩKϘP!
PROFESSOR THIMK, THEY'RE TRYING TO TELL US SOMETHING!
LET'S ADJUST OUR LANGUAGE DIALS AND LISTEN IN!
WELL, WELL! THEY WANT TO TAKE US WITH THEM... TO MEET THEIR QUEEN!
A QUEEN OF THE VENUSIAN MONSTERS! GOLLY... I WONDER WHAT SHE LOOKS LIKE?
LET'S GO AND FIND OUT!
GOOD IDEA!
HANG ON TIGHT ASTRA! WE'RE OFF TO SEE THE QUEEN!
I'VE TRAVELED BY BOAT, TRAIN AND ROCKET SHIP... BUT THIS IS THE FIRST TIME I'VE EVER TRAVELED BY MONSTER!!
WHO IS THE QUEEN OF THE VENUSIANS?
WHAT EXCITING AND UNUSUAL ADVENTURES LIE AHEAD FOR OUR BRAVE SPACE VOYAGERS?
FOLLOW THEIR MAD-CAP MISHAPS IN THE VERY NEXT ISSUE OF...
COSMO
THE MERRY MARTIAN

Katy Keene
Pep #133, 1959
by Bill Woggon

Part of the fun for readers of Katy Keene is seeing all the clothes designed by other readers and even submitting some of their own. However, as I learned while writing and drawing Katy, it's hard to find ways to use some of the more unique or unusual designs.

In this story by Bill Woggon, he finds a way to use things like an Eskimo outfit or a suit of armor by sending Katy and KO to a costume party, and by having it being thrown by an Irishman. Woggon even found a way to use some Irish and St. Patrick's Day-inspired outfits. The hope is to include as many reader designs as possible into every story, and Woggon did a good job doing that here.

--Andrew Pepoy
Eisner Award-winning writer and artist, Archie Comics

Katy Keene
by Bill Woggon
KATY'S + K.O.'S IRISH COSTUMES by RUTH B, UTAH.
THIS STORY SUGGESTED by LINDA S, KENTUCKY.
BEGORRA, KATY! AN' I'VE GOT GOOD NEWS! WE'RE INVITED TO CLANCY'S COSTUME BALL!
THAT'S WONDERFUL, K.O.! B-BUT PLEASE PUT ME D-DOWN!
SQUEEZE
CRUNCH
RANDY CAN GIVE A FANCY COSTUME BALL, BUT BEGORRA, AN' WAIT'LL YOU GO TO CLANCY'S!
OOOF! K.O.! PLEASE! NOT SO OOF HARD!
!
CRACK
CRUNCH

YEP! AN' I CAN SEE US DANCING NOW--- I'M HOLDIN' YOU TIGHT---
OOOF! PLEASE, K.O.! NOT THAT T-TIGHT--- LET'S SIT THIS DANCE OUT--
CRUNCH
CRACK
WE'LL HAVE A BALL AT CLANCY'S COSTUME BALL--C'MON! SNUGGLE UP AN' TELL ME WHATCHA GONNA WEAR, KATY!
I HAVEN'T DECIDED--
CRUNCH!
KATY'S DATE DRESS by SHARON F, KANSAS.
BEGORRA AN' I MIGHT GO AS A CIRCUS STRONG MAN--JUST FEEL ME MUSCLE!
N-NO THANKS! I FEEL ENOUGH OF YOUR MUSCLE ALREADY!
SQUEEZE
CRUNCH
I'VE GOT TO GET TO BED EARLY--BOSS LADY'S ORDERS--GOTTA KEEP IN GOOD SHAPE---'NIGHT, KATY!
SMACK
OOFF! THERE GOES MY SACROILIAC!
GOODNIGHT!
CRACK!
SLEEP TIGHT, ME LOVE, I'LL PICK YOU UP EARLY FOR CLANCY'S BALL!
2
PHEW! I HOPE I'M IN GOOD SHAPE FOR THE BALL--(GROAN) AFTER MANY DATES LIKE THAT, I WON'T BE!
LINIMENT
KATY'S NIGHTIE by DONNA K, MINN.

HMM-- NOW WHAT SHALL I WEAR? I COULD GO IN A PERIOD GOWN--THEN K.O. COULDN'T GET NEAR ME TO CRUSH ME--- BUT NO! THAT'S TOO FUSSY FOR CLANCY'S BALL!
?
PERIOD GOWN by GILBERT L., ARIZ.
HOW ABOUT A RUSSIAN COSSACK COSTUME WITH A RUSSIAN WOLFHOUND TO KEEP K.O. AND THE OTHER IRISH WOLVES AWAY?
!
?
GRRR!
COSSACK COSTUME by RASMA N, PA.
WAIT! I HAVE AN EVEN BETTER IDEA!
3

I'LL GO AS AN INUIT ---I'LL WAIT RIGHT OUTSIDE OF MY OWN LITTLE IGLOO FOR K.O. TO PICK ME UP FOR OUR DATE!
By DIANE L, N.J.
KATY KEENE
HAVE FUN AT CLANCY'S BALL, KATY!
SAY! THAT'S THE BEST IDEA YET---HE CAN GET NEAR ME TO CRUSH ME IN HIS ARMS--YES! BUT I'LL PUSH HIM AWAY AND SAY---
WAIT, STRONG BOY, INUITS DON'T KISS LIKE THAT---
CRUNCH! CRACK!
THEY KISS BY RUBBING NOSES!
?
NO! MAYBE THAT MIGHT NOT BE SO GOOD -- AFTER A WHILE OUR NOSES WOULD BE SORE -- HMMM, LET ME SEE---I HAVE IT!
4

I'LL GO AS A PIN-UP QUEEN FROM OUTER SPACE---THAT WILL KEEP K.O. AT A GOOD DISTANCE, SO HE WON'T CRACK MY RIBS! (YAWN)
HMM! LET ME THINK--THERE SHOULD BE A BETTER AND SAFER COSTUME!
OUTER SPACE GOWN by DOLORES C.
Finally Katy falls asleep.. she has picked out the perfect costume to wear...
OKAY! I'M READY FOR CLANCY'S BALL, STRONG MAN!
The END

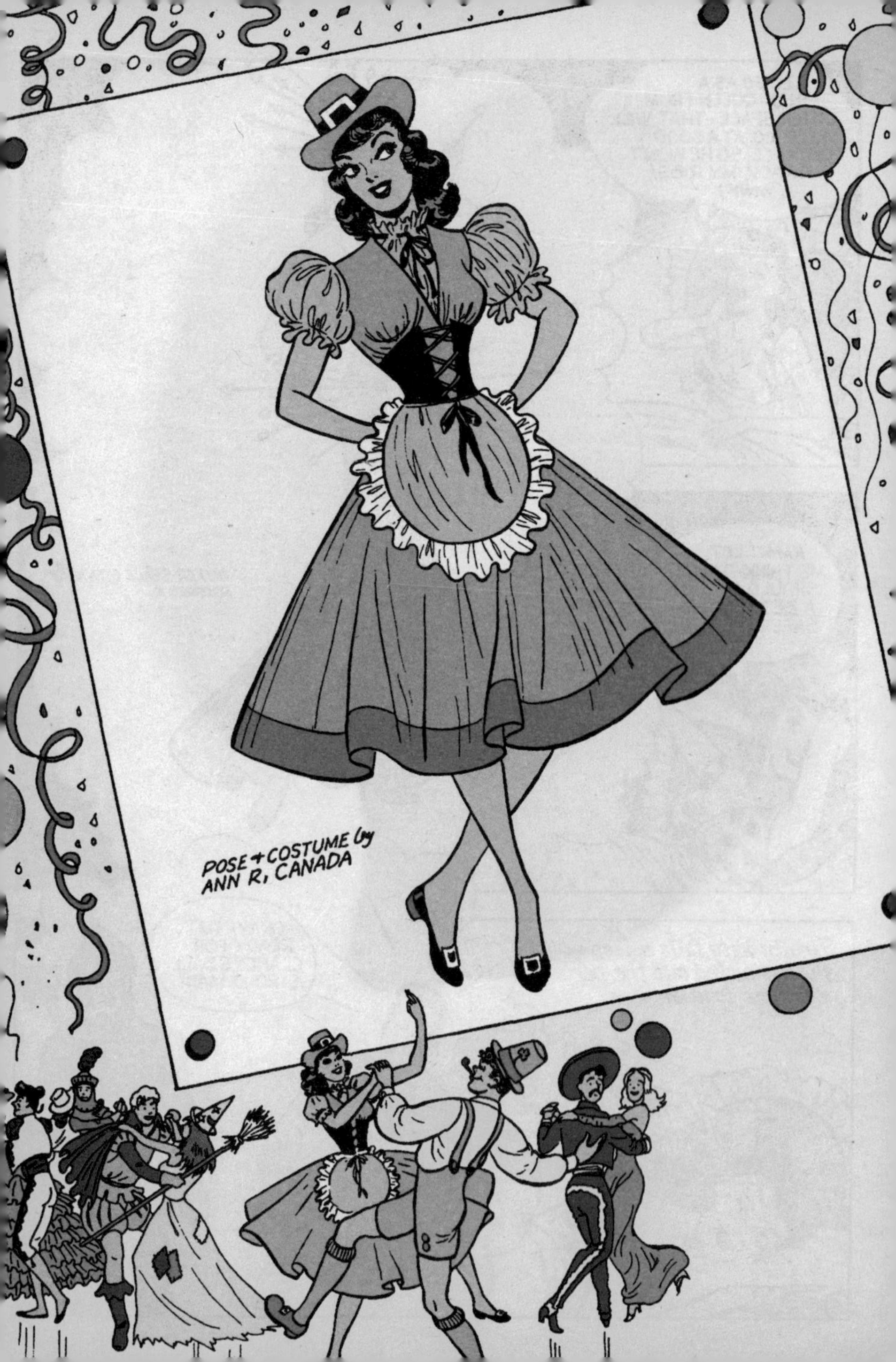
POSE + COSTUME by
ANN R, CANADA

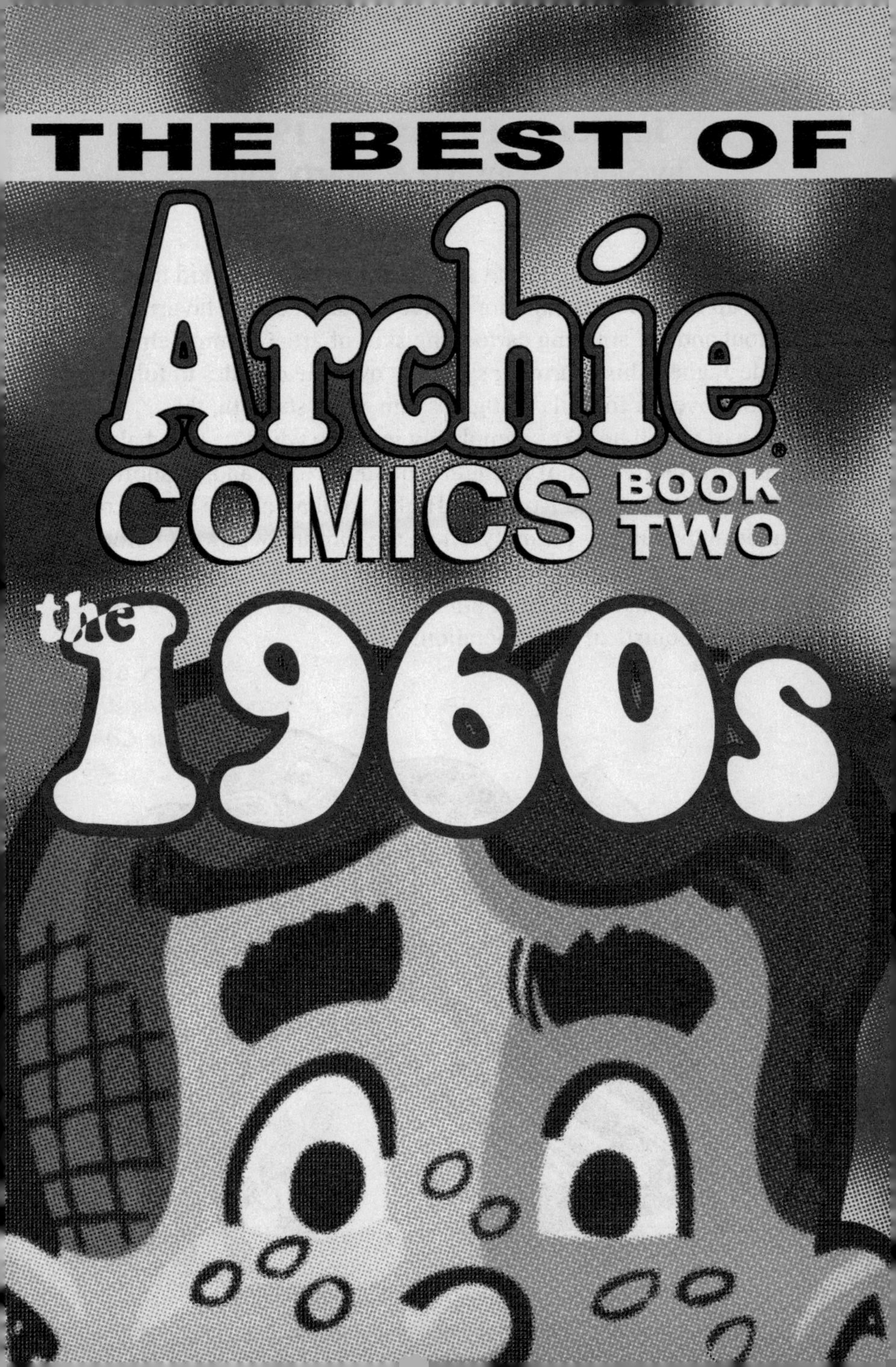
THE BEST OF
Archie®
COMICS
BOOK TWO
the 1960s

Son of Hercules
Jughead's Fantasy #3, 1960
by Samm Schwartz & Marty Epp

"Son of Hercules" is a Jughead story that I enjoyed as a kid that still holds up today for its superior characterization of our favorite lovable lout and the amazing cartooning skill of artist Samm Schwartz, who made Jughead his charming specialty over the decades to follow. Jughead discovers a formula that gives him super strength, the possession of which he takes completely in stride while he nonchalantly performs miraculous feats of strength around the town and, in short order, proceeds to become Riverdale High's football champ and hero to the adoring populace. Fittingly, when the formula wears off before the Big Game, it is Juggie's insatiable lust for food that saves the day! Bravo, Jughead and bravo, Samm Schwartz who is a hero to all discerning cartoonists of my generation!

--Terry Austin
Award Winning Artist,
Archie Comics

Jughead
CHAPTER I
PARDON MY POWER!
SON OF HERCULES
THE SCENE-RIVERDALE HIGH SCHOOL! THE TIME-MIDNIGHT! A SINGLE LIGHT BURNS BRIGHTLY, AS OUR HERO, JUGHEAD JONES, WORKS ON A TOP-SECRET PROJECT--
AND SUDDENLY
I'VE GOT IT! I'VE GOT IT!
POP--I JUST DISCOVERED THE SECRET FORMULA!
WHAT--MEASLES?
CHEMISTRY LAB.

THE SECRET FORMULA? WOW! NICE GOING, BOY! GOOD WORK! YES, SIREE! I'M SURE GLAD YOU--
HEY, WAIT A MINUTE! WHAT SECRET FORMULA?
A WAY TO MAKE HAMBURGERS OUT OF CHEMICALS!
BROTHERRR! NOW I'VE HEARD OF EVERYTHING!
THERE SHE IS, POP--THE FIRST HAMBURGER MADE CHEMICALLY!
NOW FOR THE TASTE TEST! GULP! CHOMP! MMFF!
OOP!
EEEP!
LLLP!
2

YEEEOWW!
SLOSH
ECCH! WORST TASTING THING I EVER ATE--AND THAT COVERS PLENTY!
I WONDER WHERE MY DANDY FORMULA WENT WRONG?
OH, WELL-- SWEEP IT AWAY, POP!
SOB! ALL MY HARD WORK FOR NOTHING!
CHEER UP, JUGHEAD! ROBERT FULTON AND ALEXANDER GRAHAM BELL HAD TROUBLES, TOO!
DID THEY TRY TO INVENT A CHEMICAL HAMBURGER?
SKIP IT!
3

TIRED AND WEARY, OUR WAYWARD HERO WENDS HIS WAY HOME--
SOB!
FOR A WELL-EARNED TEARFUL, NIGHT OF REST--
ZZZZZOB!
AND IN THE MORNING...
TIME TO GET UP FOR SCHOOL, JUGHEAD, DEAR!
OKAY, MOM!
GEE--I FEEL FUNNY TODAY! I DUNNO HOW--OR WHY--JUST KINDA DIFFERENT! OR SOMETHING!
R.H.S
HAVE A NICE DAY!
I WILL, MOM! SEE YOU LATER!
I CAN'T UNDER-STAND IT! I'M FULL OF ENERGY! I FEEL LIKE RUNNING--OR JUMPING!
4

WHEEEE!
BAWW
WHAT'S WRONG, SONNY?
MY BRAND NEW BASEBALL ROLLED UNDER THAT TRUCK!
TOO BAD!
I WAN' MY BALL!
NOW, NOW! DRY THOSE LITTLE EYES! UNCLE JUGGIE'S HERE TO HELP!
5

HURRY UP, SON! I DON'T WANT TO BE LATE FOR SCHOOL!
HE LIFTED DA' WHOLE TRUCK! GOSH!
FUNNY--FOR SOME REASON I DO FEEL DIFFERENT-ISH!
JOHN LOVES MARY
MARY LOVES HENRY
NUTS TO JOHN MARY!
JOHN HATES MARY
6

SCHOOL SLOW ZONE
I'M GONNA MOIDER YUH!
??
MOOSIE, YOU'VE GOT ME ALL WRONG! I WASN'T WINKING AT MIDGE! I HAD S-SOMETHING IN MY EYE!
OH, YEAH?
HONEST!
YUH CAN'T KID ME! I'M TOO **STUPID!**
LET HIM ALONE, MOOSE!
BUTTIN' IN, HUH? OKAY, NEEDLE-BEAK! HERE'S ONE FOR **YOU!**
YAWN! DEAR ME! WHY MUST YOU ALWAYS RESORT TO VIOLENCE?
PING!

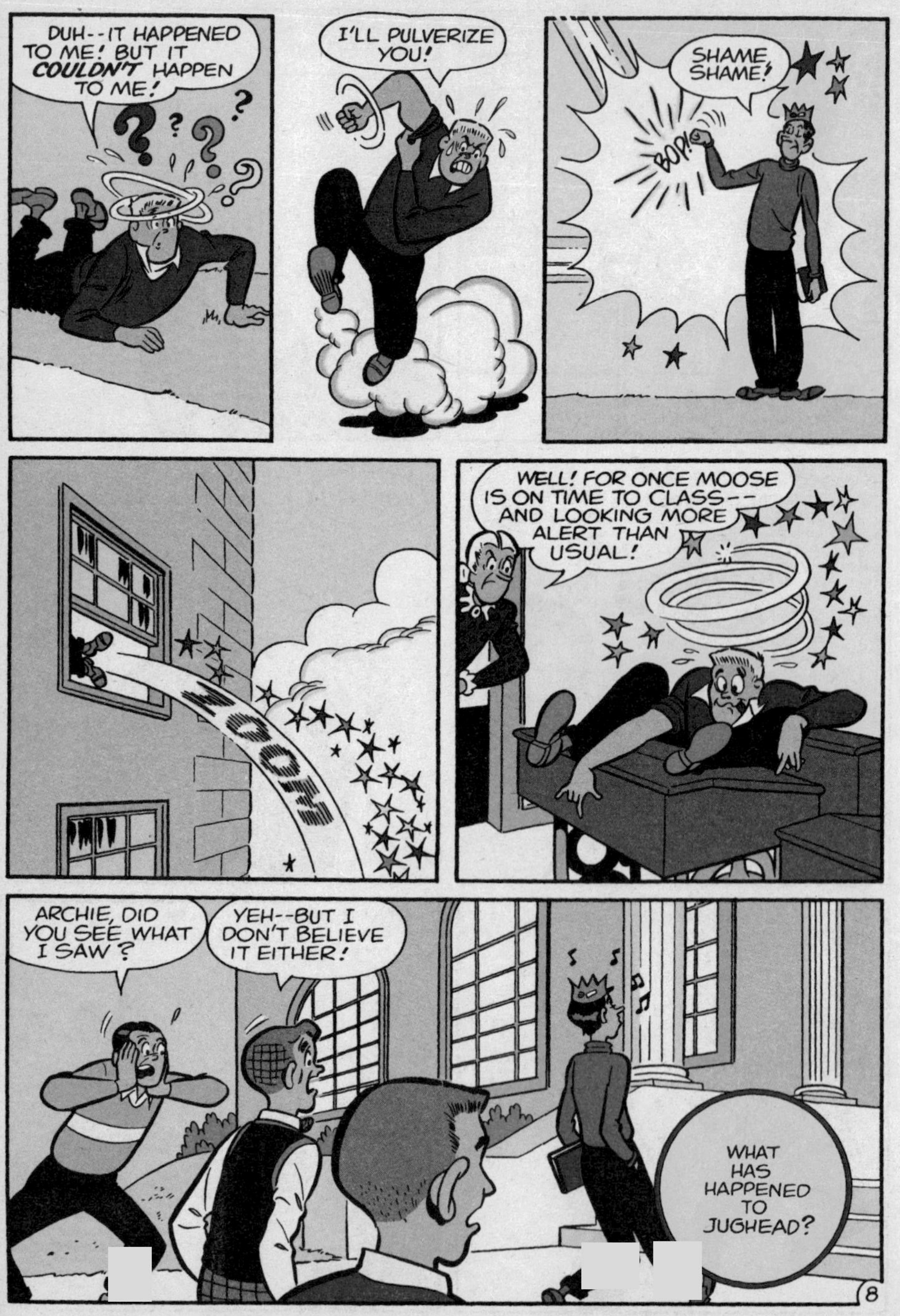
DUH--IT HAPPENED TO ME! BUT IT COULDN'T HAPPEN TO ME!
I'LL PULVERIZE YOU!
SHAME, SHAME!
BOP!
ZOOM
WELL! FOR ONCE MOOSE IS ON TIME TO CLASS-- AND LOOKING MORE ALERT THAN USUAL!
ARCHIE, DID YOU SEE WHAT I SAW?
YEH--BUT I DON'T BELIEVE IT EITHER!
WHAT HAS HAPPENED TO JUGHEAD?
8

CHAP. II -- JUGGIE THE JUGGERNAUT!
A FINE STATE OF AFFAIRS, I MUST SAY! YES, INDEED--A PRETTY KETTLE OF FISH!
ANYTHING WRONG, SIR!?
THOSE MOVERS LEFT MY NEW DESK SITTING HERE IN THE HALL, INSTEAD OF TAKING IT TO MY OFFICE!
I'LL HAVE COACH KLEATS SEND ME A FEW LADS FROM HIS FOOTBALL SQUAD!
TUT, TUT! THAT'S NOT NECESSARY, MR. WEATHERBEE!

JUMPIN' JELLYBEANS!
ARCHIE, TELL ME QUICK--DID HE DID, OR DID HE DIDN'T?
HE DID, COACH! JUGGIE SEEMS TO HAVE SUPER-HUMAN STRENGTH!
HE WAS FOOLING AROUND IN THE CHEMISTRY LAB LAST NIGHT, AND ATE SOMETHING!
GEE-- MAYBE THAT'S THE REASON!
REASON-SHMEASON! WE NEED HIM ON THE FOOTBALL TEAM!
JUGHEAD? A FOOTBALL PLAYER?
YES! JUGHEAD! NEXT WEEK IS OUR BIG GAME WITH POTTSVILLE TECH! AND YOUR JOB IS TO GET HIM OUT FOR PRACTISE!
THIS YEAR WE'RE GONNA WIN... THIS YEAR WE'RE GONNA WIN!
2

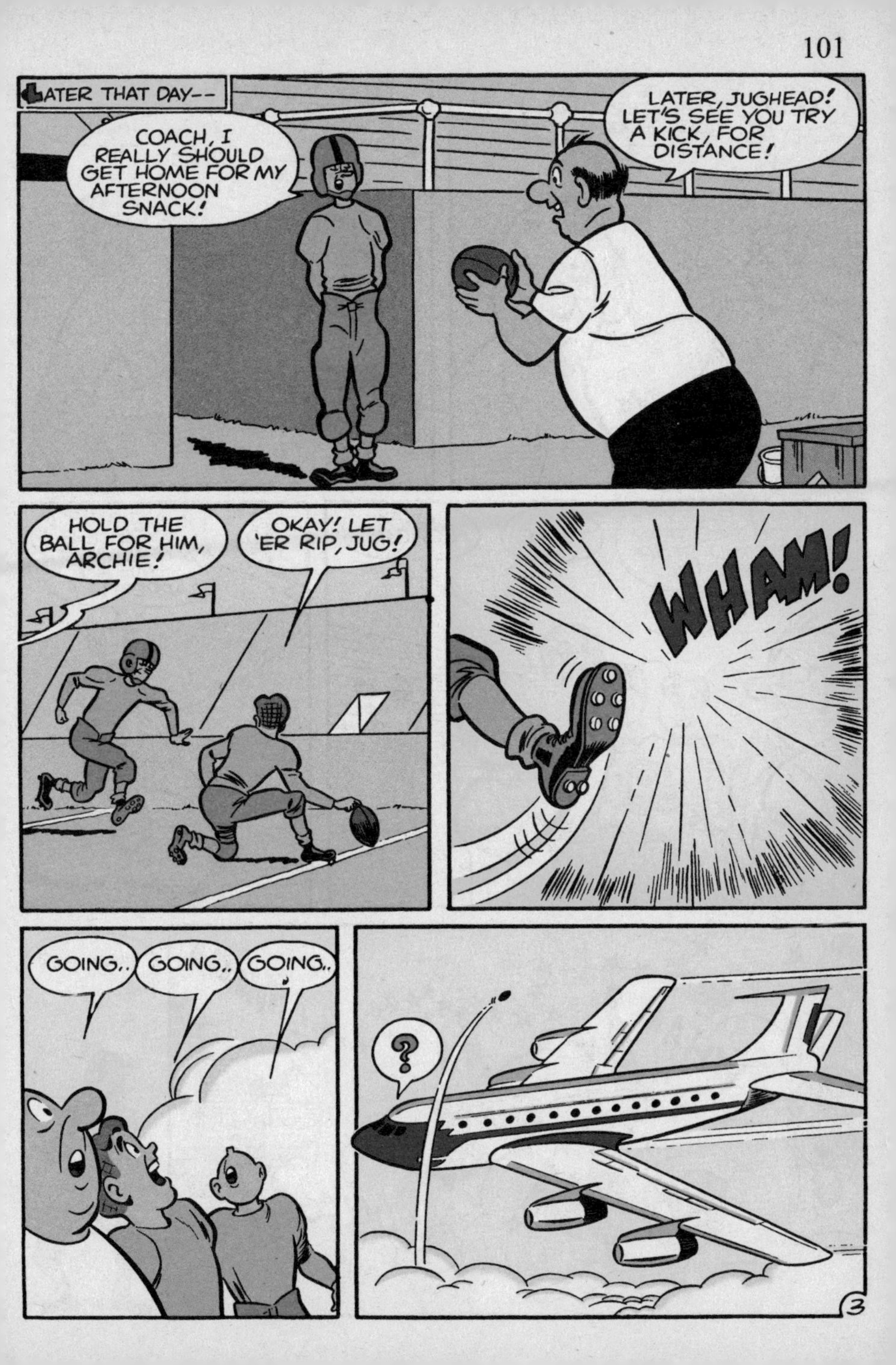
LATER THAT DAY--
COACH, I REALLY SHOULD GET HOME FOR MY AFTERNOON SNACK!
LATER, JUGHEAD! LET'S SEE YOU TRY A KICK, FOR DISTANCE!
HOLD THE BALL FOR HIM, ARCHIE!
OKAY! LET 'ER RIP, JUG!
WHAM!
GOING..
GOING..
GOING..
?
3

WOTTA KICK!
HE'S EVEN BETTER THAN I THOUGHT!
OKAY, JUGGIE! NOW FOR SOME BROKEN FIELD RUNNING!
COACH, ABOUT MY SNACK--
I WANT EVERY MAN ON THIS TEAM TO TRY AND STOP HIM... GET IT ?
SURE..
OKAY, COACH!
LET'S GO, JUG!
ALL THIS EXERCISE IS GIVING ME AN APPETITE!
WHAM
TINKLE
CRASH
BOOM
TINKLE..?
4

GOOD GRAVY! "JUGGIE THE JUGGERNAUT" HAS KNOCKED OUT EVERY SINGLE MEMBER OF THE TEAM!
NOW CAN I GO GET MY SNACK?
SNACK? M'BOY YOU CAN HAVE A BANQUET!
AT LAST, WE'RE GONNA WIN THE BIG GAME AGAINST POTTSVILLE TECH!
HMM!
I'D BETTER HURRY!
OPERATOR, CONNECT ME WITH THE COACH OF THE POTTSVILLE TECH FOOTBALL TEAM...
5

COACH-- THIS IS YOUR OLD TRAINER, MELVIN! I'VE GOT STARTLING NEWS!
HE IS?
HE CAN?
HE WAS?
HE DOES?
HE DID?
THANKS FOR THE TIP, MELVIN! I'LL INVESTIGATE AT ONCE!
LATER THAT NIGHT..
COACH! EVERYTHING MELVIN SAID WAS TRUE!
THIS GUY JUGHEAD IS ABSOLUTELY THE GREATEST!!
WE MUST BEAT RIVERDALE, BOYS! THE BIG GAME IS ONE WEEK AWAY! SO, UNTIL THEN, OUR MOTTO IS...
STOP JUGHEAD JONES!
LOOKS LIKE TROUBLE FOR JUGGIE! IN FACT, IT IS TROUBLE FOR JUGGIE!

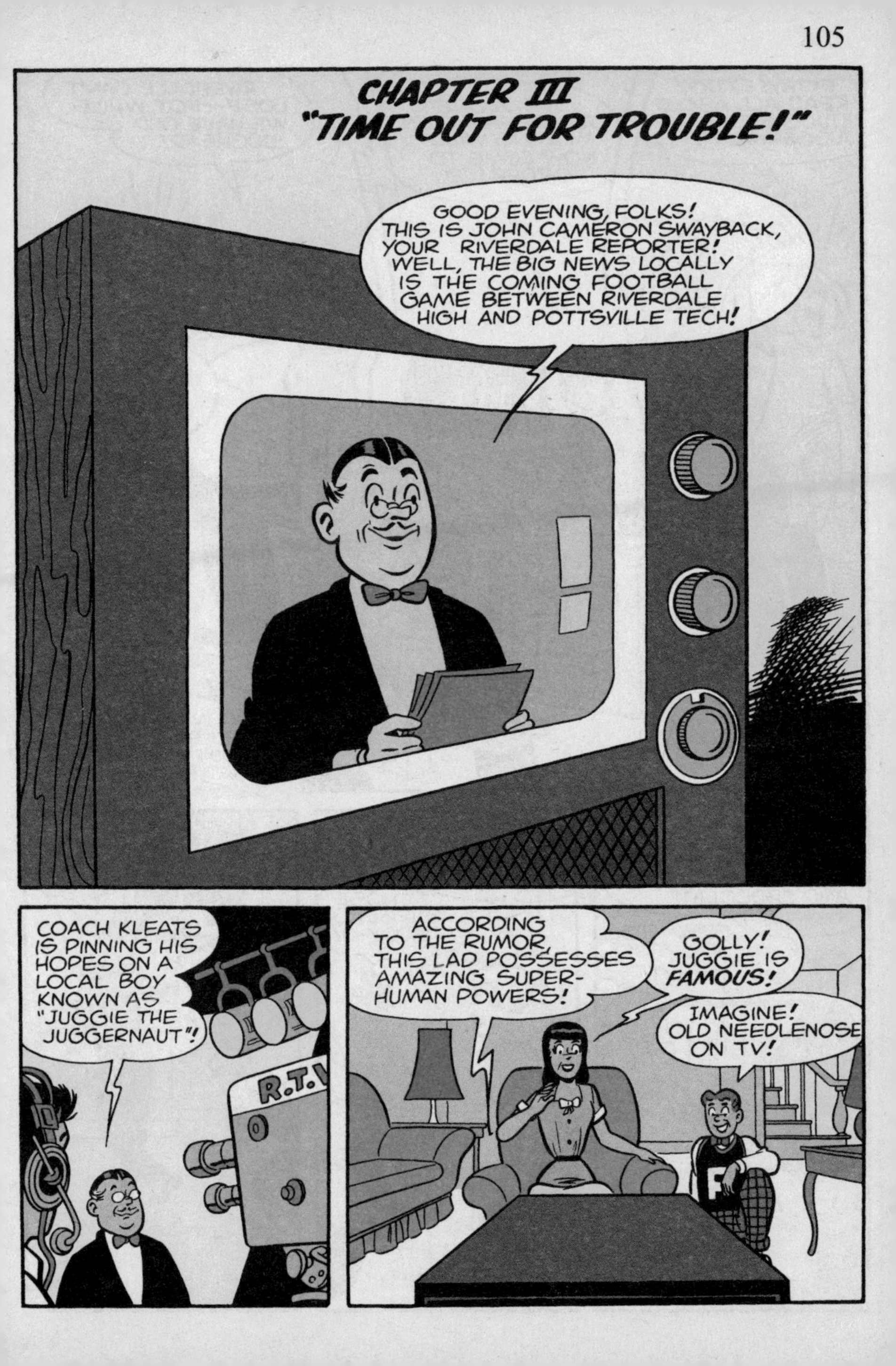
CHAPTER III
"TIME OUT FOR TROUBLE!"
GOOD EVENING, FOLKS! THIS IS JOHN CAMERON SWAYBACK, YOUR RIVERDALE REPORTER! WELL, THE BIG NEWS LOCALLY IS THE COMING FOOTBALL GAME BETWEEN RIVERDALE HIGH AND POTTSVILLE TECH!
COACH KLEATS IS PINNING HIS HOPES ON A LOCAL BOY KNOWN AS "JUGGIE THE JUGGERNAUT"!
ACCORDING TO THE RUMOR, THIS LAD POSSESSES AMAZING SUPER-HUMAN POWERS!
GOLLY! JUGGIE IS FAMOUS!
IMAGINE! OLD NEEDLENOSE ON TV!

EXTRY! EXTRY! READ ALL ABOUT "JUGGIE THE JUGGERNAUT"!
THE JUGHEAD JONES FAN CLUB MEETING WILL NOW COME TO ORDER!
J.J.f.c.
RIVERDALE CAN'T LOSE--NOT WHILE WE HAVE OLD JUGHEAD!
AND WHAT DOES OUR HERO SAY ABOUT ALL THIS?? WHAT HE ALWAYS SAYS---
TWO HAMBURGERS, POP! WITH KETCHUP, MUSTARD, MOLASSES, AND CHOCOLATE SYRUP!
COMIN (UGH) RIGHT UP!
JUGGIE, DEAR! MY LIPSTICK ROLLED UNDER THE JUKEBOX!
HOLD THOSE 'BURGERS, DADDY-O!
HO HUM!
THERE IT IS!

THAT'S HIM, COACH! THE KID LIFTING THE JUKEBOX!
HMM--I THINK I KNOW HIS ONE WEAK SPOT!
WEAK SPOT!?
YES MELVIN--HIS STOMACH!
NOW HERE'S WHAT YOU DO! JUST BEFORE THE BIG GAME, TAKE HIM INTO A BEANERY, AND BUZZ BUZZ BUZZ-WHISPER--
POTTSVILLE
SEVERAL DAYS LATER--
THIS IS IT, FOLKS! THE DAY WE'VE BEEN WAITING FOR! RIVERDALE HIGH VS POTTSVILLE TECH!
I'D BETTER GET OVER TO THE LOCKER ROOM EARLY, AND HOP INTO MY UNIFORM!
!!!
EXCUSE ME, MR. JONES! MAY I HAVE YOUR AUTOGRAPH, SIR?
3

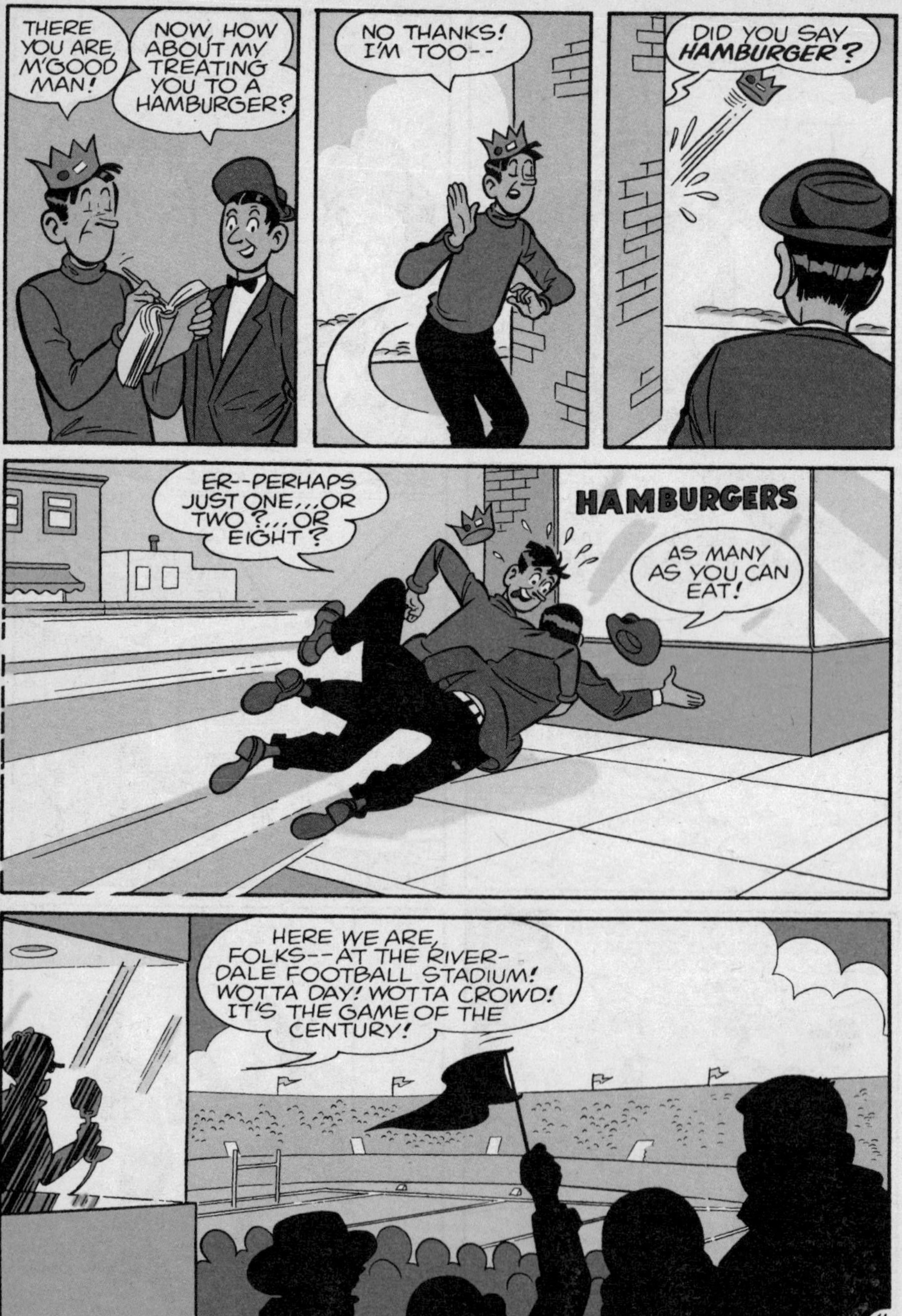
THERE YOU ARE, M'GOOD MAN!
NOW, HOW ABOUT MY TREATING YOU TO A HAMBURGER?
NO THANKS! I'M TOO--
DID YOU SAY HAMBURGER?
ER--PERHAPS JUST ONE,,,OR TWO?,,,OR EIGHT?
HAMBURGERS
AS MANY AS YOU CAN EAT!
HERE WE ARE, FOLKS--AT THE RIVER-DALE FOOTBALL STADIUM! WOTTA DAY! WOTTA CROWD! IT'S THE GAME OF THE CENTURY!
4

GOSH! IT'S ALMOST KICK-OFF TIME! WHERE'S JUGHEAD?
SOMEBODY LOOKING FOR ME?
JUMPING JELLYBEANS!
-URP-
YOU YOUNG FOOL! WHAT A TIME TO GORGE YOURSELF ON HAMBURGERS!
PLOP!
YIIIII! HE FAINTED!
MEDIC! MEDIC!
COMING, COACH!
R
WHAT NEXT FOR "JUGGIE THE EX-JUGGERNAUT" ??

CHAPTER IV
"TOUCHDOWN!"
WHERE AM I?
WHO AM I?
WHY AM I?
THANK GOODNESS-HE'S BREATHING!
MOTHER ZILCHE'S HEALTH TONIC NEVER FAILS!
OKAY, LET'S GO! WE'VE GOT A GAME TO WIN! INTO UNIFORM, JUGHEAD! CHOP, CHOP!
THE RIVERDALE TEAM IS ON THE FIELD, AND "JUGGIE THE JUGGERNAUT" IS GOING TO TAKE THE KICK-OFF!

JUGHEAD HAS THE BALL!
PLOP!
ATTA BOY, JUGGIE! GO, GO, GO! ALL THE WAY FOR A TOUCH-DOWN!
THE POTTS-VILLE LINE IS CLOSING IN! HERE COMES JUGGIE!
BOOOM!!
—AND THERE GOES JUGGIE!
RIVERDALE WAS THROWN FOR A THIRTY YARD LOSS!
WHO TOSSED THE H-BOMB?
WHAT HAPPENED? WHERE'S THE OL' SUPER-HUMAN POWER?
2

SOMETHING'S WRONG, FOLKS! THE RIVERDALE COACH HAS JUST CALLED FOR TIME OUT!
WHAT'S THE MATTER, JUGHEAD? YOU'VE LOST YOUR STRENGTH!
I BET IT WAS THAT MOTHER ZILCH'S NERVE TONIC!
HUH!
THERE WAS SOMETHING IN THE TONIC THAT BROUGHT JUGGIE BACK TO NORMAL!
GOLLY, YOU'RE RIGHT! IT MUST HAVE SET UP A CHEMICAL REACTION!
I KNEW IT WAS TOO GOOD TO LAST!
OH, OOH! THERE GOES THE WHISTLE! TOMMY-- YOU SUBSTITUTE FOR JUGHEAD!
DEAR READERS—
WE WILL SPARE YOU THE PAINFUL DETAILS OF THE NEXT TWO HOURS, AS RIVERDALE FIGHTS A LOSING BATTLE--AND JUGGIE WARMS THE BENCH —!
3

THERE'S TWO MINUTES LEFT TO PLAY, FOLKS! POTTSVILLE TECH IS LEADING – 21-18!
COACH! MOOSE IS OUT OF THE GAME!
OHH! THERE'S NOBODY LEFT ON THE BENCH EXCEPT (GROAN) JUGHEAD!
GO IN, JUGGIE! WE CAN'T WIN ANYWAY!
Y-YES, SIR!
ONLY 72 SECONDS LEFT! IT'S ALL OVER BUT THE SHOUTING!
JUGGIE, HERE'S A NOTE FOR YOU!
A NOTE?
THE GAME IS ON! IT'S RIVERDALE'S BALL ON THEIR OWN 12 YARD LINE!
THE BALL IS SNAPPED TO JUGHEAD JONES!
4

I CAN'T WATCH!
HE'S AT THE TWENTY YARD LINE--
THE THIRTY YARD LINE-- THE FORTY YARD LINE--!
PARDON ME!
COMING THROUGH!
SO SORRY!
WOW! "JUGGIE THE JUGGERNAUT" HAS JUST RUN 88 YARDS FOR A TOUCHDOWN! AND HE'S STILL GOING!
5

WE WON! WE WON! THE GAME IS OVER!
WHEEE!
COACH KLEATS-- CONTROL YOURSELF!
ARCHIE, WHAT HAPPENED ANYWAY?
JUST BEFORE THE PLAY, I HANDED JUGGIE A NOTE!
IT SAID--"DEAR JUGHEAD-ACCORDING TO MY RECORDS, I OWE YOU THREE HAMBURGERS! PLEASE COME IN AT ONCE, TO COLLECT YOUR DEBT!-- POP TATE"
ARCHIE, YOU'RE A GENIUS!
THIS IS ONE STORY THAT HAS A REAL, HAPPY ENDING!
R
PERHAPS SO, BETTY--BUT LATE THAT NIGHT, A BRIGHT LIGHT BURNS IN THE CHEMISTRY LAB--AND WE HEAR A FAMILIAR VOICE--
LET'S SEE-MAYBE I CAN REMEMBER THAT FORMULA! A LITTLE OF THIS-- A LITTLE OF THAT!
DEAR READER-LET US QUIT NOW--WHILE WE'RE STILL AHEAD...

Caramel Has A Tale
Little Archie #22, 1962
by Bob Bolling

Cats are funny creatures. Owning and helping care for seven cats, there are a handful of universal truths I've come to realize. First, cats do what they want to do, and you'll just have to get used to it. If they want your attention, they're going to get it, even if you're up late trying to write the foreword to a collection of Archie stories. Second, cats know what they want and will make sure you do too. They don't care that you're sleeping, they want their breakfast now. Finally, rules one and two go out the window when the cats lose their minds. Cats are a bundle of neurons wrapped in fur that can, and will, rocket off in any direction for no reason whatsoever! But for all their pushiness, demanding and baffling behavior, they make great companions. Betty's cat, Caramel, is about to tell us a story that sums up the spirit of what I'm talking about here. Sure, she seems like a lazy thing, but she's also an exceedingly loving creature. There's more going on within that tiny kitty brain than we sometimes give it credit for.

--Ian Flynn
Writer, Archie Comics

The House That Lodge Built
Archie #138, 1963
by Frank Doyle and Harry Lucey

One of my favorite things about Archie is the timelessness of the characters and the stories. And this story coming out decades ago feels as fresh as the day it was written, penciled, inked, lettered and colored. It's probably among my top five Archie stories of all time. It features the art of the amazing Harry Lucey, who is one of the greatest cartoonists in Archie history. This story in particular based on the classic nursery rhyme "The House That Jack Built" played perfectly into the dance between Archie, the lovely Veronica and her ever-present father Mr. Lodge. Lodge didn't dance so much as kick, as in kick Archie out of his house, on a regular basis. In addition to Harry Lucey this story happens to feature the amazing writing of Frank Doyle. Frank Doyle has written some of the very best stories in Archie history. This one has love, drama, pathos and, of course, a wonderfully twisted surprise ending.

--Mike Pellerito
President, Archie Comics

CARAMEL
"HAS A TALE"
BOY! WHAT A LAZY CAT YOU HAVE, BETTY!
YES, SHE SLEEPS MOST OF THE TIME.
AND CARAMEL ALWAYS MUSSUS UP MY BED, TOO.
SHE SURE HAS AN EASY LIFE.
CARAMEL MUST BE SMART, THOUGH, SHE LOOKS LIKE SHE UNDERSTANDS WHAT WE'RE SAYING.
HA! YES, SHE ACTS THAT WAY SOMETIMES.
TOO BAD CATS CAN'T TALK, ISN'T IT?
WHO SAYS CATS CAN'T TALK ?!?

CARAMEL!! YOU'RE TALKING!!!
YES, BUT I CAN TALK ONLY TO SMALL CHILDREN!
W-W-WE AREN'T SO SMALL!
THAT'S JUST IT! YOU'RE GROWING UP AND MY SENSES TELL ME THAT AFTER TODAY, YOU'LL NO LONGER BE ABLE TO UNDERSTAND ME!
SO THIS IS THE ONLY TIME YOU'LL HEAR ME TALK...., BUT AFTER LISTENING TO YOU, I JUST HAD TO TELL YOU SOMETHING.
BETTY, DO YOU RECALL THE NIGHT OF THE BIG BLIZZARD, TWO YEARS AGO, WHEN YOU FOUND ME LYING HURT ON YOUR DOORSTEP?
I WAS JUST A KID THEN, BUT I REMEMBER.
FROM THAT NIGHT ON, LADY LUCK HAS BEEN GOOD TO ME.
WHAT HAPPENED-
BEFORE?
WELL, I LIVED IN THE CELLAR OF AN ABANDONED BUILDING WITH MY THREE CHILDREN-
YOU HAD KITTENS ?!?
YOU WERE A MOTHER !?!?!

I CAN TELL YOU'RE STILL CHILDREN BECAUSE YOU KEEP INTERRUPTING ME.
GEE, YOU SOUND JUST LIKE MY MOTHER.
THE FOUR OF US WERE CONTENT WITH OUR HOME.
MY KITTEN'S. WELL, THEY WERE...
"HONEY" SMALL AND FLIRTY
"TAFFY" ALWAYS DIRTY
"COCOA" A BORN TROUBLE MAKER
SUDDENLY, ONE MORNING, THE WHOLE BUILDING BEGAN TO TREMBLE AND SHAKE...
THE BUILDING WAS BEING DEMOLISHED
DEMON DESTRUCTION COMPANY

WE BARELY MADE IT OUT OF THERE....
OUR HOME WAS GONE... WE WANDERED AROUND LOOKING FOR ANOTHER...... BUT WE HAD NO LUCK, UNTIL—
OUR KEEN NOSES CAUGHT THE SCENT OF FISH....
THE DOCKS WERE A WONDERFUL HOME.
EVERY DAY, WHEN THE BOATS CAME IN, WE'D HAVE A FEAST... FISHERMEN ARE KIND PEOPLE... THEY'D MAKE GOOD CATS.
BUT SOMETHING WAS WRONG... FEWER BOATS TYING UP AND THE WEATHER WAS GETTING COLDER...

LATE IN THE FALL, THE LAST FISHING BOAT LEFT....
THE BOATS WERE LEAVING FOR THE WINTER... FOLLOWING THE SCHOOLS OF FISH INTO WARMER WATERS.....
WE WERE ALONE AGAIN AND I KNEW WE MUST LEAVE THE DOCKS QUICKLY, FOR....

ALREADY HUGE, HUNGRY WHARF-RATS WERE STALKING US..

AS WE WANDERED THE STREETS ONCE MORE, WINTER'S FIRST SNOW BEGAN TO FALL....

RIVERDALE RAILROAD YARDS

THIS EMPTY BOXCAR OFFERED US SHELTER
LATER, AS WE SLEPT...
CLANG
THE TRAIN WAS MOVING! OUR LAST GLIMPSE OF RIVERDALE WAS THROUGH A CRACK IN OUR BOXCAR
WE RODE AND RODE AND GOT MIGHTY HUNGRY UNTIL—
A KINDLY BRAKEMAN DISCOVERED US AND FED US DAILY......
WE WERE HEADING SOUTH.... AND THE BRAKEMAN WOULD LEAVE THE DOOR OPEN SO WE COULD WATCH THE EVERCHANGING SCENERY......

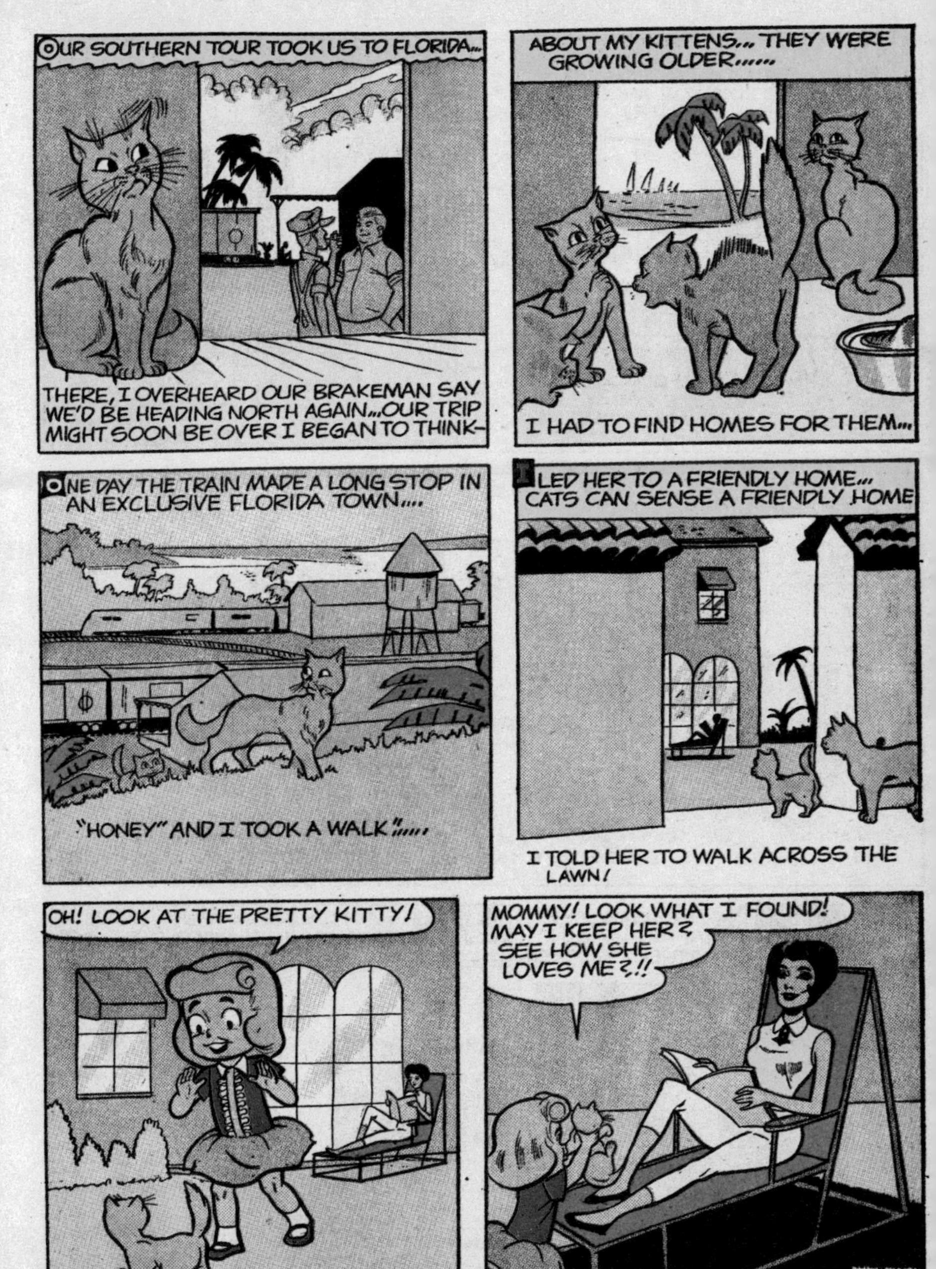
OUR SOUTHERN TOUR TOOK US TO FLORIDA...
THERE, I OVERHEARD OUR BRAKEMAN SAY WE'D BE HEADING NORTH AGAIN...OUR TRIP MIGHT SOON BE OVER I BEGAN TO THINK-
ABOUT MY KITTENS... THEY WERE GROWING OLDER......
I HAD TO FIND HOMES FOR THEM...
ONE DAY THE TRAIN MADE A LONG STOP IN AN EXCLUSIVE FLORIDA TOWN....
"HONEY" AND I TOOK A WALK".....
I LED HER TO A FRIENDLY HOME... CATS CAN SENSE A FRIENDLY HOME
I TOLD HER TO WALK ACROSS THE LAWN!
OH! LOOK AT THE PRETTY KITTY!
MOMMY! LOOK WHAT I FOUND! MAY I KEEP HER? SEE HOW SHE LOVES ME?!!

OH, ALL RIGHT, CAROLINE, SHE DOES SEEM TO LIKE YOU, AND SHE IS CUTE!
FLIRTY LITTLE "HONEY" HAD NO TROUBLE WINNING A HOME IT WAS TIME FOR ME TO GO...
TAFFY," "COCOA" AND I HEADED NORTH
WE MADE A LONG STOP IN OUR CAPITAL...."COCOA" AND I WENT WALKING.
BEING A MALE, "COCOA" WAS NATURALLY LONGWINDED...I FOUND JUST THE HOME FOR HIM.
NOW IT WAS JUST "TAFFY AND I IN A NORTHBOUND TREK.
WE STOPPED FOR A WHILE IN A SMALL COASTAL CITY THAT HAD—
A LARGE FISH CANNERY WITH A KINDLY NIGHT WATCHMAN WHO USED TO BE LONELY

IT WAS COLD AND LONELY IN THAT BOXCAR THE REST OF THE TRIP......
IN A FEW DAYS, THE TRAIN CAME TO A STOP.... IN RIVERDALE.....A WHOLE YEAR HAD PASSED....
IT WAS SNOWING AS I LEFT THE RAILROAD YARDS LATE AT NIGHT......
THE SNOW GOT DEEPER AS I WALKED THE STREETS LOOKING FOR A WARM PLACE TO STAY.
I DON'T KNOW HOW LONG I LAY UNCONSCIOUS IN THAT SNOWBANK...WHEN I AWOKE I WAS HALF FROZEN AND ACHED ALL OVER.......

IT WAS NEARLY DAWN. I SAW A LIGHT AND HOBBLED TOWARD IT.
SO THAT'S HOW I GOT HERE! NOW YOU'RE BOTH TOO OLD FOR ME EVER TO TALK TO YOU AGAIN... SO LEAVE ME ALONE, I NEED A CATNAP.
GOSH! I'LL NEVER CALL CARAMEL LAZY AGAIN!
SHE CAN MUSS UP MY BED ALL SHE WANTS! LET'S GO!
GEE, RONNIE, DO YOU THINK CARAMEL MISSES HER KITTENS?
OH, NO-
MY DADDY SAYS THAT ALL MOMMA CATS LOSE THEIR LOVE AFTER THEIR KITTENS GET OLD ENOUGH TO LEAVE THEM.
The End

Archie in The HOUSE that LODGE built
THIS IS THE HOUSE THAT LODGE BUILT!
THIS IS THE MAN WHO LIVES IN THE HOUSE THAT LODGE BUILT!
THIS IS THE THORN IN THE SIDE OF THE MAN WHO LIVES IN THE HOUSE THAT LODGE BUILT!
..NOT A REAL THORN IN THE SIDE! ..THAT'S JUST AN EXPRESSION! ..LIKE PAIN IN THE NECK! THAT DOESN'T MEAN A NECK WITH A..
--LOOK!---WHAT HE IS IS A NUISANCE! ---A PEST!
WHAM!

THAT IS-- HE'S A NUISANCE TO THE MAN WHO LIVES IN THE HOUSE THAT LODGE BUILT!
BUT NOT TO THE DAUGHTER OF THE MAN WHO LIVES IN THE HOUSE THAT LODGE BUILT!
THE MAN WHO LIVES IN THE---ETC. YOU KNOW!---LODGE!--WOULD BE LOST WITHOUT THIS PEST!
IN FACT, HE ENJOYS THIS THORN-IN-SIDE, PAIN-IN-NECK, NUISANCE!
HI, MISTER LODGE!
IT'S LIKE HAVING AN ITCH YOU CAN SCRATCH! HE ACTUALLY LOOKS FORWARD TO ARCHIE'S VISITS, BECAUSE IT FEELS SO GOOD TO EJECT HIM!
2

AND ANOTHER OF ARCHIE'S VISITS TO THE HOUSE THAT LODGE BUILT COMES TO ITS INEVITABLE CONCLUSION!
AND STAY OUT!
SLAM!
HAPPY?___ CONTENT?___JUST LOOK AT THAT GRIN!
BUT FATE* HAS A WAY OF SPOILING EVERY-ONE'S FUN!
*WE DON'T KNOW WHAT FATE LOOKS LIKE, SO DRAW YOUR OWN PICTURE IN HERE!
JUST WAIT! SOMEDAY HE'LL APPRECIATE ME!
I'M AFRAID NOT, ARCHIEKINS!
WE MAY AS WELL GIVE UP SEEING EACH OTHER!
NO!..NOT THAT!
YOU WATCH! YOUNG-LOVE ALWAYS WINS OUT IN THESE KIND OF STORIES!
YOU'RE A DREAMER, DARLING! DADDY WILL NEVER APPROVE OF YOU!
3

IT'S NO USE! I DON'T WANT TO HAVE TO CHOOSE BETWEEN YOU AND DADDY! IT'S BEST THAT WE END IT NOW!---GO!---PLEASE!
SAD! ----ISN'T IT?
SNIFF!
BUT, HARK!---LOOKA WHA HOPPEN BACK AT THE LITTLE STONE SHACK THAT WHAT'S-HIS-NAME CONSTRUCTED!
ARCHIE! LOOK BACK!---LOOK BACK!
HUH?
HEY! AS SURE AS I'M A CLEAN-LIVING, RED-BLOODED AMERICAN BOY, THAT HOUSE IS ON FIRE!
4

FIRE ALARM
OUT! OUT!--THE PLACE IS IN FLAMES!
?
RRREE-EE-EE!
CLANG!
CLANG!
5

WE WERE ABLE TO CONFINE THE DAMAGE TO ONE ROOM, MR. LODGE!
--THANKS TO THE QUICK ACTION OF THIS BRAVE YOUNG LAD!
CHIEF
DADDY!--WE OWE OUR LIVES TO ARCHIE! --ALSO THE WHOLE FABULOUSLY EXPENSIVE HOUSE IN WHICH WE LIVE!
TUT! TUT! NOT AT ALL!
I ONLY DID WHAT ANY OTHER RED-BLOODED, AMERICAN BOY WOULD HAVE DONE! YOU DON'T HAVE TO FEEL OBLIGATED TO ME---
--DAD!
THIS IS THE PERMANENT THORN IN THE SIDE, THE NUISANCE THAT WHAT'S-HIS-NAME CANNOT ABIDE--- WHO PRACTICALLY LIVES IN THE HOUSE THAT LODGE BUILT!
R-R-RIP!
The End

Dinner for One
Betty & Veronica #119, 1965
by Frank Doyle, Dan DeCarlo, Rudy Lapick, Vince DeCarlo and Barry Grossman

"The scourge of the slimy set" strikes again! As a major super-hero fan growing up, some of my very favorite Archie stories featured the students of Riverdale as the Super-Teens. From Pureheart to Superteen, it's awesome to see how the world of over-the-top heroics translates into the Archie style and tone. This is one of the most memorable examples of that transition I can think of! DeCarlo's rendition of that creepy, villainous "consumer" monster is so far out that you'd think it leaped from the pages of a space adventure title – and speaking of leaping, it's always a treat to see DeCarlo's Betty leap into action as Superteen! My favorite bit about this story, though, is that it takes Jughead's crazy appetite to send the monster packing. *Man vs. Food,* eat your heart out!

--Paul Kaminski
Executive Director of Editorial, Archie Comics

The Forest Prime Evil
Jughead #117, 1965
by Frank Doyle and Samm Schwartz

One of my favorite characters has always been Robin Hood. From Disney's animated *Robin Hood* to Errol Flynn's portrayal in *Adventures of Robin Hood,* I would watch them all. I loved the fantasy and the adventure that all of those stories encompassed. When I was a kid, I would spend many summer days at my grandmother's house. There was a huge wooded area in the back of the house and I loved running around pretending I was in Sherwood Forest trying to relive those same adventures I had seen and read about. "The Forest Prime Evil" is just one of a multitude of great Robin Hood-esque adaptations that Archie has done over the years. I would love to take all of these stories and put them into one giant Robin Hood-themed graphic novel one of these days.

--Joe Morciglio
Project Coordinator, Archie Comics

Betty as SUPERTEEN in "DINNER FOR ONE"
THE CONSUMER, THAT EVIL DEMON FROM THE PLANET DISPERSIA, WHOSE MOLECULAR STRUCTURE ENABLES HIM TO DEVOUR AT WILL WHATEVER STANDS IN HIS WAY, PAYS A VISIT TO RIVERDALE HIGH...
EGAD! THAT ARCH VILLAIN WITH THE ENDLESS APPETITE, THE CONSUMER, IS NIBBLING AWAY AT MY SCHOOL! WHERE IS THAT SUPERTEEN WHEN YOU NEED HER?
HEH, HEH! (GULP) DREAM ON, FAT BOY! I'LL HAVE THAT SUPER HEROINE FOR DESSERT
CHRISTOPHER COLUMBUS! IT'S TIME I STOPPED BEING PLAIN OLD BETTY COOPER!
SLURP!
SCRIPT: FRANK DOYLE
PENCILS: DAN DECARLO
INKS: RUDY LAPICK
LETTERS: VINCE DECARLO
COLORS: BARRY GROSSMAN
1

...AND CHANGE INTO SUPERTEEN, SCOURGE OF THE SLIMY SET!
I'LL CURE THAT FOUL FIEND'S APPETITE, OR MY NAME ISN'T...
SUPERTEEN! HOLD IT OR I'LL DO AWAY WITH THIS SILLY-LOOKING STUDENT!
!?
ULP! ARCHIE! HE'S THREATENING TO DEVOUR MY ARCHIE!
ALL RIGHT! ALL RIGHT, CONSUMER! YOU WIN THIS ROUND! LEAVE HIM ALONE AND I'LL BACK OFF!
HEH! HEH! YOU BET YOU WILL!
(GULP) THAT'S JUST TO SHOW YOU I CAN DO IT, SONNY!
MY BASKETBALL! HE ATE MY BASKETBALL!
SLURP!
2

MR. WEATHERBEE! MR. WEATHERBEE! THE CONSUMER IS RUNNING AMUCK IN MY LABORATORY!
HE CONSUMED ALL MY CHEMICALS, THE TEST TUBES, THE BUNSEN BURNER AND THE ROAST BEEF SANDWICH I BROUGHT FOR LUNCH!
SUPERTEEN! IT'S ABOUT TIME! WE... WE...
...WHAT'S WRONG WITH YOU?
I'M HELPLESS, SIR! I'M POWERLESS AGAINST THE CONSUMER!
FINK!
PHONEY HEROINE!
TURN IN YOUR SUPERSUIT!
FAILURE!
BAP!
3

(SIGH) THEY'RE RIGHT! I'M A FAILURE! A TOTAL...
SUPPLY ROOM
...OOPS!
WAP!
HA! HA! HA! HAPPY LANDINGS, SUPERTEEN!
SLURP!
YOU FIEND! YOU DEVOURED MY CHAIR!
FACE IT, KIDDO! AS A HEROINE, YOU'RE A HOAX!
WHY, YOU...
HEH, HEH, (GULP) KEEP 'EM COMING! THESE TIDBITS WILL BUILD UP MY STRENGTH!
SLURP!
CLIPS
SLAP!
NAILS
ERASERS
4

NOW LISTEN GOOD! SISTER, YOU'RE GOING TO GIVE UP BEING SUPER-TEEN! YOU'LL NEVER ASSUME THAT ROLE AGAIN!
PUFF PUFF
...OR I'LL DEVOUR THAT ARCHIE CHARACTER... AND MAYBE VERONICA, TOO!
NO!
(GROAN) SO IT'S UNCONDITIONAL SURRENDER! ALL RIGHT, CONSUMER! I'VE GOT NO CHOICE BUT TO...
WAIT!
SUPPLY ROOM
IS THIS THE SLOB THEY CALL THE CONSUMER?
YES, JUGGIE!
HAH! THAT SCRAWNY TOOTHPICK? THAT UNDERNOURISHED NOODNIK HAS EVERY-ONE WORRIED?
WATCH IT, BUSTER!
5

WHY, YOU FOUR FLUSHER! I'LL MEET YOU AT THE CAFETERIA!
YOU'LL MEET ME?
IT'S A CHALLENGE! A DUEL! I DARE YOU TO HAVE LUNCH WITH ME!
PUT YOUR MONEY WHERE YOUR MOUTH IS, BOY!
CAFETERIA
ONE HOUR LATER:
THAT'S IT, MR. WEATHERBEE! ANOTHER SUPER-VILLAIN BITES THE DUST! HE'S HAD IT THIS TIME!
LIKE TAKING CANDY FROM A BABY!...
AND, SPEAKING OF CANDY...
OOW! MY STOMACH! I'M BURSTING!
(GIGGLE) I ALMOST FEEL SORRY FOR THE POOR CONSUMER...
BUT HE'LL THINK TWICE BEFORE HE MATCHES APPETITES WITH JUGGIE AGAIN!
Z Z Z Z Z
The END

THE FOREST
PRIME EVIL
Jughead
WHAT CALL THYSELF, WOODSMAN?
LITTLE JUG! AND THOU?

ROBIN ARCH!
"ROBIN?" 'TIS INDEED A STRANGE NAME! WHY ROBIN?

HYUK! 'CAUSE I'M ALWAYS ROBIN! BUT ONLY THE RICH, OF COURSE!
1.

FUNNY MATERIAL, OUTLAW!
LAUGH THAT OFF!
CLUNK!
WELL STRUCK, LITTLE JUG! WOULDST CARE TO JOIN MY BAND?
WHY NOT? I PLUCK A MEAN ZITHER IF I DO SAY SO MYSELF!
HOW BIG IS YOUR COMBO?
NOT THAT KIND OF BAND, DOLT!
OH!
AN OUTLAW BAND!
I'M YOUR BOY, BUBU! WHAT COMES NEXT?
THAT!
2.

THESE LOUTS ARE DEPUTIES OF THE SHERIFF OF NOTTINGHAM WHO KEEPS BUGGING ME!
TAKE FIVE, VARLET! STRAIGHT SHOOTERS ALWAYS WIN!
CLUNK!
BOING!
THAT STUPID SHERIFF PUT A PRICE ON MY HEAD!
NO KID? LET'S SEE!
HMM! SEVEN POUNDS, SIX SHILLINGS! NOT EXACTLY PUBLIC ENEMY NUMBER ONE!
7£6s
FRIAR TUCK! MEET LITTLE JUG!
D-UH, HIYA!
I'VE HEARD TALK ABOUT THIS LITTLE BAND OF YOURS! ... WHERE'S THE MAID MARIAN?
WHO KNOWS?

"WHERE'S THE MAID MARRYIN'?" HE ASKS ME! I DIDN'T EVEN KNOW SHE WUZ ENGAGED! IF SHE'S MARRYIN' I NEVER HEARD OF--
NO, FRIAR! NO!
IT'S MARIAN WITH AN "I", NOT A "Y!"
OH! WELL ANYWAY SHE WENT INTO TOWN! I THINK!
GADZOOKS! THE SHERIFF WILL CAPTURE HER FOR SURE!
HE'LL SET A TRAP FOR ME WHEN I SHOW UP TO RESCUE HER!
GADZOOKS! WE'VE CAPTURED HER!
NOW TO SET A TRAP FOR ROBIN ARCH WHEN HE SHOWS UP TO RESCUE HER!
GOOD THINKING, BOSS!
4

SOONER OR LATER HE'S BOUND TO SHOW UP, AND THEN I'LL HAVE HIM!
SAY, BOSS, DO YOU HEAR MUSIC?
ZOUNDS! THAT'S A CATCHY BEAT!
LET'S GO HAVE A LOOK-SEE!
NO DUMPING
SHE LOVES ME, YEAH, SHE EVEN CUTS MY HAIR!
GO, MAN! GO!
BY MY TROTH, THOSE LADS WERE GOOD!
M'LORD! THE PRISONER IS GONE!
EGAD! WE'VE BEEN DUPED!
5

THOSE MINSTRELS! THAT WAS ROBIN ARCHIE'S BAND!
IT USED TO BE A TWO PIECE BAND! HE'S GOT A NEW ZITHER PLAYER!
WELCOME HOME, MAID MARIAN! GOOD TO SEE YOU AGAIN!
THAT WAS A COOL COMBO YOU SPRUNG ME WITH!
WE GOT A NEW ZITHER MAN TO FILL OUT THE STRING SECTION! MEET LITTLE JUG!
HI!
WILD, MAN!
GOOD CHOW! WHAT IS IT?
THE KING'S DEER!
TO HER, THE KING'S DEAR! BUT YOU SHOULD SEE THE QUEEN! WHUT A DOLL!

The Attack of the Mole Men
Little Archie #42, 1967
by Dexter Taylor
and Jon D'Agostino

Everyone equates the Little Archie adventure stories with Bob Bolling, but not everyone gives Dexter Taylor – especially in his earliest years – his proper due.

For example, take "Little Captain Pureheart and the Attack of the Mole Men!" As far as I know this is the only Pureheart the Powerful story done within the Little Archie universe – and it's absolutely ridiculous! This story deals with a muscle-bound, kid-superhero powerhouse with random mind control powers doing battle with ax-wielding under-dwelling mole people that kidnap Little Veronica so they can worship her as their 'Mole Princess.' Read that sentence out loud and I defy you to not recoil at the absurdity of it. This is Dexter Taylor in his prime!

The best Archie stories have always been the ones that are positively insane so it makes sense to apply Pureheart to the Little Archie universe. After all, what kid doesn't want to be a superhero? Still, it's a shame that there wasn't more done with the concept. Dexter Taylor had big shoes to fill after Bob Bolling moved on to other Archie stories, but this shows he had more than enough chops for the task!

--Jon Gray
Production Artist,
Archie Comics

LITTLE CAPTAIN PUREHEART
SEIZE THE CAPED INTRUDER! HE'S TRYING TO TAKE OUR PRINCESS AWAY FROM US!
PRINCESS? GOOD GOSH! HE'S TALKING ABOUT VERONICA!
WHAM!
GET SET FOR THE STRANGEST ACTION PACKED YARN OF ALL TIMES AS LITTLE CAPTAIN PUREHEART MEETS "THE ATTACK OF THE MOLE MEN"!

NIGHT HAS FALLEN! OUR STORY OPENS ON A STRANGE SCENE TAKING PLACE IN A WOODED AREA JUST OUTSIDE RIVERDALE...
THE ODD FIGURES INCH THEIR WAY TOWARD AN UNSUSPECTING TRIO...
LODGE
S'LONG, RONNIE!
GOOD NIGHT, LITTLE ARCHIE! I ENJOYED THE PARTY TONIGHT... EVEN IF BETTY DID GIVE IT!
SAY! LOOK AT YOUR DOG'S HAIR STAND UP... MAYBE HE ATE SOME OF BETTY'S CAKE!
NO! SPOTTY HEARS SOMETHING!
C-CRACK!
2

LODGE
HELP!
MFFF!
WAP!
LITTLE ARCHIE!
LODGE
LATER...
A BAND OF COSTUMED MEN JUMPED YOU? THAT BLOW ON THE HEAD MUST HAVE REALLY TOUCHED OFF YOUR IMAGINATION!
WAIT! I'M NOT SO SURE, MR. LODGE!
3

LITTLE ARCHIE HAS DESCRIBED THE MOLE MAN COSTUME TO THE LETTER!
MOLE MAN? WHAT ARE YOU TALKING ABOUT, CHIEF?
THE MOLE MEN WERE A TRIBE OF INDIANS WHO LIVED UNDER-GROUND IN CAVES YEARS AGO! THEY WERE ALMOST WIPED OUT BY A TERRIBLE FIRE WHICH SWEPT THE ENTIRE AREA!
ACCORDING TO A LEGEND A MOLE MAN WILL LIVE HIS LIFE OVER AGAIN IN 200 YEARS! THAT WOULD BRING IT TO ABOUT THIS YEAR!
THEY WERE ALSO RULED BY A SMALL WHITE PRINCESS! THAT MIGHT EXPLAIN VERONICA'S DISAPPEARANCE!
POPPYCOCK! IT CAN'T BE!
POLICE
MEANWHILE, A FEW MILES AWAY...
THE LAST FIGURE STEPS THROUGH THE STUMP AND THE STRANGE ESCAPE ROUTE IS LOST TO ALL HUMAN EYES...
...EXCEPT FOR THOSE OF A SMALL WITNESS WHO HAS FOLLOWED THEM!
4

THE NEXT DAY...
B-BUT, DAD! I WANT TO HELP FIND VERONICA!
NO! LET THE POLICE DO THAT!
THE DOCTOR SAID TO STAY IN BED!
(SIGH) PARENTS NEVER UNDERSTAND!
I'VE GOT TO CHANGE TO LITTLE CAPTAIN PUREHEART!
LITTLE ARCHIE CONCENTRATES... THE POWERS OF HIS INNER GOODNESS COME TOGETHER AND THE TRANSFORMATION TO LITTLE CAPTAIN PUREHEART BEGINS...
CONTINUED

ARF!
HUH? SPOTTY KEEPS LOOKING BACK AT ME... AS IF HE WANTS ME TO FOLLOW HIM!
MAYBE SPOTTY KNOWS WHERE RONNIE WENT!
ARF!
OH, NO! DEAD END! SPOTTY'S STOPPED BY AN OLD STUMP!
HEY! THIS STUMP HAS A COVER!
HUH? THIS STUMP IS HOLLOW! THERE ARE STEPS LEADING INTO THE GROUND!
WOW! LET'S FIND OUT WHERE IT GOES!
6

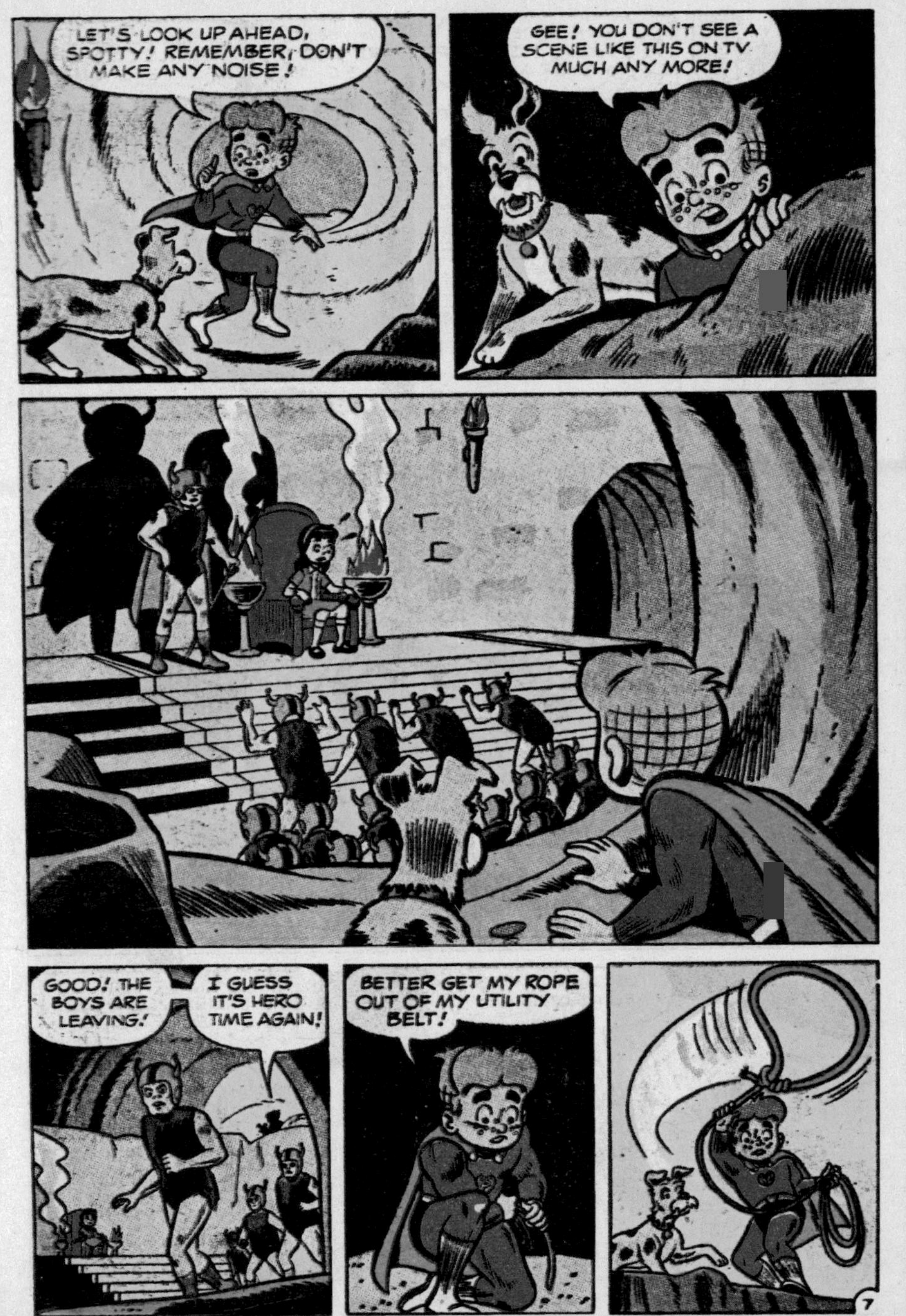
LET'S LOOK UP AHEAD, SPOTTY! REMEMBER, DON'T MAKE ANY NOISE!
GEE! YOU DON'T SEE A SCENE LIKE THIS ON TV MUCH ANY MORE!
GOOD! THE BOYS ARE LEAVING!
I GUESS IT'S HERO TIME AGAIN!
BETTER GET MY ROPE OUT OF MY UTILITY BELT!
7

WIP!
HI, RONNIE! I THOUGHT I'D DROP IN FOR A VISIT!
MY WRISTS ARE TIED TO THIS CHAIR!
THESE ROPES LOOK A LITTLE OLD! MAYBE I CAN BREAK THEM!
SNAP!
LOOK OUT! THE MOLE MEN HAVE SEEN YOU!
LET'S PLAY TAG, FELLAS! YOU'RE IT!
YOU DON'T LIKE GAMES...OKAY, BE A SORE HEAD!
WHOMP!
8

SPILLING THIS FLAMING OIL POT SHOULD GIVE THE BOYS A WARM EVENING!
SPLAT!
C'MON, RONNIE! LET'S NOT STAY TO TOAST MARSHMELLOWS!
WE MADE IT, AND JUST IN TIME!
ARF!
I'M GLAD TO SEE YOU TOO, SPOTTY!
THIS IS ONE SCENE I'M HAPPY TO LEAVE!
9

THE WHOLE TOWN'S BEEN LOOKING FOR YOU, RONNIE! MAYBE THIS LITTLE ADVENTURE WILL GET YOU ON TELEVISION!
GOODNESS! I LOOK SO DIRTY!
WELL, YOU'LL HAVE TO COME ON TV WITH ME SO EVERYONE CAN SEE YOU, LITTLE CAPTAIN PUREHEART!
ULP! I CAN'T BE SEEN ON TV!
I'D BETTER CLOUD HER MIND SO SHE FORGETS EVERY-THING!
LATER...
MY WORD, IT'S VERONICA!
I'D BETTER CHANGE AND GET IN BED FAST! SOMEONE IS COMING UP THE STAIRS!
MINUTES LATER...
GOOD NEWS! RONNIE WAS FOUND BY THE BUTLER RIGHT OUTSIDE HER HOME!
SHE DIDN'T KNOW ANYTHING ABOUT SO CALLED MOLE MEN!
I KNEW THIS MOLE MEN STORY WAS RIDICULOUS!
THE END
10

THE BEST OF
Archie
COMICS
BOOK TWO
the '70s
REX W. LINDSEY
THE REG
LOLLIPOP PUNK

An Uncle's Monkey Sabrina the Teenage Witch #1, 1971

by Frank Doyle, Dan DeCarlo, Rudy Lapick and Bill Yoshida

With a script by the irrepressible Dick Malmgren and art by the great Dan DeCarlo, "An Uncle's Monkey" is a hijinks-filled romp with that slinger of spells, Sabrina. I mean, how can it go wrong? It has the three M's that make for a classic Sabrina story – Magic, Mayhem and Monkeys!

"Magic, Mayhem and Monkeys"... what more can you ask for? I know... a rectangular-cut, peanut butter sandwich, no jelly. And that's all I have to say about that!

--Stephen Oswald
Production Manager, Archie Comics

Strange Love Sabrina the Teenage Witch #1, 1971

by Frank Doyle, Dan DeCarlo, Rudy Lapick and Bill Yoshida

There is a segment of the population for whom the name "Sabrina the Teenage Witch" conjures up that now defunct children's television show starring Melissa Joan Hart. For true diehards, though, the real Sabrina was the one you're seeing here. Impeccably coiffed with a wardrobe that put Betty and Veronica to shame, (if anyone could make a pink turtleneck pantsuit actually work, it was her) Sabrina took charge of situations. Maybe to the detriment of those around her, sure, (boyfriend Harvey might not have been the sharpest crayon in the box, but that willful ignorance was actually pretty perfect considering his choice of mate) but at least she was pro-active. She'll always be the one, the only, and the true teen witch to me.

--Betsy Bird
Youth Materials Specialist, New York Public Library

SABRINA
THE TEEN-AGE WITCH
AN UNCLE'S MONKEY
LET ME TAKE THAT TRAY FROM YOU, AUNT HILDA! I CAN HANDLE IT! YOU JUST SIT DOWN!
NO! KEEP YOUR HANDS OFF THAT TRAY! I'LL FEEL MUCH SAFER IF I HANDLE IT!
!
?
NONSENSE! WHOOPS!!
EEEEK!
OH DEAR ME! NOW I'VE GOT MILK ALL OVER MY NICE OUTFIT!
GOSH! I'M SORRY, SABRINA!

YEESH! THAT BOOB COULD TRIP OVER AN ELEPHANT!
GOLLY! I'LL GET YOU SOME WATER AND A CLOTH SO YOU CAN CLEAN YOUR DRESS BEFORE IT STAINS!
JOSIE
HERE SABRINA... WIPE IT OFF RIGHT AWAY!
GAK!
GLUB!
SPLASH
OOPS!
GOSH, I'M SORRY, AUNT HILDA! I GUESS I WENT AND DID IT AGAIN!
YOU DING-A-LING! YOU HAVE THE BRAINS OF A BABOON!
2

OH THAT BOY! I DON'T KNOW WHAT YOU SEE IN HIM! HE'S A REGULAR MISFIT! HE'S NOTHING BUT TROUBLE!
NOW AUNT HILDA, HARVEY DIDN'T MEAN IT! EVERYBODY MAKES MISTAKES! AFTER ALL, HE'S ONLY HUMAN!
THAT BIRD BRAIN ISN'T EVEN HUMAN! HE'S A BABOON! AND I'VE GOT HALF A MIND TO ZAP HIM INTO LOOKING LIKE ONE! IT WOULD MAKE A MUCH NEEDED IMPROVEMENT IN HIS (UGH) APPEARANCE!
CALM DOWN, AUNT HILDA! YOU'RE GETTING YOURSELF UPTIGHT!
I'M GOING UP AND CHANGE, AND I ASKED HARVEY TO MOP UP THE MESS HE MADE!
LOOK AT THAT IDIOT! HE'LL PROBABLY TRIP OVER THE MOP NEXT!
LA-LA-LA-LA-LA!
CONTINUED
3

WELL, THAT'S THAT!
SWAT!
GAK!
AUNT HILDA! I DIDN'T KNOW YOU WERE IN BACK OF ME!
SWAK
GULP!
OH, GIVE ME STRENGTH! GIVE ME STRENGTH!
CRASH
WHY ME? WHY IS IT ALWAYS ME? WHAT DID I EVER DO TO HIM?
SHE'S A STRANGE DUCK! WELL, I BETTER GET RID OF THIS MOP AND GET A DUST PAN!
4

HILDA! WAIT TILL YOU SEE WHAT I BOUGHT FOR YOU!
SHE'S NOT AROUND OSCAR! MAYBE SHE'S IN THE KITCHEN!
YOU SIT RIGHT THERE AND I'LL GO SEE IF I CAN FIND AUNT HILDA! IS SHE GOING TO BE SURPRISED!
CHEE! CHEE!
OH, NO!
AUNT HILDA WENT AND ZAPPED HARVEY!
CONTINUED

SPEAK TO ME HARVEY! ARE YOU ALL RIGHT? OH, YOU POOR LITTLE THING! I TOLD AUNT HILDA NOT TO DO THAT TO YOU!
?
JOSIE
DON'T YOU WORRY, HARVEY, I'LL ZAP YOU RIGHT BACK TO YOUR NORMAL SELF AGAIN!
ZAP
?
I'M GOING TO SPEAK TO AUNT HILDA ABOUT THIS!
!
THE PRESENT I HAVE FOR YOU IS SITTING IN THE LIVING ROOM, HILDA! GO TAKE A LOOK AND I'LL BET YOU'RE GOING TO FLIP OVER IT!
AMBROSE, YOU SHOULDN'T HAVE!
6

IT'S JUST A LITTLE COMPANIONSHIP FOR YOU TO HAVE BY YOUR SIDE NIGHT AND DAY!
THANK YOU COUSIN AMBROSE!
GAK!
JAPAN
CHEE! CHEE!
GOOD GRIEF! IS THIS HIS IDEA OF A JOKE? HE KNOWS I'M SICK OF THE SIGHT OF THAT HUMAN DING-A-LING!
VERY FUNNY AMBROSE! IT'S BAD ENOUGH TO HAVE TO TOLERATE HIM ON ACCOUNT OF SABRINA, BUT NOW YOU THINK IT'S AMUSING, TOO!
?
EVERYBODY IS PLOTTING AGAINST ME! YOU'RE ALL DRIVING ME NUTS!
HARVEY?
7

WAIT, HILDA! I DON'T THINK YOU SAW THE GIFT I WAS GIVING YOU, COME ON BACK DOWN AND SEE HIM! HE'S REAL CUTE!
YOU MEAN HARVEY **WASN'T** MY GIFT?
HUH?
WHO ARE YOU?
CHEE! CHEE!
YOU LOOK AWFULLY FAMILIAR FELLOW! HAVEN'T I SEEN YOU SOMEWHERE BEFORE?
MAYBE AT THE BOWLING ALLEY? I KNOW I'VE SEEN YOU SOMEWHERE BEFORE BUT WHERE?
?
HEE! HEE! YOU DON'T THINK I'D GIVE YOU HARVEY FOR A PET DO YOU, AUNT HILDA? WHAT KIND OF A RELATIVE DO YOU THINK I AM?
I WAS BEGINNING TO WONDER!
8

YAHH!
NOW THERE'S TWO OF THEM!
WHAT'S GOING ON AROUND HERE?
YOU MEAN YOU DON'T KNOW HIM EITHER?
WHO IS THIS GUY, AUNT HILDA?
CHEE! CHEE!
HELP!
KEEP THEM AWAY FROM ME!!
?
GOOD GRIEF! NOW THERE'RE TWO HARVEYS! HOW DID THAT HAPPEN COUSIN AMBROSE?
MAYBE YOU CAN TELL ME, SABRINA! ONE OF THEM HAS MY CHIMPS LEASH AND COLLAR ON!
9

A CHIMP? DON'T TELL ME THAT IT WAS YOUR CHIMPANZEE?
YES IT WAS!
IT WAS MY GIFT TO AUNT HILDA!
OH DEAR ME! I'D BETTER ZAP HIM BACK!
CHEE! CHEE!
HUH?
WHAT HAPPENED TO THE FELLOW THAT WAS HERE? AND WHERE DID HE COME FROM?
?
ZAP!
HERE'S THE PET I BOUGHT YOU HILDA... WHAT DO YOU THINK OF IT?
CHEE! CHEE!
A MONKEY? FORGET IT! THAT REMINDS ME TOO MUCH OF SOMEONE I'D LIKE TO FORGET!
THIS SURE IS A WEIRD HOUSE!
End

SABRINA
"STRANGE LOVE"
I CAN HONESTLY SAY, ETHEL, THAT AS LONG AS HARVEY AND I HAVE BEEN DATING, HE'S NEVER GONE OUT WITH ANOTHER GIRL!
I HATE TO LET YOU DOWN SABRINA, BUT THAT SURE LOOKS LIKE HARVEY ACROSS THE STREET WITH ANOTHER GIRL!
FRESH
HUH? YOU'RE RIGHT! IT IS HARVEY...AND THAT'S A GIRL HE'S WITH!
THAT'S WHAT I THOUGHT! NOW WHAT WERE YOU SAYING ABOUT YOUR BOYFRIEND, SABRINA?
HOW EMBARRASSING!!

NOW WHAT WOULD HE BE DOING WITH A STRANGE GIRL ? HE'S NEVER DONE THAT BEFORE!
I DON'T KNOW, SABRINA! WHY DON'T YOU TELL ME, SEEING THAT YOU KNOW HIM SO WELL? HEE! HEE! HEE!
POP'S
I TOLD YOU, ALL FELLOWS ARE THE SAME! WHEN THE CAT'S AWAY THE MICE WILL PLAY!
HEE! HEE! HEE!
WELL HE'S GOING TO GET A TASTE OF HIS OWN MEDICINE BECAUSE I CAN PLAY THAT GAME BETTER THAN HIM!
LET'S SEE HOW HE LIKES IT WHEN HE SEES ARCHIE FALL ALL OVER ME LIKE A LOVE STARVED PUPPY DOG!
AND HOW DO YOU INTEND TO ARRANGE THAT, PRAY TELL ?
HI, GIRLS!
2

OH I HAVE WAYS!
YOU'RE KIDDING!
ZAP
ARCHIE, HOW WOULD YOU LIKE TO BUY ME A COKE?
OH COULD I? THANK YOU! THANK YOU!
FOR YOU, SABRINA MY LOVE, I WOULD CROSS A BURNING DESERT, I WOULD CLIMB THE HIGHEST MOUNTAIN, YOUR WISH WILL BE MY COMMAND!
A COKE WILL BE SUFFICIENT, ARCHIE!
I DON'T BELIEVE IT! WAIT TILL RONNIE HEARS ABOUT THIS!
KISS
KISS
KISS
HELLO, HARVEY!
HERE'S YOUR COKE, MY LOVE! I HOPE I DIDN'T TAKE TOO LONG!
?
DO YOU WANT ANYTHING ELSE MY DEAREST? ARE YOU COMFY, SWEETS?
!?
3

MAYBE YOU WOULD LIKE ME TO BURP YOU ?
SEE, VERONICA! I WASN'T LYING! THERE HE IS WITH HER NOW!
?
SMACK! SMACK!
WHAT'S GOING ON AROUND HERE, ARCHIE ? THERE I WAS WAITING ON A COLD STREET CORNER FOR YOU,... AND HERE YOU ARE FALLING ALL OVER SABRINA!
PLEASE, RONNIE, DON'T RAISE YOUR VOICE LIKE THAT, YOU MIGHT HURT SABRINA'S BEAUTIFUL, SENSITIVE EARS!
OH DEAR ME!
WHAT ??
ARCHIE ANDREWS! ARE YOU TRYING TO MAKE A FOOL OUT OF ME!?
DON'T LISTEN TO HER SABRINA, SHE'S JUST JEALOUS OF OUR GREAT LOVE!
GOOD GRIEF! I'D BETTER UNZAP THIS SPELL RIGHT AWAY!
ZAP!

RONNIE BABY!? WHAT ARE YOU DOING HERE ? I WAS SUPPOSED TO MEET YOU ON THE CORNER!
HUH ?
COME TO THINK OF IT... WHAT AM I DOING HERE ?
YEESH! THAT DOES IT, ARCHIE!
MY FATHER WAS RIGHT ABOUT YOU! YOU DON'T HAVE A BRAIN IN YOUR HEAD!
RONNIE BABY WHAT DID I DO ? WHAT DID I DO ?
ZAP!
POOR ARCHIE! BETTER MAKE RONNIE FORGET WHAT HAPPENED, TOO!
ARCHIE ? HOW DID WE GET HERE ?
I DON'T KNOW! BUT SEEING WE ARE, LET'S SHARE A MALT!
WILL SOMEBODY MIND TELLING ME WHAT'S GOING ON AROUND HERE ?
YEAH, I'D LIKE TO KNOW TOO!
5

YOU SHOULD KNOW, HARVEY! IT'S ALL YOUR FAULT! I'VE A GOOD MIND NEVER TO TALK TO YOU AGAIN!
WHY? BECAUSE I BROUGHT MY COUSIN HERE TO MEET YOU?
?
YOUR COUSIN ?!?
THAT'S RIGHT! SUZY MEET SABRINA! THIS IS THE GIRL I WAS TELLING YOU ABOUT!
HARVEY, I SHOULD HAVE KNOWN I COULD ALWAYS TRUST YOU! WILL YOU EVER FORGIVE ME?
SURE, SABRINA!
BUT I DON'T REALLY KNOW WHAT I'M FORGIVING YOU FOR!
I DON'T GET IT! IT CAN'T BE ME POP, CAN IT? IT MUST BE LOVE BECAUSE LOVE WORKS IN STRANGE WAYS!
I AGREE ETHEL! THERE IS NOBODY STRANGER THAN MY CUSTOMERS!
The End

Little Miss Fixit

Betty & Veronica #181, 1971
by Frank Doyle,
Dan DeCarlo, Rudy Lapick
and Bill Yoshida

For anyone championing Betty as Archie's perfect match, this story easily sums up why she ought to be Archie's #1. Who wouldn't love a girl who's handy with a needle and thread? Plus it's always fun to see Veronica be taken down a peg once in a while. Jughead shows up to munch on an apple – what's that all about?

This story reminds me of my earliest memories of Archie when I discovered a dusty old digest at my Grandma's house. This story very well may have been featured in there. It still holds up twenty-some years later. That's why Archie is timeless.

--Steven M. Scott
Publicity & Marketing Coordinator, Archie Comics

The Secret of Carswell Crypt

Madhouse Glads #82, 1972
by Frank Doyle, Stan
Goldberg, Rudy Lapick
and Bill Yoshida

I remember this story so well because it was really creepy, and made a strong impression on my eight or so year-old mind. It was in an issue of *Madhouse Digest Comics*, but originally appeared in an issue of the *Madhouse Glads*. I liked it so much because I was into spooky stuff. I loved old monster movies and monster comics, and I stayed with my Grandma a lot as child and she ALWAYS told the spookiest stories imaginable. I was also a big *Scooby Doo* fan, and this story provided the same type of atmosphere. After reading it, I found that I wanted to read more of the same type of stories. I eventually did, but this one particular story stood out. I guess it was because it was the first one I read. I do believe it was drawn by Stan Goldberg, who is my personal favorite Archie artist.

--Steven Butler
Artist,
Archie Comics

Betty and Veronica
in "LITTLE MISS FIXIT"
HELLO THERE, YOU PRETTY, LITTLE BIRD! COME FLY WITH ME! COME FLY WITH ME!
ARCHIE, YOU FOOL! PUT ME DOWN! PUT ME...
DRAT! NOW I'VE POPPED A BUTTON!
YOU CRAZY CLOWN, ARCHIE! NOW LOOK WHAT YOU'VE DONE!
TUT, TUT!
COOL IT, RON! WHAT'S A POPPED BUTTON AMONG FRIENDS?
?
1

WHY THANK YOU, BETTY! THAT'S VERY SWEET OF YOU!

NO PROBLEM, RONNIE!

TRASH

SEW

WELL, LET'S GO IF WE'RE GOING!

SO LONG, GANG!

TALK ABOUT BEING DEPENDABLE! MAN! THAT BETTY IS THE GREATEST!

HMPH!

HEY! WATCH IT, YOU OLDSTERS! EXUBERANT YOUTHS COMING THROUGH!

WATCH IT, YOU ROTTEN KIDS!

LOOK WHAT THE LITTLE MONSTERS DID! THEY TORE YOUR SWEATER!

RRIP!

WHY DON'T YOU KIDS WATCH WHERE YOU'RE GOING?

YOU OUGHT TO BE MADE TO PAY FOR THE DAMAGE YOU DID!

2

NOW, NOW! NOTHING TO GET EXCITED ABOUT! BETTY WILL HAVE EVERYTHING FIXED IN A JIFFY!
HEY! HOW ABOUT THAT?
THAT'S REAL KEEN!
SAY, LADY! I GOT A LITTLE RIP IN MY PANTS! DO YOU THINK YOU COULD...
OF COURSE!
A LITTLE THING I CALL "INVISIBLE STITCHING"! YOUR MOTHER WILL NEVER KNOW YOU TORE THEM!
MAN! IF ALL GIRLS WERE AS GOOD AS THAT ONE, THEY'D BE ALMOST HUMAN!
I NEVER THOUGHT A GIRL COULD BE USEFUL!
BETTY'S ONE IN A MILLION, KIDS!
3

OH, COME OFF IT, FOR GOODNESS SAKE!
HUH? WHAT'S WRONG, CUPCAKE?
DON'T YOU APPROVE OF BETTY'S DOMESTIC TALENTS?
"TALENTS?" SHE DOES A LITTLE MENIAL WORK AND IT BECOMES "TALENTS?"
A COUPLE OF STUPID PASSES WITH A NEEDLE AND...
BE CAREFUL!
RIP!
OH! I'M SORRY!
YOU TORE MY COAT!
SOMETHING OUGHT TO BE DONE ABOUT YOU WILD, DESTRUCTIVE, YOUNG THINGS! YOU'RE ALWAYS CAUSING TROUBLE!
OH, ISN'T THAT A SHAME? YOUR LOVELY COAT IS TORN! HERE, LET ME HAVE A LOOK AT IT!
4

ACTUALLY, IT WAS A FAULTY SEAM THAT LET GO! THIS LITTLE OVERLAP STITCH WILL OUTLAST THE COAT!
NOW THAT'S WHAT ALL TEENAGERS SHOULD BE LIKE! REMINDS ME OF MYSELF AT HER AGE!
WAIT HERE, ARCHIE! I HAVE TO SEE BETTY ABOUT SOMETHING!
IF YOU CAN'T BEAT 'EM, JOIN 'EM! NOW I, TOO, WILL MAKE FRIENDS AND INFLUENCE PEOPLE!
GOOD THINKING!
LODGE
IT CAME! IT CAME! COME SEE IT! IT CAME!
WHAT CAME, DADDY?
MY NEW, INFLATABLE CHAIR! ISN'T IT GREAT? I'VE BEEN WAITING FOR MONTHS FOR IT!
5

IT'S BEAUTIFUL! YOU NEVER FELT ANYTHING MORE COMFORTABLE! TRY IT, DEAR!
POP!
HISSSSSSSSSSS
MY NEW CHAIR! YOU DESTROYED MY NEW CHAIR! H-HOW COULD YOU?
HISSSS
GULP! I-I HAD THIS NEEDLE IN MY HAND, DADDY...
YOU PLANNED IT! YOU PLANNED THIS MONSTROUS PRACTICAL JOKE!
GOLLY! NO KIDDING? WHO GAVE HER THE NEEDLE?
THAT LITTLE OL' HOMEMAKER, ME!
6
The End

A STRANGE LITTLE MAN PLEADS FOR HELP, A SCREAM AND A DISAPPEARANCE IN BROAD DAYLIGHT, CURIOUS ACCIDENTS AND A FOG SHROUDED CEMETERY, ALL PARTS OF AN INTERLOCKING HORROR WHICH THE GLADS PUT TOGETHER TO REVEAL-----
CARSWELL
CEMETERY
RIP
THE SECRET OF CARSWELL CRYPT

IT STARTED WITH A CONFRONTATION BETWEEN FRAN AND THIS TERROR RIDDEN LITTLE GUY IN THE HALLWAY OF THE APARTMENT HOUSE---
SHE WAS HEADING FOR CLYDE DIDIT'S OFF CAMPUS PAD, TO PICK UP CLYDE AND DIPPY!
HELP ME! PLEASE! YOU'VE GOT TO HELP ME!
?
THE MAN COWERED LIKE A TRAPPED ANIMAL, THE SMELL OF FEAR WAS HEAVY IN THE AIR--
W-WHAT IS IT, MISTER? WHAT'S WRONG?
BUT HIS PANIC WAS TOO GREAT FOR EXPLANATIONS, AT THE SOUND OF THE DOOR OPENING UP ABOVE, HIS EYES ROLLED BACK TO HIS HEAD, HIS SWEAT-SOAKED, RAT LIKE FACE TURNED ASHEN, AND HE BOLTED!
WAIT! WAIT! - YOU LOOK ILL!!
2

CLYDE'S LOVELY BLONDE NEIGHBOR, ANNETTE, WAS JUST ARRIVING FOR THE DOUBLE DATE WHEN FRAN REACHED THE TOP OF THE STAIRS.
HI, FRAN! THE BOYS ARE HERE ALL R---
WAIT, ANNETTE!
WHO IN THE WORLD WAS THAT ABSOLUTELY TERRIFIED LITTLE MAN WHO---
BUT THE SCREAM CHOPPED OFF HER WORDS IN MID SENTENCE---
AAARGH!
GASP! THE LITTLE GUY! SOMETHING HAPPENED TO HIM!
THAT'S HIS HAT!
SHOULDN'T WE DO SOMETHING? HE WAS TERRIBLY AFRAID, AND NOW HE'S GONE!
WHAT CAN WE DO? WE DON'T KNOW ANYTHING FOR SURE!
WE COULD CALL THE POLICE, BUT WHAT COULD WE TELL THEM?
I SUGGEST WE JUST CONTINUE ON WITH OUR DATE!
3

AND CONTINUE, THEY DID, THE FOUR OF THEM.
--- OR WAS IT ONLY FOUR ?
I'VE GOT A STRANGE UNEASY FEELING AS THOUGH THERE ARE EYES BORING INTO THE BACK OF MY NECK!
AND FOG BEGAN TO CREEP IN SINISTER SILENCE OVER THE LONELY COAST ROAD ---
THERE'S JUST ONE CAR BEHIND US!
SAY THIS FOG IS GETTING HEAVY!
HEY! SHOULDN'T THAT SIGN HAVE BEEN POINTING THE OTHER WAY ?
YOU KNOW, I THOUGHT THAT, TOO, BUT---
WILDWOOD
WATCH IT! THE ROAD JUST CAME TO AN END!!
HANG ON!
4

CLYDE'S KNOW-HOW GUIDED THE CAR IN A LURCHING, SLIDING, HAIR-RAISING PLUNGE DOWN THE ROCK STREWN SLOPE---
BUMP!
CRASH!
--UNTIL IT FETCHED UP AT THE BOTTOM IN A SICKENING, BONE JARRING STOP!
CRUNCH!
THE FOG WAS THICKENING AS THEY EXITED FROM THE DISABLED VEHICLE-
MOMENTARILY DAZED, FRAN STUMBLED AWAY FROM THE REST, ONLY TO COME FACE TO FACE WITH---

THE SCREAM OF PURE TERROR BROUGHT THE OTHER THREE TOGETHER, BUT---
WHAT HAPPENED?
THAT WAS FRAN!
AIEEEEEEEEEEEE!

--- SHE WAS GONE--
FRAN! FRAN! WHERE ARE YOU?
WE'VE SEARCHED EVERY INCH OF THIS PLACE! SHE'S JUST NOT HERE!

WAIT! - WAIT! - ISN'T THIS A PIECE OF THAT SCARF SHE WAS WEARING?

SAY! THIS WAY! HERE'S ANOTHER PIECE! I THINK SHE'S LEAVING A TRAIL!
WELL, LET'S FOLLOW IT!
CEME

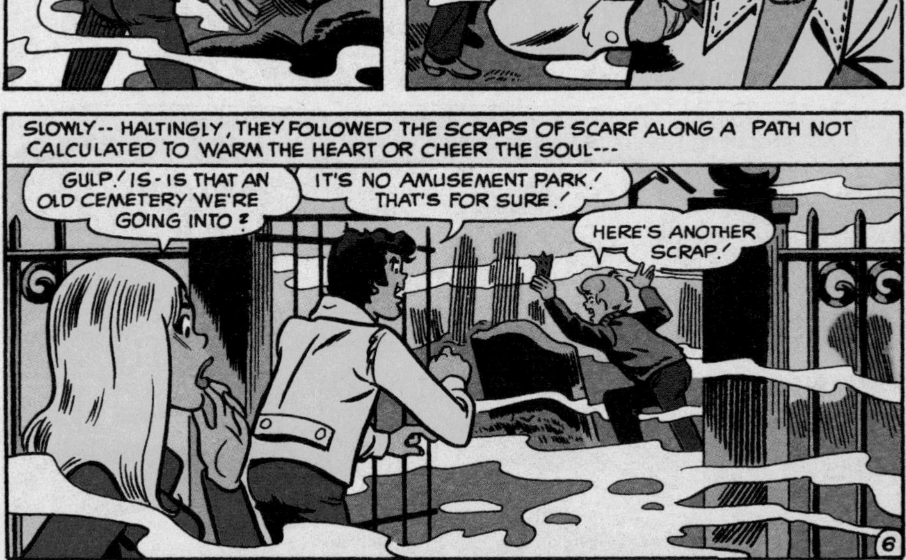
SLOWLY-- HALTINGLY, THEY FOLLOWED THE SCRAPS OF SCARF ALONG A PATH NOT CALCULATED TO WARM THE HEART OR CHEER THE SOUL---
GULP! IS - IS THAT AN OLD CEMETERY WE'RE GOING INTO?
IT'S NO AMUSEMENT PARK! THAT'S FOR SURE!
HERE'S ANOTHER SCRAP!
6

AN AIR OF DEATH AND DECAY HUNG OVER THE ANCIENT GRAVEYARD AS THE TREMBLING TRIO PROCEEDED--
I'M S-SCARED!
WE ALL ARE! BUT WE'VE GOT TO FIND FRAN!
-AND THEN!
HEY! THIS PIECE IS CAUGHT IN THE DOOR OF THIS CRYPT!
"CARSWELL?" NEVER HEARD OF THEM!
THE DOOR OPENS!
CARSWELL
THE HINGES ARE WELL OILED! SOMEBODY'S BEEN TAKING GOOD CARE OF THIS PLACE!
UGH! THIS IS NOT MY CUP OF TEA!
MINE EITHER, BUT THIS IS WHERE FRAN'S TRAIL LEADS!
HEY! STAIRS!-- WE GOT US A SPLIT-LEVEL TOMB HERE!
7

DOWN THE DANK, EVIL SMELLING STAIR-WAY, THEY CREPT, UNTIL---
HEY! DO YOU HEAR THAT SCRATCHING NOISE? IT'S BEHIND THIS DOOR!
OKAY! NOW BE CAREFUL! WE DON'T KNOW WHAT WE'RE GOING TO RUN INTO!
OPEN IT!
FRAN! WE FOUND HER! IT'S FRAN!
GET THOSE ROPES OFF OF HER!
WHEW! I'M SURE GLAD YOU FOUND MY TRAIL! WE WERE KIDNAPPED! THIS IS THE POOR MAN I MET AT THE APARTMENT HOUSE!
BUT WHY DID THEY GRAB YOU?
I KNOW! THEY THOUGHT HE TOLD HER SOMETHING IN THE HALL! THAT'S GOT TO BE IT!
8

THAT'S TRUE! THEY THOUGHT I KNEW WHERE THE LOOT FROM A RECENT JEWEL ROBBERY WAS HIDDEN!
JUST THEN AN OMINOUS COUGH FROM BEHIND, CAUSED THEM TO TURN ---
AHEM!
"THOUGHT HE KNEW?" HAH! THE LITTLE RAT PULLED THE HEIST WITH US! ONLY HE CUT OUT WITH THE SPARKLERS!
YEAH! HEH! IT TOOK A LITTLE PERSUASION TO MAKE HIM REVEAL THIS HIDING PLACE!
AND NOW, WE AND THE GEMS ARE GOING TO TAKE OUR LEAVE!
YEAH! WE'LL LOCK THE DOOR BEHIND US!
DON'T WORRY! IN A LITTLE WHILE YOU'LL ALL JOIN THE CARSWELL FAMILY!
HYUK! HAPPY HAUNTING!
9

BUT DIPPY HAS BEEN QUIETLY DISLODG-ING THE SUPPORT OF ONE OF THE LATE CARSWELLS, AND ---
ANGUS CARSWELL
SNAP!
CRUMBLE!
BACK, GANG! OUT OF THE WAY!
DOWN TUMBLED THE GROTESQUE WEAPON! THERE WAS NO ROOM FOR THE TWO CROOKS TO DODGE---
AARGH!
CREAK!
ANGUS CARSWELL
CRUMBLE!
WHEN THE DUST CLEARED THE DANGER WAS PASSED, AND OUR LITTLE GROUP OWED A VOTE OF THANKS TO A LONG DECEASED BUT STILL EFFECTIVE ANGUS CARSWELL ---
OOOOH! MY LEG!
GET THIS THING OFF OF ME!
CARSWELL
10

NICE WORK, FRAN! THAT STATUE, LOOMING UP IN THE MIST, SCARED THE HECK OUT OF HIM!
KEEP HIM COVERED, DIPPY! I'LL GO GET THE POLICE!
AND, IN A LITTLE WHILE, THE POLICE ARRIVED AND RELIEVED THE DOUBLE DATES OF THEIR HEAVY RESPONSIBILITY--
TRAPPED BY A BUNCH OF STUPID KIDS! WE'LL NEVER LIVE THIS DOWN!
IF WE EVER GET OUT, WE'LL GET YOU! YOU CAN COUNT ON THAT!
R.I.P.
HA! - MEANWHILE, AS WE SAY AT THE CARSWELL PAD---
REST IN PEACE!
I'M HUNGRY! ANYBODY GOT SOMETHING TO EAT?
HERE? -- YOU HAVE GREAT TASTE IN PICNIC GROUNDS, DAN!
CARSWELL
RIP
End

The Clean Scene
Jughead #221, 1973
by Frank Doyle, Harry Lucey and Bill Yoshida

Jughead is a pretty complex character, if you pay attention. At times, it seems like he couldn't care less about, well, anything except for food! That's the Jughead a lot of people know. There are times, though, when Forsythe P. Jones takes an interest in something noble, like doing right by his friends, or in this case, keeping Riverdale clean! And when he gets behind a cause, he's persistent as all get-out! Here, he confronts a gorilla of a man on his littering habit, and refuses to give up – even after he gets stuffed in a trash can! Now THAT'S dedication! Harry Lucey has a style like no other. The elegance of his characters and the body language they use is really something! The voice that he encoded into every drawing he did was really special, and it's something that he did uniquely well. I specifically like the way he draws hands. Also, check out Bill Yoshida's very cool sound effects in this story!

--Patrick Woodruff
Digital Media Coordinator,
Archie Comics

Delivery Dumbbell
Laugh #238, 1974
by Bob Bolling, Rudy Lapick and Bill Yoshida

After learning my craft by writing one page gags for nearly a year, I finally sold my first 6-pager and had the honor of seeing it illustrated by one of my favorite artists: the great Bob Bolling!

--Tom DeFalco
Former Editor-in-Chief,
Marvel Comics

Jughead
TSK! NO, NO, NO!
"THE CLEAN SCENE"
EP
DALE
EAN
HUH ?
WE MUSTN'T LITTER! WE MUST HAVE PRIDE IN OUR CITY!
OH GOLLY! THAT WAS CARELESS OF ME! WASN'T IT ?
WHERE SHOULD I PUT THIS ?
INTO THE NEAREST TRASH RECEPTACLE OF COURSE!
1

HAW! HOW'S THAT? I THINK I'M GETTIN' THE HANG OF IT!
HA! THAT WAS FUNNY, FELLA! -- BUT NOT VERY!
GET LOST, NEEDLENOSE!
NOT UNTIL I'M SURE YOU KNOW WHAT A TRASH RECEPTACLE IS AND WHAT GOES INTO IT!
OKAY, TEACH! I THINK YER GETTING THROUGH TO ME! THIS HERE'S A TRASH RECEP--ER--UH-- BASKET!
RIGHT!
HAW! AN' WHUT GOES IN IT IS TRASH!
FLUMP!
2

(SIGH.!) SOME PEOPLE RESIST LEARNING.!
KEEP RIVERDALE CLEAN
BUT--- IT'S A WORTHWHILE CAUSE.! ONE MUST PERSIST.!
THAT'S A NO-NO, FELLA.!
SPLIT, PUNK.!
GOOD THING THERE ARE PEOPLE LIKE ME TO PICK UP AFTER PEOPLE LIKE YOU.!
YEAH.! THAT IS GOOD, AIN'T IT?
HAW! HAW!
AREN'T YOU ASHAMED OF YOURSELF?
YEAH.!--- ASHAMED.!
JOE'S DELI
JUST KEEP TRAILIN' ALONG IN CASE I GET CARELESS.!
SLURP!
YOU KNOW WHAT TO DO WITH THAT SODA CAN.!
3

SURE! JUST LIKE BASKETBALL! I TOSS IT TO YOU, AND YOU SINK THE SHOT!
UH!--- BASKETBALL'S NOT MY GAME!
BURP!
POOL'S MY BAG! EVER SEE A GOOD CAROM SHOT?
OFF THE EIGHT BALL INTO THE CORNER POCKET!
BEAUTIFUL!
CLANK!
WHYINYA TELL ME YA WANTED TO GO 12 ROUNDS?
IT AIN'T DOIN' YA NO GOOD TO RUN IN YER HOUSE!
4

'CAUSE I'M COMIN' RIGHT IN AFTER YA!
CRASH!
POW!
HOW COME YUH RAN INTO MY HOUSE, JUG?
I WANTED TO TALK TO YOU ON A VERY IMPORTANT SUBJECT, MOOSE!
LITTERING!
OOPS!
DUH-H! SORRY, JUG! I SHOULD'NA LEFT HIM LAYIN' AROUND LIKE THAT!
WE MUST BE NEAT, MOOSE! ---NEAT, NEAT, NEAT!
THE END

Archie
"The DELIVERY DUMBBELL"
CAREFUL WITH THAT CAKE, ARCHIE! IT'S A SURPRISE FOR MY FATHER'S BIRTHDAY!
UGGHH! HOW DO I GET INVOLVED WITH THESE THINGS? THE CAKE'S SO BIG, IT CAN'T EVEN FIT INTO A BOX!
I'VE SOME MORE SHOPPING TO DO NOW! MEET ME AT HOME IN AN HOUR! DON'T BE LATE!
HAVE NO FEAR! I'LL BE THERE IN TIME TO SURPRISE YOUR FATHER WITH THE CAKE!

GEE! THIS CAKE IS HEAVY! SINCE I HAVE A LOT OF TIME, I'LL PUT IT DOWN AND TAKE A REST!
MR. LODGE WILL BE SO SURPRISED WHEN I SHOW UP WITH THE CAKE! HE MIGHT EVEN START TALKING TO ME AGAIN!
HI, ARCHIE! ARE YOU ALL READY FOR MR. LODGE'S PARTY?
YOU BET, BETTY! I WAS JUST ON MY WAY TO DELIVER HIS BIRTHDAY CAKE!
YOU HAVE MR. LODGE'S CAKE? WHERE IS IT?
IT'S RIGHT NEXT TO ME, BETTY! WHAT'S WITH YOUR EYES? CAN'T YOU SEE IT?
IT'S A BIT CHINTZY FOR MR. LODGE, ISN'T IT?
BURP!
GAK!!! THE CAKE'S DISAPPEARED! RONNIE'LL KILL ME IF I SHOW UP WITH THIS LITTLE CUPCAKE!
2

YOU WANT ANOTHER CAKE ???
YES, AND PLEASE HURRY!
RONNIE'LL NEVER FORGIVE ME IF I'M LATE WITH THE CAKE!
I STILL HAVE PLENTY OF TIME BEFORE THE PARTY, BUT I'VE GOT TO BE CAREFUL! THIS CAKE WON'T LEAVE MY SIGHT!
HEY, GANG, LOOK! TWO FOR ONE SALE AT THE CHOCKLIT SHOPPE!
WE'LL RACE! LOSER PAYS FOR THE SODAS!
LET'S GET DOWN THERE!
ON YOUR MARK! GET SET! GO!!!
KIDS RUNNING TOWARD ME! THEY'LL KNOCK ME DOWN AND TRAMPLE THE CAKE!
YOU'RE IN THE WAY, MAN!
MOVE IT, MISTER!
I'VE GOT TO HOLD TIGHT! I CAN'T LOSE THIS CAKE!
DON'T BLOCK THE STREET, RED!
3

TALK ABOUT LUCK! LOOK AT THIS! NOT A SCRATCH! I SAVED THE CAKE!
SMASH!
UUFFF!
WATCH OUT, MISTER!
YIPE!
THE SKY IS FALLING?
MOMMY, LOOK! THE SNOWMAN IS WALKING!
QUIET, HARVEY! SNOWMEN CAN'T WALK!
I KNEW YOU'D BE IN A HURRY SO I HAD ONE WAITING FOR YOU!
A FEW MORE CUSTOMERS LIKE THIS KID AND I CAN RETIRE IN A COUPLE OF YEARS!
NOW I HAVE TO RUN!
4

I HAVE TO HURRY! THE PARTY WILL BE STARTING SOON! CAN'T BE LATE!
RONNIE'S HOUSE IS JUST DOWN THE STREET! I'M GOING TO MAKE IT IN TIME! NOTHING CAN STOP ME NOW!
YEOOWW!!
CRASH!!
THE CAKE'S ALL RIGHT! I'M DESTROYED, BUT THE CAKE'S ALL RIGHT!
6

FINALLY MADE IT! I NEVER THOUGHT I'D GET HERE!
KNOCK!
A KNOCK ON THE DOOR! MUST BE ARCHIE! I'LL LET HIM IN!
KNOCK
?
DID I ARRIVE IN TIME TO SURPRISE YOUR FATHER WITH THE CAKE?
DON'T WORRY, ARCHIE!
DADDY'S VERY SURPRISED BY THE CAKE!
MY ROOF IS FALLING DOWN?
END

Big Ideas
Little Archie #85, 1974
by Dexter Taylor

You wouldn't know it by looking at him, but Little Archie is very creative and talented -- and this story is a testament to it. Who out there thought Little Archie could make a huge oversized Valentine's candy box and convince Betty to deliver it to Veronica? I know I didn't.

Little Archie Joke Page
Little Archie #85, 1974
by Dexter Taylor

This single page is jam-packed full of one-liners and sight gags. These are the kind of comic pages I loved reading as a young lad back in the mid-seventies. If there's one ingredient that's missing I have one word for you: "Skippy."

--Stephen Oswald
Produciton Manager,
Archie Comics

Nothing but the Tooth
Jughead #225, 1974
by Frank Doyle and Samm Schwartz

In this day and age, vampires seem to have gotten a bad rap. Well, at least a bad rap for what they used to be known for. Lately it seems that they're not dark, not scary, and favor romance over that whole "blood sucking" thing. Fortunately, we can always count on Jughead to bring everyone back to basics. This wouldn't be the only time he dons a vampire costume, but he does manage to make the most of this particular look… by terrifying the local neighborhood children.

--Steve Golebiewski
Production Artist,
Archie Comics

Little Archie
IN
"BIG IDEAS"
DO YOU THINK VERONICA WILL LIKE IT, JUGGIE ?
YOUR IDEA IS WAY-OUT THIS TIME, LITTLE ARCHIE !
BA BONG!
MAYBE THAT'S VERONICA NOW !
OH, LITTLE ARCHIE ! I JUST LOVE YOU !

IT'S THE NICEST VALENTINE HEART I EVER HAD FROM YOU!
AW, GEE, BETTY! IT WAS NOTHING!
BETTY
WHERE DID YOU EVER FIND SUCH A DARLING HEART BOX?
I HAD TO MAKE IT!
IT WAS A MODEL FOR THIS ONE!
VERONIC
RING!
HEY! MAYBE THAT'S VERONICA NOW!
VERONICA! WHAT? WE CAN'T SEE EACH OTHER?
YOUR FATHER IS MAD AT ME FOR LETTING HIS AFRICAN PARROT OUT OF ITS CAGE---?
-- WHY IS HE SORE? IT WAS FLYING IN THE DIRECTION OF AFRICA WHEN LAST SEEN!
2

WAIT! I'VE GOT AN IDEA HOW I CAN SEE VERONICA!
STAND BACK, BETTY! THIS SHOULD BE SOMETHING!
VERONICA
I'LL GET INSIDE THE BOX AND YOU TWO CAN DELIVER IT TO VERONICA!
NO!
VERONIC
LATER--
JUST THINK! WE'RE DELIVERING THE BIGGEST NUT IN THE WORLD!
REMEMBER! YOU PROMISED ME A DATE AFTERWARDS!
YOU'LL GET IT, BETTY!
(SOB!) I NEVER THOUGHT I'D EVER BRING LITTLE ARCHIE OVER TO VERONICA'S! (SOB!)
VERONIC
RING THE BELL, BETTY!
I CAN'T, JUG! IT'S LIKE BRINGING A PRISONER TO THE ENEMY!
VERONIC
BA BONG!
NOW BEAT IT, KIDS!
3

AH, I CAN HEAR VERONICA OPENING THE DOOR! I'LL BET SHE'S SURPRISED!
VERONICA
NOW SHE'S HAVING THE SERVANTS CARRY ME IN!
VERONICA
AT LAST! I CAN HEAR VERONICA'S FINGERS TEARING AT THE RIBBON---
--- THE BOX IS OPENING---
BE MY VALENTINE!
SURE THING!
WHERE'S THE CANDY?
THE END
4

Little Archie's
JOKE PAGE
DOES THE MOVIE HAVE A HAPPY ENDING?
YEAH! EVERY ONE WAS HAPPY IT WAS OVER!
TICKETS
"WILD TIMES"
HOW'S THE WEATHER OUT-SIDE?
IT'S SO FOGGY I CAN'T TELL!
DID YOU HEAR WHAT JUGGIE HAD FOR A FEED?
HE SWALLOWED SIX PACKETS OF SEEDS!
THE DAYS CAME TO PASS SOON HE WAS COVERED WITH GRASS
AND HE COULDN'T SIT DOWN FOR THE WEEDS!
OOOH! LITTLE ARCHIE, THAT'S A BEAUTIFUL BOW TIE!
HUH?

Jughead
nothing but the tooth
YOU MOST WISIT WITH ME EEN MY CASTLE EEN TRANSYLWANIA!
JUGHEAD, IT SEEMS TO LOSE SOMETHING WHEN YOU KEEP THAT HAT ON!
JUST TILL I LEARN MY LINES, MISS GRUNDY! I CONCENTRATE BETTER WHEN I'M WEARING MY HAT!
GO AHEAD! WEAR IT! I DON'T CARE IF YOU STAND ON YOUR HEAD IF IT WILL HELP THE PRODUCTION!
ACT: I
1

AH, YAS, MY DEAR! I KNOW YOUR FAMILY WELL! YOU HAF STRONG BLOOD LINES! TYPE "O" I PRESUME?
MAN! THAT'S CASTING! GIVING HIM THE LEAD IN THE CLASS SHOW!
GIGGLE! THIS IS REALLY GOING TO BE A HORROR SHOW!
THE FIRST BURGER-EATING VAMPIRE IN THE HISTORY OF THE THEATER!
HE GOT THE PART BECAUSE HE'S ALREADY "BATS"!
IGOR! IGOR, HAF YOU SEEN MY FILE? MY FANGS ARE BE-COMING VAIRY DULL!
WHEW! WITH THE CAST OF CHARACTERS WHO WANDER THROUGH THESE HALLS, MY JOB WILL NEVER BECOME "VAIRY DULL!"
2

IGOR! CALL THE BLOODMOBILE!
LOOK! HE DOESN'T EVEN KNOW WHERE HE'S GOING!
LET'S FOLLOW HIM!
HYOK! THIS OUGHT TO BE GOOD!
THE PUBLIC ISN'T READY FOR THIS!
BARTENDER, A BLOODY MARY!
MELVIN! MELVIN, DARLING! DON'T YOU LOVE MOMMY? PLEASE, SWEETUMS? WON'T YOU... FOR MOMMY?
NO! NO! NO! I AIN'T GONNA DO IT! FOR NOBODY! GO 'WAY!
3

WOW! NOW THAT'S A SPOILED BRAT!
A CLASSIC EXAMPLE!
I'M YOUR MOTHER! CHILDREN HAVE TO OBEY THEIR MOTHERS OR THEY GET INTO ALL SORTS OF TROUBLE!
THAT'S A LOT OF BALONEY! US KIDS DON'T GOT TO DO NOTHING WE---
WALCOME TO TRANSYLWANIA!
SCREEE

MOMMY! MOMMY!
I'LL BE GOOD! HONEST! I'LL DO ANYTHING YOU SAY!
DON'T SEND ME TO...TO... TRANSYLVANIA WITH HIM! I'LL BE GOOD FOREVER!
I'LL CLEAN MY ROOM!.. I WON'T TALK BACK! I'LL NEVER BE BAD! I'LL...
DON'T ARGUE, BOY! JUST TAKE THIS TWENTY FROM A GRATEFUL MOTHER!
TWENTY BUCKS?
COME, IGOR! LEAVE US PARTAKE OF A LEETLE REFRASHMENT!
TALK ABOUT THE LUCK OF THE IRISH-- THOSE TRANSYLVAN-IANS DON'T DO HALF BAD!
I WISH HE'D STOP GRINNING WITH THOSE FANGS!
END

Roman Holiday
Archie Annual #26, 1975
by Frank Doyle, Harry Lucey and Bill Yoshida

Archie Comics have been a constant presence in the background of my life, although I really became aware of them in the mid-1960s. When I was thirteen years old, CBS ran the animated *The Archie Show* on Saturday mornings, and I watched it every week. In my mind I can still hear the sound of Jughead's voice whenever I read the comics; as you might guess, Jughead is my favorite character. Archie represents the fun of being a kid, and I see that today, when both students and teachers reach out and pick up an Archie comic I've brought to school. I grew up liking Archie and his pals, with the kind of fun shown in "Roman Holiday" – my brother and I liked to play with words just like that, although I was already in college when this story was first published (and studying Latin – just imagine!)

--Kat Kan
Collection Development Librarian/ Graphic Novel Specialist for Brodart Books & Library Services, Librarian at St. John Catholic School, Panama City, FL

My Ideal
Betty & Veronica #243, 1976
by Frank Doyle, Dan DeCarlo, Rudy Lapick and Bill Yoshida

It's easy to forget that for decades women who wanted to read comics had very little to chose from. You had your comic strips in the newspaper and maybe a Little Lulu or two but if you wanted something a little more sophisticated than Uncle Scrooge and that didn't involve large-bosomed superladies, then the only game in town was Archie. And we all chose sides in the Betty vs. Veronica wars as well. I was a little torn since Veronica sported darker locks like me, but my name was phonetically closer to Betty's and, let's face it, unlike Veronica she wasn't some rich wannabe princess with a sense of entitlement. I was and will always be Team Betty, though as this next story shows, there was certainly something to be said for Veronica's sardonic side.

--Betsy Bird
Youth Materials Specialist, New York Public Library

ET TU, JUGIBUS?
LOOK! I'M TELLING IT LIKE IT IS, CAESAR ARCHIBUS!
Jughead
ROMAN HOLIDAY
THE SENATUS ROMANUS IS OUT TO SHAFT YOU!
NONSENSE! I AM BELOVED OF ALL ROMANS!

BUBI --- THE SCUTTLEBUT DOWN AT THE BATHS SAYS YOU SHOULDN'T MAKE ANY LONG RANGE PLANS!
OH, JUGIBUS, JUGIBUS, JUGIBUS!
DON'T YOU KNOW CAESARS ARE INFALLIBLE?
THAT MEANS WE'RE NEVER WRONG!
LOOK, OL' INFALLIBLE BUDDY-- AT LEAST GET ANOTHER OPINION!
IF IT WILL MAKE YOU FEEL BETTER!
HERE COMES REGGIO!
SIGH! THAT'S NOT THE OPINION I HAD IN MIND!
ADVICE, GREAT LEADER? I SHOULD BE HONORED TO GIVE YOU MY ADVICE!
HE LOVES ME! THEY ALL LOVE ME.
TAKE YOUR LEGIONS AND PLUNDER AND PILLAGE AN ENEMY TO THE EMPIRE!
THAT'S WHAT ALL THE PAST EMPERORS HAVE DONE!
2

I'LL DO IT! WE HAVEN'T HAD ANY FUN AND GAMES IN MONTHS!
GREAT CAESAR! DON'T BE A NOODNIK!
QUIET JUGIBUS! GOTTA FIGURE WHERE THE ACTION IS!
MAYBE YOU CAN TELL ME WHERE TO GO, REGGIO!
ER-- YEAH, FEARLESS LEADER! HAVE I GOT A WAR FOR YOU!!
THIS SOFT TOUCH IN THE NORTH RUN BY THIS WEAKLING CALLED -- ER -- ATTILA THE HUN!
PIECE OF CAKE, EH?
YOU'LL BE SORRY!
YOU CAESARS GOTTA WATCH OUT FOR THE IDES OF MARCH!
WHAT THE HECK ARE THEY?
THEY'RE THE MIDDLE OF THE MONTH BLUES WHEN LEO IS ON THE CUSP AND SCORPIO AND LIBRA ARE ON THE WANE! VIRGO IS FULL OF TAURUS AND YOUR SIGN IS IN THE HOUSE OF PANCAKES!
IT'S BAD NEWS FOR CAESARS!
3

HEY, CHIEF! THAT NUTTY ENTERTAINER OVER AT THE FORUM JUST SET FIRE TO THE PALACE!
THAT PLACE WAS GETTING TO BE A RUIN! I'LL BET THE OWNER'S TRYING TO COLLECT ON HIS FIRE INSURANCE!
WHO WOULD BE SO DISHONEST?
HEY! THERE'S THE OWNER!
REMEMBER ME, REGGIO? WE MET AT MY COUSIN'S INSURANCE FIRM THE DAY YOU TOOK OUT THAT WHOPPING BIG POLICY ON THE FORUM!
LEGIONAIRES! TAKE AWAY THIS FIREBUG!
I'M INNOCENT! IT'S A BUM RAP!
4

IT'S OUT OF HAND, JUGIBUS! THE WHOLE CITY'S GONNA GO!
YEAH! AND THAT NUTTY ENTERTAINER IS STILL OUT THERE FIDDLING AROUND THE FLAMES!
AW, COME ON, CAESAR! DON'T YOU HAVE ANY OTHER PRISONERS IN YOUR JAILS? I CAN'T PUT THIS WHOLE CITY BACK TOGETHER BY MYSELF!
PATIENCE, BABY! ROME WASN'T BUILT IN A DAY!
CHOMP! CHOMP!
CHOMP!
THE END

Betty and Veronica
IN "MY IDEAL"
BETTY, HAVE YOU EVER THOUGHT ABOUT MARRIAGE ?
CONSTANTLY!
I SOMETIMES WONDER WHAT KIND OF MAN I'LL MARRY!
I DONT!
I KNOW EXACTLY WHAT KIND OF MAN I'LL MARRY!
YOU SOUND POSITIVE!
1

IF YOU DON'T MIND MY ASKING, BETTY--- WHAT IS HE LIKE ?
AS IF I DIDN'T KNOW ?
OH, WOW! HOW DO YOU DESCRIBE PERFECTION ?
MMPH!
STATELY--- MASCULINE FIGURE! HANDSOME BEYOND ALL BELIEF!
WOMEN SWOON IN PASSION AT THE SIGHT OF HIM!
CHARM ? HE CHARMS THE BIRDS FROM THE TREES AND THE FISH FROM THE SEA!
HIS SMILE WOULD MELT YOU LIKE AN ICE CUBE ON A HOT STOVE!
SMART ? IS THE GREAT ONE SMART ?
2

"SMART?" EINSTEIN WOULD LEARN FROM HIM! HIS BRILLIANCE WOULD BLIND YOU AT TWENTY PACES!
NOW THAT IS QUITE A MAN!
I AM SURPRISED!
AND ALL THE TIME I THOUGHT YOU HAD YOUR CAP SET FOR ARCHIE!
SO DID I!
BUT I AM TALKING ABOUT ARCHIE! I JUST DESCRIBED HIM TO YOU!
MMPH!
ROAR!
WAS THERE SOME JOKE THAT I MISSED?
HA! HA!
HOO! HOO! HEE!
3

J-JOKE ? Y-YES, INDEED! I'LL TELL YOU--- MMMSLTZ!
NO, NO, DEAR! YOU MUSTN'T!
DID I SAY SOMETHING WRONG ?
ER- JUST A PRIVATE, FAMILY JOKE, MY DEAR! IT REALLY ISN'T FUNNY TO OTHERS!
OH! OF COURSE!
I - ER - THOUGHT YOUR DESCRIPTION OF ARCHIE VERY INTERESTING!
THANK YOU, MR. LODGE! I JUST CALL THEM AS I SEE THEM!
DOES ARCHIE KNOW OF YOUR MARITAL PLANS ?
I HINT A LOT!
WHY NOT TELL HIM RIGHT OUT ? USE THE SAME ACCURATE DESCRIPTION YOU DID FOR US!
GOOD IDEA! WHY HIDE IT ANY LONGER ?
4

NEXT DAY:
SIGH!
ARCHIE! DID YOU SEE BETTY YESTERDAY?
YES, SIR!
SHEESH! ALL SHE COULD TALK ABOUT WAS MARRIAGE!
NATURALLY!
SHE'S BEEN TRYING TO HOOK YOU FOR YEARS!
HMPH! THAT'S WHAT I USED TO THINK!
BUT BELIEVE ME, I WOULDN'T STAND A CHANCE AGAINST THIS DUDE SHE'S GOT IN MIND!
The END

THE BEST OF
Archie
COMICS
BOOK TWO
the '80s
CHUCKSTER
BOY
REX W. LINDSEY

In the Swing
Betty & Veronica #302, 1981
by Frank Doyle, Dan DeCarlo, Rudy Lapick and Bill Yoshida

My favorite thing about reading Archie Comics as a kid was seeing all of the great outfits worn by Betty and Veronica. No matter what the decade these girls were forever at the height of fashion. I thought the girls looked especially glamorous in the early stories and tried to emulate that in my own style. "In The Swing" perfectly illustrates the cyclical nature of fashion. It doesn't matter what year the story in each digest was created because the outfits will always come back into style.

--Kari Silbergleit
Licensing Coordinator,
Archie Comics

Hi Style Hi Jinks
TV Laugh Out #81, 1981
by Frank Doyle, Dan DeCarlo, Rudy Lapick and Bill Yoshida

There are some amazingly skilled writers in the Archie fold. There aren't a lot of people who could build a funny, interesting, complete story around the idea that a hot lady needed to be cut out of her clothes. And there's no man better to have drawn a story like that than Dan DeCarlo – a man who could make the naughty seem completely innocent. The reverse is also true of his talents of course, but you didn't hear that from me.

--Suzannah Rowntree
Features Editor,
Life With Archie *magazine*

Betty and Veronica
in "IN THE SWING"
SCHOOL PLAY, DEAR? CUTE COSTUME!
IT'S NOT A COSTUME, DADDY, DEAR!
PICASSCO
IT'S ABSOLUTELY THE LATEST FASHION!
THE PREPPIE LOOK!
1

"LATEST"?
YOU COULD HAVE FOOLED ME!
YOU LOOK LIKE SOMETHING OUT OF MY OLD HIGH SCHOOL YEARBOOK!
OF COURSE, DADDY!
LOTS OF FASHIONS ARE REVIVALS! BUT WHEN THEY'RE REVIVED, THEY'RE NEW AGAIN!
AND WHEN SOMETHING IS NEW--- I'VE GOT TO HAVE IT!
HOW WELL I KNOW!
- AND I'VE GOT THE BILLS TO PROVE IT!
2

TSK! FATHERS ARE ALWAYS SO CONCERNED WITH MONEY!
I SAY WHEN YOU'VE GOT IT, FLAUNT IT!
HE'S GOT THE MONEY!
GIGGLE! AND I FLAUNT IT!
EEEEEE!
THE PREPPIE LOOK! ADORABLE! I LOVE IT! I LOVE IT!
IT IS NEAT, ISN'T IT?
OH, I'VE GOT TO HAVE IT!!
3

OLDIES BUT GOODIES, VERONICA?
NEWIES BUT GOODIES, MR. WEATHERBEE!
IT'S MAKING A COMEBACK!
I LIKE IT! I LIKED IT THEN, AND I LIKE IT NOW!
A SKIRT IN SCHOOL? WE THOUGHT THE DRESS CODE DEMANDED BLUE JEANS!
GET WITH IT, GUYS!
TIMES CHANGE!
YOU'VE GOT TO KEEP ON YOUR TOES, FELLAS!
4

FASHION! EGAD!
IF THEY PAID THAT MUCH ATTENTION TO SCHOOL WORK!
WHAT A STRANGE SENSE OF VALUES THE YOUNG GIRLS HAVE!
FASHION IS EVERYTHING TO THEM!
RIGHT, MISS GRUNDY?
THEY ALL EXAGGERATE THE IMPORTANCE OF FASHION!
WHO'S THAT, CHIEF?
THE END

Josie in "HI STYLE HI JINKS"
HEY, GOT TO RUN, GIRLS! MY NEW HAIRDRESSER, ANTOINE, IS GOING TO MAKE ME BEAUTIFUL FOR MY BIG DATE TONIGHT!
WELL, SPLIT, CHILD! DON'T LET US STAND IN YOUR WAY OF LOVE AND ROMANCE!
OH, RIGHT OFF, JOSIE! RIGHT OFF!
ER, MELODY! I THINK THE EXPRESSION IS "RIGHT ON!"
JES' FINE!
AH, JOSEE! YOU AIR ZO PROMPT!
OUI, OUI, ANTOINE! BIG DATE TONIGHT!
1

YOU'RE GOING TO GIVE ME THAT NEW LOOK YOU WERE TALKING ABOUT, ANTOINE?
CERTAINEMENT! YOUR HAIR-STYLE-- SHE EES ZO--ZO-- UNIMAGINATIVE! NO?
VOILA! MORE BOUFFANT! ZAT EES WHAT YOUR FACE CRIES OUT FOR!
BY GOLLY! THAT'S BOUFFANT, ALL RIGHT!
IT'S GOING TO TAKE A LITTLE GETTING USED TO, BUT I THINK I'M GOING TO LIKE IT!
THE NEW ME IS MORE CHI, CHI--- MORE SOPHISTICATED! THAT'S FOR SURE!
OH, JOSIE! IT'S BEAUTIFUL! ABSOLUTELY SMASHING!
GOLLY, YES! YOU LOOK LIKE A DIFFERENT PERSON!
HOW DO YOU GET YOUR SWEATER OFF?
2

OMIGOSH!
LIKEWISE!
IT WILL RUIN THAT HAIRDO! ABSOLUTELY RUIN IT!
ALL THAT WORK FOR NOTHING!
MAYBE WE CAN STRETCH THE NECK FAR ENOUGH TO SLIDE IT OVER YOUR SHOULDERS!
IT'S WORTH A TRY!
THAT'S IT! THIS MIGHT ACTUALLY WORK! THINK THIN!
I HOPE THAT TURTLE NECK WILL SNAP BACK INTO SHAPE!
GIRLS! FANTASTIC SALE AT BONWIT'S!!
A SALE?
NO! NO! DON'T!!
OH, WOW!
STRETCH
TUG
TUG
3

OUCH!
SNAP
SNAP!
COME BACK HERE, YOU TWO, AND GET ME OUT OF THIS.!!
HA! HA! HA! JOSIE, WHAT IN THE WORLD ARE YOU SUPPOSED TO BE?
ALEXANDRA! HELP ME! I'M TRAPPED IN THIS SWEATER!
WE'LL GET A PAIR OF SCISSORS AT MY PLACE! THAT SWEATER WILL SIMPLY HAVE TO GO!
SNIFF! I SUPPOSE SO.!
WE'LL JUST CUT IT OPEN AND PEEL IT OFF YOU!
THAT WAS MY VERY FAVORITE SWEATER, TOO!
SNIP! SNIP!
4

YOU BETTER PUT THAT JACKET ON BEFORE YOU GO OUT!
THANKS, ALEXANDRA! DISPOSE OF THAT SWEATER FOR ME, WILL YOU?
I'LL BET THAT'S THE MOST EXPENSIVE HAIR SET YOU EVER GOT!
IT SURE WAS! I HOPE IT'S WORTH IT!
WHAT AM I TALKING ABOUT? A DATE WITH ALAN M. IS BEYOND PRICE!
I HOPE HE LIKES MY HAIR!
C-RACK
THAT WOULDN'T BE THUNDER! SURELY THAT WOULDN'T BE THUNDER!
DID YOU EVER HAVE ONE OF THOSE DAYS---?
The End

Little Archie and The Secret City
Little Archie Digest Annual #7, 1982
by Dexter Taylor, Rudy Lapick and Bill Yoshida

When I was a kid, I loved cryptozoology. Ahh... who am I kidding? I STILL love cryptozoology! What's that? It's the study of animals and creatures that may or may not exist like Big Foot and the Loch Ness Monster. I also love adventure stories. As much as I loved most Archie stories, which were usually funny and light, I loved the occasional adventure story where Archie would be up against bad guys or doing something thrilling, exciting and unusual. *Little Archie* was good for those types of stories. One of my all time favorite stories, "Little Archie and the Secret City," included both cryptozoology and adventure. In this one, Little Archie and the gang discover a secret undersea city which is being threatened by the Loch Ness Monster! Wow! Just writing this description makes me want to re-read this one. This was a very unusual story in that it was told in two parts over two issues, a rarity for an Archie book in those days. Continuing stories always worried me when I was a kid. I was at the mercy of the newsstands for my comic books and they weren't always very reliable. If you bought a comic one month, there were no guarantees you'd find the next issue next month. Sure enough, I read "The Secret City Part 1" in the regular Little Archie comic it appeared in but I missed the next issue containing Part 2! Arrrgh! I was at a loss! I read this great, enticing Part 1 but I'd never get to know how this great epic turned out! It wouldn't be until I picked up *Little Archie Comics Digest Annual #7* where both parts were reprinted that I finally got to enjoy the whole incredible tale and, even after that long wait, I sure wasn't disappointed!

--Fernando Ruiz
Writer / artist,
Archie Comics

AN UNDERSEA ADVENTURE
Little Archie AND THE SECRET CITY
PART 1
MONSTERS!
MAN! I'VE HEARD OF "PLANET OF THE MONKEYS" BUT THIS IS OUTASITE!
IT'S HAPPENING ON OUR OWN PLANET TOO!
YOU DON'T BELIEVE THIS SCENE? IT WAS ONE OF THE STRANGEST STORIES THAT EVER HAPPENED TO ME! C'MON! TURN THE PAGE AND READ---

THE STORY STARTED THE DAY MR. LODGE CAME UP WITH A GREAT IDEA ---
C'MON, KIDS! LET'S GO DOWN AND LOOK AT THE OCEAN!
GEE, MR. LODGE! I DIDN'T BRING MY BATHING SUIT!
CAN WE BRING A PICNIC LUNCH? (SMACK!)
BETTER THAN THAT, JUGHEAD! I'LL SHOW YOU SOMETHING YOU'VE NEVER SEEN BEFORE!
AW, I'VE SEEN ALL THE RESTAURANTS DOWN THERE!
DADDY IS TALKING ABOUT HIS RESEARCH COMPANY!
YES! PROFESSOR TRANSISTOR IS WORKING ON SOME NEW PROJECTS!
LODGE
WE'RE TRYING DIFFERENT WAYS TO HARNESS FOOD FOR MAN!
THIS COMPANY IS WORKING WITH OCEAN FARMS!
NOW YOU'RE TALKING!
LODGE LABORATORY
CHILDREN, MEET PROFESSOR TRANSISTOR!
HI, KIDS! YOU GOT HERE JUST IN TIME ---
2

I WAS JUST ABOUT TO LOOK OVER OUR FARM CROPS--- WOULD YOU LIKE TO GO?
SURE! I'LL TAKE SOME FRIED CLAMS!
YOU'VE HEARD ABOUT SNOWMOBILES --- WELL THIS IS AN OCEANMOBILE!
NEAT!
THESE ARE FISH GROWING IN SPECIAL HYDRO TANKS!
WITH SPECIAL ULTRAVIOLET LIGHT, SOME FISH GROW AS LARGE AS SHARKS!
SHARKS?
RELAX, JUGHEAD! YOU'RE PERFECTLY SAFE IN HERE!
HEH! HEH! THAT FISH LOOKS LIKE YOU, JUGGIE!
IT LOOKS SO CALM AND BEAUTIFUL DOWN HERE DADDY!
YES, BUT THERE ARE FEW FORCES MORE POWERFUL THAN THAT OF AN OCEAN!
AND, AS IF IT HEARD THE VERY WORDS MR. LODGE SPOKE, THERE IS A SLOW RUMBLE ---
RRR!
3

... EARTHQUAKE !
RUMBLE!
THE OCEAN FLOOR OPENS AS IF IT WERE THE JAWS OF A HUNGRY ANIMAL !
THE SMALL CRAFT IS DRAWN IN ---
WE'RE ALL GOING TO BE KILLED !
WHAT'S HAPPENING TO US NOW ?
I DON'T KNOW ! WE SEEM TO BE IN A STRONG CURRENT!
HEY ! WHAT A CRAZY-LOOKING FISH !
MY WORD ! THAT FISH LOOKS LIKE IT'S A MILLION YEARS OLD !
I SEE LIGHT, PROFESSOR TRANSISTOR !
WE MUST BE COMING TO THE SURFACE !
4

SPLASH!
WE SEEM TO BE IN SOME SORT OF CAVERN, MR. LODGE!
YES! JUST LIKE A GIANT DOME!
THIS IS LIKE ANOTHER WORLD WITHIN OUR OWN PLANET EARTH!
WHAT A FANTASTIC DISCOVERY!
OUR INSTRUMENTS SAY THIS AREA HAS THE SAME ATMOSPHERE AS ON THE SURFACE OF EARTH!
THAT MEANS WE CAN BREATHE OUT THERE!
WAIT'LL THE KIDS BACK HOME HEAR ABOUT THIS --- A SECRET CITY!
WHERE IS EVERYBODY?
DO YOU THINK WHO-EVER IS DOWN HERE LOOKS LIKE US, MR. LODGE?
I DON'T KNOW, LITTLE ARCHIE! THIS PLACE SEEMS DESERTED!
5

SEIZE THEM.!
LITTLE ARCHIE'S CAPTOR IS HAVING HIS TROUBLES, HOWEVER---
THE RADIO IS IN THE BACK PACK, LITTLE ARCHIE.! SEE IF YOU CAN CALL FOR HELP.!
WELL, WE KNOW ONE THING, MR. LODGE.! SOMEONE TAUGHT THEM ENGLISH.!
6

LATER ---
WOW! LOOK AT THIS PAD!
TAKE THEM TO THE SUPREME RULER!
HEY! THEIR SUPREME RULER LOOKS LIKE US, MR. LODGE!
I AM DOCTOR KOLTER, THE SUPREME RULER! I AM A SURFACE PERSON --- LIKE YOURSELVES!
I DON'T UNDERSTAND!
IF YOU ARE THE SUPREME RULER AND LOOK LIKE US, WHY DID YOUR PEOPLE ATTACK US?
I CAN TELL YOU!
YOU ARE THE ONLY SURFACE PEOPLE, EXCEPT MYSELF, THESE PEOPLE HAVE EVER SEEN!
YOU MEAN NO OTHER PERSON ON OUR WORLD HAS EVER SEEN THIS PLACE?
NO! OTHER SURFACE PEOPLE HAVE STUMBLED INTO OUR WORLD, BUT NO ONE EVER REACHED OUR CITY!
WHY NOT?
7

BECAUSE OF THE MONSTER!
MONSTER?
YOU'VE HEARD OF THE FAMOUS LOCHNESS MONSTER?
SURE! BUT I THOUGHT THAT WAS JUST A WILD STORY!
HERE'S YOUR WILD STORY--- IN PERSON!
WOW! LOOK AT THOSE TEETH!
IT HOLDS ALL OF US IN TERROR! WE ARE ALL CAPTIVES HERE!
YIIII!
YOU MEAN WE'LL NEVER SEE RIVERDALE AGAIN! (CHOKE!)
I'LL MISS ALL THOSE FUDGE SUNDAES AT THE CHOK'LIT SHOP!
READ THE EXCITING CONCLUSION IN THE NEXT CHAPTER!

AN UNDERSEA ADVENTURE
Little Archie
AND THE "SECRET CITY"
PART 2
THE STORY SO FAR-
LITTLE ARCHIE AND HIS FRIENDS EXPLORE THE BOTTOM OF THE OCEAN IN AN OCEANMOBILE! AN EARTH-QUAKE OCCURS AND THE SHIP IS DRAWN INTO AN OPENING BY A STRONG CURRENT! THEY DISCOVER A NEW WORLD AND A SECRET CITY! HOWEVER THE ENTIRE POPULATION IS HELD PRISONER BY A HUGE SERPENT-LIKE MONSTER--
WE'LL NEVER SEE RIVERDALE AGAIN, LITTLE ARCHIE!
OUR CITY IS DOOMED FOREVER!
WAIT! I THINK WE HAVE A WAY TO HELP YOU PEOPLE!
--- WE HAVE A LARGE ROCKET GUN ON OUR OCEANMOBILE---
WE USE IT TO DISCOURAGE LARGE FISH FROM ATTACK-ING OUR SHIP!

BUT OUR OCEANMOBILE IS OUTSIDE, PROFESSOR TRANSISTOR!
YEAH--- AND SO IS THE MONSTER!
PERHAPS WE COULD DIVERT THE MONSTER'S ATTENTION IN SOME WAY!
LET'S SHOW JUGHEAD TO HIM! THAT SHOULD SCARE THE MONSTER!
HEY!
THAT'S AN IDEA!
LET JUGGIE AND ME GET THE MONSTER'S ATTENTION, MR. LODGE!
I CAN'T LET YOU BOYS DO THIS!
YOU HEARD WHAT HE SAID, LITTLE ARCHIE!
AW, IT'LL BE EASY!
WE'LL GO TO THE OTHER END OF THE BUILDING AND SHOW OUR-SELVES TO THE MONSTER!
WAIT! I LOVE TO EAT--- NOT TO BE EATEN!
C'MON! LET'S DO OUR THING!
YOU FIRST, LITTLE ARCHIE!
2

YA-AH!
HERE WE ARE, BIRD-BRAIN!
C'MON! LET'S GET BACK INSIDE!
LITTLE ARCHIE AND JUGGIE HAVE THE MONSTER'S ATTENTION!
HURRY! TO THE OCEANMOBILE!
I CAN'T OPEN THE DOOR, LITTLE ARCHIE! (SOB!) IT'S LOCKED!
PULL
IT SAYS TO PULL, YOU NINNY! YOU'RE PUSHING!
AGGRG!
WE MADE IT!
GET READY TO FIRE THE ROCKET, MR. LODGE!
I'VE GOT THE MONSTER IN MY SIGHTS, PROFESSOR!
8

THE MONSTER SEES US!
FIRE ONE!
B-RIP
THAT SHOT DIDN'T SEEM TO BOTHER HIM A BIT!
THE MONSTER IS COMING AFTER US, DADDY!
ARGGGRH!
THE SIDES ARE CRUMBLING LIKE PAPER!
I'LL TRY TO DIVE!
NOW, LODGE! FIRE THE ROCKET AGAIN!
OKAY, PROFESSOR!
4

I THINK IT'S HAD ENOUGH! IT'S SWIMMING AWAY!
LOOK, PROFESSOR! IT'S DISAPPEARING THROUGH THAT HOLE!
DO YOU SUPPOSE THAT OPENING IS THE WAY TO THE SURFACE WORLD?
I DON'T KNOW, KIDS! WE'LL FIND OUT AFTER WE PICK UP LITTLE ARCHIE AND JUGHEAD!
MY PEOPLE AND I ARE GRATEFUL, MR. LODGE!
THEY'RE GOING TO HAVE A BIG FEAST IN OUR HONOR, PROFESSOR TRANSISTOR!
CAN WE STAY, HUH? HUH?
MAN! THIS IS THE BEST FEED I EVER HAD!
PSSST! EVERYONE IS LOOKING AT YOU, JUGGIE!
CHOMP SMACK!
5

THAT'S BECAUSE JUGHEAD'S EATING IS DROWNING OUT THE SPEAKER!
HEH! HEH! AFTER THIS, THEY'LL ASK US TO LEAVE!
SMACK! GULP!
WE WISH YOU WOULD STAY AND TEACH YOUR SCIENTIFIC KNOWLEDGE TO OUR WORLD!
I'M SORRY, BUT WE MUST GET BACK TO THE SURFACE WORLD!
WE ONLY ASK THAT NONE OF YOU TELL ANYTHING OF OUR WORLD DOWN HERE!
WE WON'T!
WE ONLY WANT TO GET BACK TO RIVERDALE!
LATER---
GOOD-BYE!
START THE ENGINES!
RRR!
WAIT, MR. LODGE! WE CAN'T GO! JUGGIE ISN'T HERE!
YOU MEAN THE FOOD WAS SO GOOD HE WANTED TO STAY?
NO! IT'S NOT THAT---
---JUGGIE'S SO FAT HE CAN'T GET INSIDE THE DOOR!
6

USE PLENTY OF SOAP.!
PHOOEY.! TAKE IT EASY, GUYS.! YOU'RE GETTING IT IN MY MOUTH.!
IT'S PROBABLY THE FIRST THING JUGHEAD EVER ATE THAT DIDN'T TASTE GOOD.!
PULL!
POP!
C'MON.! LET'S LEAVE BEFORE THEY GIVE JUGHEAD ANOTHER FEED.!
RIVERDALE, HERE WE COME.!
YAY!
WE HAVEN'T GOTTEN TO THE SURFACE WORLD YET, CHILDREN.!
YES.! THAT OPENING COULD LEAD TO A DEAD END.!
WE'LL KNOW IN JUST A MOMENT.!
WE SEEM TO BE RISING.!
7

WE MADE IT! WE'RE THROUGH THE OTHER OPENING!
WE'RE BACK IN OUR OWN WORLD!
GOOD NEWS, KIDS! ACCORDING TO MY CALCULATIONS WE SHOULD BE IN RIVERDALE BY TEN O'CLOCK IN THE MORNING!
GEE! THAT'S BAD NEWS, PROFESSOR TRANSISTOR!
BAD NEWS?
YEP! SCHOOL HAS ALREADY STARTED!
SO?
WELL, WE CAN'T TELL ANYONE ABOUT OUR ADVENTURE IN THE SECRET CITY---
WHAT EXCUSE CAN I USE---? I CAN'T EVEN TELL MISS GRUNDY I OVERSLEPT!
NO! BUT YOU CAN TELL HER ONE THING, JUG---
---TELL HER YOU OVERATE!
THE END

The Punk
Jughead #327, 1983
by Stan Goldberg, Rudy Lapick and Bill Yoshida

Jugheeeeaaaaad don't like it – ROCK the Casbah! ROCK the Casbah! Archie, at its best, is a snapshot of American culture from the perspective of those most affected by that culture – young people. "The Punk" is a great example of the cast getting to know a popular new movement, in this case the "punk" movement, and then going out of their way to overcome preconceived notions about that movement. It's a great way to teach kids about understanding and prejudice, and to do it in a way that doesn't feel too preachy. But let's be honest, the only thing more memorable than Archie Andrews SLAM DANCING is that overly-awesome, gone-too-soon mohawk on Jughead! I say, bring back the mohawk and the gold chain and let's get into the punk groove again right on down to Rockaway Beach!

--Paul Kaminski
Executive Director of Editorial, Archie Comics

The Image
TV Laugh Out #98, 1984
by Frank Doyle, Stan Goldberg, Rudy Lapick, Bill Yoshida and Barry Grossman

The Pussycats take a walk on the wild side in this Hollywood tale of fame and the not so fortunate. Alex Cabot continues to navigate the girls' career, often to mixed results, but that doesn't mean he's not the hardest working manager in the biz! The only thing that could have improved this story is an appearance by Alex's beautiful and talented sister Alexandra. That's based more on what I think she would want me to say than personal opinion.

The music from the Josie and the Pussycats film adaptation is the definitive soundtrack of 2001 for many fans, which goes to show how these characters can easily mix it up in different mediums to stellar effect. I know I'll be following their career.

--Steven M. Scott
Publicity & Marketing Coordinator, Archie Comics

Jughead in "THE PUNK"
BLUE AND GOLD
WRITING ASSIGNMENTS MUST BE IN ON TIME! SCOTT WRIGHT FACULTY SUPERVISOR
SOME OF THOSE PUNK HAIRDOS ARE BECOMING!
YEAH, THEY'RE BECOMING, ALL RIGHT --- THEY'RE BECOMING UTTERLY REVOLTING!

DID YOU SAY SOMETHING, MAC?
PUNK RULES
BETTY, TELL ME I DIDN'T SEE WHAT I JUST SAW!
SEE WHAT, ARCHIE?
1

I THOUGHT I SAW JUGGIE IN A PUNK OUTFIT! I MUST HAVE PUNK ON THE BRAIN!
NO, THAT WAS JUGGIE! HE'S NOT THE ONLY ONE ON CAMPUS WHO'S INTO THE PUNK SCENE!
BUT, BETTY, WE'VE GOT TO SAVE HIM!
ARCHIE, JUGGIE IS ENTITLED TO MAKE HIS OWN DECISIONS!
---NOW, ABOUT OUR NEXT ISSUE---
BETTY! DON'T YOU CARE ABOUT JUGHEAD? ISN'T HE YOUR FRIEND, TOO?
HOW CAN WE STOP HIM? AND BESIDES, WE DON'T KNOW IF THERE'S ANYTHING WRONG WITH THE PUNK MOVEMENT!
I'M WASTING MY TIME TALKING TO HER!
--- SHE'S SO COLD-BLOODED, IF A MOSQUITO BIT HER, IT'D DIE OF PNEUMONIA!
BLUE & GOLD
EDITORIAL OFFICE
SLAM!
RONNIE, DID YOU JUST SEE JUGHEAD?
YES! WHAT ARE WE GOING TO DO? WE HAVE TO SAVE HIM FROM HIMSELF!
I'M GLAD YOU SEE IT THAT WAY! BETTY ACTS AS THOUGH IT WEREN'T IMPORTANT!
MAYBE THE PUNK MOVE-MENT IS GETTING TO HER, TOO!
2

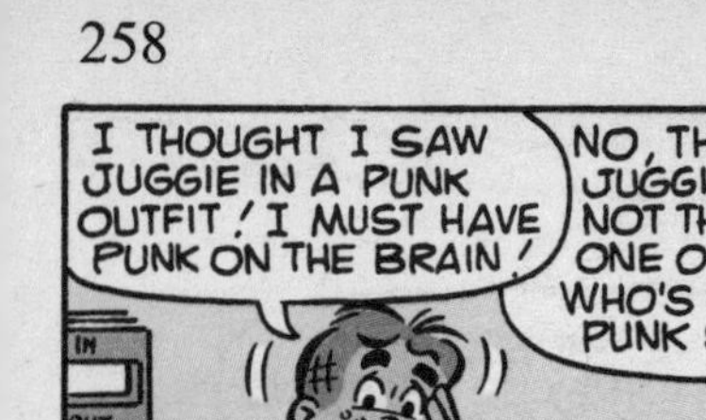

AND TO THINK I ONCE THOUGHT HIS HAT WAS TACKY! --- IF ONLY HE'D GO BACK TO HIS CUTE L'IL CAP AGAIN!
OH, NO!
WHAT IS IT, ARCH?
IT'S EITHER HOT DOG, OR A RAINBOW WITH PAWS!
A PUNK POOCH! NOW I'VE SEEN EVERYTHING!
JUGGIE --- JUG!
JUG, I'M TALKING TO YOU!
BACK OFF, NERD!
BUT, JUG--- DON'T YOU RECOGNIZE ME? YOUR OL' PAL ARCHIE?
STOP CALLING ME BY THAT RIDICULOUS NAME! MY NEW HANDLE IS 'CAPTAIN THRASH'!
'CAPTAIN TRASH' WOULD BE MORE LIKE IT!
3

AND I SUPPOSE HIS NAME IS NOW CAPTAIN BARK!
NO, HIS NAME IS 'VICIOUS'!
PUNK RULES
SHOW THESE JERKS WHY WE CALL YOU VICIOUS, PAL!
ARRGH!
I'M HUNGRY, CAP'N THRASH! LET'S GO OVER TO DINGY'S FOR SOME FOOD!
'DINGY'S'! THAT'S THE NOTORIOUS PUNK HANGOUT!
ARCHIE, IT ALL LOOKS SO HOPELESS!
I CAN'T GIVE UP ON JUGGIE! I'M GOING TO PAY DINGY'S A LITTLE VISIT!
LATER:
HAS JUGHEAD --- I MEAN "CAP'N THRASH" BEEN HERE YET?
YEAH, HE AND HIS DOLL WENT OVER TO THE CLUB CHAOS!
DINGY'S
BURGERS
YOU BETTER NOT GO OVER THERE LOOKING LIKE THAT, JACK--- OR YOU'LL BE SORRY!
GULP! IT'S TOO LATE TO TURN BACK!
CLUB CHAOS
4

THERE'S TOO MUCH SOCIAL INJUSTICE IN THIS WORLD!
YEAH, MY PARENTS MAKE ME TAKE OUT THE TRASH, TOO!
IT'S MONSTER MUSIC!
MAN! THIS ISN'T A NIGHTCLUB! IT'S A CONVENTION FOR WEIRDOS!
WHY IS EVERYONE BANGING INTO EACH OTHER ON THE DANCE FLOOR?
THAT'S THE WAY WE DANCE HERE! IT'S CALLED 'THE SLAM'!
IT LOOKS MORE LIKE A SCRIMMAGE BETWEEN THE CHICAGO BEARS AND THE PITTSBURGH STEELERS!
GULP! HE HIT JUGHEAD! HE HIT MY PAL!
YOU'RE NOT GETTING AWAY WITH THAT! YOU HIT MY FRIEND!
THAT'S THE WAY WE DANCE HERE, PINHEAD! WE LIKE TO CLOBBER EACH OTHER!
5

WHAT'S THIS SQUARE DOING HERE ?
LET'S GIVE HIM A REAL GOING OVER!
LET ME TAKE CARE OF THAT CREEP!
ARCHIE, ONCE AND FOR ALL, WILL YOU GET OUT OF MY LIFE ?
BUT JUGHEAD...
I'VE GOT NEW FRIENDS! WE SHARE THE SAME BELIEFS AND GOALS! SO LEAVE ME ALONE!
I DON'T BELIEVE IT! AFTER ALL OUR YEARS OF FRIENDSHIP, JUG THREW ME OUT OF THERE!
VERONICA IS RIGHT! IT IS HOPELESS!
CLUB CHAOS
THE NEXT DAY:
DID YOU MANAGE TO TALK SOME SENSE INTO JUGHEAD ?
NO, HE'S TOO FAR GONE!
GULP! LOOK! HE'S IN THE OFFICE WITH BETTY!
MAYBE HE'S TRYING TO TALK HER INTO JOINING THE PUNK SCENE!
LET'S STOP HIM!
6

SHE LOOKS NORMAL ENOUGH!
YOU NEVER CAN TELL!
BLUE & GOLD
I WANT YOU TWO TO READ THIS! IT'S GOING TO BE THE BEST ARTICLE OUR SCHOOL PAPER EVER RAN!
?
BLUE & GOLD
THE PUNK SCENE AT RIVERDALE HIGH
BY JUGHEAD JONES
AND WE OWE IT ALL TO OUR UNDERCOVER REPORTER, JUGHEAD FORSYTHE JONES!
, ALIAS CAPTAIN THRASH!
SO THAT'S WHY YOU THREW ME OUT OF THAT CLUB!
IF I HADN'T, YOU WOULD HAVE WOUND UP LOOKING LIKE SOMETHING KING KONG SAT ON!
GEE, JUG! IT'S GOOD TO SEE YOU LOOKING NORMAL AGAIN!
NOT QUITE, RONNIE!
RIVER HIGH SCHO
--- IT'LL TAKE A LITTLE WHILE FOR THINGS TO REALLY GET BACK TO NORMAL!
7

I BET YOUR ARTICLE REALLY TEARS INTO THOSE PUNK CHARACTERS!
NOT REALLY!
I CAN UNDERSTAND WHY A LOT OF THEM FEEL CONFUSED IN TODAY'S WORLD!
ALL THEY EVER HEAR ARE THE NEGATIVE THINGS ABOUT OUR SOCIETY!
MAYBE IT'S UP TO THE REST OF US TO CONVINCE 'EM THINGS AREN'T QUITE SO HOPELESS!
GET A LOAD OF JUG THE PHILOSOPHER!
AT ANY RATE, I GUESS YOU'RE HAPPY TO SAY ADIEU TO THE WORLD OF PUNK!
ON THE CONTRARY– I FEEL THIS OVER-POWERING URGE TO RETURN TO IT!
FOR MORE OF THEIR WEIRD PHILOSOPHY?
NO, FOR MORE OF DINGY'S FANTASTIC BURGERS! THEY'RE THE BEST I'VE EVER EATEN!
AND I WAS ACTUALLY WORRIED ABOUT HIM CHANGING!
DINGY'S
BURGER FRANKS
END

Doyle / Goldberg / Lapick / Yoshida / Grossman

YOU WERE GREAT, GIRLS! YOUR PHOTOS WILL BE IN ALL THE ROCK PUBLICATIONS!
I FEEL GUILTY!
WHAT DO YOU THINK YOU'RE DOING, JOSIE?!
CLEANING UP THE MESS WE MADE!
WHOEVER HEARD OF ROCK STARS WHO CLEANED UP THEIR OWN FOOD FIGHT?!
C'MON! CLEAN YOURSELVES UP, AND I'LL TAKE YOU TO A BIG PARTY I'M THROWING IN YOUR HONOR!
ALEX, IS ALL THIS PHONEY HYPE NECESSARY?!
TRUST ME, VALERIE!
... IF YOU EXPECT TO PLAY IN L.A.'S HOTTEST CLUB SOMEDAY, YOU'LL NEED A REAL OFF-BEAT IMAGE!
HOLLYWOOD
RED ONION
2

THE BIGGEST ROCK MOGULS ARE AT THIS PARTY! WE'LL KNOCK THEIR SOCKS OFF!
BUT WHY WOULD WE WANT THEM TO GO BAREFOOT?
HOTEL
BEFORE WE GO IN, VAL, HERE'S A PET PYTHON TO IMPRESS THEM WITH!
A 'PET' PYTHON?!
CELEBRITY ROOM
HE'S HARMLESS! I'M AN EXPERT ON SNAKES!
IT TAKES ONE TO KNOW ONE!
I'M GLAD YOU DIDN'T GIVE ME ANY BIG MONSTROSITY TO CARRY AROUND!
OF COURSE NOT!
---HERE'S YOUR PET TARANTULA!
TARANTULA!!
HA! HA! THE PUSSYCATS ARE THE KOOKIEST GROUP IN THE WORLD! DON'T KNOW HOW I HANDLE THEM!
IT SAYS HERE YOU WERE A DOG SLED OPERATER IN THE YUKON BEFORE YOU JOINED THE GROUP!
PRESS RELEASE
3

SORRY, GUYS! THE PUSSYCATS HAVE TO LEAVE!
YAWN! WE HAVE TO TURN IN EARLY!
HA! HA! GREAT KIDDER!
THE PUSSYCATS WANT TO HIT A COUPLE OF REAL WILD PARTIES!
JOSIE, ARE THOSE GUYS BY YOUR CAR YOUR BOYFRIENDS?
WITH OUR BUSY SCHEDULE, WE DON'T HAVE TIME FOR BOYFRIENDS!
HOTEL PARKING
PUSSYCAT FAN CLUB
WE ♥ THE PUSSYCATS
ALWAYS KIDDING!
ACTUALLY THOSE GUYS ARE MALE GROUPIES WHO ADORE THE PUSSYCATS!
WE ♥ THE PUSSYCATS
I'D GLADLY KISS THE HEM OF YOUR SKIRT!
SORRY! BUT WE'RE NOT WEARING SKIRTS!
ALEX, YOU OWE ME TWO HUNDRED FOR ROUNDING UP ALL THOSE NERDS!
SHHH! I'LL PAY YOU LATER!
PUSSYCAT FAN CLUB
WE ♥ THE PUSSYCATS
4

ONE WEEK LATER:
WITH THE NEW IMAGE I'VE GIVEN YOU GIRLS, YOU'RE NOW A CINCH TO BE BOOKED BY THE RED ONION!
RED ONIO
WELL, WALTER, DO MY WILD, WILD CHICKADEES APPEAR IN YOUR CLUB, OR DON'T THEY?
I REALLY LIKE THEIR MUSIC, ALEX, BUT THEIR SCREWBALL ANTICS TURN ME OFF!
IF THEY WERE MORE NORMAL I'D HIRE THEM!
DON'T WORRY! THEY'LL FAKE IT!
...I'LL TEACH 'EM TO ACT AS WHOLESOME AS MOM'S APPLE PIE!
OH, YOU LUCKY GIRLS ARE SO FORTUNATE TO HAVE ME GUIDING YOUR CAREERS!
WE'RE LUCKY, ALL RIGHT... WE'RE LUCKY ALEX ISN'T TWINS!
END

Look-A-Like Loony
Archie #336, 1985
by George Gladir, Dan DeCarlo Jr., Jimmy DeCarlo and Bill Yoshida

"Look-a-like Loony" is just that – loony – and wacky Archie stories are my favorite kind! I especially like this story because as a kid in the late '80s to early '90s, shows like *Supermarket Sweep* were popular and extremely fascinating to me. I always wanted to be a contestant on a game show that would allow me to grab as much of an item that I liked in a certain amount of time – especially if those items were records and CDs! I also enjoy this story for the humorous plays on famous people's names, like Michael Jackstone and Boy Roy – I wonder who they could have been referencing! This mega-'80s story is chock full of laughs and fun outfits to boot! Plus, Archie in eyeliner and lipstick – what's not to love?!

-- Jamie Lee Rotante
Editorial Assistant / Proofreader, Archie Comics

Rock 'N' Rassle
Everything's Archie #120, 1985
by George Gladir, Stan Goldberg, Sal Trapan, Bill Yoshida and Barry Grossman

Since I was a kid, I was a wrestling fan. Even though some older kids joked and made fun, I didn't care, I loved wrestling! I cheered my heroes and booed the bad guys. At school, my friends and I would play with our wrestling figures, which were made of heavy rubber that would hurt if you threw them at each other, which we did! Rowdy Roddy Piper, Hulk Hogan, Junkyard Dog, Macho Man, and who can forget Captain Lou Albano?! Then, out of the blue, he was playing Cyndi Lauper's father in her music video for "Girls Just Wanna Have Fun" and she appeared at Wrestlemania! Now it was cool to be a wrestling fan. Those same older kids who poked fun were suddenly wearing Hulkamania shirts and playing with the same figures we were. It was great! Cyndi Lauper had made it cool to be a wrestling fan – at least for everyone else! It was already cool to me!

--Joe Morciglio
Project Coordinator, Archie Comics

Archie in "LOOKALIKE LOONY"
MICHAEL AND I REALLY RESEMBLE ONE ANOTHER, DON'T WE?
YEAH, ALL EXCEPT FOR YOUR BANK ACCOUNTS!
WHAT'S THIS ALL ABOUT, ARCHIE?
MICHAEL JACKSTONE
DAVE'S RECORD STORE IS HOLDING A LOOKALIKE CONTEST!
ROCK STAR LOOKALIKE CONTEST
WIN RECORDS
FREE 10 MINUTE SHOPPING SPREE
DAVE'S RECORD STORE
THE WINNER GETS TO KEEP ALL THE RECORDS HE CAN CARRY OUT IN ONE LOAD!
OH, WOW!

YOU'RE MAKING A MISTAKE, ARCHIE!
---EVERYBODY IS GONNA DRESS UP AS MICHAEL JACKSTONE!
YOUR BEST CHANCE OF WINNING IS TO BE DIFFERENT! WHY DON'T YOU ENTER AS BOY ROY?
BOY ROY!!
JUGHEAD IS RIGHT!
RECORD NEWS
FORGET IT! NO WAY! IT'S OUT OF THE QUESTION!
THEN YOU'RE NOT GOING TO WIN THAT CONTEST!
BUT HOW AM I GONNA GET THE MAKE-UP, THE HAIR-DO AND THE COSTUME IN TIME? THE CONTEST IS TODAY!
I COULD HELP YOU IN THAT DEPARTMENT, ARCHIE!
SEVERAL EXCRUCIATING HOURS LATER-
YOU'RE A DEAD-RINGER FOR HIM, ARCHIE!
GULP! OKAY! WE BETTER GO OR WE'LL BE LATE!
ARCHIE, IS THAT YOU?
DO YOUR PARENTS KNOW ABOUT THIS?
ULP!
2

YOO HOO! LOOK, EVERYBODY! IT'S BOY ARCHIE!
WILL I BE GLAD WHEN THIS DAY IS OVER!
LOOK AT ALL THE CONTESTANTS!
ROCK STAR LOOKALIKE CONTES
MOST OF 'EM LOOK PRETTY GOOD!
YEAH, BUT I SEE ONE WHO'S OUTSTANDING!
Dave's Records
JUDGES' STAND
IT IS THE UNANIMOUS OPINION OF THE JUDGES THAT OUR WINNER IS---
BOY ARCHIE!--- UH, I MEAN ARCHIE ANDREWS!
YAHOO!
3

THE STORE WILL BE CLEARED FOR TEN MINUTES WHILE YOU SELECT YOUR ALBUMS!
YOU CAN HAVE ONE FRIEND ASSIST YOU!
COUNTRY
ROCK
BUT REMEMBER - YOU HAVE TO CARRY THE ALBUMS OUT OF THE STORE BY YOURSELF!
I KNOW! I KNOW!
JUG, PUT DOWN THAT BURGER AND READ ME THE LIST OF ALBUMS I WANT TO GRAB!
OKAY, PAL!
TOM-TOM TWIN
DURAN DURAN, LIONEL RICHIE, THE CARS, TINA TURNER, BRUCE SPRINGSTEEN!
HEY, ARCHIE! HERE ARE A COUPLE OF ALBUMS BY BOY ROY!
BUT I DON'T LIKE BOY ROY!
BOY ROY
BUT I DO!
4

I CAN'T CARRY ANY MORE ALBUMS! BETTER CALL IT QUITS!
WHERE'S MY HAMBURGER? I PUT IT RIGHT ON THIS COUNTER!
IT'S ON THE FLOOR! YOU MUST HAVE KNOCKED IT OFF!
I BLEW IT! I BLEW IT!
I MANAGED TO HOLD ON TO ONLY TWO ALBUMS!
BOY ROY
KISS
THANKS, ARCHIE! THOSE ARE THE TWO BOY ROY ALBUMS I WANTED!
5

WE TAPED THE ENTIRE CONTEST... ...WE WANT TO USE THE HIGHLIGHTS FOR OUR T.V. COMMERCIAL!
A T.V. COMMERCIAL ?!
TV
THERE'S NO END TO MY SHAME AND DISGRACE!
NOW EVERYONE IS GONNA SEE ME ACTING LIKE A BIG CLUMSY GOON!
IF YOU SIGN THIS RELEASE, WE'LL LET YOU KEEP ALL THE ALBUMS YOU DROPPED!
YOU WILL!? OH, BOY!
WHEW! AT LAST, ALL MY PROBLEMS ARE OVER!
I DON'T THINK SO, ARCHIE!
THERE HE IS, GIRLS! LET'S TAKE HIM APART FOR SOUVENIRS!
HERE COME A BUNCH OF FANS WHO REALLY THINK YOU ARE BOY ROY!
The END

THE Archies IN "ROCK 'N' RASSLE"
ARCHIE, WHAT ON EARTH ARE WE DOING PLAYING AT A WRESTLING MATCH?
HAVEN'T YOU HEARD- THE COMBINATION OF ROCK AND WRESTLING IS THE HOTTEST THING AROUND!
SCRIPT: GEORGE GLADIR PENCILS: STAN G. INKS: SAL TRAPANI LETTERING: BILL YOSHIDA COLORING: BARRY GROSSMAN EDITOR: VICTOR GORELICK EDITOR-IN-CHIEF: RICHARD GOLDWATER
I HOPE NO ONE GETS INJURED!
RELAX, RONNIE! WRESTLERS ARE IN EXCELLENT CONDITION! NO ONE EVER REALLY GETS HURT!

AND NOW, FOR OUR NEXT BOUT...
LADIES AND GENTLEMEN, FROM NEW YORK CITY - BROADWAY BOB AND HIS VALET, JEANNIE JEANS!
... AND HIS OPPONENT FROM HOBOKEN, NEW JERSEY THE MASKED MARVEL!
OKAY, GUYS, THAT'S OUR CUE! WE'RE SUPPOSED TO PLAY THE MASKED MARVEL'S THEME SONG!
HOW DARE YOU PLAY THE MARVEL'S THEME SONG WHILE MY BROADWAY BOB IS STILL TAKING HIS BOWS!
EEOW!!
THWACK
SO, NO ONE GETS HURT?
WELL, ALMOST NO ONE!
2

IS THE REF BLIND? CAN'T HE SEE THOSE FOULS?
HEY! TAKE IT EASY, MAC! I'M NOT THE REF!
SORRY, PAL! I GOT CARRIED AWAY BY THE FIGHT!
A FEW MORE BOPS AND I'LL GET CARRIED AWAY... BY THE MEDICS!
AND NOW FOR THE BOUT YOU'VE ALL BEEN WAITING FOR!
FROM THE BEACHES OF SOUTHERN CALIFORNIA, WEIGHING 240, MALIBU MAL!
THAT'S ME! THAT'S ME!
OOPS! DROPPED MY GOOD LUCK CHARM!
OUCH!
BUMP!
... AND HIS OPPONENT FROM PITTSBURGH, P.A., THE WORLD CHAMPION, STEELER STAN!
CHAMP
3

BETTY, I'D LIKE YOU AND RONNIE TO HOLD ONTO MY CHAMPIONSHIP BELT!
THANK YOU, STAN!
CHAMP
LET ME TOUCH STAN'S BELT!
I'M THE VICE-PRESIDENT OF HIS FAN CLUB! I SHOULD HOLD IT!
CHAMP
DON'T MIND MY FANS! NOW AND THEN THEY GET A LITTLE EXCITED!
I'D HATE TO BE AROUND WHEN THEY GET REAL EXCITED!
I AM SENDING MALIBU MAL BACK TO THE BEACH!
KRASH!
I'M SORRY, GUYS! DID I HURT ANYONE IN YOUR GROUP?
NO, BUT YOU SURE TOTALED OUR DRUM!
4

LOOK! THEY'VE DISQUALIFIED STEELER STAN FOR FOULING MALIBU MAL!
THEY CAN'T DO THAT TO OUR HERO!
THAT MAKES ME SO MAD!
THWACK!
HERE COMES ARCHIE AND HIS PALS BACK FROM THE WRESTLING MATCH!
I WONDER IF WRESTLING IS REALLY AS VIOLENT AS IT LOOKS ON TV!
YES, IT IS, DAD!
---BUT ONLY FOR THE SPECTATORS!
The End

Wieners over Riverdale
Archie 3000 #1, 1987
by Rex Lindsey, Jon D'Agostino and Barry Grossman

Fast forward into the future of Riverdale! This hilarious tale is jam-packed with flying cars, robotic chairs, and... hot dog pills?

Boy, Jughead's food antics certainly haven't changed, have they? This is definitely one of the best stories in the Archie library, especially if you are a fan of movies or shows that give you a glimpse of what lies ahead. It just goes to show that no matter what year they're in, Archie and his friends remain the most timeless characters in comic book history.

--Vincent Lovallo
Assistant Editor, Archie Comics

In The Dark
The New Archies #5, 1988
by Joe Edwards and Barry Grossman

Despite not being the brightest bulb in the room, Moose does come up with some good lines.

It's like he's Rain Man with Henny Youngman's timing.

Now where's my peanut butter sandwich?

--Stephen Oswald
Production Manager, Archie Comics

Archie 3000!
WIENERS OVER Riverdale!
THIS IS RIVERDALE! DON'T BELIEVE IT? WELL, IT IS! RIVERDALE SOMETIME IN THE FUTURE! GOT IT? GOOD! NOW, ON WITH OUR TALE...
GOODBYE, ARCHIE!
SEE YA, BETTY! SORRY I CAN'T STAY AND TALK, BUT I GOTTA FLY!
SCRIPT/PENCILLING: REX LINDSEY
INKING/LETTERING: JON D'AGOSTINO
COLORING: BARRY GROSSMAN
POP TATE'S
HOLOGRAM CINEMA
BIJOU
CITY BANK
CHOCKLIT SHOPPE
AND FLY IS RIGHT... THIS JET-CAR OF MINE SURE IS FAITHFUL!! VINTAGE 2088!
ZIPP!
1

OH, MAN! RIGHT SMACK INTO RUSH HOUR TRAFFIC! TIME FOR AUTO PILOT!
A LITTLE LATER AT THE DIGS OF JUGHEAD JONES...
15
HIYA! JUG! TAKIN' IT EASY, I SEE!
EASY? YOU THINK IT'S EASY THINKING OF THINGS FOR THESE HANDY HANDS TO DO?
HOT DOG
PIZZA
SAY, CARE FOR A BURGER OR HOT DOG FROM MY INSTA-FOOD MACHINE?
2

NO THANKS, I JUST ATE A SYNTHO-NUTRIENT DINNER!
EECH! WELL, I'LL HAVE ONE! HANDY HANDS TWO, ONE HOT DOG, PLEASE... WITH THE WORKS, OF COURSE!
SORRY, MASTER JONES, ALL OUT OF DOGS...REPEAT, ALL OUT OF DOGS...REPEAT, ALL OUT...
OKAY, JUG... THAT DOES IT! GETTING MORE HOT DOGS WILL BE A GOOD EXCUSE FOR A LITTLE EXERCISE!
BUT WE'VE GOT TO HURRY BACK! I'VE A DATE WITH RONNIE AT SEVEN SHARP!
15
SWISH!
IT'S DOWN THERE IN THE MALL, ARCH! IT'S MY SECRET SHOP. HIGHLY EXCLUSIVE FOR THE 20th CENTURY CONNOISSEUR!
3

LATER, IN THE SECRET SHOP...
GREETIN'S, JUG! WHAT'S ON YOUR MIND, TODAY?
A NEW SUPPLY OF HOT DOG PILLS, FRANKO!
ROUTE US 66
HERE YOU ARE! REMEMBER, KEEP THIS LID ON TIGHT!
I KNOW, AS SOON AS THEY'RE EXPOSED TO AIR... POP! INSTANT HOT DOGS! WITH THE WORKS, OF COURSE!
MICHAEL WHO...?
METS
ROCK N ROLL
GEE, JUG... I DON'T KNOW WHAT YOU SEE IN ALL THAT WEIRD STUFF!
"WEIRD STUFF"? THOSE ARE PRIME ANTIQUES, ARCH! REALLY UNIQUE ITEMS OF THE PAST!
BUT I WOULDN'T WANT TO LIVE BACK THEN, WHAT WITH TODAY'S MODERN CONVENIENCES AND ALL...
YEAH, THINGS SURE HAVE CHANGED IN OLE RIVERDALE, U.S.A.!
WELL, I THINK I'LL CHANGE THIS RADIO STATION! WHICH BUTTON IS IT AGAIN?
KLICK! KLICK! KLICK!
4

CAREFUL, JUG! THIS BABY'S OLD BUT SHE'S GOT SOME FANCY FEATURES...
...TWIN JETS, REAR SEAT TRAP DOOR FOR EASY ACCESS, AUTO ANTI-GRAVITY...
BUT UNKNOWN TO OUR HEROES, THE TRAP DOOR BUTTON WAS PRESSED... SPILLING OUT THE "YOU KNOW WHAT"... WITH THE WORKS, OF COURSE!
POP! POP! POP! POP! POP!
MEANWHILE, SOMEWHERE BELOW, AT REGGIE'S...
AH, SHININ' LIKE A QUASAR! THESE WINGS ARE LEAGUES AHEAD OF ARCHIE'S OLD SKY BUCKET!
SPEAKING OF ARCHIE, I'VE GOT TO GET OVER TO VERONICA'S HOUSE FIVE MINUTES BEFORE HE DOES, AND TELL HER HE SENT ME INSTEAD! HEH, HEH!
5

BUT, AS FATE WOULD HAVE IT...
YIPES! WHAT'S HAPPENING? MY NEW WAX JOB!
SPLAT!
SPLAT!
SPLAT!
SPLAT!
SPLAT!
SPLAT!
SPLAT!
I'LL NEVER MAKE IT TO RONNIE'S NOW! BUT... WHAT IS THIS STUFF?
MUST BE GARBAGE FROM THAT NEW POWER STATION, DROPPED BY THOSE LOW-FLYING WASTE DISPOSAL TRUCKS!
I HATE PROGRESS!!
BACK AT JUG'S HOUSE, THEY DISCOVER THE HOT DOGS ARE MISSING...
MAYBE YOU LEFT THEM AT THE SHOP! YOU THINK IT OVER, I'VE GOT TO PICK UP RONNIE!
YEAH, OKAY...
?
ZOOM!
?
6

LATER, JUST BEFORE SEVEN...
I WONDER WHO REGGIE IS TAKING OUT TONIGHT! WITH HIS LUCK, I'M SURE HE'S GOT HIS HANDS FULL!
AH! THERE GOES ARCHIE TO PICK UP VERONICA... SOME GUYS HAVE ALL THE LUCK! ...THAT WIENER!
...AND REPORTS OF AN UNKNOWN GOOEY SUBSTANCE THAT FELL OVER A SECTION OF RIVERDALE TODAY, STILL HAVE RESIDENTS BAFFLED... IN OTHER NEWS...
GEE, THAT'S FUNNY. I WONDER WHO'S RESPONSIBLE? OH, SOME SIMPLETON, NO DOUBT! HEH, HEH!
7
THE END

MOOSE IN THE DARK
GRRRR... MATH AGAIN!
199 x21
JOE EDWARDS
MOOSE! WHY DO YOU DISLIKE MATH SO?
WELL, MISS GRUNDY, LET ME PUT IT THIS WAY! MATH TO ME IS LIKE DIALING A TELEPHONE IN THE IN THE DARK!!
VERY COLORFUL! HOW DO YOU FIGURE THAT?
YOU GET TOO MANY WRONG NUMBERS!
End

THE BEST OF
Archie
COMICS
BOOK TWO
THE
'90s
KING OF THE WORLD

The Putt Down
Betty & Veronica #33, 1990
by Frank Doyle, Dan DeCarlo, Henry Scarpelli and Bill Yoshida

I love golf. This story is so much fun to read because in golf, as in life, if you "overthink" something you do not perform to your utmost capabilities. Just make it happen, as the saying goes. Betty & Veronica are effortless in their abilities to putt the golf ball, while Mr. Lodge, with all his practice, just can't seem to get it right.

Archie and golf – my two favorite pastimes. It doesn't get any better than that for me.

--Jonathan Goldwater
Publisher / Co-CEO, Archie Comics

Boatwrongs
Archie #405, 1992
by George Gladir, Stan Goldberg, Rudy Lapick and Bill Yoshida

Archie Comics has a long standing tradition of seafaring stories. This has partly to do with the publishers (at that time Richard Goldwater and Michael Silberkleit) who were avid yachtsmen. They were always trying to find a way to mix business with boating. There were even times when they would get us employees involved! Mostly scrubbing and painting their boats, but it was always a fun day at the dock capped off with lunch and a company cruise.

--Ellen Leonforte
Senior Art Director, Archie Comics

Betty and Veronica
IN "The PUTT DOWN"
DADDY! WHY ARE YOU GOLFING IN THE HOUSE ?!
NOT GOLFING, DEAR! PUTTING! THE PUTT IS THE MOST IMPORTANT SHOT IN THE GAME OF GOLF!
POK!
THE PUTT IS THE SHOT THAT FINALLY PUTS THE BALL IN THE HOLE!
THRILLING, I'M SURE!
YAWN!
SOMEDAY, A SILLIER GAME WILL BE INVENTED - AND I'LL BET MY DADDY WILL TAKE IT UP!
IS HITTING A LITTLE BALL INTO A LITTLE HOLE ANY SILLIER THAN SHOOTING A BIG BALL INTO A BIG BASKET?

NONSENSE, GIRL! GOLF IS A FAR SUPERIOR GAME TO BASKETBALL!
YOU DON'T SEEM TO BE DOING TOO WELL AT IT!
CLUNK
PLUNK
THAT LOOKS EASY, DADDY! MIND IF I TRY?
NOT AT ALL, DEAR!
PIECE OF CAKE!
BEGINNER'S LUCK!
CLINK
THAT'S FIVE IN A ROW! IT IS EASY!
MAY I TRY IT?
CLINK
CLINK
CLINK
CLINK
CLINK
GO AHEAD! LET'S SEE IF YOU'RE AS LUCKY AS VERONICA!
2

POK
WHAP
CLIP
SOK
PLUNK! PLUNK! PLUNK!
PLUNK! PLUNK!
SUFFERING SANDTRAPS! WHAT PHENOMENAL SHOT-MAKING!! I'VE NEVER SEEN THE LIKES OF IT!
I'M GOING TO ENTER YOU TWO IN THE PUTTING CONTEST AT THE COUNTRY CLUB! YOU'LL BEAT THE SOCKS OFF THAT YOUNG UPSTART!
UPSTART?
THE NEW PRO! ALWAYS LOOKING DOWN HIS NOSE AT US OLD TIMERS! THINKS HE'S SO GREAT!
BAH!
WHEN YOU TWO TAKE HIM TO THE CLEANERS, I'LL BE MAGNANIMOUS IN MY GRATITUDE!
WE DON'T WANT TO PASS THIS UP, BETTY!
NO WAY!
3

SOON... AT THE CLUB!
HERE WE ARE, GIRLS! THIS IS GOING TO BE BEAUTIFUL! GO OUT THERE AND PUTT THE PANTS OFF HIM!
PUTTING GREEN
KEN, I'VE BROUGHT ALONG SOME COMPETITION FOR YOU! GIRLS, MEET OUR CLUB PRO KEN BROWN!
KEN! BETTY AND VERONICA!
MY PLEASURE, GIRLS!
OH, WOW, RON! HOW DOES THAT HUNK GRAB YOU?
OOOH! IF HE ONLY WOULD!
PREPARE TO BE DETHRONED, YOUNG FELLA!
THEY PUTT WELL, DO THEY, MR. LODGE?
THEY HAVE EYES THAT ARE THE ENVY OF EAGLES!
SHALL WE DO IT? LADIES FIRST!
4

RON, HOW CAN I KEEP MY EYE ON THE BALL WITH HIM STANDING THERE?
YOU'RE SO RIGHT, BETTY!
I THINK HE'S WHAT THEY CALL A NATURAL HAZARD! GO ON! GIVE IT YOUR BEST SHOT!
SIGH! HOW DID I DO?
PROBABLY BETTER THAN I'LL DO! D-UH!
YOU CALLED IT, PARTNER! THAT WAS EVEN WORSE THAN YOUR DAD'S PUTTING!
WHACK
WE WERE PRETTY BAD! DO YOU GIVE LESSONS?
THAT'S WHAT I DO!! TEACH GOLF!
SIGH! AND BESIDES GOLF?
MR. LODGE, SIR! YOU'RE BENDING YOUR PUTTER!
PRO SHOP
END

JUG, I JUST BOUGHT A BOAT!
DOES IT COME COMPLETE WITH OARS?
THIS IS NO ROWBOAT, JUG! IT'S A VERITABLE YACHT!
YES, BUT IS IT A VIABLE YACHT?
Archie IN BOATWRONGS
THIS SHIPWRECK IS YOUR YACHT?
IT'S A FIXER-UPPER!
IT LOOKS MORE LIKE A SINKER-DOWNER!
JOE'S BAIT SHOP
1

ALL IT'LL TAKE IS A LITTLE PAINT AND SOME SPARE PARTS!
AND A LOTTA LUCK!
AND WHEN I GET IT SHIPSHAPE, I'LL NAME IT AFTER YOU!
ME?
IT WOULD BE KIND OF NICE TO HAVE A BOAT NAMED AFTER ME!
THAT'S JUST WHAT HESPERUS SAID!
I COULD GET YOU ALL THE SUPPLIES YOU NEED! ARE YOU SURE YOU KNOW HOW TO MAKE THIS BILGE BUCKET SEAWORTHY?
YOU'RE LOOKING AT ANDREWS AND JONES, MASTER BOATWRIGHTS!
OR MAYBE BOAT-WRONGS!
LATER...
WELL, JUG, I GOT ALL THE SUPPLIES AND A BOOK ON BOAT BUILDING!
I HOPE IT FLOATS!
2

THE BOAT?
NO, THE BOOK!
OKAY, NOW, JUG, YOU PAINT THE HULL! I'LL GO INSIDE AND DO SOME CARPENTRY WORK!
AYE, CAPTAIN... OOOPS!
BOAT PAINT
DO YOU WANT ME TO PAINT THE WHOLE HULL?
WHAT DID YOU SAY, JUG?
OOPS! SORRY, ARCH!
SPLOOP!
NOW, IS THIS MAST A MIZZEN?
NO, IT'S NOT A-MIZZEN! IT'S RIGHT OVER THERE!
JUG, BE CAREFUL WITH THAT!
CRUNCH
3

JUG, YOU PUT YOUR FOOT THROUGH THE BOTTOM OF THE HULL!
AT LEAST IT PROBABLY SCARED AWAY THE BARNACLES!
HI, BOYS! WHAT ARE YOU DOING?
WE'RE DISCOVERING WHAT WE DON'T KNOW!
ACTUALLY, WE'RE TRYING TO FIX UP THIS BOAT!
CAN YOU USE A HAND?
IT'D BE BETTER THAN JUG'S FOOT!
I USED TO DO REPAIR WORK ON MY UNCLE'S BOAT!
WELCOME ABOARD, MATEY!
LATER...
BETTY, YOU DID A GREAT JOB! I REALLY OWE YOU... HEY, I KNOW WHAT...
I'LL NAME THE BOAT AFTER YOU!
OH, ARCHIE! HOW THRILLING!
4

YOU SHOULDN'T HAVE DONE THAT, ARCH! YOU'RE IN BIG TROUBLE!
WHY? WHAT DO YOU MEAN?
YOU ALREADY PROMISED VERONICA YOU'D NAME THE BOAT AFTER HER!
OMIGOSH! I FORGOT! I AM IN BIG TROUBLE!
WAIT! I KNOW! I HAVE THE SOLUTION!
SNAP!
JOE'S BAIT SHOP
THE NEXT DAY...
I GOTTA ADMIT IT, ARCH, THIS GENERIC NAME IS A STROKE OF GENIUS!
ROOT BEER
THE SEA FOX
I CHRISTEN THEE "THE SEA FOX"!
CRASH
THE SEA FOX
MAYBE YOU SHOULD HAVE CHRISTENED IT "THE UNDERSEA FOX"!
GLUB GLUB
GLUB
END

Blarney Blues
Jughead #57, 1994
by Mike Pellowski, Stan Goldberg, Rudy Lapick and Bill Yoshida

Why? Why would I choose this story? I asked this question because I'm a father of a three-year-old daughter who's obsessed with the "Purple Dinosaur" show. As a result of this obsession, I endure four to five hour "Purple Dinosaur" marathons, of course, it's the same two or three episodes played over and over again… aarrgghhh!! Then there's the screaming and crying tantrums, naturally associated with toddlers, when it's time to turn off the colorful dino and go to sleep – that's a marathon that can last an hour or two… aarrgghhh!!! Wait a second, I know the answer to my question, it's because this story reminds me of my daughter who I'll always love and cherish through the good times and the bad, stressful and annoying times, usually caused by that infernal purple dinosaur… aarrgghhh!!!

--Carlos Antunes
Editor, Archie Comics

Win Some, Lose Some
Cheryl Blossom #20, 1999
by Dan Parent, Jon D'Agostino, Bill Yoshida, Barry Grossman

I really enjoyed writing and drawing this story, because it encompassed two of my favorite things: TV and Cheryl Blossom! This story was so much fun because we see the true Cheryl in this story. There's the girl who seeks celebrity attention, the girl who wants to steal Archie from Betty and Veronica, and the girl who will throw her wealth around to get what she wants. Cheryl seems like she was the pre- Kim Kardashian here! In fact, I think she could learn a thing or two from Cheryl!

--Dan Parent
Wrtier / artist, Archie Comics

THAT'S IT, JELLYBEAN! CRAWL OVER HERE AND GET THE BALL FROM BIG BROTHER!
GOO! GOO!
Jughead's IN "BLARNEY BLUES!"
HI, BOYS AND GIRLS! WELCOME TO MY SHOW!
LET'S ALL SING A SONG!
PLOP!

OH, JELLYBEAN! I GOT THE BALL! REMEMBER?!
I LIKE YOU! YOU LIKE ME!
WE'LL BE ONE BIG FAMILY...
OH, JELLYBEAN! EARTH TO JELLYBEAN!
WITH A VERY BIG SQUEEZE AND A SMACK FROM ME TO YOU...
JELLYBEAN!!
WHAT'S ALL THE YELLING ABOUT IN HERE?!
I WAS TRYING TO BREAK THAT GRAPE LIZARD'S SPELL OVER MY LITTLE SISTER!
BUT I CAN'T DO IT!
IT'S JUST UNNATURAL, HER ATTRACTION TO THAT THING!
OF COURSE IT'S NOT! ALL THE KIDS LOVE BLARNEY!
THERE MUST BE SOME SUBCONSCIOUS MESSAGE IN IT, OR SOMETHING! HOW ELSE COULD IT HOLD A BABY'S ATTENTION LIKE THAT?!
OH, DON'T BE SILLY!
2

SOON...
WAH!
OH, DEAR! THE SHOW'S OVER WITH!
OH, WHERE IS IT?! WHERE IS IT?!
WHAT ARE YOU LOOKING FOR, MA?!
TOY CHEST
THIS! ONE OF HER BLARNEY VIDEOTAPES!
THIS SHOULD KEEP HER PACIFIED FOR A WHILE LONGER!
WAH!!
WA...
HI, BOYS AND GIRLS! I'M BLARNEY!
OH, BROTHER!
I CAN'T TAKE ANYMORE OF THIS! WHAT'S IN TODAY'S PAPER?
HEY, WHAT'S THIS?!
"A SUPPORT GROUP FOR BLARNEY LOVERS AND THEIR FAMILIES!"
"GET THAT PURPLE DINO OFF YOUR KID'S BACK!"
3

"CONTACT BLARNEY LOVERS ANONYMOUS!"
I BELIEVE I HAVE A PHONE CALL TO MAKE!
THAT NIGHT...
HI! I'M RICK WATSON AND MY LITTLE BROTHER IS A B-L-A-R-N-E-Y LOVER!
WHY'D YOU SPELL BLARNEY?!
SCREECH!
WAHHHH!
THANK YOU VERY MUCH, MR. JONES! THERE'S ONLY ONE THING WE CAN DO NOW!
HI, BOYS AND GIRLS! WELCOME TO MY SHOW!
THERE! THAT SHOULD SATISFY THEM!
MR. JONES, I REALIZE YOU'RE NEW TO THE GROUP! BUT WE CAN'T SPEAK HIS NAME OR WE GET THAT REACTION!
4

DOC! WHAT CAN WE DO?! THAT VIOLET VELOCIRAPTOR SEEMS TO RULE THEIR LIVES!
HERE'S MY THEORY...
WHEN IT BEGINS TO GET CLOSE TO SHOW TIME, TRY TO MAKE SURE TO GET THEIR ATTENTION WITH SOMETHING ELSE!
HMMM! MAYBE JELLYBEAN'S FAVORITE FOOD WOULD MAKE HER FORGET!
GOOD NIGHT, EVERYONE! AND JUST REMEMBER, I'M ONLY A PHONE CALL AWAY!
G'NIGHT, DOC!
JUG
THE NEXT DAY...
UH-OH! IT'S GETTING CLOSE TO SHOW TIME, AND JELLY-BEAN'S ASSUMING THE POSITION!
THIS CALLS FOR A KITCHEN RUN!
RING
RING
PLOP!
HI, DR. FLYNN! YEAH, SHE'S ANTSY, BUT I'M GOING TO TRY TO ENTICE HER WITH HER FAVORITE DISH!
GAH! GAH!
JELLY
A PEANUT BUTTER AND JELLY SANDWICH!
GAH?!
5

HEY! I'VE GOT HER ATTENTION! THIS IS GONNA WORK!
THAT'S IT, JELLYBEAN! EAT UP THAT PRETTY BROWN AND PURPLE SANDWICH!
?
WAH!
YEAH! I KNOW! I SAID PURPLE! I'M SORRY!
HERE YOU GO, JELLYBEAN! NOW PIPE DOWN!
HI, KIDS! TODAY CHEF JULIA KIDD IS GOING TO SHOW US HOW TO MAKE A TASTY BLARNEY BURGER!
MS. FLYNN! JULIA KIDD'S ON THE SHOW AND SHE'S GOT THIS GIANT... GULP!... HAMBURGER!
JUGHEAD! LOOK AWAY! DON'T STARE AT THE SET!
I LIKE YOU! YOU LIKE ME!
JUGHEAD?! JUGHEAD?! PICK UP THE PHONE! JUGHEAD?!
END

Cheryl Blossom
in "Win Some, Lose Some"
CLASS, I'M PLEASED TO ANNOUNCE THAT PEMBROOKE WILL BE ON THE GAME SHOW "WHEEL OF DUMB LUCK"!
WE'LL BE COMPETING AGAINST OTHER SCHOOLS FOR CHARITY!
PEMBROOKE WILL BE UP AGAINST RIVERDALE HIGH!
OOH!!
WE WILL BE REPRESENTED BY OUR TOP 5 STUDENTS!
JENNA, BOB, CRAIG, PRISCILLA AND HUMPHREY!

PRISCILLA! YOU'VE GOT TO LET ME TAKE YOUR PLACE!
W-ELL! YOU KNOW MY PRICE! DATE WITH JASON!
OKAY, OKAY! I'LL WORK ON IT!
NOW I CAN SQUARE OFF AGAINST THOSE RIVERDALE GOONS!
AND...
WELCOME TO "WHEEL OF DUMB LUCK!" TONIGHT, IT'S PEMBROOKE HIGH...
... VERSUS RIVERDALE HIGH!
GOODY! BETTY AND VERONICA ARE ON THE TEAM!
AND THERE'S ARCHIE IN THE AUDIENCE!
YOO HOO! ARCHIE HONEY!
CHERYL! PLEASE! WE'RE ON LIVE TV!
ER... MR. SETBACK! VIANNA BEIGE IS STUCK IN TRAFFIC!
2

THEN WHO WILL TURN THE LETTERS?
I WILL! I WILL! I WILL!
BUT YOU'RE COMPETING...
I'LL GIVE $ 2,000 TO OUR CHARITY IF YOU LET ME BE VIANNA!
WELL, WE CAN'T REFUSE AN OFFER LIKE THAT!
YOU'RE ON, CHERYL! JUST TURN THE LETTERS AS THEY LIGHT UP!
SOON...
I WANT TO GUESS THE PUZZLE! IT'S "NICK OF TIME"!
ER... WRONG!
N C
OF
T M
BUT THE SQUARES LIT UP!
IT'S JUST AN ELECTRICAL MISTAKE!
TURN THE LETTERS, CHERYL!
OKAY, OKAY, DON'T GET SO TOUCHY!
OF
3

RIVERDALE WINS THAT ROUND!
HMPH! OH, THERE'S ARCHIE!
SO, ARCHIE, HOW DO YOU LIKE THIS GOWN ? IT'S A BIT...
CHERYL! WE'RE READY TO PLAY, IF THAT'S OKAY WITH YOU!
SPIN THE WHEEL, VERONICA!
THESE HEELS ARE KILLING ME! I'LL KICK 'EM OFF!
BONK!!
UH-OH!!
BONK!
GIGGLE! I COULDN'T HAVE PLANNED THAT BETTER MYSELF!
LET'S MOVE ON!
I'D LIKE A "T"!
THERE ARE THREE "T's"!
4

HELLO! I'M HERE! I'LL TAKE OVER NOW!
OH, NO! IT'S VIANNA!
SINCE I STARTED, I GUESS I'D BETTER FINISH!
THAT'S OKAY! I'M THE ONE PEOPLE TUNE IN TO SEE!
WELL, MAYBE THEY WANT SOMEONE YOUNGER!
W-ELL!
REMOVE CHERYL! PUT HER BACK WITH HER PEERS!
JUST A COUPLE MORE LETTERS PLEASE...
SO...
CHERYL, GIVE US ANOTHER LETTER!
A "C"!
I'LL GUESS THE PUZZLE NOW! IT'S "CENTER OF ATTENTION"!
NOW THAT'S IRONY!
CENTER
OF
ATTENTI
END

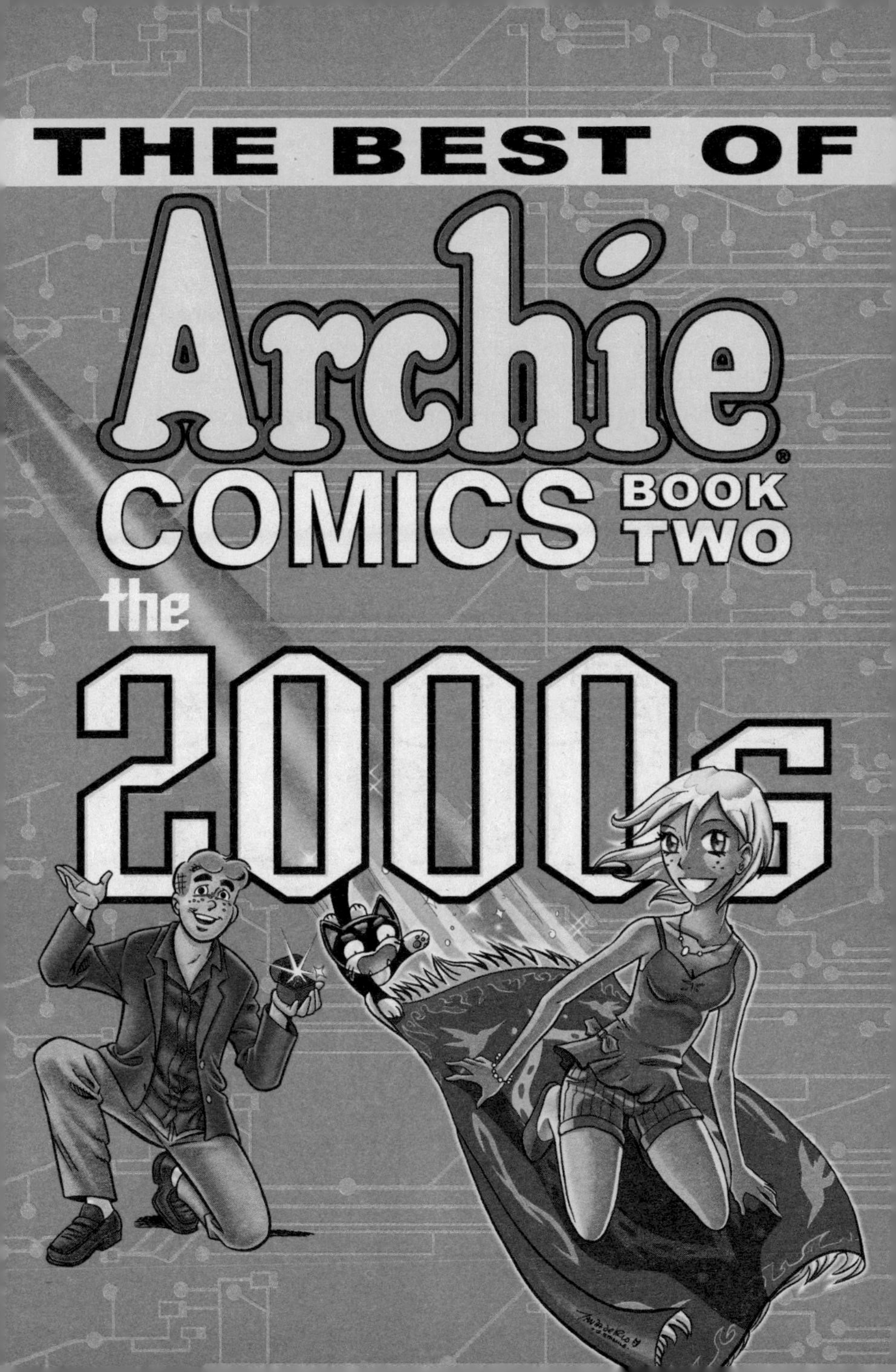
THE BEST OF
Archie
COMICS
BOOK TWO
the
2000s

Maid of Money
Josie & the Pussycats #47, 2001
by George Gladir, Stan Goldberg, Rudy Lapick and Bill Yoshida

The entire premise of this story is about lovely, acorn-brained Melody Valentine dressing in nothing but dollar bills and a skimpy bikini while unwittingly stripping bit by bit in front of a slathering gaggle of teenage boys. If you don't find this to be a recipe for hilarity then there is simply no help for you. :)

--Jon Gray
Production Artist,
Archie Comics

MELODY SAID SHE MIGHT BE A LITTLE LATE GETTING HERE TONIGHT!
I HEARD SHE HAD TROUBLE FINDING A DRESS FOR THE DANCE THAT SHE LIKED...
...NOT TO MENTION ONE SHE COULD AFFORD, AND...
OMIGOSH! VALERIE! LOOK!
GULP LOOKS LIKE SHE MANAGED TO SCRAPE A FEW DOLLARS TOGETHER AFTER ALL!
HI, EVERYONE!
Josie AND THE PUSSYCATS
IN "MAID OF MONEY"
-OR-
"HERE COMES THE MILLION DOLLAR MELODY!"

HOT MOMMA! I WANNA CLOSE LOOK AT THIS!
JACK?!
MOVE IT, JACK!
MONEY MAY NOT BE ABLE TO BUY HAPPINESS, BUT IT SURE CAN DRESS IT UP!
WHAT SAY, MELODY?
HOW 'BOUT A LOAN?
SURE !!!
RIP
HERE'S FIVE ONES! WILL THAT DO?
HOLY MOLEY! CAN YOU SPARE ANY MORE?
YE GADS! WE'VE GOT TO GET MELODY AND THAT DETACHABLE DRESS OUT OF HERE BEFORE SHE WREAKS HAVOC!
RIGHT... BECAUSE IF THE BOYS DON'T MOB HER---
---THEIR GIRLFRIENDS WILL!
C'MON, MELODY!
MIDVALE HIGH
FALL PARTY

C'MON, GUYS! DON'T LET 'EM GET AWAY!
RIGHT! WE'VE STILL GOTTA BREAK THE BANK!
IN HERE! QUICK!
SEND OUT THE MONEYTREE!
SPOILSPORTS!
GIRLS LOCKERS
MELODY! WHY IN THE WORLD DID YOU WEAR A DRESS LIKE THAT TONIGHT?
BECAUSE I NEEDED A DRESS FOR THE DANCE, JOSIE!
YOU'LL BE LUCKY IF YOU SURVIVE THE DANCE!
WHERE DID YOU GET THAT THING, ANYWAY?
I MADE IT!
SO WHY TEAR IT APART ON DEMAND?
3

HE ASKED ME FOR A LOAN!
AND WHAT WERE YOU PLANNING TO DO WHEN YOU RAN OUT OF MONEY, YOU DING-DONG?
IT'S OKAY! I'M WEARING A BIKINI UNDERNEATH! THE MONEY'S JUST TAPED ON!
HEY!
I JUST CAME TO TELL YOU THAT THE GUYS HAVE BEEN PARADED BACK TO THE GYM BY THEIR GIRLFRIENDS--
...SO IF YOU WANT TO SMUGGLE FEATHER-BRAIN HOME, DO IT NOW WHILE THE COAST IS CLEAR!
GREAT!
THANKS, ALEXANDRA! WE OWE YOU ONE FOR THIS!
A FEW FIVES OFF MELODY'S DRESS SHOULD COVER IT!
MELODY, WE THOUGHT YOU WERE GOING TO BUY A NEW DRESS FOR THE DANCE!
I COULDN'T AFFORD IT!
JONES
4

SO I USED THE MONEY TO MAKE A NEW DRESS INSTEAD!
YOU'LL BE LESS SOLVENT WEAR-ING ONE OF YOUR OLD DRESSES!
GOOD THING YOU ONLY USED ONES AND FIVES ON THIS THING!
IMAGINE THE FEEDING FRENZY YOU'D HAVE CAUSED IF YOU'D WORN LARGER BILLS!
NOT TO MENTION ANGRY GIRL FRIENDS!
HOTTEST DANCE OF THE YEAR
THANK HEAVENS MELODY'S THE ONLY ONE DUMB ENOUGH TO...
UH, JOSIE...
THE ONLY ONE?
HMPF! NO FAIR! I THOUGHT OF IT FIRST!
WOW! LOOK AT ALL THE HUNDREDS!
WOW! OL' ULYSSES S. NEVER LOOKED SO GOOD!
A THOUSAND! I'VE NEVER SEEN A THOUSAND BEFORE!
END

Rings and Things
Archie Digest #171, 2002
by George Gladir, Fernando Ruiz, Bob Smith, Bill Yoshida and Barry Grossman

When I read this story, I instantly felt like I did when I first heard the news that there was going to be a series of movies based on J.R.R. Tolkien's *Lord of the Rings* trilogy. As a kid, I had loved *The Hobbit* and once I saw *The Hobbit* cartoon in my 5th grade English class I was hooked. I still remember lining up at the theater for a midnight showing of *Fellowship of the Ring*, the first movie in the trilogy, with my wife, brother-in-law, and three of my best friends. Sitting in that theater I can clearly remember saying, "I want to be Aragorn!" Now in the book I never cared for him, but on the big screen he was portrayed as such a cool and mysterious character. Plus, (SPOILER ALERT!) he's destined to be king! Needless to say, when we left the theater we pretty much did exactly what Archie and Jughead did.

--Joe Morciglio
Project Coordinator, Archie Comics

Oh, What A Knight
Archie & Friends #53, 2001
by Bill Golliher, Holly G! and John Costanza

As a comic book artist and writer, I always strive to add a dimension of personal truth to my work. Gleefully I did this with all my Archie work! In the "Oh, What a Knight" story I drew heavily (hee hee pun intended) from my uber-geeky love of Ren faires, Medieval dinner theatre, and dragons!! Many of my birthdays were spent dressed in armor or Camelot attire, joyously gnawing on a giant turkey leg – so having the Archie gang enjoying the same was a hoot! I hope you enjoy what I believe was one of the early Archie adventures I illustrated. I know I did! So let the joust begin!!!

--Holly G!
Writer / Artist, Broadsword Comics

Gladir / Ruiz / Smith / Yoshida / Grossman

AHH... THERE'S NOTHING LIKE CURLING UP IN A COZY HOBBIT HOLE AFTER A BIG SCRUMPTIOUS MEAL... BURP!
YO! WAIT UP, ARCH! WHAT'S THE RUSH?
I WANT TO GET TO POP TATE'S! BESIDES, IT LOOKS LIKE IT MIGHT RAIN!
WELL YOU DON'T HAVE TO TAKE SUCH LONG STRIDES!
HEY! I'M JUST LIKE THE ROYAL RANGER IN THE STORY!
YOUR NAME SHOULD BE HOP-ALONG INSTEAD OF STRIDE-ALONG!
GULP! CAN I HELP IT IF I BUMPED INTO A TREE STUMP AND HURT MY KNEE?
2

TELL ME, AREN'T YOU THE KING WHO CARRIES THE SWORD THAT IS BROKEN?
YUP! THAT'S ME! I'M ARCHAGONE!
HOW DID YOUR SWORD GET THAT WAY?
WELL... TO TELL THE TRUTH, SOMETIMES I'M A BIT CLUMSY! I ACCIDENTLY SNAPPED THE TIP OFF!
RIGHT! BUT WE'D STILL HAVE TO RECRUIT A TRICKY ELF AND A TOUGH DWARF!
HA! HA! A FINE FELLOWSHIP WE'D FORM!
POP TATE'S
CHOCOLATE SHOPPE
HUH?
DUH... YOU KNOW I DON'T LIKE PRANKS, REG!
HEH! HEH! I WAS JUST JOKIN', MOOSE!
I'M A DORK
ARE YOU THINKING WHAT I'M THINKING?
OH, ABSOLUTELY!
3

NOW THAT WOULD BE ONE FUNNY FELLOWSHIP!
FELLOWSHIP? WHAT ARE YOU GUYS TALKING ABOUT?
WE JUST SAW "MASTER OF THE RINGS"!
HOW WAS IT? I READ THOSE BOOKS IN JR. HIGH AND LOVED THEM!
SO DID I!
IF YOU LOVED THE BOOKS, YOU'LL ADORE THE MOVIE!
I ALWAYS ENVISIONED MYSELF AS THE QUEEN OF THE ELVES!
I HAVE A MAGIC RING... IN FACT, I HAVE LOTS OF EXPENSIVE JEWELRY!
4

I RATHER ENVISIONED MYSELF AS THE BRAVE KING'S DAUGHTER WHO BECAME A WARRIOR PRINCESS!
OH YEAH! THE ONE WHO FOUGHT THE LEADER OF THE DARK ARMY!
I CAN DEFINITELY SEE YOU IN THAT ROLE, BETTY!
HA! HA! NO MAN CAN DESTROY ME!
REALLY? WELL SURPRISE, SURPRISE! I'M NOT A MAN!
WHOA! LISTEN TO THAT THUNDER! IT'S A REGULAR CLOUDBURST! THAT ENDS MY DAYDREAMING!
BOOM!
HEY, WAIT, ARCH! WE FORGOT SOMEONE VERY IMPORTANT!
WHO?
5

YOU KNOW... THE WIZARD!
YEAH! THE WIZARD! WHO COULD BE OUR WIZARD?
BOOM!
YIKES! L-LOOK! IT'S HIM!
POP'S
WHEW! LUCKY I HAD THIS HOODED RAINCOAT IN MY CARTODAY! IS MY ORDER TO GO READY, POP?
I HAVE IT RIGHT HERE, WALDO! I'LL PUT IT ON YOUR TAB!
POP'S
STAY DRY AND ENJOY YOUR BURGERS AND ONION RINGS!
HA! HA! AS SOON AS I GET HOME I'LL MAKE THEM DISAPPEAR LIKE MAGIC!
WELL ARCH, WHAT DO YOU THINK OF OUR FANTASY FELLOWSHIP? WOULD THE BEE MAKE A GOOD WIZARD?
I THINK...IT'S TIME TO RETURN TO REALITY, JUG!
END

Archie & FRIENDS
"Oh, What a Knight"
'A NIGHT AT THE ROUND TABLE'! I'VE ALWAYS WANTED TO CHECK OUT ONE OF THESE MEDIEVAL TYPE MEALS AND SHOWS!
YEAH, BUT I FEEL SILLY BEING THE ONLY NON-PERFORMERS DRESSED IN COSTUMES!
OH, COME ON! IT'S FUN...
A Night at the Round Table...
DINNER/SHOW
SCRIPT: BILL GOLLIHER
PENCILS: HOLLY G!
INKS: JOHN COSTANZA
ME AS THE PRINCESS, BETTY AS MY LADY-IN-WAITING, REGGIE AS THE DUKE, AND YOU AS MY BRAVE KNIGHT!
WHERE'S THE FOOD?
AND OF COURSE NO COURT IS COMPLETE WITHOUT IT'S FOOL!
FUNNY, I THOUGHT HE WAS JUST THE VILLAGE IDIOT!
HAR HAR!
HMPH!

OH, YEAH? WELL, YOU LOOK LIKE A COUPLE OF PLAYING CARDS GONE BAD!
THE TRUMPETS! THINGS MUST BE STARTING! LET'S GO!
TA-DAH
HEAR YE! HEAR YE! THE KINGDOM OF CAMELOT WELCOMES YOU TO THIS EVENING'S ROYAL BANQUET!
YOU WILL BE SERVED A MEAL FIT FOR ROYALTY AND TREATED TO ENTERTAINMENT EXTRAVAGANZA!
HOW EXCITING! A KING!
MMM! THIS LOOKS DELICIOUS! CORNISH HEN, BREAD, AND FRESH VEGETABLES!
LET'S DIG IN!
WAIT A MINUTE, SERVER! WHERE'S OUR SILVERWARE?
THERE IS NO SILVERWARE, M'LADY!
TONIGHT IT'S THE MIDDLE AGES AND WE EAT HOW THEY DID! WITH OUR FINGERS!
CHOMP! CHOMP! CHOMP!
2

THAT'S BARBARIC! I'M A PRINCESS, FOR GOODNESS SAKE! THERE HAS TO BE SILVERWARE AROUND HERE, SOMEWHERE!
ARCHIE, AS MY ROYAL KNIGHT, I COMMAND YOU TO FIND ME SOME!
BUT WHERE AM I SUPPOSED TO LOOK?
I ASSUME IF THERE'S FOOD, THERE'S A KITCHEN, AND IF THERE'S A KITCHEN, THERE'S SILVERWARE!
WELL, IF YOU PUT IT THAT WAY!
WHAM!
ALL THE SERVERS ARE COMING FROM THIS DIRECTION! I'LL CHECK OUT THIS HALLWAY!
EMPLOYEES ONLY
AH-HAH! THERE YOU ARE!
HUH?
YOU MUST BE THE NEW GUY THE TALENT AGENCY SENT OVER! AND JUST IN THE NICK OF TIME! THE SHOW'S ABOUT TO START!
BUT...
3

PUT THIS HELMET ON!
WE'LL TALK LATER!
MUFFLE! MUFFLE!
KLONK!
GET HIM SAFELY ON THAT HORSE! IT'S TIME TO BATTLE THE DRAGON!
DRAGON!?
HERE'S YOUR LANCE!
MEANWHILE...
ARCHIE MUST'VE GOTTEN LOST! DIG IN, RON!
IT'S AGAINST MY BETTER JUDGEMENT, BUT IT DOES LOOK TASTY!
SAY, THIS ISN'T SO BAD! SLURP! CHOMP!
KEEP IT DOWN! THE SHOW'S STARTING!
THERE WAS A TERRIBLE DRAGON WHO TERRORIZED THE KINGDOM!
WOW! THAT MECHANICAL DRAGON LOOKS PRETTY CONVINCING!
YOU CAN EVEN FEEL THE HEAT!
THEN ONE DAY, A BRAVE KNIGHT CAME TO FACE HIM...
EASY, BOY! ULP! THE HORSE SEEMS TO KNOW WHAT HE'S SUPPOSED TO DO!
SNORT!
4

THAT SUIT OF ARMOR WITH THE "A" ON IT LOOKS FAMILIAR!
OF COURSE! THAT'S ARCHIE!!
TOO LATE TO STOP NOW!
IF IT'S A SHOW THEY WANT, THEY'LL GET IT! I'LL STAB THAT DRAGON WITH MY LANCE!
RRRR!
TAKE THAT!!
BING!
BZAT!
THWAK!
WHAT'S THAT KNIGHT DOING? HE'S NOT SUPPOSED TO DO THAT!
IT'S A NEW GUY!
YE GADS!! HE MUST'VE SHORTED SOMETHING OUT!
THE DRAGON IS OUT OF CONTROL!
BZAT!
RRR!
POOF!
HE'S GETTING TOO CLOSE! I'M OUTTA HERE!
FINE, I'LL FINISH YOUR DINNER THEN! SLURP!
ROAR!
EEK!
ROAR!
RONNIE'S IN TROUBLE! I'VE GOT TO DO SOME-THING!
5

THIS LANCE IS AN EXCELLENT POLE VAULT POLE!
YAHOO!
EEK!!
ZIP
SPROING!
DON'T WORRY, VERONICA, I'VE GOT THIS DRAGON UNDER CONTROL!
SPUTTER!
WHORRR!
CRUNCH
ARCHIE! YOU DID IT! YOU SAVED ME FROM THE DRAGON! YOU ARE MY KNIGHT IN SHINING ARMOR!
SMOOCH!
HE WON'T BE AFTER WE SUE THE ARMOR OFF HIM FOR "SLAYING OUR DRAGON!"
HOLD IT, FRED... ER... KING! PERHAPS THIS COULD BE GOOD PUBLICITY FOR US!
NEXT DAY...
DID YOU GUYS SEE TODAY'S PAPER?
WE SURE DID! PRETTY COOL!
WHEW WHAT A NIGHT!
SIGH! YOU CERTAINLY ARE!
RIVERDALE TIMES
LOCAL BOY SLAYS DRAGON SAVES DAMSEL
END!

Four-Color Fun
Archie & Friends #107, 2007
by Andrew Pepoy, John Workman and Rosario "Tito" Peña

Right from the start "Katy Keene" was always a family tradition for me. Both my parents read comics as kids, and my Mom's favorite was Katy. So when I was asked to update and bring back Katy, one of the first people I talked to was my Mom. I wanted to find out what made Katy special to a reader in her original run and try to keep that spirit in its update. Besides, I knew I'd hear about it if I didn't get it right.

Once my new Katy stories started appearing I started to hear from kids whose moms read Katy in its '80s version and had some of the moms thank me for bringing her back. I even heard from one great-grandmother, who had been one of Katy Keene's earliest fans in the 1940s, who saw her great-granddaughter reading one of my new stories. So Katy and a love of comics really was a tradition handed down in families.

With this in mind, I wrote this story about Katy visiting a large comic book convention to promote her latest Web movie -- something movie stars do these days. I added the subplot about Katy trying to find that one missing issue of the collection started by her grandmother and continued by her mother of another classic Archie Comics character, Suzie, continuing her own family tradition of loving comics.

--Andrew Pepoy
Eisner Award-winning
writer and artist,
Archie Comics

Katy's outfit by **Sara O.**, Michigan
Katy's purse by **Elizabeth A.**, Tennessee

THAT DEALER LOOKS LIKE HE HAS SOME REALLY OLD COMIC BOOKS.
TOP-NOTCH
ZIP
PEP
BLUE RIBBON
JACKPOT
GOT TO FIND THE "S" BOX!
HI! CAN I HELP YOU?
DO YOU HAVE ANY "SUZIE" COMICS?
"SUZIE?" MAYBE. HEY! YOU'RE KATY KEENE. I DIDN'T KNOW YOU COLLECTED COMICS.
I DON'T, REALLY, BUT I'VE ALWAYS LIKED THEM. "SUZIE" WAS MY GRANDMA'S FAVORITE COMIC BOOK. SHE HAD ALMOST EVERY ISSUE.
SHE HANDED THEM DOWN TO MY MOM, WHO TRIED TO FIND ANY MISSING ISSUES. BY THE TIME SHE HANDED THEM DOWN TO ME, SHE WAS ONLY MISSING # 62.
IF YOU KNEW SUSIE LIKE WE KNOW-
SUZIE
Comics
10¢
SO I OWE IT TO THEIR MEMORY. I'VE JUST GOT TO FINISH THE SET!
WELL, I'M AFRAID I CAN'T HELP YOU WITH THAT ISH, BUT TRY "COMICS COMICS" TWO AISLES OVER. THEY MIGHT HAVE IT.
THANKS.
COMIC
RING RING
HELLO?
KATY, IT'S JIM. IT'S TIME FOR OUR PANEL.
OKAY. I'LL BE RIGHT THERE.
GUESS I'LL HAVE TO LOOK FOR "SUZIE" LATER.

Katy's outfit by
Mike M.,
North Carolina

NOW WE'LL OPEN THE FLOOR TO SOME QUESTIONS.
UM...I HAVE A COUPLE OF QUESTIONS...UM...FOR KATY. WHAT DO YOU THINK OF THE CONVENTION?
CAPTAIN SENSIBLE
THIS IS MY FIRST, BUT IT'S JUST AMAZING! AND IT GIVES ME A CHANCE TO LOOK FOR A COPY OF "SUZIE" #62.
AND NOW THAT YOU'VE PLAYED THE GIRLFRIEND IN TWO SUPER-HERO MOVIES, WOULD YOU WANT TO STAR IN YOUR OWN SUPERHERO MOVIE?
HMMMMM...
SURE, BUT I'M MAINLY JUST LOOKING FOR GOOD ROLES, WHATEVER THEY ARE... DOCTOR, COWGIRL, SPACE EXPLORER, FAIRY PRINCESS...I PLAYED A PIRATE IN "JOHNNY THE PIRATE III." BUT IF THE RIGHT SUPER-HERO SCRIPT CAME ALONG, I'D LOVE TO DO IT!

Superhero Costume also by **Mike M.**, North Carolina

AFTER THE PANEL...
HEY, TOPHER, WHAT TIME DO YOU WANT TO MEET UP TONIGHT TO GO TO "THE WEB RETURNS" PREMIERE?
WHAT ARE YOU TALKING ABOUT?
I THOUGHT WE WERE SUPPOSED TO GO TO THE PREMIERE AND WORK THE RED CARPET TOGETHER.
YOU MISSED YOUR CHANCE WITH ME WHEN WE WERE FILMING. I'VE ALREADY GOT A DATE WITH SOMEONE SMART ENOUGH TO APPRECIATE ME... GLORIA GOLD!
IT'S NOT LIKE I WANTED TO GO WITH YOU. I THOUGHT I HAD TO.
NOW WHAT AM I SUPPOSED TO DO ABOUT A DATE? K.O.'S IN NEW YORK... LITTLE SIS MACKENZIE IS IN MICHIGAN VISITING FRIENDS...
SOON, INSIDE THE CONVENTION...
I'LL HAVE TO WORRY ABOUT A DATE LATER.
I'VE ONLY GOT A LITTLE TIME TO FIND THAT "SUZIE" COMIC.
RING RING
HELLO?
KATY? JIM. TIME FOR THE SIGNING UPSTAIRS.
ALREADY ?!
OKAY. I'LL BE THERE IN A FEW...
OOF!
WAM!

OH, NO! LOOK AT ME!
WHAT ABOUT MY--
HEY! YOU'RE KATY KEENE!
YEP. KLUTZY KATY. SORRY ABOUT THAT.
UM, YEAH, WELL, THIS SHOULD COVER IT... GOTTA GO. SORRY.
WOW! KATY KEENE BUMPED INTO ME!
BACK AT THE HOTEL...
GOTTA PICK SOME-THING TO WEAR.
HOW 'BOUT THIS?
THIS'LL WORK.
NOW FOR SOME SHOES.
Outfit by Donnelly R., Ohio
Outfit by Mike P., New York
Dress by Kathryn P., California
Shoes by Elle V., Iowa

BACK AT THE CONVENTION...
SORRY I'M LATE!
WELL...LOOK WHO FINALLY DECIDED TO BLESS US WITH HER PRESENCE.
A
Ultravox!
WEB
I RAN INTO SOME--
AT LEAST SOME OF US KNOW HOW TO TREAT OUR ADORING PUBLIC.
HERE YA GO.
THE WEB
DVD
TOPHER'S RIGHT, DARN IT. IT'S NOT RIGHT TO LET THE FANS DOWN. BUT HOW TO...?
SO KATY STAYS LONG AFTER THEIR SCHEDULED TIME, AND TOPHER'S LEFT, TO MAKE SURE EVERY FAN IN LINE GETS A SMILE AND AN AUTOGRAPH.
THANKS FOR STOPPING BY.
LATER, AFTER EVERYONE IS GONE...
OH, I'M EXHAUSTED. AND DOES MY HAND HURT.
AND HERE IT IS... THE END OF THE DAY... AND I HAVEN'T HAD A CHANCE TO THINK ABOUT A NEW DATE FOR TONIGHT'S PREMIERE.

AND THE WORST THING IS... I NEVER FOUND THAT "SUZIE" COMIC...
UM, EXCUSE ME, MS. KEENE...
OH, NO! NOT ANOTHER AUTOGRAPH!
UM, I REALLY LIKE YOUR MOVIES, AN' I WANNA BE AN ACTRESS LIKE YOU WHEN I GROW UP.
OH, THANKS! IS THAT A "WEB" COMIC YOU'VE GOT THERE? DID YOU WANT ME TO SIGN IT?
NO, THIS IS ONE OF THE SPECIAL SIGNED ONES THEY GAVE AWAY AT YOUR PANEL.
WEB
I WANTED TO GIVE YOU THIS.
IF YOU KNEW SUZIE LIKE WE KNOW-
Archie
SUZIE
Comics
APRIL 10¢
NO. 62
WOW!
HARRY the TALKING DOG
Al Fagaly
A "SUZIE" # 62?
YEAH. I HEARD YOU SAYING HOW YOU REALLY WANTED IT BECAUSE OF YOUR MOM AND GRANDMA. I'M SORRY IT'S SO BEAT UP, BUT IT'S THE ONLY ONE I COULD FIND AND AFFORD.
ALL MY COMICS LOOK LIKE THAT BECAUSE THEY'RE SO LOVED, AND THEY'VE BEEN READ SO MANY TIMES--IT'S WONDERFUL! I WANT TO PAY YOU BACK!
NO. I JUST WANTED YOU TO HAVE IT...!
SUZIE
WOW!

ISN'T THERE SOMETHING I CAN...?
I HAVE AN IDEA. LET'S GO FIND YOUR PARENTS.
LATER, AT THE STAR-STUDDED PREMIERE OF "THE WEB RETURNS"...
AND WHO'S WITH YOU TONIGHT, KATY?
THIS IS MY NEW PAL MICHELE AND HER PARENTS. SHE'S THE ONE YOU SHOULD INTERVIEW BECAUSE SOMEDAY SHE'LL BE THE BIGGEST STAR ON THE RED CARPET.
GEE!
Katy's dress by **Margaret M-F.**, California
Hostess' gown by **Julia M.**, California
Mom's dress by **Erin D.**, Washington

Manga Magic
Sabrina the Teenage Witch #58, 2004
by Holly G!, Jim Amash, Teresa Davidson and Jason Jensen

When Archie hired me to give Sabrina a "manga makeover" in 2003, we needed a way to explain her shift from the classic Archie style to her new look, which began with issue #58. Luckily, being a teenage witch means that Sabrina can use magic to become anything and anyone she wants to be – a skill she's taken full advantage of over the years! Of all the Archie characters, Sabrina has probably enjoyed the most transformations and unique looks since Dan DeCarlo and George Gladir first created her in 1962. Her Japanese-inspired transformation occurred during the height of the manga boom in the US, so the timing was just right to have Sabrina segue into a world of drama, romance and mystery where the stakes were higher than ever before!

--Tania Del Rio
Writer / artist,
Archie Comics

The Adventures of Young Salem Cover Gallery
Sabrina the Teenage Witch #101 - 104, 2009
by Ian Flynn, Chad Thomas, Jim Amash, Teresa Davidson and Jason Jensen

When Mike Pellerito called and asked me if I would be interested in continuing the tales of Salem after a short arc on Sabrina, I jumped at the chance. I mean it was Harry Potter meets Tom Sawyer! How could I turn such a premise down? Talking frogs, lizard men, heaps of treasure and an evil velociraptor wizard were just a few of the things I was tapped to draw, and that was just the beginning of the world Ian Flynn was creating. Here's hoping (fingers crossed) we get to see more of Young Salem and company again some day.

--Chad Thomas
Artist,
Archie Comics

Sabrina
"Manga Magic!"
WHAT ARE YOU LOOKING AT?
OH, I'M JUST CHECKING OUT SOME OF MY FAVORITE MANGA STORIES!
BEAR Fancy
Return Polic
Teen! Girl
MANGA? WHAT'S THAT?!
DON'T YOU KNOW? IT'S REALLY POPULAR! IT'S COMICS DRAWN IN A JAPANESE STYLE!
OH, COOL!
SALE
YEAH, "MANGA" ACTUALLY MEANS "WHIMSICAL PICTURES," SO IT CAN COVER A WIDE RANGE OF STYLES!
WHAT ARE YOUR FAVORITES?
COME HOME WITH ME AND I'LL SHOW YOU!
Book Bargains

WOW, SABRINA! THESE ARE REALLY COOL!
I KNOW! THEY'RE SO FULL OF ROMANCE, FASHION, DRAMA AND ACTION!
I JUST CAN'T GET ENOUGH!
I WONDER WHAT OUR LIVES WOULD BE LIKE IF WE WERE IN A MANGA!
HMM... THAT GIVES ME AN IDEA!
OH, NO, SABRINA! I DON'T LIKE THE SOUND OF THIS!
COME ON! IT WILL BE FUN! READY, GUYS?
YEAH!
HERE WE GO!
サブリナ!
HEY, 'BRINA! YOU LOOK REALLY COOL!
SO DO YOU, LLANDRA!
:ACK: WHAT ABOUT ME?! I LOOK LIKE A STUFFED ANIMAL!
HEY, THAT'S A GOOD THING! NOW YOU CAN COME TO SCHOOL WITH ME AND NO ONE WILL KNOW YOU'RE A REAL CAT!
I'M NOT HELPING YOU ON YOUR HISTORY TESTS, YOU KNOW!
HA HA! ANYTHING IS POSSIBLE IN MANGA! I CAN'T WAIT TO SEE WHAT HAPPENS!
END

SABRINA THE TEENAGE WITCH PRESENTS:
the magical tales of
young
SaLeM
THOMAS
AMASH '08
JENSEN

SABRINA® THE TEENAGE WITCH PRESENTS:
the magical tales of
young SaLeM
THOMAS-AMASH JENSEN

SABRINA THE TEENAGE WITCH PRESENTS:
the magical tales of
young Salem
THOMAS! AMASH

SABRINA® THE TEENAGE WITCH PRESENTS:
the magical tales of
young SaLeM®
THOMAS -Amash JENSEN

The Proposal
Archie #600, 2009
by Michael Uslan, Stan Goldberg, Bob Smith, Jack Morelli and Barry Grossman

It was such a perfect idea, I was almost certain it'd been done before.

About three years ago I'd just stepped in the door as the Co-CEO of Archie Comics. I met with the creative minds behind our comics and told them, plain and simple, to cut loose, be creative, make change... Archie needed it. With the all-important issue #600 looming, we had to do something epic – something important.

Enter Michael Uslan, the uber-talented producer of all the Batman films and an excellent writer to boot. When we sat down and figured it out, the story fell into place smoothly, like it was meant to be... Archie was getting married. But even at the altar, America's favorite teen redhead couldn't decide, so we soon split the narrative into two alternate realities. One in which Archie marries Betty and another where he marries Veronica. The story was great and we were excited about a new era for Archie and his friends. Boy, were we surprised!

The media reaction was huge. The story became an international sensation – TV news, daily papers and the Internet were all abuzz about Archie, for the first time in years. He was at the forefront of pop culture again, and it felt right. Not only had we created a great comic, which is what we've always been about, but we made it matter. That's Archie today, in a nutshell. We tell stories that are important and fun, and always entertaining – for everyone. Just wait 'til you see what we do next!

--Jonathan Goldwater
Publisher / Co-CEO,
Archie Comics

THE PROPOSAL
ARCHIE MARRIES VERONICA
the Archies
GREAT SET, ARCHIEKINS!
HAD TO BE FOR OUR FINAL GIG HERE AT RIVERDALE HIGH!
AUTOGRAPHS
THAT WAS AMAZING! THE ABSOLUTE BEST-- ALL OF US HERE TOGETHER!
YEAH! EVERY-THING'S PERFECT!
EVERYTHING'S ARCHIE, YOU MEAN! YOU'RE THE CENTER OF THE RIVER-DALE UNIVERSE, DUDE!
WE CAN'T BREAK UP THE ACT! WE ALL GOTTA HANG HERE AFTER GRAD-UATION!
"Oh, AUNTIE EM...THERE'S NO PLACE LIKE HOME!"
1

MOM! DAD! I'M HOME!
HI! HOW'D IT GO? WAS EVERYONE SAD?
SAD? MARY, IT WAS THEIR LAST HIGH SCHOOL ROCK CONCERT, NOT A FUNERAL!
IT WAS THE OPPOSITE OF A FUNERAL! IT WAS AWESOME!
STATE COLLEGE
AND NOW THAT IT'S OVER, YOU CAN'T PUT THIS OFF ANY LONGER!
GULP! COLLEGE BROCHURES?
HILLSIDE COLLEGE
STATE U
ARCHIE, MY VERY OWN PETER PAN! EVEN A BOY WHO DOESN'T WANT TO GROW UP HAS TO FACE REALITY!
AWWW... I GOT PLENTY OF TIME!
THE OLDER YOU GET, THE FASTER TIME PASSES!
Huh? WHAT DOES THAT MEAN?
YOU'LL UNDERSTAND WHEN YOU'RE OLDER!
ALL I UNDERSTAND IS THIS PRESSURE! I GOTTA TAKE A WALK! BACK IN AN HOUR!
RIVERDALE H.S.
ZIP UP YOUR JACKET! IT'S VERY CHILLY!
2

COLLEGE... NO MORE ARCHIES... THE GANG SPLITTING UP...
MEMORY LANE! I'VE WALKED DOWN THIS STREET BEFORE! IT LOOKS LIKE IT NEVER WANTED TO GROW UP EITHER!
MEMORY LN.
RIVERDALE
I LOVE IT!! REMINDS ME OF RIVERDALE WHEN I WAS YOUNG!
MEMORY LN.
VIC'S BLOOMS
BELMONT BOOKS
FLORAL SHOP 599
601
STAMPS
603
MIGHTY COMICS SHOP (FORMERLY RADIO COMICS)
605 SHORTEN SWEET SHOPPE
607
SILBERKLEIT & SON TRAVEL
DAILY JET SERVICE TO MONTANA
609
GOLDWATER FOR PREZ
MLJ FOR USA
RIVERDALE H.S.
HEY! I'VE NEVER WALKED UP MEMORY LANE, ONLY DOWN! THINK I'LL EXPLORE THE OPPOSITE DIRECTION THIS TIME!
MEMORY LN.
SOMETIMES YOU GOTTA TRY SOMETHING NEW! THERE'S A YELLOW WOOD UP AHEAD!
hmm... MEMORY LANE BECOMES TWO DIRT ROADS HERE. I THINK I'LL TAKE THE LEFT ONE AND SAVE THE RIGHT ONE FOR ANOTHER DAY!
RIVERDALE H.S.

MAN! I FEEL LIKE I'VE BEEN WALKING FOREVER! BETTER HEAD HOME! GOTTA FACE THE BIG DAY TOMORROW!
GRADUATION DAY
STATE U
SORRY MY WALK TOOK SO LONG! THOUGHT YOU'D BE ASLEEP!
SLEEP? TOO EXCITED! MY LITTLE BOY IS ABOUT TO GRADUATE!
BUT WITHOUT A JOB LINED UP! I WISH YOU LISTENED TO ME AND MAJORED IN BUSINESS!
BUT I LOVE HISTORY, POP!
NOT A BIG JOB MARKET THESE DAYS FOR PEOPLE WHO CAN RECITE LINCOLN'S GETTYSBURG ADDRESS BY HEART!
I'LL FIND SOMETHING! I'LL DO THE BEST I CAN!
I KNOW YOU WILL, SON! I'M PROUD OF YOU GRADUATING FROM COLLEGE!
VERONICA IS INSIDE. SHE'S BEEN WAITING FOR YOU!
REALLY? RONNIE'S HERE? WELL ALL RIGHT!
STOP THE PRESSES!
DID MR. ANDREWS SAY ARCHIE WAS GRADUATING FROM COLLEGE? WHAT HAPPENED TO HIGH SCHOOL? BY WALKING UP MEMORY LANE, HAS ARCHIE WALKED INTO HIS OWN FUTURE?
4

HI! WHAT A SURPRISE! I--
Oh, ARCHIE! GRADUATION DAY SHOULD BE THE HAPPIEST DAY OF OUR LIVES! BUT WHY DO I KEEP CRYING!?
IT'S OKAY, RONNIE! WE'VE ALL BEEN FRIENDS SINCE WE WERE LITTLE KIDS, AND NOW, WELL...
WE'RE ALL GOING OUR SEPARATE WAYS! SNIFF! Oh, ARCHIE... SOB!
MY DAD CALLS IT "GROWING UP!" I THINK I'LL GO BACK TO BEING A KID!
BUT THERE IS NO GOING BACK, IS THERE?
MOST EVERYONE BUT JUGHEAD IS TALKING ABOUT LEAVING RIVERDALE AFTER TO-MORROW!
WHAT?! YOU'RE KIDDING?! I DIDN'T HEAR THAT! BETTY? BETTY, TOO?
YOU'VE BEEN TOO BUSY WITH YOUR FINALS TO NOTICE, RED! BUT YEAH...
AND WHY SO INTERESTED IN WHERE BETTY'S GOING?
UH...
I'LL TALK TO EVERYONE AT GRADUATION... ASK THEM ABOUT THEIR PLANS. I HAVEN'T DONE THAT...
BRACE YOUR-SELF, ARCHIE! AFTER TOMORROW... IT'S NO LONGER JUST ALL ABOUT YOU!
MY FATHER SAID THAT ABOUT ME EARLIER TONIGHT. AND YOU KNOW WHAT? IT'S TRUE!
SO THIS IS "GROWING UP"?
5

YOUR GRADUATION GOWN LOOKS GREAT, SON--BUT DON'T FORGET TO PUT PANTS ON UNDER IT!
OKAY, SO FOR THIS ONE LAST DAY IT'S STILL ALL ABOUT ME!
BUT WITH ALL THE GRADUATION SPEECHES, I MAY NOT EAT AGAIN FOR HOURS!!
NO MORE "BIG MAN ON CAMPUS!" NO MORE ROCK BAND GUITARIST! JEEEEZ-- I MAY NEVER BE "REGGIE" AGAIN!!
GROAN!
I'M NOT GOING!! MY FRIENDS HERE LIKE ME! AFTER TODAY I'LL BE JUST ANOTHER NERD TO PEOPLE!
JUST KEEP BEING YOU, AND YOU'LL MAKE NEW FRIENDS, DILTON!
YOU KNOW WE'LL ALWAYS BE THERE FOR YOU, BETTY!
I HAVE THE FEELING WONDERFUL THINGS ARE JUST AROUND THE NEXT CORNER FOR ME! I CAN'T WAIT!
6

GRADUATION DAY IS HERE! AND NO ONE'S LIFE WILL EVER BE THE SAME!
SO REMEMBER... "WHAT LIES BEHIND US AND WHAT LIES BEFORE US ARE TINY MATTERS COMPARED TO WHAT LIES WITHIN US!"
STATE UNIVERSITY
THANK YOU FOR AN INSPIRING VALEDICTORIAN SPEECH, MR. DOILEY!
NOW I DECLARE YOU ALL TO BE GRADUATES OF STATE UNIVERSITY! GOOD BYE AND GOOD LUCK!
HOORAY!!
WE GRADUATED, JUGGIE! WHY NO SMILE?
JUST WONDERING WHAT HAPPENS TO US ALL NEXT!
GRADUATION PARTY AT MY MANSION--
NOW!

HAPPY GRADUATION VERONICA
WELL, OL' PAL...WE MAY BE THE ONLY TWO STAYING IN RIVERDALE!
WOOF!
WELCOME, GRADS! I SEE THE WHOLE GANG MADE IT! ARCHIE'S HERE! BETTY'S HERE, VERONICA TOO!! REGGIE'S HERE"...
JOSIE AND THE PUSSYCATS
AND HERE COMES JUGHEAD AND HOT DOG, TOO!
NOW EVERYTHING'S ARCHIE!
SO, RONNIE... I'M GONNA DO AS I SAID... FIND OUT EVERYONE'S FUTURE PLANS!
GOOD BOY!
THOUGHT I'D START WITH YOU!
WELL, DADDY'S GRADUATION GIFT IS A WORLD CRUISE! AFTER THAT, HE SAYS I CAN RUN LODGE CHARITIES IN LONDON OR HONG KONG!
AND WHAT ABOUT YOU?
ME? GULP! I'M GONNA LOOK FOR A JOB!
8

I'M GONNA MANAGE MY UNCLE JOE'S "UP AND DOWN BURGER" ON STATEN ISLAND!
MY FOLKS CO-SIGNED A LOAN FOR MY OWN "NAILS" PLACE IN BAYONNE!
I'M GOING TO M.I.T. FOR A DOCTORATE IN QUANTUM MECHANICS!
A DOCTOR AND A MECHANIC? THAT'S A LOTTA SCHOOLING JUST TO HEAL A CAR!
I HEARD ATLANTA WAS COOL. SO I LINED UP A JOB THERE SELLING USED CARS!
Hmmm... I ALWAYS THOUGHT YOU'D MAKE A GOOD USED CAR SALESMAN!
STATE U
ME? I DUNNO, ARCH. POP TATE SAYS I CAN GRILL BURGERS TILL I FIGURE THINGS OUT!
S'OKAY, JUG! WE GOT ALL THE TIME IN THE WORLD!
STATE U
I THOUGHT YOU KNEW! I'LL BE A BUYER TRAINEE AT SACKS FIFTH AVENUE!
GREAT, BETTY! BUT... YOU'RE GONNA MOVE TO NEW YORK CITY?!
IT'S NOT TOO FAR, ARCHIE... YOU'LL... YOU'LL COME AND VISIT ME?
VISIT? SURE. YOU'LL SEE ME IN NEW YORK CITY BEFORE YOU KNOW IT!
9

ENOUGH PARTYING...! I GOTTA THINK... HARD. IT'S LIKE THE FUTURE IS HERE!
M.I.T.
STATEN ISLAND
BAYONNE
ATLANTA
NEW YORK CITY
LONDON OR HONG KONG
FACE REALITY!
A JOB!
PRESSURE ...SO THIS IS GROWING UP!
GO OUR SEPARATE WAYS!
AND HERE COMES OUR GRADU-ATE!
HOW WAS VERONICA'S PARTY?
I DUNNO. CONFUSING. SCARY.
WELL, MAYBE THIS WILL MAKE THINGS LESS CONFUSING... LESS SCARY FOR YOU!
IT'S YOUR GRADUATION PRESENT, ARCHIE!
A...A CHECK?
WOW! TH-THANKS FOLKS!!
DO YOU KNOW WHAT YOU'LL USE IT FOR?
SAVE IT!
I THINK... THIS MAY CHANGE EVERY-THING!
10

A FEW WHIRLWIND WEEKS WHIZ BY, AND...
THANKS FOR COMING WITH ME JUG!
OKAY... BUT WHY SO MYSTERIOUS? WHAT'CHA MEAN YOU'RE A "MAN ON A MISSION"?
5TH AVE
ONE WAY
I'M A MAN PETRIFIED! IS THERE LIFE AFTER COLLEGE? WOMEN? A JOB? A DENTAL PLAN?
ENOUGH! YOU'RE SCARING ME!
PIER 41
I TOLD BETTY I'D MEET HER FOR LUNCH NEAR HER NEW JOB. SURE YOU CAN'T JOIN US?
NOT NOW. TOO LATE. MEET ME HERE AT 3PM!
GOOD LUCK WITH YOUR MYSTERY MISSION. I'LL TELL BETTY YOU SAID "HI."
YEAH... GULP!
THE LODGEMOBILE, RIGHT ON TIME!
ARCHIEKINS! YOU CAME TO SEE ME OFF!
I KNOW YOUR SHIP LEAVES AT 3PM, RONNIE, BUT I REALLY, REALLY NEED YOU FOR AN HOUR!
NOW SEE HERE, ARCHIE--
SIR, I PROMISE I'LL HAVE HER BACK IN ONE HOUR.
HMMM... YOU'VE DEVELOPED SOME BACKBONE, ANDREWS!
ONE HOUR. NOT ONE MINUTE MORE!
11

OSTERIA AL RÖSEN
GREAT TO SEE YOU, JUGGIE! I THOUGHT ARCHIE--
HE'S BEING VERY SECRETIVE, BUT I THINK HE HAD A BIG JOB INTERVIEW. HE SAYS "HI."
YOU--YOU MEAN HE MIGHT MOVE TO NEW YORK?
DUNNO... YEAH, MAYBE. I GUESS...
MY TURF, MY TREAT. WALK ME BACK TO THE OFFICE.
THANKS! I CAN TELL YOU LOVE THE CITY AND YOUR JOB!
GOOD GOIN', BETTY!
Spiffany's
39 MINUTES LEFT! C'MON, RONNIE!
SPIFFANY'S? YOU NEED MY HELP PICKING A CHARM FOR YOUR MOM'S BRACELET?
CAB
SCREECH
THIS PLACE IS TOO EXPENSIVE FOR YOU, SWEETIE! LET'S TRY MALL-WART'S INSTEAD!
THAT'S NOT WHY WE'RE HERE!
WELL, THEN WHY ARE WE--
'CAUSE YOU'RE LEAVING TODAY FOR 3 MONTHS AND I HADDA MAKE A BIG CHOICE!
SPIFFANY'S! LET'S LOOK AT THEIR DIAMONDS IN THE WINDOW!
I'D RATHER LOOK AT THE BURGERS IN THE DRIVE-THRU WINDOW AT McDANIEL'S!
12

NO!
VERONICA... WILL YOU MARRY ME?
YES!
5TH AVE
13

IT'S BEAUTIFUL! AND BIG! YOU CAN'T AFFORD THIS, ARCHIE!!
I... UH... CAME INTO SOME MONEY RECENTLY...
DADDY!! WE HAVE TO TELL DADDY!!
UH... MAYBE WE SHOULD BREAK IT TO HIM LATER ... LIKE ON OUR 50th ANNIVERSARY!!
EASY, GIRL... I KNOW IT'S A SHOCK. FOR ME, TOO. HE NEVER TOLD ME!
OH, JUGGIE... THE HOPES AND DREAMS I HAD SINCE I WAS LITTLE... ALL GONE!
C'MON, LET'S GO FOR A LONG WALK...
I CAN'T, I HAVE TO GO TO WORK... THEN I'M GOING FAR, FAR AWAY FROM HERE!
NYC TOU
BETTY!!
BETTY...
NA
NYC TOURS

57 MINUTES AND 30 SECONDS...
HE WON'T MAKE IT, SIR. I HAVE FAITH!
WELL, WELL, WELL! FIRST TIME FOR EVERYTHING! MAYBE THAT BOY HAS ACTUALLY GROWN UP!
FIDDLE FADDLE, SIR!
CAB
DADDY! SMITHERS! DADDY!!
DID THAT SCOUNDREL HARM YOU?!
HARM ME? NO! HE--
CALM DOWN, DEAR. TELL ME ONCE WE'RE ON BOARD!
NO! NO!!
HERE! LOOK!
MMM-HMMM... LOVELY. DID I GIVE YOU THAT FOR YOUR 16th BIRTHDAY?
NOPE. ARCHIE JUST GAVE IT TO ME... FOR OUR ENGAGEMENT.
HOW NICE. NOW LET'S HURRY AND BOARD THE--
ENGAGEMENT?!!
ARCHIE?!
15

VERONICA... HERE'S MY CHECKBOOK. TELL THE CAPTAIN TO DELAY SAILING, AND PAY HIM WHAT HE ASKS!
SMITHERS, TAKE NOTES.
YES, SIR.
AND NOW, MY PROSPECTIVE SON-IN-LAW... WE'RE GOING TO HAVE A LITTLE CHAT!
ARCHIE, DO YOU LOVE MY DAUGHTER?
YES, SIR. I THINK I ALWAYS HAVE.
DO YOU HAVE A JOB?
UH... NO.
AN INCOME?
NO.
A HOUSE?
NO.
A HEALTH PLAN?
NO.
A SAVINGS ACCOUNT ?!
NO.
SO IF YOU LOVE HER, THEN HOW DO YOU PLAN TO CARE FOR HER?
I'LL FIND A JOB AND WORK HARD, MR. LODGE!
YOU WILL NOT!
I--I WON'T?
CERTAINLY NOT! NO SON-IN-LAW OF HIRAM P. LODGE IS GOING JOB-HUNTING WHILE MY DAUGHTER SUFFERS!
STARTING TOMORROW, YOU WORK FOR ME!!
16

OH, DADDY! I'M SO LUCKY TO HAVE YOU!
HONEY, YOU'RE AN ADULT NOW. YOU MUST KNOW YOUR HEART AND LISTEN TO YOUR HEAD. ALL I WANT IS YOUR HAPINESS!
YOU HAVE MY FAITH, TRUST, CONFIDENCE AND LOVE.
AND AS FOR YOU...
AS OF TODAY, I WILL NO LONGER JUDGE YOU. YOU'RE A MAN NOW, ARCHIE. YOUR ACTIONS WILL SPEAK FOR THEMSELVES!
PIER 41
NOW YOU MAY KISS THE BRIDE-TO-BE GOOD-BYE!
UPON OUR RETURN THERE WILL BE A WEDDING! BY GEORGE--
--THE BIGGEST WEDDING IN RIVER-DALE HISTORY!

JUGHEAD! GUESS WHAT I DID TODAY.
WILD GUESS? PROPOSED TO VERONICA. DESTROYED A GIRL'S LIFE. DISSED OUR FRIENDSHIP.
WHY DIDN'T YOU TELL ME?
HOW THE HECK DID YOU KNOW?
AW, JUG... I WAS NOT SURE I'D GO THROUGH WITH IT, AND I DIDN'T WANT YOU TO THINK I WAS A COWARD!
LAME EXCUSE.
AND WHADDAYA MEAN "DESTROYED A GIRL'S LIFE"? RONNIE WAS THRILLED!
BETTY! SHE WAS THERE! SHE SAW!
OMIGOSH! I'LL GO TO HER RIGHT NOW AND EXPLAIN!
NO! NO, ARCH! YOU JUST NEED TO STAY AWAY FROM HER NOW. LET HER HEAL AND MOVE ON!
SHE WAS MY FIRST FRIEND IN RIVERDALE. I NEVER MEANT TO HURT HER...
BETTY...
CAN YOU FORGIVE ME FOR NOT TELLING YOU, AND BE MY BEST MAN?
BEING IDIOTS SOMETIMES HAS NEVER INTERFERED WITH OUR FRIENDSHIP!
SUBWAY
DOWNTOWN
UPTOWN
18

MOM! DAD! I'M...
DID YOU DO IT? DID YOU ASK HER?
DID SHE SAY "YES"?
CONGRATULATIONS ARCHIE ON YOUR ENGAGEMENT!!
UH... YEAH... AND... UH...
YEAH!
PARENTS ARE SORCERERS! THEY KNOW ALL... AND SEE ALL... ALL THE TIME!
THE BANK CALLED TO VERIFY YOUR VERY LARGE CHECK!
SPIFFANY'S?! THAT LARGE A CHECK MEANT A VERY LARGE DIAMOND! WE REALIZED THAT MEANT VERONICA!
MAD AT ME, POP? I SPENT ALL THE MONEY YOU GAVE ME!
WELL, I CALL IT AN INVESTMENT... A GOOD INVESTMENT IN YOUR FUTURE, SONNY BOY!
BUT... WELL... YOUR MOTHER AND I WERE WONDERING...
WHAT ABOUT BETTY?
19

YES! JUGHEAD JUST TOLD ME!
WOW! THE PRESSURE IS ON US NOW, MOOSIE!
UH... WHAT ABOUT BETTY?
I'M SO HAPPY FOR THEM!
POOR BETTY!!
OH, WELL... YOU WIN SOME, YOU LOSE SOME! BETTY MUST BE DEVASTATED!!
HOORAY!
IT'S TRUE, GANG!!
IS BETTY OKAY?!
CHUCK
I'LL E-BLAST AND TEXT-BLAST THE NEWS TO EVERYONE!
UH... MAYBE I'LL JUST DELETE BETTY FROM THIS ONE!
fazebook
20

JOANN, AS MY WEDDING PLANNER, THIS CANNOT BE AS LOW-KEY AS THE OBAMA INAUGURATION BALL! I WANT LIVE COVERAGE FROM THE LODGE ESTATE ON NETWORK TV!
BROOKLYN BROS.? MEASURE MISTER ANDREWS FOR 7 WORKWEEK SUITS. ALSO, MY DAUGHTER HAS STRICT WEDDING TUXEDO REQUIREMENTS FOR HIM, HIS USHERS AND BEST MAN!
ROBY WILL DESIGN MY WEDDING GOWN. SARAH USLAN WILL DO MY MAKE-UP. THE BAND WILL BE THE STONES OR JOSIE AND THE PUSSYCATS!
JOE? START CONSTRUCTING ARCHIE'S OFFICE. MAKE IT ONE QUARTER THE SIZE OF MINE.
THEN ADD A NEW FLOOR IF THAT'S TOO BIG FOR THE BUILDING!
KATY KEENE MUST TRAIN MY 22 BRIDESMAIDS!
BRIDESMAIDS! NOT GUESTS! WE'RE FIGURING 2,000 GUESTS. SIGH! WE COULDN'T INVITE EVERYONE!
BEN? START GROOMING ARCHIE FOR HIS JOB... VP OF LODGE INTERNATIONAL'S OIL HOLDINGS IN NEW YORK! YES, I KNOW WE HAVE NONE IN NEW YORK, BUT IT'LL KEEP VERONICA CLOSE BY!
BLAM
21

SO, REGGIE, MOOSE, DILTON ...I'D LIKE YOU GUYS TO BE MY USHERS IN THE WEDDING PARTY...
POP'S
Duh... PLEASURE'S ALL MINE, RED!
ARCHIE, I AM SO HONORED! YOU LIKE ME! YOU REALLY LIKE ME!
POP'S
STATE
I CANNOT BELIEVE YOU ACTUALLY WOUND UP WITH VERONICA. MY SUPER-EGO IS TAKING A BEATING HERE!
THANKS FOR YOUR GOOD WISHES, REG.
POP'S
Menu
WHAT'RE WE SUPPOSED TO WEAR TO THIS PARTY?
um... YOU'D BETTER GET A TUX. RONNIE WOULD PROBABLY WANT EVERY-ONE IN SOME SORT OF TUXEDO.
WHERE ARE YOU GETTING MARRIED?
NO CLUE. I'M GUESSING IN THE GARDEN IN RONNIE'S BACKYARD... OR MAYBE IN RIVERDALE PARK. THAT'S REAL NICE.
HOW MANY PEOPLE?
GEE... IF YOU ADD UP MY FAMILY... OUR MUTUAL FRIENDS... THEN ADD HER FAMILY... MAYBE A HUNDRED.
WHAT JOB DID MR. LODGE OFFER YA, ARCH?
uh... HE DIDN'T SAY. I GUESS WHEREVER A HISTORY MAJOR CAN BE VALUABLE TO HIS COMPANY.
22

OH, BETTY, DARLING -- I'M SO SORRY. I'LL BE ON THE FIRST TRAIN FOR NEW YORK TOMORROW!
NO, MOTHER...
BUT HONEY, IF YOUR OWN PARENTS CAN'T BE THERE FOR YOU WHEN YOU NEED US, WHO CAN?
DAD, I KNOW YOU AND MOM ARE THERE FOR ME. JUST KNOWING THAT IS ALL I NEED!
I'M AN ADULT NOW. I CAN DEAL WITH THIS.
WE LOVE YOU, BETTY. WE WISH WE COULD TAKE YOUR PAIN AWAY...
I KNOW YOU DO! CALL COMING IN. I LOVE YOU BOTH. BYE.
BZZZZZTT
HELLO?
EARTHPHONE OPERATOR. I'M CONNECTING A CALL FROM THE QE4!
ISN'T THAT A CABLE NET-WORK?
PLEASE STAND BY...
BETTY? IT'S VERONICA!
23

HEY, RONNIE. I--I KNOW WHY YOU'RE CALLING...
SOMETHING HAPPENED TODAY, AND I WANTED YOU TO BE MY FIRST FRIEND TO KNOW.
I DON'T EVEN KNOW HOW TO SAY THIS... I MEAN YOU AND ME AND ARCHIE... ALL THESE YEARS...
THEN I'LL SAY IT. ARCHIE PROPOSED TO YOU AND YOU SAID "YES!"
CONGRATULATIONS, RONNIE... YOU-- YOU WON.
WHAT? YOU'RE BREAKING UP. I THINK YOU SAID "I WON...DER?" YEAH, BETTY... I WONDER IF YOU'LL BE MY MAID OF HONOR?
HELLO, BETTY? BETTY?!
DON'T MISS THE STORY THE WORLD HAS BEEN WAITING MORE THAN 60 YEARS TO READ! GET YOUR GOWN READY... PRESS YOUR TUX! NEXT: ARCHIE MARRIES VERONICA PART TWO...
The Wedding

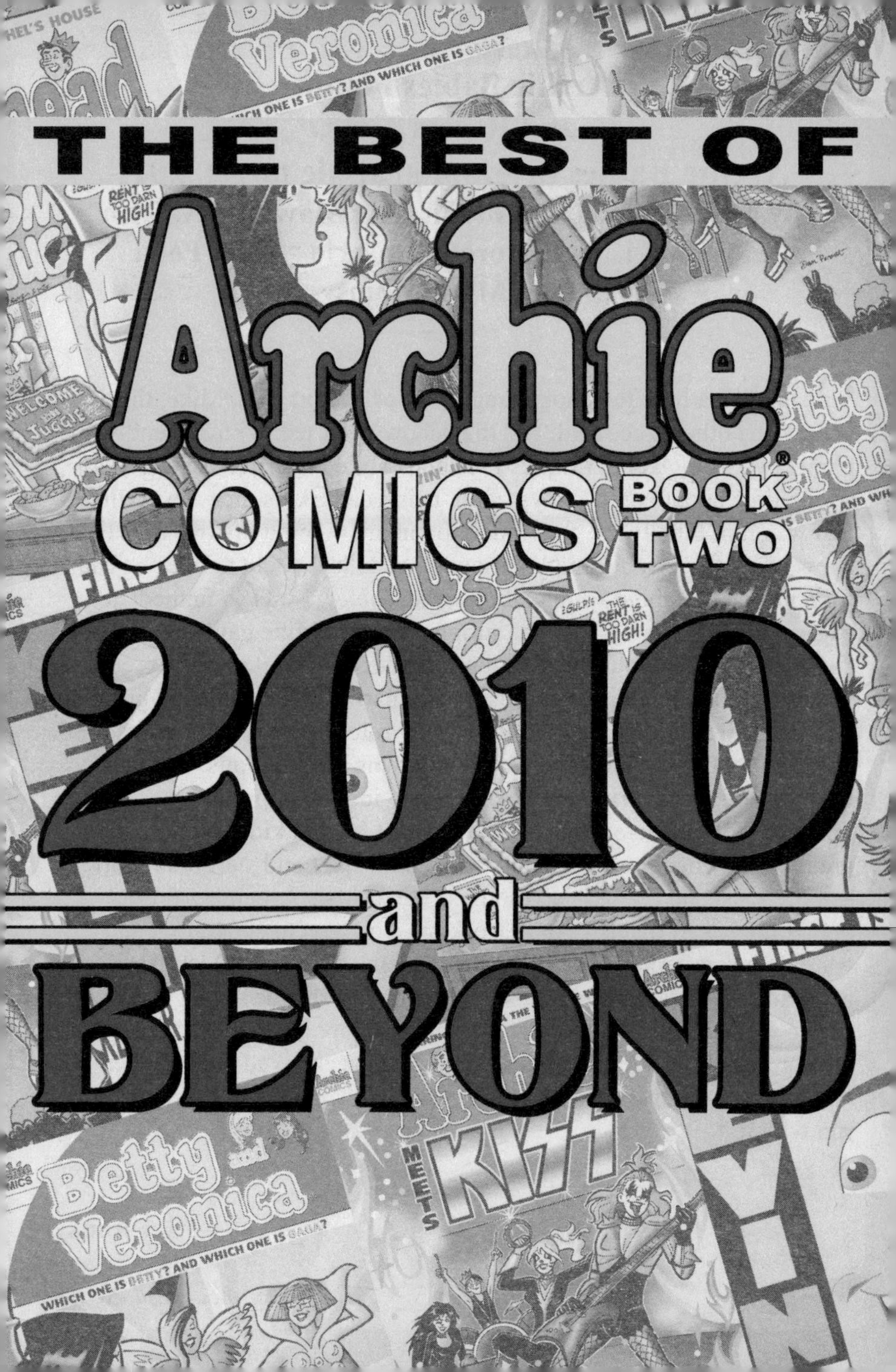
THE BEST OF
Archie®
COMICS
BOOK TWO
2010
and
BEYOND

Archie Babies Pinups and Recess Time

Archie Babies original graphic novel, 2011

by Mike Kunkel, Ian Flynn, Art Mawhinney, Rich Koslowski, Jack Morelli, Rosario "Tito" Peña and Matt Herms

Once upon a time the phone rang. "Hello?" I said. "Hi, Mike, this is Mike," the other voice said, and that's how it started, with a friendly phone call from Archie Comics President Mike Pellerito. We talked for a long time about comics, toys, food, being dads, kids, life... everything that was fun. Finally we got around to one more thing that we BOTH knew was fun... Archie and his friends. We talked about an idea he had for a new series about Archie, the *Archie Babies*. I was so immediately excited to help him with it. The simple directive Mike gave me was "have fun, and let your imagination run with it," and that was exactly what I did. Imagination always had to be part of it. I so enjoyed bringing Archie's wild creative mind to life. So I wrote stories that gave Archie and his friends adventures to enjoy with their imaginations. This has been one of my favorite sandboxes to play in. The opportunity to create in a world of characters that I'd loved since I was a kid was more than great... I now had the chance to create and inspire and start their world as little kids, and that was awesome. I will always remember this as one of the best projects I got to work on. And then to stand back and watch it be crafted by such an amazing team... Art, Rich, Matt, Jack, and Paul... it came out so great. I'm honored to see the stories come to life so wonderfully. And to you, the fans... I hope you enjoy these new adventures of the *Archie Babies* as much as we enjoyed making them. Always remember what Mike said... "have fun and let your imagination run with it."

--Mike Kunkel
Writer / creator,
Herobear and the Kid

THE Archie BABIES
ALIEN PLANET RECESS

USA
A
ARCHIE AND HIS FRIENDS WILL FIND ADVENTURE...
...WHEREVER THEY GO AND NO MATTER WHAT THEY DO.
THE BEST OF FRIENDS, AND ALWAYS EXPLORING...
...WHETHER IN A DARK JUNGLE OR AT A BIG ZOO.
IT'S A GIFT IN THEIR BRAINS TO ENJOY MADE-UP CREATIONS...
...FOR THEY NEVER STOP BELIEVING IN THEIR OWN IMAGINATIONS!

POEM
Rain, rain go away,
come again another day.
But if you stay
and we must play
in the inside room all day,
we'll have such fun
as we do play
and happy times
are here to stay!

RECESS TIME
HOW DO YOU MAKE GOLD SOUP?
YOU PUT FOURTEEN CARROTS IN IT!
WHAT ANIMAL DOESN'T PLAY FAIR?
A CHEETAH!
CONNECT THE NUMBERED DOTS IN ORDER, AND YOU'LL FIND A SPECIAL FRIEND!
CAN YOU HELP MISS BLOSSUM TO CONNECT EACH OBJECT--
--WITH HER WEE TOTS STUDENT WHO MIGHT ENJOY IT THE MOST?
WHAT DOES "MINIMUM" MEAN?
A VERY SMALL MOMMY?
WHEN DOES THURSDAY COME BEFORE WEDNESDAY?
WHEN IT'S IN THE DICTIONARY!

MORE
RECESS TIME
WHAT DO YOU GET WHEN YOU CROSS A CENTIPEDE WITH A PARROT?
A WALKIE-TALKIE!
E
S
T
I
A
CAN YOU HELP JUGHEAD FIND THE RIGHT PATH TO HIS LUNCH?
THEN FILL-IN THE BLANK BOXES ON THE CROSSWORD PUZZLE... AND REVEAL THE NAMES OF SOME OF ARCHIE'S PLAYMATES!
WHAT HAS FIVE EYES..
--AND SLEEPS IN A WATER BED?
THE MISSISSIPPI RIVER!
WHAT KIND OF EARS DOES A TRAIN HAVE?
ENGINEERS!

RECESS TIME
KNOCK, KNOCK.
WHO'S THERE?
WET.
WET WHO?
WET ME IN! IT'S RAINING OUT HERE!
WHAT VEHICLE IS SPELLED THE SAME BACKWARDS AND FORWARDS?
I DON'T KNOW!
RACECAR!
KNOCK, KNOCK!
WHO'S THERE?
HOUSE.
HOUSE WHO?
HOUSE IT GOING TODAY? ARE YOU HAVING FUN?

Archie: Cyber Adventures Cover Gallery

Archie & Friends Double Digest #1-5, 2011

by Stephen Oswald, Joe Staton, Bob Smith, Jack Morelli, Rosario "Tito" Peña, Jason Jensen and Joe Morciglio

Getting to write a story where Archie and the gang have a great big adventure was something I always wanted to do. I took certain themes from some of my favorite movies like *Tron*, *The Wizard of Oz* and the *Lord of the Rings* trilogy and formed the basic story structure. There are heaps of *Back to the Future*, *Highlander* and video game references as well! Though the story could have stood on its own without all the pop culture nods, it was fun to pack in as many "extras" as I could, rewarding re-reading of the book by noticing things you may not have the first time around. Of course none of this would have been possible without the immensely talented group of artists that I had the privilege of working with on this project. My only regret is not putting in more of America's finest sport: pinball!

--Stephen Oswald
Production Manager, Archie Comics

Fitting In ~and~ It's Complicated

Jinx original graphic novel, 2011

by J. Torres, Rick Burchett, Terry Austin, John Workman, Mark McNabb and Jason Jensen

Mike Pellerito asked me to come up with some one-page gag strips in the tradition of the classic Li'l Jinx comics. They were to be used as preview and promo material for the new Jinx. "Fitting In" (originally titled *"Daddy's Little Girl"*) is probably my favorite of the bunch. I think it not only encapsulates Jinx's relationship with her father, Hap, but even if you didn't know anything about them or their comic, even if you're not the father of a teenage girl, you can relate in some way because haven't we all wanted a ride on the coin-operated pony way past that age?

--J. Torres
Writer, Archie Comics series Jinx

Archie: Cyber Adventures Part 1 cover

Archie: Cyber Adventures Part 2 cover

Archie: Cyber Adventures Part 3 cover

Archie: Cyber Adventures Part 4 cover

Archie: Cyber Adventures Part 5 cover

JINX IN FITTING IN
COME ON, LI'L JINX! HURRY UP!
I HAVEN'T GOT ALL DAY.
DA-AAD! STOP CALLING ME "LI'L JINX"!
ESPECIALLY IN PUBLIC!
IN CASE YOU HAVEN'T NOTICED, I'M NOT SIX ANYMORE. I'M A HIGH SCHOOL FRESHMAN NOW. I'M NOT A CHILD. I BABYSIT OTHER PEOPLE'S CHILDREN.
I'M A RESPONSIBLE, GROWN-UP, YOUNG WOMAN NOW.
GASP!
DADDY, CAN I HAVE A QUARTER, PLEEASE?
25¢
END

JINX™ IN IT'S COMPLICATED
YOU KNOW, EVERYONE AT SCHOOL THINKS YOU'RE MY GIRLFRIEND.
GIRL FRIEND AS IN "GIRL SPACE FRIEND," OR GIRLFRIEND AS IN "GIRLFRIEND," ONE WORD?
UM...WHAT'S THE DIFFERENCE?
WELL, WITHOUT THE SPACE, YOU HAVE TO PAY FOR MY TICKET AND POPCORN.
OH...
...THEN I'D LIKE SOME SPACE, PLEASE.
OH, REALLY? WHY, GREG? AM I SUFFOCATING YOU?
AM I HOLDING YOU BACK?
DO YOU WANT TO SEE ...OTHER PEOPLE ???
END

Archie Meets KISS Part 1: Riverdale Rock City
Archie #627, 2012
by Alex Segura, Dan Parent, Francesco Francavilla (variant covers), Rich Koslowski and Jack Morelli

"Gene Simmons wants to do an Archie/KISS comic." That's how this all started – at least for me. I was sitting in our CEO Jon Goldwater's office, doing my usual PR routine. We were talking about where to announce one thing or another when Jon dropped this fact on me. I almost missed it. "He called us?" Turns out Gene, who's a huge comic book fan, was also an Archie fan. The concept of Archie and his friends crossing paths with the Demon, Starchild, Catman and Spaceman seemed off-the-wall and crazy enough to work. This could be bigger than *Archie Meets Punisher*, I thought. "Who's drawing it?" I asked. "Dan," Jon said, meaning Dan Parent, our top artist and a longtime KISS fan. I knew this would be a dream come true for him. "Can I write it?" I blurted out the question without giving it much thought – it was pure impulse. At that point, I'd been with the company as their PR and marketing person for a few months. In that time I'd written one entire comic – a well-received comic convention-themed story, sure, but probably not enough to merit getting the keys to the new car. I was expecting a quick, polite "No." "Sure, why not? Write up a proposal." So, I did. That started a chain of events so fun, bizarre, surreal and exciting that I'm hard-pressed to fully describe them in just one 500-word intro. Dan and I wanted to create a story that brought these two icons of American pop culture – Archie, the everyman teen and his friends, and KISS, the larger-than-life rock group that are as close to real-life superheroes as we can get – together for a romp that was part '80s monster movie and part comic book mega-crossover. We wanted BIG action with a heart of gold. We're all honored it was selected for inclusion as part of *The Best of Archie Comics Book Two*. Welcome to Riverdale Rock City!

--Alex Segura
Vice President - Marketing and Publicity, Archie Comics

WHERE DID THEY GO?!
RIVERDALE ROCK CITY
1

I THINK THEY WENT THIS WAY!
WHO WERE THOSE GUYS?
NO CLUE! DID YOU SEE THEIR OUTFITS?!
SO, YOU'RE PROBABLY WONDERING HOW THINGS GOT TO THIS POINT.
Y'KNOW... FOUR DUDES IN SCARY MAKE-UP AT THE CLUBHOUSE? FOR THAT, WE HAVE TO GO BACK A FEW DAYS!
IT ALL STARTED AT A MEETING OF THE RIVERDALE MONSTER SOCIETY!
R M S
GUYS, RIVERDALE IS IN DIRE NEED OF A PROTECTION SPELL!
PROTECTION SPELL, SABRINA?
YEAH, DOOFUS. SOMETHING TO KEEP GOONS LIKE YOU AWAY!
NOT EXACTLY.
IT'S A MAGICAL SPELL TO PROTECT THE TOWN FROM MONSTERS!
THEY'RE HERE, SO I GUESS THE OLD ONE'S NOT WORKING!
I'LL NEED FOUR OF YOU TO HELP ME CAST IT.
I'D LOVE TO HELP!
Ahem!
GREAT, BETTY! HOW ABOUT YOU, ARCHIE, JUGHEAD, DILTON?
SORRY, VERONICA. YOU AND REGGIE HAVEN'T BEEN TO A MEETING IN WEEKS! THIS IS A TRICKY SPELL!
HOW HARD CAN IT BE IF YOU CAN PULL IT OFF?
2

I DIDN'T WANT TO BE PART OF THIS SILLY GROUP ANYWAY!
YEAH, SERIOUSLY! EVERYONE KNOWS MONSTERS ARE STUPID!
YOU'RE THE EXPERT!
THANKS, JUG!
WHERE TO NOW, RON? POP'S?
NO, YOU IMBECILE! WE'RE GOING TO FIGURE OUT HOW TO CAST OUR OWN SPELL!
I HOPE RON'S NOT TOO UPSET.
I'M SURE IT'S FINE!
WHAT'S THE WORST THAT COULD HAPPEN?
3

IF YOU ONLY KNEW, CARROT-TOP!
WE'LL SHOW THEM! THE NERVE-- KICKING US OUT OF THEIR STUPID GROUP!
IT WAS KINDA BORING ANY-WAY. MAGIC'S DOPEY!
THAT'S NOT THE POINT! NO ONE KICKS VERONICA LODGE OUT OF A CLUB!
AH! HERE IT IS! I KNEW ALL THESE DUSTY BOOKS WERE GOOD FOR SOME-THING!
WHAT IS IT? A GROOM-ING GUIDE?
SPELLS
IT'S A SPELL BOOK, REGGIE! MY FATHER COLLECTS THESE OLD BOOKS FOR SOME SILLY REASON!
TO READ THEM?
LET'S SEE...
SHE WAS TRYING TO CAST A PROTECTION SPELL, RIGHT? OR WAS IT "PROJECTION"?
hmm?
4

A FEW DAYS LATER, AT THE NEXT MEETING OF THE RIVER-DALE MONSTER SOCIETY... THINGS GOT INTERESTING!
R Mo S
WE'LL SHOW THEM HOW TO CAST A SPELL!
WE WILL?
SPELLS
OF COURSE! STOP BEING SUCH A WIMP! IT CAN'T BE THAT HARD!
SPELLS
OKAY, IT SAYS WE JUST SAY THE MAGIC WORDS IN THE RIGHT ORDER, AND WE'RE SET!
ARE YOU SURE WE'RE CASTING A PRO-JECTION SPELL?
LET ME DO THE THINKING, REGGIE. YOU JUST SIT THERE AND LOOK PRETTY!
ALRIGHT, GUYS! HERE GOES... BE VERY QUIET WHILE I UTTER THE MAGIC WORDS... ANY MISTAKES COULD ALTER THE ENTIRE SPELL!
5

ONCE I CAST THE SPELL, WE SHOULD BE SAFE FROM ANY MONSTER PROBLEMS ON HALLOWEEN!
BEYOND THE USUAL ONES, LIKE RONNIE AND REGGIE!
WHY THAT BURGER-STUFFED BUFFOON! I'LL STRANGLE HIM!!
DID YOU GUYS HEAR SOME-THING?
QUIET! WE HAVE TO BE CAREFUL!
LOOKS LIKE SHE'S ABOUT TO START!
YOUR ATTENTION TO DETAIL, REGGIE, IS REMARKABLE!
ZINGBAT POLLYWOK SNICKLE DOODLE FRITZ--
--BILLI RUBINA WATANEGI CONSU-UPI PA TI--UPI PA MI--
--ISBIN YODDLE CROW SNIL DAK BRO--
6

SHE'S DOING IT WRONG! WE HAVE TO FIX IT!
SPELLS
NO, WAIT! SHE'S CASTING A PROTECTION SPELL, NOT...
SHIMMY SHIMMY COCO POP!
SPELLS
RON?
NO! YOU'VE REVERSED THE SPELL!
KRASH
OH, NO!!
NO, I FIXED YOUR MISTAKE! YOUR PROJECTION SPELL WAS WAY OFF! YOU'RE WELCOME!
PROJECTION? NO, RONNIE, SHE WAS CASTING A PROTECTION SPELL!!
OH.
GUYS... WHAT'S THAT SOUND?
7

KRAKOW

COOL.
MY BANDAGES ARE, LIKE, TOTALLY TORN! giggle!
EVERYTHING MAKES ME SAD.
THIS...THIS IS IDEAL!
ARCH... ARE YOU SEEING WHAT I'M SEEING?
I WISH I WASN'T!
WELL, IT'S BEEN REAL... BUT WE'VE GOT WORK TO DO!

IT'S GOING TO BE, UM... TOTALLY COOL TO, UH...
DRAIN THIS PLACE OF ANY PERSONALITY? SHOULD BE EASY ENOUGH!
ARE YOU HAPPY NOW, RON? YOU'VE UNLEASHED MONSTERS ON RIVERDALE!
OH, BETTY, DON'T BE SO NAIVE! THOSE AREN'T MONSTERS, THEY'RE NERDS!
YEAH, SERIOUSLY! THEY'RE PROBABLY BIDING TIME BETWEEN RENAISSANCE FAIRS!
THIS DIVE WILL BE PERMAN-ENTLY LAME AND BORING!
SABRINA, WHAT WERE THOSE THINGS?
I'M NOT SURE, BUT THEY'RE NOT FROM AROUND HERE!
AND, JUDGING FROM THE INSTABILITY THAT PORTAL CAUSED UPON OPENING, WE MAY BE IN A HIGHLY TEMPERA-MENTAL GEOGRAPH-ICAL AREA, AKIN TO A WORMHOLE!
DILTON. ENGLISH.
UM... GUYS? I HATE TO SOUND LIKE A BROKEN RECORD, BUT...
10

AND, JUST WHEN WE THOUGHT IT COULDN'T GET ANY WEIRDER...
...IT LOOKS LIKE THOSE FOUR WEREN'T THE ONLY THINGS COMING TO VISIT!
SABRINA, ANY ADVICE ON HOW TO STOP THIS?!
CROSS YOUR FINGERS AND THINK HAPPY THOUGHTS, KIDDO!
FWOOM

SO, THIS IS HOW WE GOT HERE... WITH FOUR MONSTERS ON THE LOOSE IN RIVERDALE, AND THESE DUDES IN OUR CLUBHOUSE!
Whoa.
WE'VE BEEN SUMMONED, STARCHILD!
LOOKS LIKE THEY'RE ON THE LOOSE AGAIN!
WHO?! WHAT'S ON THE LOOSE?!
DON'T YOU KNOW? YOU LET THEM OUT! WHAT KIND OF WITCH ARE YOU?!
I-IT WAS AN ACCIDENT!
DOESN'T MATTER! THE DAMAGE IS DONE!
12

WHO ARE YOU GUYS?!
I'M THE DEMON! THIS HERE IS STARCHILD. THAT'S SPACEMAN AND CATMAN...
WE'RE KISS!
NO TIME FOR PLEASANTRIES.
HOW RUDE!
RUDE?! YOU DON'T KNOW THE HALF OF IT, GIRLIE!
gulp!
SHOOM
AM I THE ONLY ONE WHO THINKS THIS IS TOTALLY WEIRD?
I LIKE THEIR MAKE-UP!
THEY SEEM KIND OF COOL!
DID YOU SEE THAT GUITAR?
Uh... WE'RE MISSING THE POINT HERE, GUYS!
13

YOU REALLY HAVE NO IDEA WHAT YOU'VE UNLEASHED, DO YOU?
SO THERE ARE A FEW EXTRA WEIRDOS IN RIVERDALE! BIG WHOOP! MAYBE YOU CAN INVITE THEM TO YOUR HOUSE FOR A FREAK SLUMBER PARTY!
RON! THEY'RE MONSTERS! ON THE LOOSE IN OUR TOWN!
THIS IS SILLY.
ARCH?
GUYS! WAIT UP!
Hmh?
HOW ARE YOU GONNA STOP THOSE... WHATEVER-THEY-ARE?
THE ONLY WAY WE KNOW HOW...
14

WITH ROCK!!
WE'RE GONNA ROCK THOSE MONSTERS BACK WHERE THEY CAME FROM.!!
Whoa. WOW. BUT WHAT ARE THEY?
THEY'RE MONSTERS, MAN! THEY'RE GOING TO CHANGE THIS TOWN FOREVER IF WE DON'T STOP THEM.!
WHAT DO YOU MEAN?
YOU EVER BEEN TO A LAME PARTY? WHERE EVERYONE WAS BORING AND NO FUN?
YEAH, SURE! EVERYONE HAS!
IMAGINE THAT WAS PERMANENT! NO FUN. NO FRIENDS. NO PARTYING. THAT'LL BE THIS DIVE IF THOSE CREATURES GET THEIR WAY.!
NO FUN IN RIVERDALE?
15

RIVERDALE WITHOUT FUN? HOW IS THAT POSSIBLE?!
WHEN WAS RIVERDALE FUN?
WE HAVE TO HELP KISS STOP THOSE MONSTERS, GUYS!
OR AT THE VERY LEAST HELP THEM WITH THEIR OUTFITS!
SABRINA'S RIGHT! WE SHOULD RECONVENE TO-MORROW MORNING AND PUT A PLAN TOGETHER!
IN THE MEANTIME, I'LL DO SOME RE-SEARCH ON THESE GHOULS AND SEE WHAT I CAN FIND!
I'LL DO THE SAME-- THERE HAS TO BE SOME WEBSITES WITH INFO ON HOW TO STOP THEM!
TRY WWW. DESTROY-LAME-MONSTERS-.NET!
CUT THE WISE-CRACKS, FOOD PIT!
AS MUCH AS IT PAINS ME, REG IS RIGHT, JUG! LET'S GET HOME AND TACKLE THIS BEFORE SCHOOL TOMORROW!
16

SEE YOU GUYS TOMORROW!
I'D BETTER STOCK UP ON FOOD!
COME ON, BETTY... SMITHERS CAN DROP YOU OFF.
GOOD LUCK, EVERY-ONE--IF MY CALCULA-TIONS ARE CORRECT, WE'LL NEED IT!
NEED SOME COMPANY?
OH...YEAH. THANKS, ARCHIE.
IT'S NOT YOUR FAULT. YOU COULDN'T HAVE KNOWN RONNIE WAS GOING TO BURST IN LIKE THAT!
THAT'S TRUE, BUT I SHOULDN'T HAVE BEEN MUCKING AROUND WITH THAT KIND OF MAGIC. IT'S DANGER-OUS, AND MY AUNTS WILL BE FURIOUS!
I'M SURE THEY'LL UNDERSTAND, BUT MAYBE WE CAN GET THIS FIGURED OUT BEFORE THEY EVEN NOTICE!
YEAH, THIS TOWN IS JUST FULL OF VAMPIRES, MUMMIES AND WERE-WOLVES!
17

HEY, YOU NEVER KNOW. WHAT DO YOU THINK YOU'RE GOING TO DO?
I REMEMBER MY AUNTS TALKING ABOUT A GROUP OF POWERFUL MONSTERS THAT PREY UPON FOOLISH YOUTHS, AND TAKE AWAY THE ONE THING THEY HOLD DEAR. BUT I DON'T REMEMBER THE DETAILS!
DOESN'T SOUND LIKE MUCH FUN!
DO YOU HEAR SOMETHING?
NO... WAIT, YEAH. SOUNDS LIKE SOMEONE IS COMING TOWARDS US.
HEY, WHO'S THERE? HELLO?
MAYBE SPLITTING UP WASN'T SUCH A GREAT IDEA!
18

Josie!
WOW! WHAT A RELIEF TO SEE YOU!
WE THOUGHT IT WAS ANOTHER MONSTER!
JOSIE?!
WELL, THAT WAS WEIRD.
YEAH. SHE'S USUALLY A BIT MORE... LIVELY.
19

WELL, I'LL SEE YOU TOMORROW. THANKS FOR WALKING WITH ME.
NO PROBLEM. AND DON'T BEAT YOURSELF UP OVER THIS.
WE'LL FIGURE IT OUT.
WE ALWAYS DO!
MGGHMPHH!!
POOR SABRINA! I HOPE THE GANG CAN FIGURE OUT A WAY TO STOP THOSE CREEPY CREATURES BEFORE THEY DO ANY REAL DAMAGE!

SO BEAT. A FEW HOURS' SLEEP SHOULD DO THE TRICK, THOUGH.
RING
WHO COULD BE CALLING THIS LATE?
HELLO?
HAVE YOU BEEN OUTSIDE?
HEY, BETTS...YEAH, I JUST GOT HOME. WHAT'S UP?
IT'S TERRIBLE, ARCHIE! I'M SO GLAD THAT YOU'RE OKAY!
Huh? WHAT HAPPENED?
STAY SAFE INSIDE! THEY'VE GOT EVERYONE!
Oh... Oh, MY!
21

THEY'RE TURNING RIVERDALE INTO A TOWN FULL OF--
MINDLESS ZOMBIES!
NEXT TIME:
CAN KISS HELP THE ARCHIES SAVE RIVERDALE? OR HAVE THINGS GONE TOO FAR?!
FIND OUT IN:
Archie MEETS KISS
ON SALE NOW!
22